i

Murder At Red Gem Farm

Louise Furley

Murder at Red Gem Farm

ISBN: 979-8-218-07320-6 (Paperback)
ISBN: 979-8-9859963-9-5 (eBook)

Cover art by: *Pixel Mischief Design*
Photo: *Courtesy of Shutterstock*

ALSO BY LOUISE FURLEY

Murder at Red Gem Farm

Chapter One

Shanti Lane walked the customer to the door, nodding politely at the woman's chattering, wishing she'd hurry up and leave. She had exciting news to tell her sister and she couldn't wait to get next door to their family-owned restaurant and spill her news.

But now, over the past few weeks Mrs. Davison had developed the annoying habit of coming in daily and absently wandering around the warm shop for an hour waiting for her kids and husband to come in off the slopes. She touched everything, but bought nothing.

Shanti cringed every time Mrs. Davison picked up a fragile vase with her pudgy fingers. She'd turn it upside down to peer at the price sticker on the bottom then plunk it back down on the counter. This wasn't the only late evening she'd kept Shanti long after the shop normally closed.

The pair hesitated under the lit exit sign. Just as Shanti reached for the brass door knob, Mrs. Davison's beady, mud-brown eyes turned up and caught sight of the oil painting hanging to the left of the cedar door.

The heavy lady feigned interest in the painting of mutely colored sailboats lining a canal, each loosely tied to the weathered dock.

The sun had just been thinking of rising. Lanterns on the boats strung like Christmas lights reflected on the still dark water. The sails seemed to be moving, different shapes and sizes and colors of silk billowing in the early morning breeze.

A gifted artist, Shanti's distinctive style pulls the viewer into the scene. Her paintings invoke a dreamlike quality that give people that warm fuzzy feeling they are always searching for, without losing any of the realism.

"Oh, Miss Lane!" the woman gushed. "Is that one of the paintings you were working on during that- that horrible murder you were involved in?"

Shanti blanched at the woman's tactless words.

Mrs. Davison unbuttoned the top button of her oversized tweed coat and pulled the plaid scarf from around her thick neck. Droplets of sweat glistened in the peach fuzz above her upper lip, fleshy jowls jiggled as she moved her head back and forth pretending to admire the art.

The fact was, she was eager to hear firsthand the juicy inside tidbits about the famous killings of three members of a wealthy family in Napa Valley.

The local rag was all a-buzz that Shantilly Lane had been present during the murders. She had been commissioned to paint a picture the historic winery.

She also happened to have solved the murders. Unable to continue painting during the investigation, she had discreetly nosed around and pondered the clues until she figured out 'Who Dunnit'.

She presented her views of the evidence to the police who at first were reluctant to believe this young woman knew what she was talking about, until they put all her gathered information together and finally arrested the nephew for the crime.

The nephew had a gambling habit and owed some bad men really big and couldn't wait for everyone to die before he got his inheritance. Shanti was briefly extolled in a corner of the local newspaper as a kind of young J. B. Fletcher.

"Mrs. Davison, if you read the papers you would know that I was not involved in the murders, I just happened to be there painting a picture of the winery for the owner Sir Duke Rothschild-"

Mrs. Davison's head cock slightly to one side. With some type of 'mother radar' she could hear her husband and children coming noisily up the walk.

Before they could come inside and join Mrs. Davison, Shanti grabbed the cold doorknob and yanked the door open oblivious to the tinkling of the silver bell that hit the door over their heads.

Shanti briskly ushered the lady outside before she could even wrap the wool scarf back around her dirigible-sized neck.

Quickly turning over the Closed sign in the front window, Shanti grabbed a sweater off the back of a chair, dropped it over her shoulders then returned to the door.

Opening the door for one last time this evening, Shanti flipped off the lights and stepped outside. The chill of the evening hit her immediately.

Shivering, she leaned over and locked the door, dropping the key into her pants pocket. As soon as she took a step away from the shelter of the dark shop, the cold wind snapped, whipping her blonde hair so hard it stung her face.

Pulling her head into her shoulders to block the wind, she drew her sweater more tightly against her slim body and hurried the few yards from the shop to the restaurant next door. Although it was California, it still could be freezing in February.

It was especially cold this time of year in White Cedar. Framed by saw-toothed mountains, the small resort town is snuggled next to Snow Lake in a secluded verdant valley.

A few powdery snowflakes danced and twirled about in the wind. The late evening sky was already sprinkled with stars. There were no streetlights on the winding lake road.

The only illumination came from the cool silver moon and lights from cottages, shops and the many restaurants that dotted the lake. Even the marina was only dimly lit.

Winter leaves rustling and scraping along the cobblestone path crunched under Shanti's feet as she quickened her pace to the restaurant that was only a few yards from Fleurtique her tiny shop of handcrafted wares.

Welcoming beacons of amber lights glowed through windows that were dusted with freshly fallen snow. The soft lights beckoned her to hurry to the cozy restaurant.

As soon as she opened one of the double front doors, the warmth of the small restaurant enveloped her, instantly the goose bumps vanished from her arms.

Brushing a few feathered snowflakes from her thick yellow hair, she looked around for her sister.

Only a handful of customers were scattered around the dining room, their quiet murmuring and the background music lilted in her head as she scanned the room.

There was only one waitress in view. She was standing idly at a table, her hands tucked in her white apron. Listening with interest, she was smiling at the weary but happy customers as they relayed their day on the slopes.

On the other side of the dining room, the kitchen door swung open. Shanti's twin sister, Summer, bustled into the dining room.

"Hey sis," Summer smiled a welcome. Her eyes narrowed. Shanti's face was flushed rosy and her eyes sparkled. Double sapphires gleamed happily at Summer.

"Okay, what's up, I can tell you have some good news."

Shanti chuckled. "You know me so well. Let's sit." Their favorite spot was by the fireplace. When they were little they loved the crackling and sparking and the fiery brilliance of the lively flames in the fireplace.

Shanti pushed her hair behind her ears then haughtily held out a hand pretending to study her nails. "I, dear sister, have been commissioned to do another painting." Unable to hold back her glee any longer, she broke into a huge grin.

4

"Yahoo!" Summer yelped. "I'm so happy for you! Tell me all about it!"

"Well, a few months ago, an elderly couple was here on holiday, they had lunch in the restaurant and then the gentleman came into the shop. He asked a lot of questions about my paintings. He asked if I ever hired out to do personal work. I told him certainly I do."

Summer waved to a server who was cleaning up after the last customer that had just left. "Emily honey, will you be a dear and bring us a pot of ruby-black tea?"

Good-natured Emily winked and headed for the coffee stand by the kitchen.

"Anyway," Shanti leaned in closer to her sister, "apparently the man is a wealthy, gentleman farmer and his house was built in the 1800's. He told me his family has lived there for generations. He said he would just love to have a painting of the estate home and part of the grounds.

"The best part of course," she grinned at Summer, "is that he's sending me a plane ticket and will pay me quite handsomely for my work!" Shanti sat back, her face relaxed in satisfaction while she waited for her sister's reaction.

Emily stopped at their table and set down a flowery china pot of tea, two matching teacups and a plate of chocolate chip cookies. She put up a quick hand to stop their thanks.

"You girls work so hard and I know you barely had any dinner. I'm going back now to put up the clean dishes." Heading back towards the kitchen, the long skirt of her flower-printed uniform swinging like a pendulum brushed the tablecloths along the way.

"Oh Shanti, I'm so happy for you! It's been a while since you've had a commission. After that nasty business of the murders and all- well it was hardly your fault that you were present." Summer poured tea into two cups then pushed one cup across the table within her sister's reach.

Shanti scooped up a lump of brown sugar from a bowl on the table and dropped it into her cup and then stirred the tea automatically.

Summer chose a cookie. "Anyway, that horrible event is in the past, it certainly isn't likely to happen again. Lightning does not strike twice in the same place thank goodness! So, how long do you think this new project will take?" She plucked off the sugar encrusted flower that sat atop the cookie and popped it into her mouth.

The flower was the theme of the restaurant, named Crystal Petals. Edible flowers encased in sugar garnish all the dishes.

"Well, believe it or not, I'm going to Idaho-"

"Idaho!" Summer blurted, interrupting her sister. "Who the heck living in Idaho would want a painting of their house for heaven's sake? I mean, is there anything there except potatoes?"

Shanti laughed at her sister's aghast expression. "Actually, I'm going to a sugar beet farm-"

"A what? A dirty old farm?" Summer broke in again, her disapproving eyes wide and mouth open.

"Listen Summer," Shanti said patiently. "Mr. Lawton doesn't exactly go out and dig in the dirt anymore you know, he's rich and pays people to do that. The way he describes the house, gosh, it sounds like a mansion, with servants and such. I think it sounds quite exciting!"

Summer snorted. "Shanti, have you forgotten it's February for heaven's sake, you're going to freeze your butt off! I can't believe-"

"Oh Sum, you know the cold never bothers me. He, I mean, Langston Lawton, that's his name, and his wife, Maud, um, Mary, no, Maeve, I think her name is, anyway, he says I will be treated as a guest. He said I could go snowmobiling and skiing and horseback riding and-"

"Okay, okay I get you. When are you going to have time to work?" Summer asked, laughing at her sister. "It sounds like all play and no work to me!"

"I can only paint during a short period of time in the day, you know, sunlight and shadows and all that. I'll have plenty of free time on my hands," Shanti explained, nibbling a cookie. Flurries of crumbs flew out of her mouth as she bit the sweet treat. She set the half eaten cookie on a china plate.

"Anyway," Shanti continued, licking her lips. "I just got off the telephone with him. He asked me if I'd be interested. I said yes, I'd love to, of course. We went over details like time and airplanes and stuff.

"That customer, Mrs. Davison, you remember, with the four unruly brats that have been in every day for the past two weeks? Well, she was browsing like a bull in a china shop as she always does, and never buying anything like she always does, she kept interrupting me and asking questions.

"I felt I was being so rude to Mr. Lawton, but he didn't seem to mind. He said he'll send me my ticket in the overnight mail, I'll be leaving on Saturday."

"Saturday? Gee Shanti, that's so soon! Have you checked this guy out? He could be a big fake and wants to kidnap or murder you or something! He's a stranger for heaven's sake- I can't believe you're serious. You really need to be careful-"

"Yeah, yeah, I know, bad people are lurking out there everywhere waiting to have their way with me, or worse, rob and kill me!" Shanti laughed at her sister's concern.

She reached over and patted her hand. "I called the BBB and he's listed and very well reviewed. They confirmed he and his family have owned the land and farm for generations. The original homestead was actually started as a log cabin in the 1700's. There's no need to worry.

"Now, let's close up shop, come and help me pack. I don't want to forget anything." Shanti gulped the last of her tea, wiped her fingers on the cloth napkin and jumped up.

Chapter Two

*A*s soon as she stepped off the plane and onto the ramp, Shanti could feel the difference in the temperature.

At home it was chilly, here it's downright frigid! Good thing she had packed her warmest and sturdiest clothing.

When she reached the inside of the terminal, the air turned suffocatingly stuffy. She unbuttoned her coat and pulled off her knit hat and gloves then shoved them into a pocket.

Yanking her carry-on bag back up on her shoulder, she pushed her long hair out of her eyes and looked around for the sign for baggage claim.

While she waited for the first of the bags to come around on the turntable, she set down her carry-on filled with her art supplies and canvases and pulled a folded piece of paper out of her pocket.

Unfolding the paper, she read the lines:

Dear Miss Lane, we are thrilled you are able to do this project for us, and so looking forward to your arrival. As soon as you collect your luggage, our man, Geoffrey Montgomery, will be waiting for you by the exit door of your airline. Geoffrey is in his mid-fifties, has a mustache and is slightly greying, (but don't tell him that!). He will be wearing a black suit with a red tie and holding a sign with your name on it. We wait in anticipation of your arrival.

Yours truly,
Langston J. Lawton.

Shanti refolded the paper and put it back in her pocket. She looked up just in time to see one of her pieces of luggage come around the bend on the conveyor belt.

When she had retrieved both bags and her carry-on, she headed for the escalator.

Geoffrey Montgomery stood as still as a statue, holding up a white paper with **Shantilly Lane** printed in big black letters on it. He always hated when he had to do this. He felt like a damn store mannequin. *Oh well, stiff upper lip, old chap.*

Sighing imperceptibly, he perused the people straggling off the escalator. His eyes fell on the first young woman he saw. *That must be her. A face as plain as a turnip, with a plywood body to match, she sure won't be keeping any young man warm during this long, cold winter.*

Exactly what he expected a young female artist from a small town to look like. Probably will be a dried up old raisin someday. He held his up sign, trying to catch her eye.

A vacant look plastered on her homely face, the woman moved right past him. *Damn the chit,* he cursed under his breath.

"Miss Lane, oh Miss Lane!" he called out to the plain girl. His mustache twitched in aggravation as the girl continued to plod away from him. *I'm going to have to run after her- damn the-*

He felt a tug at his sleeve. Turning in annoyance, his mouth parted to voice his complaint, but he immediately pressed his lips together. Through years of training he was able to keep his expression totally void. But he couldn't hide the surprise that widened his eyes.

A beautiful young woman was smiling up at him with the most pristinely white teeth he'd ever seen. Shiny blonde hair cascaded in disarray around her shoulders, while striking blue eyes laughed at him.

"Yes Madam?" He looked down his nose at the woman, trying to hide his impression of her under a bored tone and heavy-lidded eyes. "I don't mean to be rude, but I must hurry and catch my party-"

He had forgotten about the homely girl he was supposed to bring back to the estate. *Damn*, he cursed under his breath again. She had blended in with other people.

Anxiously swinging his head back and forth, he searched frantically for her. Mr. Lawton would have his head if he lost his guest. Again he felt a tug at his sleeve. "What?" he snapped.

"Hi," the voice lilted sweetly, "are you Mr. Montgomery? I'm Shantilly Lane." Dropping the handle to one of her pieces of luggage, she held out a hand.

Red crept up Montgomery's neck as he realized the mistake he'd made. Embarrassed at his rude behavior, he took her small hand completely covering it with his gloved one, and shook it vigorously. "I am so sorry, Miss Lane, I uh, I thought that girl, I mean-"

Shanti giggled at his stammered apology. "Please call me Shanti, Mr. Montgomery, all my friends do. It's okay," she patted his arm, "you couldn't be expected to know what someone you've never met looks like!"

Shanti smiled at him and reached for her luggage. Quickly collecting himself, Montgomery also reached for the luggage.

"Allow me Miss, uh, Shantilly, that's my job." Easily picking up all three bags, he turned on his heel and quickly strode towards the exit, curtly calling over his shoulder, "Follow me."

She tried to keep Montgomery's tall, arrow-straight figure in sight as she darted around people, practically running to catch up with him. He moved purposefully through the airport and out the automatic sliding doors.

A gust of freezing wind blasted her so fiercely the second she exited the terminal, Shanti was almost pushed right back inside. She stopped abruptly and gasped, her eyes opened wide.

A freshly waxed, midnight blue Rolls Royce was parked right outside the exit. Hard snowflakes were starting to pelt the stunning car.

Montgomery, not wearing an overcoat of any kind, was already putting Shanti's luggage into the trunk. Another man, smartly attired in a chauffeur's uniform, stood beside the driver's door.

The chauffeur was staring at her slyly. Montgomery glared at him and moved to Shanti's side.

"Miss Shantilly Lane, Dario Lantana," he introduced the pair.

Dario's dark eyebrows shot up. He and Montgomery had discussed the visiting artist on the way to the airport. They'd shared a snicker or two over what they figured she'd look like.

Picket-fence teeth, pointy nose, and flat chested as a barn door, they had agreed on. They certainly hadn't expected this beauty whose gleaming eyes matched their master's glossy car.

Shanti didn't notice the raised eyebrows. She never paid much attention to her looks. Having a twin sister was like walking around with a mirror in front of her all the time. She became habituated to their appearance at a young age.

Dario sucked in his stomach and reached for the rear passenger door. He pulled it open then stood to the side, his eyes straight ahead like a soldier's.

"Please get in, Miss Lane." Dario swooped his arm towards the door motioning for her to climb into the car. He and Montgomery exchanged glances over the top of the vehicle as Shanti gracefully slid into the honey-beige, leathered interior.

Dario closed the door trying not to sneak another peek at the girl inside. Montgomery slid inside without seeming to bend his back at all, and sat next to Shanti.

"How was your flight, Miss, uh, Shantilly?" Montgomery politely inquired. He could hear Dario choking back a chuckle in the front seat as he turned the car on.

The experienced chauffeur effortlessly pulled the big car from the curb and onto the perimeter road, heading away from the airport.

Shanti settled back, luxuriating in the buttery softness of the leather seat. She laid her head back, resting it on the back of the seat. Her eyes drifted closed.

Montgomery took the opportunity to study her.

She had unbuttoned her coat. One black trousered leg crossed over the other, golden hair splayed across the seat. The locks shone in the light streaming in through the back window.

The butler took in her heart shaped face, now relaxed, full lips slightly turned up at the corners. Long lashes, darker than her lemon colored hair, laced soft cheeks that were flushed pink from the cold air. Her nose was small and straight.

His gaze traveled down her long, slim neck to her chest. With the thick clothing on, it was hard to tell, but Montgomery thought she was well endowed- he jerked his eyes off the girl and stared straight forward feeling like a creeper. He heard stifled laughter coming from the front seat.

Looking up, he saw Dario had been watching him checking out the girl. He frowned at the chauffeur, trying to keep the red from crawling up his neck again.

Shanti ran her fingers through her hair trying to smooth out the tangles. Sitting up, she turned to Montgomery and grinned at him.

Again, her perfectly straight, snow-white teeth took him aback. Wondering if they were inherited or cosmetically fixed like the circle of aristocrats he worked for, he'd forgotten he had asked her a question.

"The flight was very pleasant, Mr. Montgomery, thanks for asking. It was on time and there was hardly any turbulence. I've never been to Idaho so I chose the window so I could see a bird's eye view."

"Well then, uh, young lady, what did you think of our state from the air?" Montgomery stiffly cracked a polite smile.

"Actually," the blonde turned towards Montgomery, her expression serious, "it's really difficult to say what one thinks of a place when it's dead winter. Unless there's newly fallen snow, the bareness only accentuates the bleakness. But then, my artistic eye tends to see things in a different light."

She smiled at the man sitting next to her. She didn't see Dario watching her in the rear view mirror. Montgomery turned to her with sincere interest.

"Oh really, Miss, um, Shantilly, what do you see in this barren time of year?"

Shanti turned towards her side window and silently looked out as the car sped along the highway.

It had been just like any other busy city when they were near the airport, but after some miles, they left the red brick buildings and traffic behind and were now traveling along a country road. Her head swiveled back and forth as she watched the passing countryside.

It wasn't snowing very hard, fleeting nubs of flaky ice only occasionally pelted the windows, melting almost upon impact. Weak rays of the winter sun struggled to push light and heat through the few clouds to the cold earth.

Drab, round hills blocked the horizon. Grass the color of wheat, withered and waved from blotchy, liver-brown fields. Plain houses devoid of summer flowers and green trees stood like lonely square boulders against the foothills.

Mile long patches of farmland stretched between towns. Dark grey clouds hovering like helicopters cast shadows across cows grazing in cinnamon pastures. Shanti didn't notice Montgomery's light sarcasm.

"Oh, Mr. Montgomery, there's beauty in everything, sometimes you just have to look for it. For instance, look at that tree out there in the middle of that field."

Montgomery followed her pointing finger. Centered way out in the empty field far from the road, stood a lone enormous tree, its gnarly branches bereft of leaves.

He shrugged. "So what. A big ugly tree."

"Come on," Shanti coaxed, "use your imagination. Look, there's another one like it."

Her voice dropped, the tone serious. "Stare at it. See the tree, a single sentry in the desolate field, its bare branches, black silhouettes against the blue sky, stretching, grasping for the sun, the cows gathered against it to block themselves from the sharp wind."

Her voice softened, "But now, imagine a huge, loving old grandmother, her long, crooked fingers reaching out to gather in her children; the cows, and the grass, and the birds, sheltering them, keeping them safe against her woody breast."

Dario snickered.

Montgomery blinked then shook his head. *Damn*, he cursed to himself, the girl had drawn him right into her poetic picture. Actually, it wasn't all that of an unpleasant experience. He looked at Shanti.

Her eyes dreamy, lips slipping into a half-smile, she still stared out the window. For a second, Montgomery was envious of the way she was able to look at dismally plain things and see beauty there.

Shanti tried to take in everything she could see, it was so different from where she was from, but the flight and now the long, gently bumping ride were lulling her to sleep. Her head started to tilt back against the seat, until unconsciously, her eyes closed.

Montgomery looked over at her, then up at Dario watching in the mirror. Without a word, Montgomery reached into a side pocket on the door and pulled out cell. He settled back and quietly read the news.

Chapter Three

"Here you are, sir."

Langston Lawton looked up from the book he was reading. A maid stood in front of him holding a silver tray.

He took his glasses off and set them and his book on the rosewood table next to his chair. Ahh, tea was just what he'd been thinking about.

"Thank you, Serafina. You can set it right here on this table." He gestured to a space next to his book.

The girl set down the tray containing a steaming cup of tea, a tiny pitcher of cream, and a plate of cheese and crackers. A silver teaspoon wrapped in a napkin was beside the teacup.

She stood up, wiping her hands on her crisp apron. Nervously, she reached up and tucked a lacquer black hair back into her bun. She'd forgotten to put the white maid's bonnet on. Darn. She was always forgetting it. If the Missus saw her, she'd have her head! Her eyes darted guiltily towards the door to the library.

Langston chuckled. "Don't worry, Serafina. Mrs. Lawton is in the kitchen checking with Mrs. Li about dinner. If you hurry and use the back staircase, like you're supposed to," he gently admonished the maid, "you're pretty likely to miss her. Go on now." He motioned for her to leave.

The girl smiled, her dark eyes thanked him for not giving her away. She hurried to the doorway, peeked out, then disappeared, leaving the French doors, a design of galloping horses beautifully etched in the glass, wide open.

The creamy white walls of the library were stocked floor to ceiling with books. All types of books lined the rosewood shelves that were as highly polished as the other tables in the room. Maeve, Langston's wife of 50 odd years had quite a collection of inlaid rosewood tables.

Not large, yet roomy enough to hold a sofa and two matching, overstuffed chairs covered in hunter green chintz, the library was Langston's favorite room. The servants kept the fireplace in the library lit most of the time knowing the Master spends most of his time there.

The black-veined marble fireplace stood out against the mellow colors of the walls and tied the other masculine elements of the room together.

Langston could be found most afternoons sitting by the fire with either a snifter of brandy or a cup of tea, reading a book, or just drowsing and pretending he's sitting atop one of the horses in the many hunting pictures that decorated the walls, ready for an adventure.

Chuckling to himself again, Langston reached for his tea. He poured some of the delicious rich cream in, absently stirring with the silver spoon. *That girl*, he shook his head, *she'll never learn.*

Serafina had been with them for two years, right out of high school. He had been encouraging her to apply to the local college, but she was dragging her feet. Sometimes she acted like she'd been standing behind the door when God was handing out brains!

The maid was pretty, blessed with an appealing face and a voluptuous figure. Her black hair and gypsy eyes were striking, but it was her lush red lips that men couldn't take their eyes off.

It was surprising her body hadn't gotten her into trouble yet. It must be her extreme shyness that puts up a safety wall around her, Langston mused. At least Serafina was better than that other maid, Daisy.

No matter how hard his wife, Maeve, and their housekeeper, Mrs. Tii Li, worked with her, Daisy couldn't remember where to put the good silver, and she could be as clumsy as a newborn calf.

The other maids were always covering for her, trying to keep her from Maeve and Mrs. Li's wrath. Both women were perfectionists and neither of them had a lick of patience or an even temperament.

Both considered Red Gem Farm to be exclusively theirs. Mrs. Li never actually exhibits a bad temper, she just glares right through people with fathomless black eyes and lets their imagination do them in.

Oh well, the old man sighed, *not my problem*. But he couldn't help it if he felt sorry for people that were constantly beaten down and he does try to help when he can. Sighing again, he reached for his book. He put his glasses back on, opened the book and leisurely sipped his tea.

"Granddaddy!"

Langston jumped at the shriek. He must have dozed off. Dazed and struggling to sit up, his glasses landed in his lap and the book that was resting on his knee fell to the plush carpet with a thump.

"Wha-wha-" disoriented, he grabbed his glasses and slid them onto his aquiline nose. A crop of white hair fell over his forehead and into his eyes. Blinking rapidly, he shoved the loose hair aside and peered at the cause of the disturbance.

A flurry of flame-red hair bounced across the room and hurled itself onto the couch. Langston's eldest granddaughter, Dawn, threw herself onto her stomach.

Her chin was propped on her fists, elbows pushed into the couch with legs bent at the knees, her feet kicked back and forth in the air. Green eyes pleaded with her grandfather. She was behaving much younger than her twenty years.

"Granddaaaaddy…" the shriek ground into a whine.

With the slowness of old age, Langston reached down, resisting the urge to groan, and picked up his book. Calmly, he placed the book on the end table and smiled indulgently at his granddaughter.

"What is the problem now, Dawn?" He folded his arms across his chest and waited for his granddaughter's plea. He knew she wanted something.

Dawn spent little effort or time with anyone unless they could be of some benefit to her. She was almost the complete opposite of her younger sister, Chloe.

Always cheerful and helpful, Chloe hummed when wandering the vast halls of the estate. Bird watching and working in the extensive gardens were Chloe's two loves. Once or twice, when her grandmother hadn't caught her, the girl had appeared at the dinner table with dirt smudges on her cheeks.

Most afternoons she could be found right alongside their landscaper, Pablo, clipping rosebushes and planting tulip bulbs.

Dawn on the other hand was always off somewhere with her friends, lunching, shopping or getting her hair and nails done.

Once a month she sits through a vigorous facial to get rid of the ginger tossed freckles she was cursed with. Oh, how she wails about the sprinkling of tiny spots that cover her face and arms. She is never outdoors without a wide-brimmed hat to protect her skin from the sun.

Just the opposite, her sister Chloe spends hours in the sun and gets nary a freckle nor does she tan. Her siblings call her The Albino. Her russet brown hair and matching eyes stand out prettily against the foil of her bone-white skin.

What the girls do share along with their brother, Jaime, are their tall thin builds and limbs. They also have identical rowboat shaped feet, bony shoulders and piano key fingers. Nonetheless, they are all extremely attractive siblings.

Jaime's brown hair lacks the luster of Chloe's russet color, and he definitely does not share Dawn's brilliant coloring and cursed freckles. However, Jaime and Dawn's self-centeredness is about equal.

"Oh Granddad, Grandmother says I have to stay for dinner this evening. But I have *plans!*" Dawn's green eyes were as wide open as she could stretch them, begging for him to understand her plight and assist her in some way.

Grandmother makes the rules in the mansion and everyone that wants to live there abides by them. And no one wanted to take the slightest chance of being disinherited.

"Ashley and Britney and Suzanne and I are going to that new pub in town, you know, Starry Nights, it's not like there's all that much to do in this one-horse town. We're so tired of the Club and Winter's Wren at the lake, for crying out loud.

"Please Granddaddy, please talk to Grandmother and tell her I just have to go. I don't need to be at some stuffy ol' dinner party with the same old family and the neighbor Vaughns, just to meet some spinster artist."

Dawn gave her grandfather her most engaging smile. Swinging her legs around, she sat up and held out her hands, palms pressed together, begging.

Langston sighed. It's a good thing he had a little nap. "Honey, I'm sorry, you know when your grandmother gives an order no one can disobey and still keep their head. The last time you ignored her instructions to be at Jaime's 19th birthday party, and you chose instead to go skinny dipping with your friends at the lake, well, you surely remember the repercussions!"

Smiling wryly, he dropped hands covered with age-spots onto the arms of his chair to brace himself against her fury. His granddaughter comes by her fiery temper honestly.

She inherited it and the red hair from his wife. Although now Maeve's hair was totally grey, actually it was mostly white, but the temper hadn't lessened one tad.

"I certainly have no desire to incur her wrath, and I'm sure, neither do you. Besides, I think you will enjoy our guest. I was quite taken with her work. She has the most unique approach to painting, her pictures have a…make you feel…well, they're just hard to explain. You have to experience them yourself.

"I've hired her to paint the estate as you know, but I also expect her to be treated as a guest-and-" he held up a hand to stop her response, he could see her mouth opening, her red brows furrowing. "She is a lovely young woman, somewhere around your own age I think, and I found her an absolute pleasure to speak with."

"Ugh," Dawn groaned, slamming her back against the couch. Her hands fell to her side, rowboat feet flopped to the floor. She leaned forward. "Granddad, please-"

Langston took his book off the table and opened it. Flipping through the pages, he searched for where he had left off reading before he fell asleep. The conversation was over.

He heard Dawn's resigned groan, but didn't look up as she flounced out the door. His slight smile was barely noticeable.

Dawn stalked down the hall. Stamping each foot as hard on the carpet as she could, she was glowering at the floor and didn't see her brother coming around the corner.

"Look out!" Jaime yelled, grabbing her arms to keep her from crashing into him. "What the hell's your big hurry?" he huffed, thrusting her away.

Dawn glared at her younger brother. Jaime was the middle child with Dawn as the eldest and Chloe the youngest. "Oh, I have to stay here with you and our stupid family to have stupid dinner with our stupid guest."

Laughing, Jaime said, "Gee Sis, don't hold back, tell me how you really feel!"

"Oh sure, it's fine for you, it's not like you have a girlfriend or anything, Jaime. I was supposed to meet Jonathan later at that new nightclub. Now I'm stuck here."

Whining like a petulant child, Dawn crossed her arms over her chest and threw herself against the wall. She hit the wall so hard in her tantrum a painting almost lurched off the wall.

"Hey, watch it-" Jaime jumped up and grabbed the painting, steadying it. He stood back.

"Little do you know, missy, I do have a girlfriend-" he held up a hand when Dawn started to question him, "and who she is, is none of your business. Just do like you always do," he suggested.

"It's not like you're not proficient at sneaking out you know. Just wait until everyone gathers in the living room for coffee after dinner and claim your normal headache. Leave your car way down at the end of the driveway, and don't turn on the lights until you're well off the estate drive and halfway down Red Boulder Road."

Dawn's sullen face immediately cleared, her eyes lit up. "Thanks little brother, you always know how to get around things!"

She stood on tiptoe and kissed his unshaven cheek. Happy now, she skipped off down the hall to her room to decide what clothes will fit in her large bag. She'll have to change in her car.

She needn't worry about her mother noticing anything she did, she was so wrapped up in her fourth husband, that smarmy gigolo, Logan Thayne, she couldn't see beyond his greasy head.

"And don't call me 'little brother!'" Jaime called off after her. He hated that, made him sound like a little boy. He headed off to his room, he had his own plans to prepare.

Chapter Four

Maeve Lawton strode towards the kitchen. Tall, her back straight even into old age; Maeve comes from sturdy Viking stock. Her family claims ancestry to King Jovann of 15th century Norway.

They may be farmers, but they are old money and claim ancient titled royalty. The Lawtons have never had a problem getting into any elite clubs, universities or political offices in Idaho.

As Maeve approached the partially open door, she could feel the warmth emanating from the room. Obviously, the ovens were already on.

Mrs. Li's distinctive voice could be heard through the doorway. Normally her tone was low, devoid of any emotion or expression, sometimes it was hard to understand her because she barely opens her mouth when she speaks, and her words are heavily accented. But right now, she sounded like she was reaming someone out.

Maeve pushed the door open and walked in. Mrs. Li and one of the Vaughns' permanent field hands, Miguel, immediately stopped talking, both heads turned at Maeve's entrance.

Abruptly, Miguel dropped his head and stared at the floor. His callused hands were thrust deeply into well-worn, dungaree pockets.

Mrs. Li slowly turned her entire body towards Maeve. She glanced back at Miguel and said, "You can go."

Immediately Miguel turned and without a word, quickly exited out the back kitchen door.

Mrs. Li nodded slightly in deference to the lady of the house. "Yes Mrs. Lawton?" As always, her face was totally blank. Her lips pressed together, she stared unwavering at Maeve.

Although she was curious as to what they had been talking about, Maeve knew better than to question Mrs. Li. The housekeeper was notoriously closed mouthed. She used very few words. Stating facts and then moving out of sight so quickly, sometimes one wondered if she'd been standing there at all.

Mrs. Li does not engage in unnecessary conversation. The rest of the Lawtons' help tell tales that Mrs. Li has special evil powers. Langston laughs this off. He tells his servants they are way too modern and educated to be superstitious and believe in hocus-pocus.

Maeve never makes a comment either way. Mrs. Li is the best housekeeper they've ever had, she runs the mansion just the way Maeve wants it run. Mrs. Li stays out of Maeve's way and never argues with her. If she disagrees with any of Maeve's ideas, she keeps it to herself.

After receiving instructions, the housekeeper always nods briefly, and turns a quick heel to do Mrs. Lawton's bidding. Mrs. Li's expressionless face never gives anything away.

As long as the house runs smoothly and she does as Maeve instructs, Maeve could care less if she's sticking pins in voodoo dolls in the back room or making love potions for the silly housemaids.

Maeve assumed Mrs. Li was advising Miguel what time to tell the Vaughns to be over for dinner. The Vaughns have the neighboring farmstead. Their farm has also been in their family for generations. However, they farm potatoes while the Lawtons' main crop is sugar beets.

"Where is Cook?" Maeve asked Mrs. Li looking around the enormous kitchen. No one except the housekeeper was present. It looked like someone had just cleaned up after lunch and was preparing for the evening's small dinner party.

The oven's red light was glowing, advising it was on, and several pots were steaming on the burners. Maeve could see the silver was laid out and the polish and several cloths were on the solid oak kitchen table that the help ate and worked on.

Mrs. Li moved effortlessly towards the kitchen door. It was never apparent how tiny she really was; being so formidable and severe, she seemed ten feet tall.

"Cook is in the larder, and the girls are cleaning the dining room before they get started on polishing the silver. I'm going to go find that lazy girl, Serafina. Libby and Daisy are already out there. No one has seen Serafina since she brought the Master his tea. She's probably out in the beach house banging Mr. Thayne."

Mrs. Li pretended not to see the shocked look on Maeve's face. Without waiting for a response from her mistress, the housekeeper left.

Maeve's silver eyebrows rose so high they almost hit her hairline. Well! She wasn't the least bit surprised at Mrs. Li's foul language. She knew the Asian lady did it deliberately to shock people.

She didn't, however, want to hear about her fourth son-in-law, Logan Thayne's, possible indiscretions. Her daughter, Camelia, was a giddy, brainless woman who drinks too much and gives blondes a bad name.

It seems she's desperately trying to run through her daddy's money as fast as she can with greedy immoral men who are at least ten years younger than she. The last one, Dalton Smith, Maeve had to get Graham, their foreman, to yank off her granddaughter, Dawn.

Graham had grabbed Smith by the belt and shirt collar; dragged him to the door then threw him out onto the steps. The well-muscled Graham followed Smith out the door, kicking him down the hard cement steps.

Smith was screaming and holding his head that was bleeding profusely from a nasty gash over one eye. He begged Graham to stop, but his pleas fell on deaf ears. Without saying a word, Graham continued kicking, pushing and dragging the man across the lawn and then down the winding drive.

Maeve watched until Mrs. Li disappeared through the gate. Shrugging, she closed the door. She didn't care what Graham had done to Dalton Smith, as long as Smith knew not to come back to the estate or come near her daughter or granddaughter again.

She had ignored Camelia's wails as she forced her to sign divorce papers. Maeve paid Smith a paltry sum to send him on his way, advising him not to try to claim anything further from her gullible daughter.

Understandably, her granddaughter, Dawn, probably had a hand in enticing Smith to come on to her. But, she was screaming and struggling quite realistically when Maeve had unexpectedly entered the parlor and saw Smith lying atop her, trying to rip off her silk blouse.

None of Maeve's three grandchildren were yet married, although they had passed the age of consent. Maeve didn't know whether that was good or bad. None seemed to have any common sense at all, and it was trying enough to keep paying off her daughter's men and bailing her out of trouble, she couldn't imagine tripling that effort with her grandchildren.

At that moment, Cook bustled into the kitchen, her arms full of butter, mayonnaise, salad dressing, tomatoes and a can of bread crumbs. She jolted when she saw Maeve standing there with an intent expression, her green eyes hard.

"Ma'am?" Cook asked, dropping her armful onto the closest counter. "Is something the matter?" Never taking her eyes off Maeve, she stretched out a short arm to catch the mayonnaise jar that rolled towards the edge of the counter.

Maeve turned her eyes up towards the ceiling. Sighing, she lowered her eyes, taking in the rotund cook's nervous manner. Cook had been with them for several years.

Cook easily blustered at the help that worked at the Manor, including the field hands and seasonal migrant workers, but she was respectful of the Master and Mistress of the house. They were her bread and butter. To be dismissed from their household would mean death in the entire city, probably the state too. No one would ever hire her.

The Lawtons were very well known and long established members of the Idaho community and sugar beet commission. They were great contributors to the University of Idaho, and generous benefactors of the local hospital and library.

Basically, they're farmers. But they are the cream of the society, aristocrats of deeply ingrained generations of local inhabitants. Their family name, as well as their neighbor's, the Vaughns', was emblazoned on the Town Hall as well as bridges, the library and wings in the hospital.

Cook's roly-poly cheeks were tomato red from her exertions and the heat of the kitchen. Barely five feet, she was as wide as tall. It was apparent she tasted all of her dishes before they were served to the family. Aware Maeve was studying her, she anxiously wiped stubby fingers on her stained apron.

Ignoring the nervous cook, Maeve passed her and went to the stove. Lifting a lid off a pot, she stood back as a burst of steam whooshed out. Bending her long neck over the pot, she closed her eyes against the heat and sniffed at the contents. "Hmmm." was all she murmured.

Opening the oven door, her slim, ramrod straight body leaning over further, she breathed in deeply. The delicious aroma of roasting garlic and baking potatoes drifted into the room. Maeve closed the door, trapping the luscious odors inside.

Turning suddenly, she caught Cook's piggish eyes riveted on her back, her tongue sticking out. She hadn't quite hid the hateful expression, or tongue aimed at her mistress fast enough.

Maeve didn't acknowledge Cook's disdainful behavior. She wished she could fire the unpleasant fat cook, but she was one of the best around and kept out of her way. But, once she makes a real glaring mistake, out she goes and good riddance.

"How long has the meat been marinating?" Maeve asked her.

Trying to make up for getting caught making a nasty face at her mistress, Cook grinned as wide as she could. She shouldn't have bothered. Her crooked, nubby teeth looked like they'd been ground down and yellowed by long years of poor care.

Seeing Maeve's look of revulsion, Cook snapped her mouth closed and stared down at her feet, wishing she'd taken the time to polish the scuff marks off her sensible shoes. "16 hours," Cook mumbled.

Maeve looked down at the top of Cook's grimy salt and pepper hair. "And the chestnuts for the stuffing? Have you roasted them yet?"

"Yes Ma'am. The girls shelled them early this morning."

"Carry on then, I can see Mrs. Li has everything under control," Maeve said, heading for the door. She couldn't wait to get away from the repugnant cook. As she left the kitchen she called out, "And put on your chef's hat."

Cook cringed, controlling herself from poking out her pointy tongue again at Maeve's parting back. Damn hat. She hated wearing the stacked chef's hat. She spotted the offending hat over on the counter near the back door.

Snatching it off the counter, she threw the hat on the floor, then jumped up and down on it.

Bending her girth with difficulty, she plucked the hat off the floor. Ignoring the black shoe marks that now graced the hat, she gleefully shoved it on her head.

Chapter Five

$\mathcal{J}$ust waking from her light nap, Shanti sleepily peeked through thick lashes out the window of the car.

Block-long stately homes, each more elegant than the last with manicured sprawling lawns, zoomed by as they rode through the neighborhood.

Dashing by acres of woods, they now passed grass brown from the winter. Beyond the grass, Montgomery pointed out the crops of sugar beet fields where they'll be planted next season.

The Rolls stopped at a closed, iron gate. A sign announcing the name of the estate spread in a wrought iron arch over the security gate.

They'd finally arrived at **Red Gem Farm**. Dario pushed a card into the metal guard box and the gate slowly swung open. As soon as the car passed through, the gate automatically closed behind them.

The gleaming luxury car glided up the curved driveway. Shanti sat up, her eyes widened in awe as she took in her grand surroundings.

The massive three-story estate made of stone with wings spreading in two directions stood as magnificently as a castle at the top of the expansive grounds.

"Oh my…" Shanti drawled. She couldn't believe the magnitude of the mansion and the acres of lawn, pasture and forest surrounding it.

Montgomery hid his smile at the girl's obvious surprise and dismay. He was long used to the grandeur of his employer's vast home.

Shanti swung her head to Montgomery. "You should have warned me!" she accused Montgomery.

His eyebrows rose in feigned affront.

"Warned you about what, Madame?" He pretended aloofness at her ingenuousness. Actually, he found the young woman quite refreshing. The usual people that visited were so blasé at the Lawtons' wealth. Most of them had grown up in equal luxury and were unimpressed with the estate.

"I…uh…you know, Montgomery!" Shanti swiped a glove playfully at his arm. She wasn't fooled, she knew the estate was quite awesome and her reaction totally appropriate.

Montgomery put his arms up in mock protection, as if the slight young woman on the seat next to him could really do him any harm.

Life was going to be different for a while around the Manor, he was thinking. Wait until Dawn, Chloe and Jaime get a look at their grandfather's guest. The reactions of the help should be interesting as well.

Shantilly Lane is to be treated as a guest according to the old man, but in reality, she is an employee. That ought to really stir things up! He caught Dario's raised eyebrows in the rearview mirror.

Dario wasn't used to seeing the normally stiff Montgomery engage in any kind of frivolity, unless it had something to do with the dogs.

Montgomery turned his nose up at people, but he loved the Lawtons' dogs. He helped Graham, the foreman, with the training of the canines for security and for hunting.

The car came to a stop at the top of the circular driveway, directly in front of the mansion. The front door immediately swung open.

A tiny Asian woman seemed to magically appear in the doorway.

Dario hopped out of the car and ran around to the trunk. He removed Shanti's luggage, setting them on the ground next to the car.

Montgomery emerged and came around to Shanti's side of the car. She was busy pulling on her hat and buttoning her coat. She was stalling to gain her composure. She knew Langston Lawton was rich, but this was astounding!

Suddenly she was worried about her casual appearance. And what if her manners weren't up to snuff? She knew enough to watch the host to see what fork to use when in doubt, but this, this grandeur was so unexpected!

She drew a deep breath and had a smile ready for Montgomery as he opened her door.

Shanti placed her hand in the one he held out, exiting the car as gracefully as she could. Was that a wink? She looked sharply at Montgomery. She could have sworn he winked in encouragement at her! Her eyes narrowed, but his gaze was fixed on the woman standing in the doorway.

When Shanti followed his glance, she saw that another woman, with a queenly bearing and much taller than the Asian woman, was now standing in the doorway as well. She had met Langston when he'd visited her shop but Maeve hadn't been with him.

Montgomery took her elbow and drew her towards the mansion. When they reached the door, nodding to both women, Montgomery pulled Shanti gently forward and presented her to the ladies.

"Mrs. Lawton, Mrs. Li, meet Miss Shantilly Lane." He nodded again then turned to Shanti. His job done, he squeezed her arm lightly, then turned to help Dario with the luggage.

Mrs. Lawton stepped forward and held out her hand. "A pleasure to meet you, Miss Lane. This is our housekeeper, Mrs. Tii Li. She will see to all of your needs during your stay here. Please feel free to ask her for anything you require." Maeve regally shook Shanti's hand.

Mrs. Li slightly inclined her head with an unsmiling welcome, her hands stayed clasped behind her back.

"How do you do, Mrs. Li? What a unique necklace. Does it represent something?" Shanti pointed at the pendant hanging on a chain around the housekeeper's neck.

A rectangle of horizontal stripes was framed in gold. The two stripes on the outside were red, the next two inner stripes were white and then a blue stripe. Mrs. Li touched the necklace.

"It is the flag of my country." After she said the few short words, she clamped her lips together, took a step back and stared blankly at Shanti.

Shanti felt like shivering. Mrs. Li's black eyes seemed to have no reflection. She felt as if the housekeeper had looked right through her.

Maeve took Shanti's hand and pulled her inside. "Welcome to my home, Miss Lane. I hope you'll be comfortable. Please feel as if you are in your own home."

Shanti stifled a giggle. Yeah, like one bathroom in this mansion is the size of my whole house! Shanti pulled off her hat and coat.

Mrs. Li immediately stepped forward. She took Shanti's outdoor clothing and left the room without speaking a word.

Shanti turned her most engaging smile to Mrs. Lawton. "Please call me Shanti, Mrs. Lawton. I know it sounds silly, but my Daddy nicknamed me when I was just a toddler."

Maeve, melting a bit, returned a half-smile. "As you wish, dear. I shall show you to your room myself and see that you get settled. I know after your long trip you may wish a shower and perhaps a nap." Her mouth twitched at Shanti's grin of gratefulness.

"One of the maids will bring you some refreshment now, and around seven, someone will fetch you for cocktails. We will get to know one another over drinks, then dinner will be served at eight. Does this suit you?"

Shanti smiled. "It all sounds lovely, Mrs. Lawton. I don't want you to go to any trouble for me."

"Oh heavens dear, we love to 'trouble' here. We all like fresh blood, um…I mean a new person is always a treat to us in this small community. Now, come along, I'll show you to your room." She turned swiftly and moved across the foyer.

Shanti barely had a second to take in the opulent foyer before she hurried after Mrs. Lawton. She caught a flash of white marble and white tile with a blue design that flowed as far as the eye could see.

A gold-veined white marble table stood in the center of the foyer. A massive display of brightly colored flowers arranged in a huge shining gold vase on the table seemed to stretch all the way up to the cathedral ceiling.

Numerous halls and doors led in all directions from the foyer like spokes on a wheel. Ancient looking paintings of people lined the walls. When she had time later, Shanti thought, she'd love to look at them more closely and see who they were.

Mrs. Lawton trod with little effort up the carpeted staircase. At the top of the stairs she hesitated, "Someone will show you around the estate and grounds later after you've rested. But, if you want to wander around on your own, you don't need to wait for someone to retrieve you. As I said, we want you to feel at home."

The triple wide, blue carpeted staircase was in the center of the room rather than against one wall. It widened at the top of each floor, flowing off in either direction to a wing.

The staircase was perfect for a ball. Shanti could imagine the grand ladies of the house dressed like princesses in an array of gorgeous gowns and jewels, all eyes on them as they strolled elegantly down to the waiting guests.

"Miss Lane!"

Shanti looked up.

Mrs. Lawton stood on the second landing staring down at her. She realized she'd been day dreaming and Mrs. Lawton was standing there waiting for her. Red faced, she hurried up the stairs. When she reached Maeve, she blurted out an apology.

"I'm so sorry for keeping you waiting, Mrs. Lawton! Your home is so beautiful, well, I'm just beside myself. I don't mean to be rude, but I really can't wait to see the rest of the house and grounds."

Maeve smiled at Shanti's guileless sincerity. "I am pleased you like our home, Miss Lane. We've worked for a long time on the estate, making it as comfortable and attractive as possible.

"Here, your room is down towards the end of what we call the 'South Wing.' You'll get the early morning sun, really the prettiest time of the day. When you look out the window you'll be able to see the sun rise over the river that runs behind the manor."

She moved more slowly down the hall, allowing Shanti to get a look at the paintings along the walls. Some of the doors to rooms were open and Shanti quickly peeked in as they passed by. All she could see were flashes of color of uniquely individual rooms.

"The horses are let out in the pasture before the sun comes up. I don't know if you're an early riser, but if you are up, go out onto your balcony, you can watch Graham Duncan, our foreman and the farmhands bring the horses in. It's a wonderful sight. The dew on the grass sparkles like diamonds in the mist and the horses are quite frolicky that time of day."

Frolicky? Shanti giggled to herself. That word sounded funny coming out of the austere Maeve Lawton's mouth. Heavens, she thought, what a long way to her room. But, she was getting excited. A balcony of her own overlooking a river, how lovely!

"We've put you in the middle of the wing, Miss Lane. We didn't want you to feel so very far away from the rest of the house, but we thought you might like some space from the normal noises of the household."

The thick carpeting muffled their steps. They passed several more rooms before Mrs. Lawton stopped outside an open door.

Stepping inside, she waited for Shanti to follow her. "Here we are, dear."

Shanti followed the older woman inside, trying not to look surprised at the size and grandeur of the room.

"Mrs. Lawton, it's so beautiful!"

"Thank you dear. Now, there is a key right there on the dresser. You certainly don't need to lock your door, you're quite safe here. However, we don't know how you'll feel in a strange place, so we put the key handy in case you wanted to use it. Now, over here," Maeve moved across the room.

Shanti wondered how she walked on the plush, pale rose carpeting in heels without tripping.

The walls of the bedroom were the shade a mother-of-pearl opalescence. Victorian lampshades fringed with glass beads matched the pale rose of the carpet.

A rosy colored bed skirt matching the curtains surrounded the lower half of the bed with a cream duvet covering the top. A rose and cream silk quilt was folded neatly across the foot of the bed, and rosy throw pillows mingled with cream pillows at the head.

Soft light shone through the room diffused by the white sheers covering the windows of the French doors.

The room contained a blonde wooden dresser, matching bedside table, a rocking chair and a small desk and chair.

"This is your bathroom." Maeve opened a door and turned on a light so Shanti could see.

The room, creamy white with white marble counters held two shell-shaped pink colored sinks with glistening gold faucets.

Shanti eyed the huge Roman tub with a whirlpool over by the window. It looked inviting to her after her long trip. She was already picturing herself luxuriating in the warm, bubble-filled swirling water.

Maeve turned off the light and left the bathroom. She walked over to the glass French doors opposite the door they came in. Shanti followed close behind.

Maeve pushed the white sheers aside, and grasping each glass doorknob, pulled the doors open. The cold air rushed inside, blowing back both women's hair and clothes.

"I know it's chilly, dear, but step out here for just a second." Maeve stood outside the doors, waiting for Shanti to join her.

Shanti's mouth dropped open.

The view was amazing. She had the urge to pull her paints out right now.

An extensive garden encircled a patio and a turquoise pool shimmering in the sunlight. Of course there were no flowers now, but Shanti recognized rose bushes and rhododendrons even from her distance up on the balcony.

The grounds spread out a few hundred yards until they reached the river. The water looked rough but exhilarating with its rushing, dark winter waters.

Way beyond the river stretched a row of trees. That must be the beginning of the forest they'd seen on the drive in. The sun was swinging down, it was almost four by now.

The bare limbs of white birch trees reflected light from the sun. Streaks of sunlight drew across the grass leaving yellow striped trails. Light even glinted off birds flying by.

Movement caught Shanti's eye.

Over to the north, she could see some horses with riders coming in from the fields. They headed towards the stables off to the left of the estate. White puffs of air from the riders' and horses' breaths became visible as they came closer.

They headed to the stables. Shanti couldn't tell if the riders were male or female, they were so bundled up against the frigid air.

Maeve stepped back inside the warm room. Shanti reluctantly followed her even though she was beginning to shiver.

Closing the doors and while walking, Maeve pointed to another set of double glass doors ahead of her.

"Mr. Lawton thought this room would suit you especially well because there is a small studio on the other side of the sitting room."

Inside the double doors was another smaller room. A sofa, an easy chair, ottoman and coffee table, all in matching gold, rose and cream looked pretty and comfortable. An entertainment center took up one wall.

A small refrigerator, sink, coffee machine and microwave were on the farthest wall. An armoire covered the entire third wall, and beyond that, there was yet another opening. Maeve disappeared through the archway of the opening.

Inside was a tiny studio, perfect for an artist on a temporary visit. "Oh my," Shanti couldn't help the words that slipped out as she looked all around.

Paints and brushes were lined up on a counter ready to be used, and stacked near the door, were numerous canvases of varying sizes.

"I don't mean to gush, Mrs. Lawton, but this is so incredible! Every need I could think of is here, and so beautiful too!" Shanti almost twirled in a circle trying to take in everything.

Mrs. Lawton smiled patiently. "These are considered technically, apartments, dear. We do want our guests to be as comfortable as possible. My grandchildren are in this wing as well." She paused while Shanti viewed the room with glowing eyes.

"Camelia, my daughter and her, uh, husband, Logan Thayne, have apartments in the north wing nearer Langston and myself. Most of the help live on the third floor near the center of the main house. Of course if there is anything you need," she gestured for Shanti to follow her as she went back into the bedroom, "just pull gently on this."

She pointed to a flowered bell pull hanging by the bedroom door. As did all the furniture, curtains and bedding, the bell pull matched the gold, rose and cream motif.

"And someone will be right here to get you what you want." She moved to the door. "I'm going to leave you to your shower and nap now, dear. Is there anything you can think of that you may need before I go? I can send Libby or Serafina up."

Grinning, Shanti shrugged. "Mrs. Lawton, I don't think there's anything in the entire world that isn't in this room that I could possibly need right now!"

"Fine then, as I said, around seven," she lifted her wrist and glanced at her watch. "That's several hours from now. I'll have someone come and fetch you for cocktails. All right?" She raised a brow in question. Moving out of the room, she quietly closed the door behind her.

"Wow!" Shanti said out loud. Kicking off her shoes she flopped on the queen-sized bed. "Uhh…" she moaned, rubbing her arms and legs against the silk of the comforter covering the bed.

Fluffing the silk covered pillows, no less than five of them, she plopped her head down, sinking as deep as she could in the silky cocoon. Letting out a deeply held breath of air, Shanti finally relaxed.

She was uncomfortable in Maeve Lawton's presence. The elderly woman was such a severe grand dame, she felt she needed to be on her very best behavior at all times when she was near her. Shanti was used to being herself, a well-bred, shy, yet free spirit that enjoyed life.

Her eyes settled on the side table next to the dresser. A pitcher of ice water and a bowl of fruit were on the table. She could see a small, sharp paring knife and a linen napkin there as well. They think of everything, she thought to herself, impressed beyond belief.

Her luggage was already in the room. How on earth had Montgomery managed to beat them there, she wondered then realized there were probably back staircases for the servants' use. She jumped at a sudden knock at the door.

Climbing off the high bed, she shuffled to the door in her socks. Slowly opening the door, she peeked through the crack. When she saw a maid's uniform she opened the door wide.

A smiling girl entered the room carrying a tray. She set the tray on an end table that was beside the bed.

"Hi!" Shanti greeted her. "I'm Shanti, who are you?" She watched the pretty girl with black hair and the reddest lips she'd ever seen move things around on the tray before she turned to Shanti.

Her gypsy eyes widened when she looked at Shanti. Then she laughed. "Wait until Miss Dawn and Master Jaime get a look at you!" she said with a giggle. A slight accent marred her words.

Shanti didn't recognize her accent and was too polite to ask what Serafina's heritage was. Shanti's brows drew together. Serafina was the second person to say those words.

"I don't understand, Serafina, why do you say that?"

Serafina laughed again. "You own a mirror, do you not?" She shook her head at Shanti's puzzled expression. *The beautiful girl has no clue as to what she looks like*, Serafina thought to herself, *Miss Dawn is going to be awfully jealous. She's used to being the local head-turner.*

Neighbor Tori Vaughn, with her dark brown hair running poker straight to her waist is a pretty girl in her own right, but Miss Dawn usually wins beauty contests hands down with her flaming hair and slightly slanted, contrasting emerald green eyes.

"Never mind honey. If you do not know what I mean, you will never know. Now," she pointed to the tray.

Shanti stood next to the shorter girl and looked down.

"Here is a mug of hot chocolate, a blueberry muffin, some cookies, and a couple of pieces of cheese. There are fruit and ice water over on the dresser. That should hold you until cocktails."

Patting Serafina's arm, Shanti said gratefully, "Thank you so much Serafina. I hope we can become good friends during my stay here."

Serafina smiled wryly at her words. "We can be friends in private, Miss, but when we are in public, I am a servant and you are the guest." She held up a hand at Shanti's rebuttal.

"Really Miss Shantilly, it is better this way. Everyone knows their place, and it makes everyone more comfortable that way. I will come by later and visit with you for a while, tell you about the estate and town if you would like." She moved towards the door.

"Okay, Serafina, I understand, I think. It'll take a little getting used to being waited on I guess. And yes, I'd love it if you'd stop by and give me some history of the town. And, before I forget, how am I expected to dress for dinner?"

Serafina laughed at Shanti's ingenuousness. "Here, the men wear ties at dinner. Mr. Lawton wears a suit and tie. Always. The ladies dress nicely, but normally you do not need to be too fancy.

"Miss Dawn and Miss Chloe often wear jeans to the table, Mrs. Lawton hates that. But, because we are having a small dinner party tonight, in your honor," Shanti winced, "and the Vaughns next door are coming, you will like them, they are nice people, it will be pretty dressy.

"Mrs. Lawton will wear floor length, her daughter, Camelia may as well, but the girls, they are around your age I suspect, they will wear knee-length. Does that help?" she asked with a kind smile.

Shanti nodded, her wardrobe running through her head. It's a good thing she picked up some extra dresses before she left.

"Yeah, I'll be fine. Thanks so much, Serafina. You run along now, I know you must have tons of work to do, and I'm keeping you with my foolish questions. You've been so kind and helpful."

Shanti closed the door behind the maid. Yawning, she headed for the bathroom. Feeling a little sticky, that tub was beckoning her, she could hear it calling her name.

Chapter Six

"Daisy!"

The young maid jumped, her hand flew to her chest. "Lordy, Miz Lawton, yer nearly scared the life outta me!" The chubby maid fanned her pudgy fingers in front of her face.

Then she caught the stern look on her mistress' face. Her own normally cheerful face fell. She followed Maeve's narrowed eyes. She was staring at the table. Her thin arm was rigidly pointing at the wine glasses.

"Those are *not* the proper Burgundy glasses!" she scolded the hapless maid. "Daisy, you've been here four, five years now-"

Cringing under her mistress' formidable demeanor and angry stance, she mumbled, "Uh, four ma'am...I'm sor-"

"Four years and you don't yet know what the proper stemware is! Get Mrs. Li immediately! Now!" she ordered when the maid didn't move fast enough.

Daisy didn't know whether to set down the glass she had been wiping with a cloth, and then go get Mrs. Li, or take the glass with her. Her face flushing, she moved her hand back and forth undecided, starting to set the glass down, and then she stopped herself, and then started to set it down again.

"Daisy!" Mrs. Lawton practically shrieked.

The maid jumped about two feet in the air.

Suddenly, a calm, clipped voice cut through like a knife.

"What is the problem?" Mrs. Li had entered the room.

Neither Maeve nor Daisy had seen her enter.

Daisy just about had a heart attack right then and there. She fully believed Mrs. Li had special powers, you could tell by the way she was suddenly in a room without anyone noticing her coming in.

And those eyes, black as midnight- they were so freaky- and here she'd just popped in again- *my God*- Daisy could feel the room swimming under her, she knew she was going to faint any second-

"Daisy! Get a grip. Stop the theatrics right now." Maeve's iron voice was the strength the maid needed to clear her head. Blinking rapidly, she tried to meld herself into the table, hoping both imperious women would forget she was there.

Maeve turned and faced Mrs. Li.

The Asian woman stood straight as a metal beam, hands clasped behind her back, her eyes fixed unblinking at Mrs. Lawton. The only person in the town not afraid of Mrs. Li was Maeve.

She stared her down. "Mrs. Li, it is your job to train the help properly. And look-" her arm swept the table that was partially set for the evening's party.

Mrs. Li looked at the table. Her brows knifed together. She turned to Daisy, the poor girl wilted under the stare. "I am sorry for the ineffectiveness of the staff, Mrs. Lawton. I will see immediately to the correction. Daisy, come with me," she directed the girl to follow her as she headed for the kitchen.

Daisy didn't dare sneak a look at Maeve. She kept her round head down, curly, mousy brown hair covering round brown eyes and pimply skin.

Without looking back at Daisy, Mrs. Li snapped, "Stop dragging your feet." Daisy picked up her wide feet and scurried after the tiny woman.

That settled, Maeve went down the long hall to the library. She peered in before entering. If her husband was asleep, as he often was, she didn't want to disturb him.

He saw her in the doorway. "Hello Maeve dear, do come in." He set his book and eyeglasses on the table, giving her his full attention.

"Hello Darling, how are you feeling?" Maeve sat on the firm couch, her legs crossed at the ankles and to the side. She folded her hands in her lap.

Langston Lawton yawned behind a hand. "I'm feeling pretty perky today actually, my dear."

"Your guest has arrived safe and sound, Langston. She's all settled into the Rose Room as you wished," Maeve told him.

"Well, now that you've visited with her a bit, what do you think? I mean about her, you haven't seen as much of her work as I have." Langston glanced over at the fire that had dwindled. He was feeling a bit chilly.

Maeve noticed his glance. She got right up and went right over to the bell pull by the door and pulled it three times.

There was a bell pull in every room of the house. Each pull is connected to a wire that runs to the kitchen where it strikes a bell. The servants can tell by which bell rings, which room to go to.

Duplicate cords go to Mrs. Li's room as well. All of the maids have cells of course, but the continuous ringing even buzzing on silent annoys Mrs. Lawton. She prefers the old time bell pulls. And if she catches anyone on a cell phone while on the clock- look out!

"Shantilly is a beauty, there's no doubt about that. Funny, but she seems totally unaware of the effect she has on people. Her vocabulary is excellent as well as her manners, one can tell she is well brought up," Maeve replied.

"And it's obvious she has quite a good intellect. If Jaime wasn't such a scoundrel, I'd be hard pressed not to fix up the pair. Unfortunately, I think our jaded grandson would eat the poor dear up and spit her out without blinking an eye."

Langston nodded in wry agreement.

Jaime was to the manor born with very little guidance or discipline. He's never had to work, and he seldom lifts anything heavier than the silver spoon to his mouth.

Langston had for years tried to get him interested in the farm, but the boy wouldn't think of dirtying his hands. Watching Polo is as close to the horses as he will get.

He considers sugar beets to be well beneath his stature in the community. That a root vegetable provides his wealth embarrasses the heck out of him.

Jaime's mother, Camelia, an empty headed woman that keeps marrying the wrong kind of man managed to have the same man father all three of her children. Sadly, by time Chloe, the youngest, was born, the millionaire Kurtis Crawford was long gone.

The children really never knew their father. And the succession of stepfathers, the next as bad as the last, were poor father figures to the children. The kids were just annoyances to be shuttled out of the way.

After Camelia's last husband, her third, dumped her, she came back home to the Manor to live. The damage was done by then.

Jaime was a playboy. His sister, Dawn, little better than the town whore, and Chloe, sweet, but has no goals other than to while away the days digging in the dirt with Pablo, the groundskeeper.

Much to Langston's chagrin, none of the grandchildren were interested in the workings of the farm.

Libby, one of the maids, trepidatiously entered the room in answer to the bell pull. "Yes Mum?" she asked.

"Libby, please see to the fire." Maeve nodded at the fireplace.

The girl went right to it, knelt down and picked up chunks of dry wood lying in the copper holder next to the fireplace.

"Who shall we have show Shantilly around?" Maeve asked her husband.

Langston absently pulled on his pursed lips as he thought. "I think Chloe would perhaps be our best choice."

Maeve nodded in agreement. "Dawn would complain that she was being given a chore, and I don't think it's quite right to thrust Jaime on the unsuspecting innocent. Graham can probably show her the grounds and stables if he isn't busy."

"That sounds fine, however, Chloe knows the fields and forests as well as any of the men, you know." Langston reminded his wife of their granddaughter's love of the outdoors.

If only they could channel that love into interest in the farm. When they die, there'll be no one to carry on with the family business. Maeve knew that terribly disheartened her husband.

Hearing the metal screen scraping, Maeve looked over and saw Libby was able to get the fire going.

Of all her servants, Maeve was the most pleased with Libby. She chewed gum like a cow and slept with half the field hands, but she learns quickly and Maeve had not yet had any complaints about her.

Even Mrs. Li never says her name. That's a positive thing. Mrs. Li doesn't mention anyone unless she has a complaint.

Libby stood up, brushing her hands on her apron. She stared at the fire for a minute, making sure it had really caught. When she was satisfied she turned to Maeve.

"Is there anything else I can do for you?" Chewing and snapping her gum loudly, she waited politely for Maeve's dismissal.

"That's fine, Libby, you may go."

The girl turned towards the French doors.

"Wait," Maeve called out.

The girl stopped, turning back to her mistress, her face was placid. Surprisingly, the girl never had an annoyed look on her face, no matter how much she was asked to do.

"Libby, you know I don't want you chewing gum when you're serving tonight."

The girl solemnly nodded.

"And your hair, please see that it is tightly pulled back and tucked neatly under your bonnet. In fact, you'd better wear a hairnet. And you know I frown on my girls wearing so much makeup when they're serving."

Libby unfortunately had wispy, baby fine, straw-colored hair that slipped out of any restraints. She wears so much makeup, that at the end of the day when she washes her face, a stranger looks back at her in the bathroom mirror. Plenty of men have done a double take when they've woken up next to her the morning after.

The girl shrugged, *whatever.* "Yes Ma'am, I'll use extra hairspray and clean my face." She waited for further instructions. Maeve nodded and turned back to her husband. Dismissed, Libby left the library.

"Whew!" Libby blew out a loud sigh of relief as she entered the kitchen.

Serafina and Daisy looked up from their work. Numerous silver bowls and flatware were laid out in front of them. They were about halfway through polishing the heirloom pieces needed for tonight's small dinner party.

"What did they want?" Daisy asked. She tried to blow a curl of sweaty hair out of her eyes, but it didn't move. Pushing the lock back with the back of her plastic-gloved hand, she added one more smear of polish to her forehead. She was covered almost more than the dishes in silver polish.

"Oh, the fire had just about gone out in the library. The poor old Sir was practically turning blue." The three girls giggled.

"I do not think it is the fire that turns the old man blue, I think it is Mrs. Lawton breathing her ice on him that does it!" Serafina said, the girls erupted in gales of laughter.

"What is going on here?" A steely voice halted the laughter.

All three maids' eyes turned down immediately. Libby hurried to the table and picked up a cloth, reaching for the silver polish at the same time as Daisy, they bumped hands. Daisy's face blushed beet red, almost dropping the chafing dish she was holding. The girls said not a word.

Mrs. Li stood in the doorway of the kitchen, her hands on her hips. None of the girls dared look in her direction.

Daisy knew if she attempted the tiniest peek she'd be turned to stone. Even the normally unflappable Libby kept her eyes down, pretending to be busy. They ignored the nasty chuckling coming from the stove.

Cook had one hand on a fat hip, the other stirred a wooden spoon around a large, heavy bottomed pot. Cook loved it when someone was in trouble, as long as it wasn't her.

Mrs. Li's head whipped around at Cook. The gross woman shut her mouth and stared at the pot she was stirring.

"Libby, forget the silver, get a clean cloth and wipe the water spots off the crystal."

Libby dropped the cloth and ran to the cupboard to get a clean cloth. She pulled a cloth off a stack and hurried back to the table. The stemware was already laid out to be cleaned. She picked up a wineglass, furiously attacking it, not wanting to be the brunt any further of Mrs. Li's wrath.

Mrs. Li stood still, glaring at the three maids and the cook, making sure they were all hard at work. The only sound in the kitchen was the stirring by the stove and the gentle clunk as a clean glass or freshly polished dish was set on the table.

Satisfied, the housekeeper left the room as soundlessly as she entered.

There was silence in the kitchen for a long time, until the women were sure she was gone. Libby and Serafina peeked at the door to make sure she was gone, but they didn't dare slow up on their chores.

Daisy kept her head down, only occasionally swiping at the sweat that dropped from her forehead with the polishing cloth. If they heard the cook's snort, they ignored it. They knew she feared the enigmatic housekeeper as much as they did.

Chapter Seven

$\mathcal{A}$ soft knock at the door pulled Shanti gently from dreams.

Rubbing her eyes, she looked around, temporarily forgetting where she was. The rose and cream room was dark, but outside lights shone through the glass doors of the balcony.

A second soft knock encouraged her to slide off the bed and flip on the light next to the door. Heaven knows what she looks like, she thought. Her hair must be a mess. Looking down, she realized she was wearing only her bra and panties.

Hurrying to the foot of the bed, she grabbed a white terry cloth bathrobe and quickly pulled it on. She was still tying the belt and pushing her hair off her face when she opened the door.

A young woman, possibly around her own age with wavy mahogany hair in a dark cloud around her head, was smiling shyly at her.

"Hi, I'm Chloe. I hope I didn't wake you." Concern suddenly clouded her eyes when she saw Shanti hide a yawn behind her hand. Shanti swallowed the yawn and smiling a welcome, she stood aside for Chloe to come inside.

"I was only taking a short nap. I'd already had one in the car on the way here. What time is it, do you know?" Shanti watched the pretty girl as she perched on the edge of a thickly cushioned chair.

"Oh," Chloe looked around the room. "It's only about 6:00. I thought we could talk a bit before we have to get ready for cocktails." She smiled at Shanti as she broke into chatter.

"This is one of my favorite rooms, the colors go well without being cloying. My room is almost identical except in lilac. But I don't have the extra studio. Granddaddy said you'd need that for your work. I can't wait to see what you've painted. Granddaddy was quite glowing about your work."

Shanti sat on the edge of the bed, opposite Chloe, waiting for the girl to take a breath.

"Well, I hear you are quite the creative one in the garden, Chloe. Your grandfather was very expansive on your knowledge and care of the plants and flowers here. He said most of the design of the gardens is from your touch." Shanti tucked her hair, still damp from her earlier bath behind her ears.

Chloe shook her head, her wavy hair bounced off her shoulders, tickling her arms. "Working in the dirt is hardly the same as bringing something alive on a canvas!" she spurted, surprised that Shanti could think of her toiling around in the gardens as serious as painting.

Shanti stood up. "Oh but it is. Art is art, you know. Even a hair stylist or a chef or a gardener can be an artist!"

Chloe was amused by Shanti's animation. *Damn what a pretty girl, she thought. Dawn's going to be in quite a pickle!* The thought brought a sly grin to her face.

"Besides, I love flowers. I hope you'll show me around, Chloe." Shanti studied the other girl.

Her face was a little too long to be considered really pretty, but she was attractive with her youth, and the color of her hair made Shanti think of the deepest part of a forest, the dark mahogany of the redwoods. Her large eyes reflecting the light from the room were shining with health and almost the same brown-red of her hair.

Chloe smiled warmly at Shanti, her slender hands and tapered fingers motioned gracefully when she spoke. Long, slim legs twisted in a pretzel in front of her chair, were clothed in neat, navy blue slacks, a white, cashmere turtleneck sweater hugged her trim body.

Chloe leaned forward. "I hear you're from a lovely town, Cedar Woods or something, Granddaddy says it's really quaint, and that your family owns a restaurant and a store on a lake."

Shanti laughed. "My town is called White Cedar. It's touristy because of the lake and nearby mountains. And it's a shop of my paintings and jewelry and pottery, not a store actually.'

"Sounds charming," Chloe grinned, "I'd love to see it. Tell me about your restaurant."

Happy to talk about it, Shanti replied, "Our restaurant is kind of ole Englishy with items like cucumber sandwiches, vegetable-stuffed salads, scones with clotted cream and a large selection of flavored teas, and an endless supply of home-baked cookies."

"Wow, it sounds so homey and organic." Chloe smiled.

Shanti nodded. "Yeah, it kind of is. Most of the vegetables used in the restaurant are grown in an extensive garden behind the restaurant. Canning in the fall provides a variety of dishes throughout the winter.

"Our restaurant, Crystal Petals, was started by my mom and dad. They're both gone now, but my sister and brothers work there too." Shadows dimmed her sapphire eyes, saddening at the memory of her parents when they were alive and still ran the restaurant.

Always sensitive to another person's feelings, Chloe could see the sadness in Shanti's face. She jumped up. "Listen Shantilly, show me what you're planning on wearing tonight."

Shanti's face cleared. She could tell she was going to like Chloe.

"Well," she walked over to the armoire. She had unpacked after her shower and had already hung up her dresses. "Serafina was here earlier and she was helping me think about what I should wear, I-"

"Oh honey, not Serafina!" Chloe laughed, cutting her off. She came and stood beside Shanti. "She'll have you looking like a belly-dancer right out of Gypsy Rose Lee!"

Shanti nodded. "Yeah, I can see that possibility." The darkly flamboyant looking maid could probably be quite decked out in vivid colors of ruffles and fringe when she wanted to.

Chloe started rifling through Shanti's dresses. She pulled one out, studied it, shook her head and shoved it back in the armoire. She pushed hanger after hanger aside until she stopped again.

"Here, this is it!" She held the dress up to Shanti. "Oh honey, this totally matches those striking eyes of yours, you've got to wear it!"

Brooking no argument, Chloe laid the dress across Shanti's outstretched arms. She reached out and lifted a few strands of Shanti's hair. "What are you going to do with your hair?"

Shanti sighed. "Uh, well, I was just going to leave it loose, down, you know, kind of like it is now, uh…" she trailed off when she saw Chloe shaking her head.

"This is not exactly a ball or anything, Shantilly, but you really want to knock 'em dead your first night here. I think you-"

"Wait, wait," Shanti held up a hand to stop her. "Listen, first of all, please call me Shanti, Shantilly is too, you know, lacy, and Chloe, gee," she walked over and set the dress on the bed.

"I'm here to work, not show off or anything. I don't want to 'knock anyone dead.'" She smiled weakly at Chloe, hoping she'd understand.

Chloe laid a hand on Shanti's arm. "I'm sorry, Shanti, I didn't mean to go off full tilt, it's just that, well, you are so beautiful, yes you are," she insisted when she saw Shanti embarrassingly shake her head.

"I just wanted to stir up my sister and brother. I guess that's mean and at your expense and all, but, there's nothing wrong with a person looking their best, is there?" Chloe held her flattened palms up and grinned.

"Come on, at least let me do your hair, okay?" Chloe pleaded.

Chapter Eight

$\mathcal{T}$ he doorbell rang and rang.

Serafina in her dressier black maid's uniform, and Geoffrey Montgomery impeccably attired as always in a black suit and tie, were standing ready at the door.

It was just seven and the Lawtons' guests had arrived. Everyone passing through the security gate either needed to have a card to pass through the code detector or they had to push the button on the call box.

Montgomery buzzed the Vaughns in.

Dorothy Vaughn was the one unnecessarily ringing the bell. She had her arms full of chocolates and a couple of bottles of vintage wine. She always brought something when they came for dinner.

They were the Lawtons' closest neighbors and had known each other their entire lives. They saw each other frequently, but when they were invited to a more formal dinner or party, Dorothy, or Dolly, as her close friends and family call her, brings a gift.

Dolly's daughter, Tori, had an arm laced through her mother's arm and her head rested on her mother's shoulder.

Tori's brother, Matthew was still at the car with his father, Tobias, helping him help his grandfather get out of the car.

Magnus Vaughn was getting up in years, and in the damp winter his arthritis acts up. Everyone is always after him to move to sunny Florida or at least to drier Arizona, but he will never leave the family potato farm.

The elderly man was born and raised in the house he still lives in. His estate isn't quite as opulent as the Lawtons', he prefers less hoity-toity surroundings. His son, Tobias Vaughn and Tobias' wife Dolly are as solid and down to earth as a wealthy country couple could get.

"Good evening Mrs. Vaughn, Miss Tori," Montgomery greeted the ladies and gestured for them to come inside.

"Hello Montgomery, hi Serafina," the ladies returned the greeting, while wiping their feet on the small rug just inside the door.

Serafina took their overcoats and hats. She waited for the rest of the Vaughns to come in before putting up the coats. Montgomery stepped outside to assist the men.

"Oh Montgomery," Tobias Vaughn blustered. "Go back inside man, you have no coat on and it's cold as the belly of a snake slithering on a sno-cone out here."

They shook hands. Montgomery's was surprisingly warm. Montgomery stepped in front of Tobias and greeted Tobias' father, the patriarch Magnus Vaughn.

In the dark, early evening sky, puffy snowflakes fluttered around, flickering in the moonlight before landing lightly on the men's hair like light white dust.

"How are you this evening, sir? Let me give you a hand." Montgomery reached in and firmly grasped both of the elderly man's arms above the elbows and effortlessly lifted him out of the car.

He held him until he was sure the old fellow was steady on his feet. Magnus grinned a full set of still white teeth and everyone his own, of thanks at Montgomery.

"Langston was so lucky the day he came upon you, son. I don't know where he found you, he refuses to tell, but I wish there were two of you!" Magnus shook Montgomery's hand.

Montgomery flashed a brief smile. His past life was a secret between him and Langston Lawton. A pact they'd kept, no matter how hard people tried to get it out of them.

Everyone knows there was something odd between the two men, yet neither would ever tell how they met. But, the word was that Langston Lawton saved Geoffrey Montgomery's life a long time ago, and Montgomery will be grateful until he goes to his grave. Or vice versa.

Montgomery saluted Magnus and then ran back up the now lightly snow covered steps and into the mansion.

Tobias and his son Matthew followed more slowly, flanking the elderly Magnus. When the three men got inside, they handed Serafina their hats and coats. The weighted down girl struggled off to the parlor to deposit the coats.

"Dolly, Magnus, welcome." Maeve grasped each of their hands, holding them briefly before letting go. She kissed Tobias on the cheek and hugged Dolly.

"Hello Tori, honey, how are you? Matthew?" She leaned in and kissed both young people on their cheeks as well. "I think Jaime and Dawn are already in the drawing room, dears, if you'd like to go join them."

"Okay Mrs. Lawton, thank you." Tori and her brother left to find their own way to the drawing room.

"Welcome!" Langston entered the foyer as quickly as his old legs would carry him to greet his guests.

"It's too damned cold in this marble castle, come on let's join the youngsters in the drawing room. Libby's had the fire rarin' and goin' for over an hour now, getting ready for us. Cold enough for you, Magnus?" He laughed, his arm around his old friend, leading him down the hall to the drawing room.

Dolly, Tobias and Maeve followed the older men.

"Where's this artist we've come to meet, Maeve?" Dolly asked her hostess.

"Oh, I think you're in for a treat, my dear. She's around the grandchildren's age, I think, and very charming. Langston was quite taken with her work when we were in California."

"Oh dear," Dolly remarked with a twist to her lips. "California you say. Is she one of those plastic, platinum blonde, would-be actor types? I can't see Langston going for that. Her paintings must be quite spectacular in that case."

Everyone was moving very slowly as they were following Magnus and Langston. Langston, still very spry, but in deference to his old friend, moved slowly along with him. They discussed the steers Tobias had just purchased at auction.

Magnus' son, Tobias liked to diversify his interests.

Langston had no desire to add to his sugar beet production. Magnus has Tobias and Matthew to help him move into additional projects, but as Langston constantly laments, he has no one to carry on after he goes.

"Tori looks darling tonight, Dolly, of course so do you. Has she caught the interest of any young man yet?" Maeve admired Tori's taste in clothes.

The girl was young and wants to dress her age, but she still manages to maintain a refined appearance. Tonight she was wearing a sleeveless, knee-length black dress with a gold sequined, transparent blouse over the top.

Her dark hair with thick bangs just touching the tips of her eyelashes, ran poker straight down her back to her waist. A gold necklace and earrings pulled her outfit together. She looked sexy yet still demure.

Her mother though, poor thing, Maeve thought to herself, *has no taste whatsoever.*

Dolly and her husband, Tobias were middle-aged plump. Dolly's floor-length dress, covered with teeny little flowers was too homespun with its big, white lacy collar and sleeves. *You can take the girl out of the country but you can't take the-*

"Oh thank you Maeve. Doesn't she just take your breath away? My beautiful little girl is all grown up. I think those debutante balls were all a waste of time. They did none of the children any good. Tori was seeing that Stanton boy all summer, but after he got that scholarship to the University of Miami, he has so many girlfriends now Tori gets pushed to the wayside."

Dolly went on with affection for her daughter, "She's just too nice, you know, she lets everyone walk all over her. Keeps her nose in too many books, I say. I keep telling her 'girl, you've got to get out and live life! It won't come looking for you, you know.'

"She just looks up from her books, all dreamy-eyed, and says, 'Yes, Ma, I know, as soon as I finish this chapter I'll go do something, I swear,' and then plop, right back into the book. She lies there, twirling her hair and reading romance novels.

"I'm sure she's fantasizing that she is the damsel in distress and some handsome knight on a white horse is coming to her rescue." Dolly chuckled. "I used to be the same way. But the girl never moves except to help me in the kitchen. She's not going to find any white knight that way!"

Maeve tried not to picture the plump Dolly sitting on an old nag, waving her flannel scarf beguilingly at some poor knight weary from a battle-

"Oh well, dear, Tori's a nice girl, she'll give you those grandchildren you want soon enough." Maeve patted her hand.

"Is Camelia here tonight?" Dolly asked Maeve about her daughter.

Maeve was actually closer to the elder Magnus Vaughn's age than Dolly who was nearer to Camelia's late forties, but with few other neighbors nearby the two women had become close friends.

Huh," Maeve grunted. "Yes, she and that gigolo-, I mean her husband are upstairs still getting ready."

"What's his name again?" Tobias asked, speaking for the first time. He was trailing behind the women, hands clasped behind his back, looking down at his feet as he walked.

A man of few words, his sole interest lies in the farm and little outside of it. He couldn't keep Camelia's husbands straight, there always seemed to be a new one.

He had squired Camelia to a few dances when they were in high school and college, but she was way too flaky for him. She was a party girl that liked drinking and going to Lover's Leap every Saturday night with a different guy. Sturdy, steady Dolly was much more his cup of tea.

Dolly had pursued him. She even had to tell him to buy her a ring when they got engaged. Tobias was a plain, hardworking man, ignorant of the finer things in life. His children try their best to keep him up to date like buying him a snappy shirt at Christmas occasionally instead of the same old plaid flannel he prefers.

"Yes, Maeve, I can't remember either, is this her fourth or fifth?" Dolly asked.

Maeve's laugh was derisive. "It is in fact her fourth marriage. His name is Logan Thayne."

"Huh," Tobias muttered.

"What does he do? My, his name sounds kind of made up, doesn't it? I mean like a movie star or something." Dolly giggled at the thought.

"Actually, Dolly dear, I'm not sure what he does. He said something about the import export business when she first brought him home. However, I've never seen him get up in the morning and go anywhere. He and Camelia sleep in long after breakfast.

"They have one of the girls bring up lunch and they eat in their room. They've only been married six months, but they've already gone on two trips. For their honeymoon they went to France, and now they've just returned on Monday from Hawaii."

They slowed as they reached the drawing room.

"Here we are then, come in and make yourselves comfortable. I see the children already have." Maeve nodded pointedly in the direction of her grandchildren, Camelia's offspring.

Jaime, wearing a winter cream suit with a powder blue silk tie and matching handkerchief in his breast pocket was leaning against the mantel of the fireplace. His hair was slicked back, it looked wet, but upon closer inspection he'd run some gel through it to keep the curls tamed.

It was obvious he'd already put back a few. He seemed totally oblivious that he'd knocked over a framed picture with his elbow that had been sitting on the mantel. He was alternating taking drags from an imported Turkish cigar and pulling swigs from the brandy snifter.

"Montgomery," Maeve called to the butler.

He came over immediately. "Madam?" he inquired. His bow was slight.

"Please see what the Vaughns would like to drink. I see Magnus and his grandson Matthew are already set. Then see to Mr. Lawton. I'm going to slip into the kitchen for just a second. I don't see the hors d'- oh, here's Libby and Serafina now with them."

Both maids were dressed in the more formal black uniforms with starched, white aprons, stiff collars and cuffs. Their bonnets were perfectly secured to their heads with not one escaping hair.

Maeve could tell Mrs. Li has been busy. She would see that Daisy was kept in the kitchen helping Cook. Way too clumsy to help serve, Daisy gets so nervous she sweats which is hardly appealing at a dinner party. She's better kept working behind the scene.

Maeve looked over at the loud laughter coming from the fireplace. Jaime let out a huge guffaw then threw back the rest of his drink.

Matthew Vaughn's black suit fit his trim body nicely. He and his sister, Tori, were laughing at whatever joke Jaime had just told.

Maeve's granddaughter Dawn was sitting in front of her brother, Jaime on the marble encircling the fireplace. Her hair, a lion's mane around her face, competed with the color and brilliance of the flames in the fireplace.

Her dress was so tight, Maeve wondered how she could breathe. The dress was a vivid red, totally in contrast to her hair, but somehow it didn't clash.

It did, however clash horribly with Maeve's floor length crushed velvet, burgundy dress. The brocade neckline would be too heavy a design on most people, but Maeve carried it off with her height and stature.

Maeve's eye followed the neckline of Dawn's dress. Matthew was doing the same as it plunged nearly to her navel. For heaven's sake, the girl might as well be naked. She always had to have all the attention in the room. And she was getting it.

Dawn stood up, looking like the fire had jumped right out of the fireplace all laughing and wiggly, it was hard to take one's eye off of her.

The family was used to her, but although Matthew grew up living next door, he saw her infrequently enough he seems mesmerized every time he sees her.

Maeve sighed. If Dawn wasn't more careful, she'll get a reputation and they'd never marry her off.

Libby was standing in front of her with a tray of hors d'oeuvres. Maeve waved her off.

"See to the guests first, Libby, you know that. Go."

Libby hurried over to Dolly Vaughn who swiped up several shrimp puffs at once.

Maeve looked around.

Everyone seemed comfortable. Magnus and Langston, both in dark suits and ties, were deep in conversation over by the window nearest the fireplace.

Each already held a drink, and had a cocktail napkin with a shrimp puff and cracker dolloped with caviar balanced on one knee. They looked like two elderly peas in a pod, sitting comfortably in matching thickly cushioned easy chairs.

Tobias was standing in front of some bookshelves with one hand in his pocket. Montgomery handed him a drink. He took it, nodding his thanks then turned to peruse the books on the shelves. Clearly Tori got her love of reading from her father.

Camelia and Logan Thayne noisily swaggered into the room. Camelia was hanging onto Thayne's arm like she was in danger of falling if she let go. They'd also already been hitting the bottle.

Camelia's make-up was smeared and she was laughing too loud. Curly blonde hair flopped over her flushed face, covering one heavily mascaraed eye.

Thayne apparently thought he was a cowboy because the silver on the tips of his pointy-toed boots matched the enormous silver buckle on his belt. Instead of a tie, he had chosen to wear a silver bolero. The gleaming white shirt accentuated the swarthiness of his skin.

The couple sloshed over to Magnus and Langston to make their greetings. They avoided Maeve.

Thayne was always spoiling for a fight, but Camelia could see the disapproving look in her mother's eye and knew better than to go near her.

The noise in the room elevated as it filled. Dawn was now standing as close to Matthew as she could get without touching him. She batted her red eyelashes teasingly at him, trying to perfect her femme fatale act.

She actually had no interest in Matthew, but since he was the only other male there her age except her brother Jaime, she decided to practice her wiles on him. She knew it was taking everything he had not to stare down into her cleavage.

She pretended to unconsciously jiggle her breasts that were scarce inches from his chest. The young temptress knew her teasing was working. Matthew's face was as red as the tie he was nervously tugging.

"So Tori, what have you been up to lately?" Jaime asked Matthew's sister, Tori. She shrugged, twisting a long hair around one finger, trying to think of something exciting to tell him.

"Yes darling, do tell us what you Vaughns have been doing lately. Have you gone to any parties? I haven't seen either of you in the local haunts." Dawn tipped her head back so she was peering at Matthew with half closed eyes. She ran her tongue around her lips.

Matthew's eyes followed her tongue's slow journey, wetting her already glossy lip-sticked mouth.

Tori jabbed her brother in his side with her elbow. He blinked, then gulped, then quickly looked down at the floor.

Tori smiled at Jaime. She'd had a crush on him for as long as she could remember. But, he always had a girlfriend, even though he changes them as often as he changes his socks.

She knew Jaime thought of her just as 'the girl next door,' with no more interest than he would have for one of his sisters. She planned on working this winter on changing his mind. She wished she had the nerve to dress and act like Dawn.

Shaking her head, her lips twisted wryly. Tori just didn't have Dawn's audacity, and no one could compete with that startling hair of hers. She sighed deeply.

Before she could answer Jaime, she realized he wasn't even listening, He'd turned to light another cigarillo. She saw Dawn smirking at her. Dawn turned back to Matthew. Placing her red-tipped fingernails on his chest she leaned forward to whisper in his ear.

Jaime was laughing at his sister Dawn's antics.

Giving up, Tori huffily went over to the bar to get another drink.

Dolly had joined Magnus and Langston. Standing awkwardly. She looked around for her husband Tobias. He'd found a book that interested him. Sitting down in an easy chair with a good light in an unobtrusive corner, he was already engrossed in the book.

Maeve surveyed the room. All that was missing was her other granddaughter Chloe and their guest of honor. She'd sent Chloe to go retrieve Shanti an hour ago.

What could be keeping those two, she wondered.

Chapter Nine

"Oh!" Someone's sharp intake of air caused heads to turn towards the door.

Chloe was wearing a floor length, body hugging, sparkly silver gown. The silver was an electrifying foil for her dark hair; the mahogany highlights reflected off the shiny dress. Silver earrings winked and twinkled every time she moved her head.

Maeve never thought Chloe would have the nerve to wear that gown her mother had talked her into buying ages ago, but apparently their guest has been a bit more persuasive.

Chloe had changed in seconds from 'nice little Chloe' to a strikingly, vibrant young woman. Maeve could see what had taken them so long to get ready. The results were interesting.

Both girls had their hair done in loosely full, French braids. Since it was the first time she'd ever seen her granddaughter in a French braid, it must also have been their guest's handiwork.

Shanti's hair, also in a chic modern braid, had some loose wavy wisps of blonde hair off and down one side of her face. Two miniature, sapphire blue blows entwined in her hair, pulled one side back.

The girls entered the room. Chloe was actually pulling Shanti who was struck by shyness as soon as she realized everyone was already there and they were all staring at her! All she could see was a sea of unfamiliar faces.

"My dear, do come in." Langston Lawton pushed himself out of his chair and trod across the room to greet Shanti.

Shanti recognized the old fellow and smiled gratefully at him. He reached her side and took her hand.

"Welcome to our home, Miss Lane. How was your trip?" He nodded patiently while she described her flight and car trip to his estate. Smiling, his eyes crinkled when she told of her so far brief images of the manor.

"Mr. Lawton, your home is quite impressive. I really can't wait to get started painting it." She was smiling radiantly, unaware of the silence in the room.

Everyone was watching and listening, but she was only aware of Langston's interest in her words. Then she suddenly frowned.

"There is one thing that bothers me, sir."

Langston's white eyebrows shot up. "What is that my dear?" he asked, leaning in closer to her.

Shanti put a fingertip to her lips. Now she was becoming aware of the other people in the room and realized she was the center of attention. Her eyes widened as she looked around.

Jaime and Matthew's interest was apparent, they both stared unblinking at her, looking her up and down, head to toe.

Tobias had glanced up at her entrance, but already he was back into his book. Dolly was smiling politely, thinking maybe if the girl was really good she could do a family portrait of them.

Maeve stood stately by the door, watching everyone.

Chloe's smile was smug. Her eyes sparkled impishly as she watched her sister, Dawn's reaction.

It was all Dawn could do to clamp her lips together and not shout out to get the attention off this California intruder and back on herself. Humph! Her eyes swept the blonde beauty at the door.

Red brows daggered down over narrowed green eyes as Dawn took in the off-the-shoulder, sapphire dress that hugged Shanti's figure but was not skintight. The hem didn't quite hit her knees, showing off Shanti's shapely legs.

Matching high heels and earrings were the exact color of her big eyes.

That blonde hair can't be natural, Dawn decided.

"And what bothers you, dear?" Langston prodded Shanti back to their conversation. Shanti blinked, swinging her gaze back at the elder man.

"Oh, um, well, the good thing is that it's winter and I can get an unobstructed view of the estate. But the bad thing is, I don't know if you want the picture to be a winter scene. I may be wrong, you may prefer snow covered trees and bushes, but um," she looked hesitantly at Langston, he was earnestly following her every word.

"Well, I see that tremendous garden all along the back of the estate, and I can see you love flowers, um, do you want me to imagine what I think the manor looks like in the spring or summer and, you know, put those flowers and green bushes and trees in full bloom like I'd think they'd be?"

Shanti tried to word her question carefully. She wanted the painting to be what they envisioned, not what she would imagine since she'd never seen the property before.

Langston pulled at his lower lip thoughtfully. "Well, I can see your point, I think..." His brows drew together, then lifted. He smiled, nodding. "Of course we want the splendor of the spring flowers in the painting. Our rhododendrons are the finest in the town!"

Other heads in the room nodded in agreement with him.

"We have photos I'm sure. I think Chloe can help in that department. Can't you, honey?" He turned to his granddaughter.

Chloe stepped nearer to Langston and Shanti. "Sure Granddaddy I'd love to help Shanti! When do we start?" she asked eagerly. She'd felt in a slump for a long time and this was just the thing to get her blood going.

Langston chuckled at his granddaughter's excitement. "Settle down girlie, there's plenty of time to get to work. First someone needs to show Miss Lane around the house and grounds and then there-"

"I can do that, Granddad!" Jaime broke in. He set his drink on the mantel and with long strides quickly joined the small group.

He missed the pained look Tori shot him. "It would be an honor to-"

"I think," Langston said, tilting his head at his granddaughter, "that Chloe would really be the best one to show our guest around. The girls have obviously hit it off."

Chloe and Shanti smiled warmly at each other.

"And Chloe knows the stables, gardens and forest pretty much better than anyone here, except maybe Graham. She would be the best to describe our flowers in the summer and what they look like in full bloom wrapped around the manor."

"But Grandfather-" Jaime protested, but Langston shook his head.

"Miss Lane," Langston turned to Shanti, lightly touching her arm. "Do you ride horses?"

Shanti's face lit up. "Oh yes, sir, I ride at home every chance I get."

"Jaime, you know you only ride if you have to, and your sister loves the horses. So it's settled then." He pretended not to see his grandson's crestfallen face.

"The important thing right now, though, is that we get you a drink and you meet everyone, don't you think?" Langston took Shanti's hand and squeezed it lightly. "Montgomery-"

"Sir?" Montgomery was at his elbow.

"Oh, there you are, what would you like, Miss Lane?" Langston inquired.

"Well, I don't usually drink much, but since I haven't far to drive," Langston and Chloe laughed at her quip. "I guess maybe a little white wine, um..." Shanti imagined Montgomery's heels clicking together as he turned and headed for the bar that curved along one side of the room.

Affronted at his grandfather's dismissal of his offer to help, Jaime stalked huffily to the bar and poured a fresh drink. Switching from brandy to scotch, he didn't bother with a shot glass, just poured the scotch until there wasn't much room left for the ice and chaser. After adding one ice cube and a thimble full of water, he slugged the drink right down.

Tori had returned to the fireplace. Leaning against the warm stones, her smile belied her loneliness as her eyes followed Jaime's movements.

Matthew approached Shanti with his hand out. "How do you do, Miss Lane? I'm Matthew Vaughn, we have the house next door."

Shanti took his hand and shook it. Montgomery handed her a wine glass filled with Chardonnay.

"I know where you live, Matthew, thank you Montgomery." Shanti frowned at Montgomery, she could swear he winked at her again! But he'd already turned and was asking Tobias if he needed another drink.

"Chloe has told me all about your family. I'm looking forward to seeing your home- I mean- if, if I'm invited." Shanti took a big gulp of her wine, embarrassed that is sounded like she was inviting herself to the Vaughns' home.

Oh! The wine, which she seldom drinks, was gently burning a trail down her throat and into her belly. Suddenly, she felt deliciously warm.

"Oh, Miss Lane, I- I mean we, we would love to have you visit our home. Right Mother?" Matthew's face was slightly pink. He wasn't exactly a ladies man. He was handsome enough with dark hair and eyes, but he'd spent most of his youth in private boys' schools and then studied hard at the university.

He hadn't dated much, the town was small and he spends most of his time on the family farm when not in school. There's always work to do, dawn to dusk, doesn't leave much time for partying.

Plus, he shares his sister Tori's shyness. He ducked his head, silently pleading with his mother to say something.

Dolly came to her son's rescue. Holding out a beefy hand, she pumped Shanti's hand enthusiastically. "Oh honey, you are welcome in our home any time. Chloe will show you where we live. You can get there easily on horseback. We'll plan an evening, maybe a sleigh ride or dance or something, what do you think,

Tori?" Dolly glanced over at her daughter, trying to draw her into the group.

Tori smiled weakly. Reluctantly, she came over and joined the group. She saw the friendliness in Shanti's blue eyes and relaxed.

Maeve hovered near the doorway, still watching.

Tobias as always wasn't interested in visiting, and Langston had returned to his chair next to Magnus. The two old gents resumed their conversation about the weather and Tobias' new steers.

Dolly, Tori, Chloe and Matthew were getting to know Shanti, and Jaime reached yet again for the bottle of scotch and poured another healthy drink.

Other than Camelia and Logan, the only one who hadn't moved, nor introduced herself to Shanti was Dawn. She still stood by the fireplace. She was staring down at the drink in her hand.

Swirling the clear liquid, she reached in and using a cocktail pick stabbed a fat green olive, its pimento sticking out one end, and brought it to her lips. She sucked on the olive, while peering at the group in the middle of the room through her red eyelashes.

Viciously, she bit the olive off the miniature sword she'd stabbed it with. Chewing the olive loudly, then swallowing it, she drank the rest of the martini in one gulp, tossed the sword in the glass and set it on the mantle next to her brother's glass.

Dawn ran her hands down along her sides, smoothing her dress down, it had crept up to the top of her thighs when she'd been sitting on the border of the fireplace. Running long tapered fingers through the tangle of flame-red hair, she licked her lips wet again, took a breath and strolled confidently over to the group surrounding Shanti.

"Hello there, I'm Dawn, I must welcome you to our dreary old home," Dawn drawled, holding out her hand. Her nails were newly manicured, blood red and glossy.

Shanti flashed her a megawatt smile and shook her hand. "Thanks. But I'd hardly describe this incredible place as dreary!"

Primping her hair, Dawn looked bored. "Oh, you get used to it. I'd much rather live in California. Isn't that where you're from?" She slid her glance back to Shanti. She decided Shanti must be wearing contacts. No one had eyes that blue naturally.

"Oh yes, I'm from a lovely town, White Cedar. My family owns a restaurant called Crystal Petals and I run a shop there. You must come and visit some-"

"Oh yeah, sure honey, I'd love to come visit. Oh Matthew-" Dawn cut off Shanti, and without another word she sauntered, hips swaying dangerously from side-to-side, over to Matthew who had left the group and was talking to his father, Tobias.

Shanti was embarrassed at Dawn's blatant rudeness. She looked down at her drink then took a tiny sip.

"You have to ignore her, Shanti," Chloe said, wrapping an arm around Shanti's bare shoulder. "That's just Dawn, she's not interested in anything that isn't about her. Come on, let's grab the last of those shrimp puffs."

She pointed at the tray Libby had left on the coffee table. The two maids had gone to help Cook and make sure everything was ready as it was almost time to serve dinner.

The two young women gracefully sat down on the thick cushioned sofa. Montgomery approached them and asked if they needed a refill.

Camelia and her husband were sitting on the loveseat that was positioned kitty-corner to the sofa Shanti and Chloe were sitting on.

But the Thaynes took no notice of the girls. He and his wife were kissing as if they were not in a room full of people. Camelia had one leg crossed over the other, her body twisting to face Logan.

Her black, floor length gown had a slit up each side nearly to the hip. The dress parted at one of the slits when she crossed her legs. Logan had his hand on Camelia's bare thigh, squeezing it. His hand was slowly moving up. Maeve decided it was time to go in to dinner.

"Everyone, let's head into the dining room, I think Cook has everything ready. Why don't you check, Montgomery?

The butler left the room without a word.

Langston and Magnus slowly pushed themselves up from the comfortable chairs, never hesitating in their conversation. They left their glasses and crumpled napkins on the table.

Jaime and Dawn had already disappeared. Tori, Matthew and their parents walked down the hall together with Shanti and Chloe following them.

Camelia and Logan didn't notice everyone except Maeve had left.

"*Camelia,*" Maeve hissed harshly between her teeth.

Camelia pulled her head back from Logan and turned drunken dazed eyes to her mother. Then she looked around the room.

Realizing the room was empty except for the three of them, she pushed Logan's hands away, quickly trying to pull her dress together at the thigh and neck. Logan's hands had traveled everywhere.

Logan sat there, his legs spread loosely apart, one arm draped over the back of the loveseat, the other lay limp on his thigh. He smirked at Maeve.

"Camelia, go wash your face then meet us in the dining room. Now," Maeve ordered.

Camelia blinked blurry eyes at her mother, then she struggled to her feet and without looking at Logan, stumbled to the door.

Falling against the doorframe, she put her hands up against the wall, using it to hold her up and to guide her. They could hear her sliding along the wall all the way down the hall.

Maeve stood in front of Logan, her face hard as cement.

"Listen Mr. Thayne, as long as you are in my h-" Maeve pointed a finger at the man, but he cut her off.

Not even bothering to sit up, he tilted his head back and arrogantly scoffed at her, "No, you listen, old woman. I am married to your daughter now."

He suddenly stood up in one quick move and got within a few inches of Maeve. Shoving his face so close to hers that she could smell the liquor on his breath, he pointed his finger in her face.

"You've been bossing everyone around here for too long. No one died and made you queen. That old man isn't going to disinherit his daughter. So you can harangue me all you want. I'm not going anywhere so you can knock off the threats."

Sneering, he jabbed his finger at Maeve's chest, he didn't touch her but it felt like he had.

Maeve sucked in her breath, her lips pressed tightly together.

Thayne headed for the door, then stopped and looked back at Maeve.

"And you can stop bossing around Camelia too. You scare her, but you don't scare me, you old bag of wind," he spat, leaving the room.

Maeve stood rock still, sputtering, "Why, the nerve of the man!" Her brows knit together, she crossed her arms in front of her chest. Her mind raced with ideas of how to dispose of the rude, abominable man.

He was just a lowlife thug. She'd had Montgomery investigate him. The slimeball has been in trouble with the law since his teens. Mostly petty offenses, theft, gambling, minor cons.

But as much as she tried to talk to Camelia, warn her, her daughter just blew her off. Something about the man's badness attracted Camelia. That he'd done time in prison only excited her more.

By the time Maeve reached the dining room, everyone was already seated.

Langston sat at the head of the table. She had placed Tobias at the other end. Respectfully, she should have put Magnus there, but she had him sitting on Langston's left because she knew the two elderly men enjoy chatting with each other.

Knowing Langston would also want to get to know Shanti better, she'd placed her on his right. Then it was boy-girl boy-girl after that.

She'd moved Dawn two people away on the same side as Matthew. It was too painful watching her granddaughter tease the young man when she had no intentions of following through. And Matthew was way too green to realize that until too far down the road after his heart was already stomped on and broken.

She'd also separated Shanti and Jaime. She didn't want any trouble in that avenue either. Maeve took her place next to Magnus.

A bowl of steaming she-crab soup, the dollop of cream sherry and few sliced spring onions still floating on top, was ready for her to dip into.

"Let's please say grace, giving thanks for our food, family, good friends, good health and our guest." Maeve held her arms out, lightly taking Magnus' and Jaime's hands in hers.

Everyone followed suit, bowing their heads as she said a prayer of thanks. Then, Maeve picked up her soupspoon, the signal it was okay to start eating.

Everyone heartily enjoyed the hot soup. The clink of spoons hitting the side of china bowls and polite slurping sounded like musical chairs around the rectangle table. Candles flickered off the highly polished silver and sparkling, crystal clear stemware.

As soon as the last person set down their soupspoon, Maeve picked up a bell that was next to her place setting and gave it a light twitch between two fingers.

Before the sound of the ringing bell had ceased, Libby was standing in the doorway of the kitchen. The maid had used half a can of hair spray on her recalcitrant hair and she still had to use a hair net to hold in some escaping baby fine wisps.

A wad of pink bubblegum was pinched between two fingers behind her back. She stared blankly at Maeve waiting for her instructions.

"We're ready, Libby," Maeve announced to the maid.

Libby nodded briskly and immediately gathered all the soup bowls on a tray and returned to the kitchen.

Within seconds, Libby and Serafina entered the dining room, their arms laden with platters and serving bowls. They approached each person from the left, allowing the guests to serve themselves from the dishes they held.

Shanti looked all around, her eyes shining. *Wow*! She thought, *so this is how the rich live*! It was all so exciting and overwhelming.

She turned slightly as Serafina stopped next to her holding out a platter of wine-infused, pepper encrusted beef loin. It looked so luscious, Shanti tried not to be a pig with her helping. When she was done, she whispered a thank you to Serafina.

The maid winked at her before moving on to Matthew.

Libby stopped next with bowls of garlic mashed potatoes and sautéed asparagus swimming in butter and sprinkled with toasted almond slivers.

Salad, flaky hot rolls, a relish tray, tins of horseradish, and chestnut stuffing were already on the table. Between courses, everyone chatted amiably, but as soon as their plates were full, the dining room quickly hushed, everyone intent on the food in front of them.

Matthew speared a crisp asparagus. Before putting it in his mouth, he turned to Shanti. "I hear you're from California. How do you like living in all that commercial glitz?" he asked, biting the asparagus in half, he chewed, waiting for Shanti's response.

Shanti had just eaten a heaping spoonful of garlicky potatoes. She held a finger up, chewing and swallowing quickly.

She replied, "Matthew, the town I'm from, White Cedar, is very far from the 'Hollywood' part of California you're talking about."

Matthew nibbled on his asparagus then reached for a toasty roll. Tearing it in half, he lathered on sweet butter and shoved half of it in his mouth. Munching thoughtfully, he raised one eyebrow in curiosity at what Shanti said.

Shanti took a sip of wine. "The only thing that keeps my town from being totally rural is the heavy tourist trade. But they come in bunches, mainly during holidays so the town isn't swollen with people all the time."

"Are you near the mountains? We all love to ski here, but we have to travel a bit to get to the mountains," Matthew asked.

Shanti nodded her head. "Actually, we live in a big valley, surrounded on three sides by mountains. Skiing is a very avid sport in White Cedar. My family owns a restaurant and a small shop on a beautiful lake called Snow Lake.

"In the warmer weather of course we sail and water-ski and stuff, you know, all the summer sports. They've finally outlawed those jet-ski things on the lake, they're so noisy and they damage the flora and wildlife."

"Oh but I loved those jet-ski machines when we vacationed in Florida!" Dawn said with exuberance. "The speed, the wind tearing through your hair, oh, the danger was so invigorating, I get delightful shivers just thinking about it!"

Dawn shimmied in her seat, jiggling what she could jiggle. Out of the corner of her eye, she could see Logan Thayne peering discreetly at her breasts.

Thrusting her chest out as far as she could, Dawn leaned over the table, reaching for the black olives on the relish tray. She pretended she was unaware of Matthew and Logan's eyes drawn to her cleavage. Grabbing a handful of olives, she tilted her head back, tossing in one at a time.

Dawn knew she has a swan-like neck, every man that ever sucked on it told her so. The long line of her pale neck led straight down to her breasts. She knew the men couldn't help but follow the line down.

"Dawn!" A shrill voice coming from Camelia cut into her musings, she almost choked on an olive. Her head jerked forward and she started coughing.

Next to her, a concerned Tobias slapped her hard on her back several times, his huge, burly hand just about knocking her contacts off her eyes.

"I'm okay Mr. Vaughn, I'm okay! Stop!" Dawn squawked while still coughing. Her eyes watering, mascara ran down her rouged cheeks. She turned to her mother blinking tears out of her swimming eyes.

"What Mother?" she sputtered, glaring across the table at her mother.

Camelia was smiling innocently at her daughter. "Oh, darling, I was just going to say, remember the time we went sailing in Key West, what a lovely time we had?" She smirked at her daughter.

Dawn sat back, sucking in hacking gulps of air, trying to catch her breath. Pushing her damp hair back, she fanned her face. Sweating slightly from her choking attack caused her orange hair to go from wavy to curly.

The hair around her face was starting to frizz. She knew she must look a fright. *Damn you Mother*, her furious wet eyes screamed at Camelia.

Clearing her throat, Dawn said snidely, "Why yes, Mother dear, I remember, what a wonderful time we had! Remember when your second husband, what was his name now? Oh yeah, Stanley. Remember when Stanley was practically chasing me around the deck and you came after him with a wine bottle and tried to clock him in the back of the head?"

Dawn laughed meanly, wiping the wet mascara from under her eyes. Her red eyelashes were spiky from the tears she shed while choking.

At Camelia's aghast gasp, "But," Dawn continued, "you missed his balding pate and fell over the side! One big yelp, a splash, and no more Mommy!" Dawn broke into gales of laughter.

Camelia glared at her daughter.

Logan sat back, one corner of his mouth turned up. What a family he'd gotten himself involved in, he thought. His eyes swept Dawn.

Even frazzled and angry, that little red-haired siren looked like she could be a real spitfire in the bedroom. It was hard to get alone with her though, either Camelia or the old broad was always watching him.

He slid his glance over to Shanti. Hmm, blondie there looks a good piece too. Then his gaze moved to Chloe. Boy, that little girl cleaned up nicely. He turned back to the scene between mother and daughter.

"*Ladies*, decorum, please," Maeve said laconically, reaching for the bell again. It tinkled lightly.

Camelia and Dawn both clamped their lips together. Arms crossed resentfully in front of their chests they glared squinty eyes at each other.

"Madam?" Serafina stood in the doorway.

"Yes, I believe we are ready for dessert and coffee. We shall adjourn to the drawing room. Everyone?" Maeve folded and placed her linen napkin next to her empty plate and stood up.

Everyone stood up as well. Embarrassed over the scene between the two women, Dolly was chatting too fast in a high-pitched voice.

"Libby told me earlier we're having pecan topped ginger cake for dessert. I hope there's whipped cream for the top, and I just loved that Pinot Grigio we had with the pears charlotte. Are you smoking a cigar with your brandy, Magnus? You know what the doctor said, he said you shouldn't-"

"Dolly dear, I hear your church is holding their annual winter bazaar next weekend. Are you involved in it?" Maeve cut off Dolly's ramblings. She took Dolly's arm and led the group into the drawing room.

Chloe tapped Shanti on the shoulder, holding a finger to her lips when Shanti opened her mouth to speak. Chloe wiggled a finger to Tori and Shanti to follow her. The three girls slipped down a hallway, away from the drawing room.

Dawn had already stormed up the stairs to her room. It would take her hours now to get ready all over again for her late date with Jonathan. She had to sneak out to see Jonathan because her grandmother disapproved of him.

He came, as she would say, from the wrong side of the tracks. He liked to do drugs, and he's been arrested a few times for other minor crimes. Following in her mother's footsteps, the seamier the man the more exciting she found him.

74

Chapter Ten

Shanti could have sworn she'd closed the curtains over the glass doors to the balcony, yet streams of sunlight shined through, gently prodding her heavy eyes open.

She sniffed. Coffee.

Sitting up in the silky bed, she rubbed her eyes and yawned. Something on the table next to her caught her eye. Oh my! A delicate china cup of coffee, sugar, cream and a local newspaper were on a tray.

A red rose bud peeped from a glass vase on the tray. *What a lovely way to wake up, I could sure get used to this*! Snuggling back onto the soft pillows, Shanti sipped her hot coffee and skimmed the paper.

Finishing, she set the cup down, folded the newspaper, laid it next to the cup on the tray and reached for her cell to check more news.

Suddenly, she remembered what Maeve had said about the horses in the pasture.

Leaping up, she grabbed her white terry robe and pulled it on as she slipped into furry slippers, then hurried to the glass French doors. Ignoring the frigid air, she pulled open a door and stepped out onto the balcony.

Drawing the cowl of the robe tightly up around her neck, her hair blew back in the wind. It was cold, but stimulating. The sky was already brightening from the early sun. Shanti looked out over the railing, she cupped her hand over her eyes to cut the glare of the morning brightness.

A hundred or so yards out, she could see the horses. Most were standing in the glistening, dew-covered grass, necks down, chomping on what little bedraggled grass they could find.

Out in the pasture, two men were playing with a couple of horses. The horses would approach the men, snap their heads down, paw at the dirt, then they would throw their large heads back, shaking their beautiful manes. Shanti could just barely hear their whinnies.

One of the men held out something red, an apple maybe, to one of the horses. Recognizing the golden coat and white mane and tail of a Palomino, Shanti laughed when the saucy horse tripped lightly up to the outreached arm. First he sniffed the apple in the man's flat palm, then he quickly snapped up the apple.

A short man hurried across the field, joining the two men.

Shanti recognized him as Miguel, the farmhand that had driven the Vaughns to the estate last night.

The horses galloped off at the man's abrupt intrusion. The men gave Miguel their attention.

Miguel was waving his arms as he spoke, obviously agitated about something.

Shanti figured the man he was talking to might be the Lawtons' foreman, Graham Duncan. He seemed composed and in charge.

The other man that had been in the fields with him was very short and dark. He appeared to be Mexican. He stood silently while the other man continued to wave his arms about. Graham, listening at first, was now trying to calm Miguel.

Losing interest because she couldn't hear what they were saying, Shanti looked over to the glorious river.

Such a deep blue it turned violet in the deeper waves. Chloe told her last night the water moves too rapidly to fully freeze over.

Shanti looked back at the three men in the field. One of them pointed up at her. She waved. Graham waved back, the other two men ducked their heads and immediately strode away, in the direction of the Vaughns' farm.

Realizing she no longer could feel her hands and feet, Shanti swiftly stepped off the balcony into the cozy warmth of the bedroom.

After showering and dressing, wondering where everyone was, it was early still but not extremely so, when Shanti reached the dining room she realized she had the room to herself. It was quiet, but she could hear dishes clanging and voices from behind the closed door of the kitchen.

She recognized Serafina's voice but not the others. The room was lovely and bright, decorated in the same royal blue as the foyer. The upper half of the walls was the same opalescent cream as her bedroom. The chair rail, slightly darker than the cream of the walls, circled the room.

A glass chandelier draped over the long dining table. It wasn't quite as spectacular as the one hanging over the main staircase in the foyer, but it was gorgeous nonetheless. The sun sparkled on each diamond shaped piece of glass spreading rainbows all over the table and the walls.

Clasping her hands behind her back, Shanti wandered around the room enjoying the various other paintings adorning the walls. Bushes of green ferns flowed out of gold-plated vases filled in the corners of the room.

Her stomach rumbled. Thankful no one else was there to hear, she decided it was okay to get started eating instead of waiting for someone else to come.

The long table in the center of the room was set for breakfast. She could see some places appeared to have already been removed, while others held silverware and napkins. Just inside the doorway, along one wall, was a buffet table completely set for breakfast.

Steam drifted from the spout of a silver coffee urn and a china teapot. Coffee cups, teacups, juice and water glasses lined like dominoes ready for use. China plates and bowls were stacked at one end of the table. Silver chafing dishes with tiny burners under them keeping the food warm, beckoned Shanti.

Shanti grabbed a plate, still hot from the dishwasher, spooned on some eggs then covered them with the spicy salsa. She added a couple of pieces of bacon. Plopping a blob of orange marmalade on a piece of toast, she forked a few pieces of melon.

Pouring a small glass of juice, she set her plate down and took a drink of the fresh squeezed orange juice. She reached for her plate- then squeaked with a startled jump as she felt a hand snake around her waist.

"Apparently I'm not the only early bird around here this morning," a masculine voice whispered in her ear. The arm slid down Shanti's waist, almost to her hip.

Shanti took a step back, holding her plate and juice glass up in front of her as shields.

"Um, well good morning Mr. Thayne, uh, how are you?" Shanti's voice shook uncertainly. She wasn't used to a man brazenly touching her.

Logan Thayne maneuvered so that he was facing her, he stepped in close.

Shanti took a step back, but she came up dead against the table. Thayne leaned over, placing one hand on either side of Shanti, caging her against the table.

Realizing she was trapped, Shanti still held up her glass and plate, unsure of what to do. Thayne leaned in closer, his lips close to her ear-

"Well, children, how are we this bright early morn?" A chipper voice with a slight elderly quaver came from the doorway.

Shanti turned and saw Langston standing there calmly watching, his hands tucked in his trouser pockets. He looked deliberately at Thayne.

Chuckling drily, Thayne dropped his arms and moved back from Shanti. Shanti took the opportunity to hurry to the table. She flashed Mr. Lawton a grateful smile. He nodded to her then frowned at Logan.

Shanti pulled out a chair and sat down, not sure what to do next. Langston came over and sat at the head of the table where he sat last night. There was no silverware at his place, he'd obviously already eaten.

"I hadn't finished reading my paper so I thought I'd come back and enjoy the warm light that comes in through the dining room windows." He looked pointedly at Thayne. There was no paper on the table.

Thayne shrugged. "I don't eat breakfast, I'm just having a cup of coffee." He turned back to the table and poured a cup. Without saying another word, or looking in Shanti's direction, he left the room.

Shanti was staring intently at the tablecloth. Langston patted her hand.

"Honey, I don't think you really need to fear anything from that department," he nodded towards the door. "But if you ever feel you are in an uncomfortable situation, you just let out a holler and Graham or I will hear you. You got that?" He patted her hand again, smiling.

Shanti smiled gratefully at the kind man. What a lovely old soul, she thought.

His eyeglasses made his eyes big and soft, the laugh lines around his eyes and mouth crinkled when he smiled. Shanti felt warm and welcome whenever he was around.

"You go ahead and eat dear, others will be down soon. I'm going to the library and hunt down that book I was reading." With a gentle pat to her shoulder, he pushed his chair back and left the room.

By the time Shanti was almost finished with her breakfast, Chloe appeared, bouncing into the room. Her long dark hair was loose, swinging around her shoulders. She was wearing blue jeans and a fluffy yellow sweater.

"Hi! How'd you sleep?" she greeted Shanti, helping herself to some toast and coffee.

"Oh Chloe, I slept like a dream. Your home is so fabulous. Quiet and peaceful, you're so lucky to live here!"

"You get used to it. Besides, I think your home sounds really neat with mountains and lakes, and different people to see all the time. We see the same old people all the time. It's exciting to meet new people."

She spread strawberry jam on her toast and took a bite. Making fast work of her toast, she wiped her mouth on a napkin and gulped down the rest of the coffee. "C'mon, let's go horseback riding? Want to?" Chloe grinned at her new friend.

Shanti wiped her mouth and agreed cheerfully, "Let's go!"

"Okay, put on something really warm, hat, gloves and boots too if you have them. I'll meet you out by the back door." She ran off so fast Shanti didn't have a chance to ask her where the back door was.

Chapter Eleven

*B*undled in her powder blue, goose-down jacket, Shanti held her gloves and knit hat in her hands, her hair was pulled back into a ponytail. She'd tucked her blue jeans into black, knee-hi boots.

The door to the kitchen was closed. Cautiously, she pushed it open an inch or two and peeked in.

Chloe was chatting amiably with Serafina. Serafina had a towel in her hands, she was drying the good crystal. Chloe saw Shanti as soon as she peeked in, she beckoned to her. "Hey! You all ready?"

"Yeah, I'm ready. Looks pretty chilly out there, but it'll be invigorating I think!"

"How did you sleep, Miss Shantilly?" Serafina asked. She'd pinned up the sides of her lustrous black hair, the back tumbled in large curls down past her shoulders.

"I slept wonderfully, thanks. And dinner last night was incredible, as was breakfast. I wanted to thank the cook, but I don't see her."

"Cook is already to the market, she goes early to get the freshest food," Serafina told her. "You will probably meet her around lunchtime. Unless you girls would like a picnic, I can prepare something very fast if you would like?" Serafina set down the glass and cloth and walked quickly to the refrigerator.

'No, no Serafina, that's okay. It's like freezing outside. I don't think we'll be gone more than an hour if that. We'll be back in plenty of time for lunch. You ready?" Chloe asked Shanti, pulling on her hat and gloves.

Shanti was zipped up to her neck. "I'm ready, let's go. See ya later, Serafina!" She waved at the maid as the two women went out the back door of the kitchen.

"Oh my!" Shanti gasped as the frigid air hit her.

Chloe laughed. "You sissy Californians aren't used to 'really cold' weather, are you?"

Shanti pulled her hat more tightly on her head and shoved her gloved hands deep into her pockets. "Oh, it gets cold enough where I'm from. Maybe not this cold, but enough that you look forward to a toasty fire at the end of the day!" Shanti trudged quickly to keep up with Chloe.

A dusting of snow had covered the lawn since Shanti had looked out her balcony window. Their breaths exhaled in white vapor as they walked briskly towards the stables. The blue sky was more than half filled with clouds, but it was only lightly snowing.

Just as the girls reached the stable, a man came out holding two reins, two horses and two German Shepherds followed him. The dogs came right up to both girls, allowing them to scratch their ears.

Quickly losing interest, the two dogs ran off chasing each other, zig zagging across the open fields. Shanti recognized the beautiful Palomino from this morning. He looked frisky, but not overly so. He came right up to her. Pulling off one glove, she held her hand out; the horse nuzzled it.

"You are so beautiful," she whispered in his ear. She rubbed his nose, then his head. She scratched his ears, then ran her hand down his soft, white mane. The horse stood quietly, obviously enjoying her ministrations.

"How long have you had this problem with horses not liking you?" the man said with a lopsided grin.

Chloe laughed. "Yeah. Really Shanti, it's quite clear that horses have an innate distrust of you. It's so sad." Chloe reached for the reins of the other horse, a lovely Chestnut. She patted his head and stroked his long nose.

The horse obviously recognized her, he came right to her and tried to poke his nose in her pockets. Laughing, Chloe pushed him away, then pulled out two carrots, the greens still attached to the ends. She handed one to Shanti. "Here, give this to Goldie and he'll be your friend for life."

Chloe nodded at the man standing patiently. "Shanti, this is Graham Duncan, our foreman. He's been with us for a couple of years. He's originally from Scotland, so when you realize you can't understand what he's saying, that's his Scottish burr getting in the way!"

Graham frowned in pretense of annoyance at Chloe, then held out a hand to Shanti. "It's a pleasure to meet you. I think I saw you early this morning out on the balcony."

The foreman was a stalwart man with a handsome face if somewhat weather-beaten and rugged. Short dark hair combed back with twinkling blue eyes, his grin was welcoming.

They shook hands. "That's Manfred," he informed her, pointing to one of the dogs, "and that's Wolf," he gestured towards the other. Shanti knelt and patted both dogs as they rushed back to visit more.

Standing up, Shanti went over to the golden horse and held out her carrot to him. The horse immediately gobbled it. "Yes, that was me, freezing my, uh, butt out there. The pasture is very lovely in the morning. Mrs. Lawton told me to look out when the sun starts to rise. She said it's the prettiest time of the day, boy was she right!"

Chloe looked at Shanti, puzzlement pulled her eyebrows down. "Our Mrs. Lawton, my grandmother said that? I didn't think she knew what the word 'pretty' meant, much less ever bothered to look outside and enjoy the world!"

"Now, Miss Chloe, you shouldn't disrespect your grandmother that way. She's stern but she has feelings. It's not easy running as large an establishment as the estate and farm. There's a lot to keep track of and she does it very well," Graham admonished the young woman.

Chloe pulled in one side of her mouth and chewed on her lip at the mild rebuke.

Graham had already saddled the horses, they were ready to ride. Chloe had called him earlier. The dogs stood waiting eagerly, tails wagging, tongues hanging, they hoped they were going too.

"You've already met Goldie," Chloe told Shanti, pointing to the horse that was swallowing the carrot she'd given him. "I have Brandywine, isn't he beautiful?" She stroked his nose again. He nodded his large head up and down when he heard his name.

Shanti nodded vigorously. "They are both gorgeous animals, but I know why you chose Brandywine, did you do that because he so identically matches your mahogany hair?"

Chloe laughed, caught red-handed. "Yeah, I know he matches me. But, I chose Goldie for you because I knew you'd look great sitting on him, your hair matches him as well. Although that wasn't my sole reason for choosing him, he is highly spirited, but easily controlled. He loves to run and jump, but is even-tempered.

"Besides Brandywine, he's my other favorite horse." She took the reins to her horse and drew him outside of the barn. Shanti and Graham followed her.

Graham came up to Chloe and held out his cupped hands next to the stirrups. Chloe tucked a booted foot into his hands and he thrust her up onto the large horse. Graham checked the saddle straps to make sure they fit and were secure. Satisfied, he turned to Shanti. "Ready Miss Shantilly?"

Shanti nodded, standing next to Goldie. Graham cupped his hands and helped Shanti up on her horse. He checked her saddle straps and stirrups as well. When he was satisfied they fit and were secure, he patted the horse's rump.

"Okay ladies, you're ready to go. You sit a horse well, Miss Shantilly, like you've been on one your whole life." The foreman complimented the young woman. "Stay," he commanded the dogs.

Shanti grinned perfect white teeth at him. "Thanks Graham. I love to ride. I think I was probably less than three when my daddy first put me on a pony!"

Chloe pulled her reins to the right, the horse easily complied. "Let's go!" She took off at a canter. Shanti smiled at Graham then quickly followed Chloe.

Graham watched the girls trot off through the fields, then turned and went back into the stable. He inclined his head to Miguel standing behind the door on the opposite side of the barn. The dogs followed him into the barn.

The girls trotted silently, side by side, across the field lightly covered with snow. Ochre colored grass peeked through the thin layer of snow. Only a few snowflakes drifted down, swirling in the wind.

The grey fields were vast, dormant, waiting for the warm spring to be planted. After several hundred yards, they reached the river. Trotting alongside the water, both girls had their eyes peeled for wildlife.

"Look!" Chloe whispered, pointing to a bare oak tree. Sitting on a snow floured branch was a snowy owl. The girls pulled gently on the reins, the horses stopped. Shanti stared in awe at the startling, pure white owl.

The owl swiveled his head around without moving his body and stared his bright, golden yellow, cat's eyes at them. Shanti's horse snorted.

Immediately the owl spread wide wings and swooped off, heading for the woods on the other side of the river where he disappeared into the white forest.

"Oh my gosh, Chloe, he was so incredible!" Shanti exclaimed in delight.

Chloe nodded in agreement, still staring off wide-eyed to where the bird had disappeared. "Believe it or not, that's the first one I've ever seen. He was fabulous wasn't he?" She shook the reins, and gently kneed her horse in the side, he turned and they continued on alongside the rushing river.

"What river is this?" Shanti asked.

"It's part of the Snake river. It's actually a branch of it, it goes through the state and into Utah." They continued in camaraderie silence until they reached a covered bridge.

"Oh how lovely, a covered bridge, cool!" Shanti said as she followed Chloe into the bridge. The horses' hooves clomped on the wooden beams. It was dark inside, but they could see the light at the other end of the bridge.

"It's covered so it'll stay dry and not ice over in the winter. It'd be too slippery to cross then," Chloe informed her, speaking loudly so Shanti could hear her over the clippity- clop of the horses.

They clip-clopped out the end of the bridge and onto the snow covered grass. The icy grass crunched beneath the horses' hard hooves. A few hundred more yards and they reached the woods.

"Did you name the woods? Are they part of your property?" Shanti asked.

Nodding, Chloe replied, "Yeah, we have hundreds of acres. I've explored most of it, summer and winter. There's always something different to see, you know."

"What's its name?"

"Sweetbriar Forest. Isn't that lovely? Sweetbriar is a wild rose. I think Grandmother's grandmother named it. Grandmother sure didn't. Not a romantic bone in that skinny old body!"

"Now, come on Chloe. Your grandmother, severe as she seems, has been welcoming and gracious to me. Besides, she had nothing but nice things to say about you, you know."

"Me?" Chloe looked shocked. "You've got to be kidding. She hardly ever even says a word to me!"

"Well, she told me that the garden's beauty and design were entirely due to you. She said that for years it was just a jumble of bushes with a couple of flowering plants tossed in. They paid the landscaper primarily to keep things clipped and neat."

Chloe blinked in surprise at Shanti's words.

"She said you used to come out when you were around seven or eight, visiting with your mother and Jaime and Dawn, and you'd go tell Pablo to put a rose bush here, and a lavender wisteria-draped walkway over there..." Shanti gestured in the air at an imaginary garden.

"You're kidding," Chloe said, shaking her head in disbelief.

"No, I'm not. She said since you guys came and lived here permanently, that you go out every day and instruct Pablo what to buy and where to plant it. And that a good majority of the gardening work, except for the mowing is yours."

Chloe looked at Shanti with her mouth open. "I didn't think anyone noticed. I work in the gardens for myself. No one else seems to care. I love the feel of the rich earth flowing through my fingers, and the smell of fertilizer. I'm not kidding!" she insisted at the funny look Shanti shot her.

"Well, not just your grandmother told me, but your grandfather says you are quite the artist in the gardens. I swear!" She held up her hand at Chloe's disbelief.

"I think people notice you and what you do a lot more than you think, you know. You just have a really closed-mouthed family, they don't seem quick to compliment anyone."

Chloe nodded in agreement. They had entered the forest, immediately picking up a trail they followed it, heading deep into the woods. Even though the snow had covered some of the ground, patches of the dark trail could be seen.

Since there were no leaves on the trees the sun streaked through the clouds and tall trees with spindly branches, lighting the falling snow like fairy dust.

Cobwebs stretching between trees glistened like strung teardrops, sunbeams picked out spotted toadstools hiding next to tree stumps, and a few late falling red and orange leaves closed up like clenched fists sparkled in the dappled light.

"This is heaven, Chloe. The snow and trees totally blanket out sound. All you can hear are the horses and the birds calling in the distance. I feel like I'm in a loose cocoon."

"I come out here nearly every day, except if it's raining or too freezing. I've spotted a couple of deer and some little foxes on occasion."

Shanti looked at her friend. "I've seen birdhouses and feeders near the manor. Who put those there?"

Chloe smiled. "I love birds so I bought the feeders and had Pablo hang them. There's a couple right next to my bedroom window hanging off branches of a sugar maple."

"I'm with you, Chloe, I love birds too. I have hummingbird feeders at home."

Chloe smiled. "We plant yellow flowering plants in the summer, those attract butterflies, I bet you like those too?"

Shanti nodded. "Oh yes, I watch them fluttering from bush to bush, like a handful of colorful tossed confetti. I talk to them, my sister laughs at me."

"I think I'd laugh too, Shanti if I saw you chasing a butterfly around a yard yakking at it." They giggled together.

They trotted silently for a while through the normally dense woods. Shanti shivered slightly, but Chloe caught it.

"We'd better head back. Once you start feeling the cold, it'll only get worse, c'mon, follow me." They trotted more quickly, heading back the way they'd come until they reached the entrance to the woods.

Stepping outside, the sun hit them more brightly, no longer diffused from the trees. As soon as they crossed the river and exited the bridge, Chloe slapped her horse's rump with the reins, the horse bolted, hurtling across the pasture.

Shanti did likewise, racing to catch up with Chloe's head start. She could hear Chloe's laughter carried back to her by the wind.

The girls galloped across the open field. Shanti snapped her horse to get into high gear and it burst leagues past Chloe.

When she approached the barn she pulled back on the reins.

Graham hearing the pounding hooves nearing, was already outside waiting. He grabbed the reins, holding the horse steady as Shanti slid off the big Palomino.

"Well? How was it? Was Goldie good?" Graham asked.

Shanti panting from the hard fast ride patted the horse's neck. Goldie was panting too, his legs were still moving, sorry that the ride was over. He tried to nudge Shanti's arm, hinting for her to get back on.

"That's enough now, boy," she told the beautiful horse, still petting him. "We had a wonderful ride, Graham. We rode through the fields and into the pasture, and then Chloe took me into your enchanting forest. I can't wait to go again!"

Chloe came to a screeching halt in front of the pair. Both horse and rider were breathing hard. Still holding Goldie's reins, Graham grabbed Brandywine's too.

"Hey! How'd you learn to ride like that, girl?" Chloe demanded as she jumped from her horse, sliding with a thud to the hard, muddy earth. Shanti laughed at her friend. Chloe was all out of breath, her windblown hair flying in her eyes.

"I told you, I've ridden since I was practically a baby. If I had the space I'd have my own horse."

"I'll take care of the horses, Miss Chloe, I think they have lunch almost ready." Graham took the two horses and headed back inside the stables to brush them down and give them some feed.

"Lunch! My goodness, we must have been out longer than I thought! We'd better hurry, Grandmother does not like it when you're late!"

The young women giggled, racing each other again but to the manor now.

Chapter Twelve

$\mathcal{E}$veryone was already at the table, waiting, when Chloe and Shanti, after stopping for a quick face and hand wash, rushed to the dining room.

Pretending not to see Maeve's disapproving glare, the two young women slid unceremoniously into their chairs. Dawn smirked smugly at the pair. She gets a tickle when someone other than her for a change is in the doghouse.

"How was your ride, Shantilly?" Langston's friendly inquiry deflected any bad feelings in the room.

Shanti picked up her napkin and shaking it out, set it across her lap. Smiling her thanks once again at the kind old man, she said, "It was great. We got to see a good deal of your property."

"I doubt that," Jaime said. "The property goes for miles and miles. Take you the better part of a day just to cross most of it if you went as the crow flies." He sipped his ice water. He didn't look too worse the wear for what he drank last night. His eyes appeared tired, but they still glinted mischievously.

"Anyway, what we saw of it was incredibly beautiful." Shanti thanked Serafina as she helped herself to pasta dribbled in a creamy white sauce and topped with plump pink shrimp.

Serafina smiled moving onto Jaime. Shanti looked around, "Where's Camelia and Logan?" she asked politely, seeing their seats empty.

Dawn smirked again. "Darling, they never join us for meals except for dinner. They have the girls bring breakfast and lunch to their rooms. They're still on their honeymoon, apparently." She snickered.

"Dawn." Maeve frowned at the redhead.

Dawn picked up her fork and twisted the long creamy pasta around it. "Well, what do you think they're doing, Grandmother, playing cards?"

Jaime's crooked grin confirmed what his sister was saying.

"Ahem." Langston cleared his throat, bringing the attention back to him. "What are your plans today, Shanti?"

She smiled her pearlies at him. "I'm going to take some photographs first of the exterior of the manor, just to keep the color constant when I'm working inside. Then I-"

"Excuse me." Montgomery entered the room. He leaned down and whispered in Langston's ear.

Concern scribbled over the old man's face, he looked shaken, his face whitened.

"Langston, what is it?" Maeve asked, her grey brows lifted.

The old man struggled to his feet. Montgomery stifled the urge to help him knowing it would make Langston look weak in front of the others.

Langston stood, his hands clutching the edge of the table for support. He looked towards the open door of the dining room.

Matthew Vaughn was standing there. He came forward at Langston's nod.

Taking a deep breath, Langston said, "Apparently, some of the workers at the Vaughns' farm were going through the potatoes in cold storage to check for any signs of rot, and, well they found," he paused, looking at Matthew.

Matthew cleared his throat then explained, "They...uh...the hands...uh, well there's at least a quarter of the stored potatoes are...decayed." He tucked his hands in his trouser pockets and stared down at the table as he heard gasps all around.

He looked up at the group. "It looks like, but we're not sure yet, like Potato Rot Nematode." His lips compressed and his eyes dropped again at the round of gasps.

Shanti asked, "What's wrong? What's Potato Neme, Nemata-"

Even Jaime looked distressed at the words.

Langston turned worried eyes to his guest. He told her, "It's infrequent, but it happens. The potatoes somehow get infected. There are no above ground symptoms, it's usually not apparent until the potatoes are in storage. They, well they just rapidly decay."

Langston shrugged. "Sometimes you can't tell as much by sight as by touch. They can be soft, but then as the infection progresses, the potatoes get splits and some actually crumble." He looked at Matthew. "Any signs of secondary infection, fungi or fusarium?"

His lips compressed, Matthew shook his head. "It's too early to tell that yet. We've only just realized. I'm here because, well, I know the hands will talk amongst themselves and word will get back to you. But for now, we've instructed them, and we're asking you, that, well...we're asking that the County Extension Agent and the Potato Commission not be informed until we've completed our own investigation."

Wordless, Langston's brows arched in question.

"If word gets out to our buyers in Venezuela, Italy, Thailand, or our investors, well, you know how that can hurt us, what damage it'll cause." Matthew looked around at everyone at the table, pleading with them to understand.

Langston stared down at the table, shaking his head. Then he looked up and out the window. A few slow blinks behind his glasses, then he said, "I need to speak with Tobias and Magnus first, Matt. You know what you're asking. The farm needs to be quarantined. What about the spuds that have already gone out?"

"Well, sir, we've discreetly checked around and it looks like the early group is okay. But, that's less than 10%. We've kept the majority later than the normal February 1st deadline, the shippers weren't ready."

Langston sighed deeply. One-by-one, he made eye contact with everyone at the table. "For the time being Matt, I and my family will keep this under our hats, right?" He raised his eyebrows at the group.

Everyone nodded their acquiescence except Dawn, who was studying her nails, looking bored out of her mind.

"Dawn?" Langston questioned, sounding unusually stern.

She turned languid eyes towards Matthew, primping her hair. She rolled her eyes then answered, "Yes Granddaddy." Yawning, her tone bored, she said, "Like I have nothing to talk to my friends about except a bunch of nasty ol' rotting potatoes. My lips are sealed."

Clearly uninterested in the entire conversation, she picked up her fork and stuck it into her pasta, swirling long strands around the fork's tines.

"Thanks, you know, well, thanks." Matthew nodded to the group. His eyes bleak, mouth pinched.

"I'll walk you to the door, Matthew," Langston said, he and Montgomery ambled out with the young man.

The manor was unusually quiet for a few days.

Shanti saw little of anyone as she took her pictures of the house and prepared her canvasses.

The third day after Matthew Vaughn's visit, Shanti woke to a timid knock at her door. Opening the door, Shanti looked in dismay at Chloe's white face that greeted her.

"Chloe, what's wrong? Come inside." She took her friend's hand and pulled her into the room. She gently helped her to sit on the bed.

Chloe looked close to tears. Her russet eyes were brimming, ready to spill, her lower lip quivered.

Shanti put a consoling arm around arm around her shoulder. "Tell me honey, what's the matter?"

Chloe started shaking, her words trembled out, "It's Grandfather. He…he's very sick, they don't know what's wrong…" Tears spilled over, she started sobbing.

Oh no, Shanti slapped a hand over her heart. "Okay, okay," she murmured, hugging her friend, she petted her hair.

Chloe cried against her shoulder.

"I…I'm so scared, Shanti, he' so old, you know," she cried.

"But what's wrong, did he go to the hospital?"

"Yeah, they took him a few minutes ago, against Mrs. Li's wishes. She- she said she has…some, um, medicine, hokey-pokey stuff, you know? She usually can work miracles on anyone, no matter how sick, but this time, I…I…it looks bad Shanti…"

Shanti continued trying to comfort Chloe. When her sobs subsided somewhat, she asked again, "But what's wrong, what are his symptoms? Is it a heart attack?"

Chloe shook her dark head back and forth. "No, no…not a heart attack, he's horribly sick to his stomach, has been for a couple of days I guess. But now he's delirious and so weak he can't even sit up. Oh Shanti, I couldn't stand it if something happened to him!" Chloe wailed, burying her face in Shanti's shoulder again.

Silently, Shanti stroked Chloe's hair, there was nothing she could say to help.

An hour or so later, Chloe left to go to her room to lie down. She was exhausted from the stress of her grandfather's illness.

Shanti slipped downstairs to the dining room. The house was hushed. Everyone tiptoed about, not wishing to disturb anyone else.

Maeve was there, a cup of coffee in front of her. "Please join me, Shantilly, I'll ring for Serafina to-"

Shanti shook her head. "No, that's okay, I'll just have coffee for now, thanks. How is he?" she asked, fearing to hear the worse.

Maeve shrugged, but worry lines creased her forehead. "Still the same." She took a sip of coffee.

She gave out a small cough, then a deep breath before saying, "Listen dear, I think it would be best, for the time being, at least until Langston gets better, that you go back home. As soon as he recovers, we'll send for you." Her voice was cold, but her eyes regarded Shanti warmly.

Shanti blinked in surprise then nodded. "Yes, yes of course you're right, Mrs. Lawton. I'll pack immediately. I'll leave as soon as I can get a flight. You will keep me informed of his progress?"

"Of course dear. We will obviously take care of the cost of the ticket. There's a flight at 12:00. Montgomery will have the car ready out front at 9:00, will that give you time?" the older lady asked.

"Oh." Shanti was surprised, so soon. "Of course, I'll go pack now. I don't think I have an appetite for breakfast anyway. Excuse me." When Maeve nodded, returning to her coffee, Shanti turned and fled the room.

At the front door, Chloe hugged her tightly, tears running down her cheeks. "What will I do without you? Hurry back, okay?" She hic-cupped, stuffing a fuzzy mitten in her mouth to still her crying. The girls had become close in their short time together.

Shanti hugged her hard, holding back her own tears.

Jaime, Serafina, Libby, Maeve and Chloe were outside to see her off.

Serafina, wiping at her eyes hugged Shanti. "We will all miss you, Miss Shantilly, God Speed." The maid smiled weakly and stepped back.

"I'll miss you guys, too. Write me, okay?" Shanti said to Serafina and Chloe, her voice choked with tears.

They all nodded miserably.

Montgomery held the door open and followed her out.

Dario was already in the car with the heat going. She climbed in, Montgomery sat next to her, just like when they'd arrived, seemed like years ago yet it was barely a week.

The big blue car swung around the circular drive and then headed out towards the outer gate. Shanti pressed her face against the window, her hand held up in a wave.

The group on the step waved back, their faces sad and forlorn.

Chapter Thirteen

$\mathcal{S}$hanti heard the bell tinkle out in the shop, but didn't stop painting. She didn't even look up when she heard movement at the door of her workshop.

"Sis."

She still didn't look up at the sound of her sister's voice.

Summer walked over to the stool Shanti was sitting on and stood next to her. "Come on Shanti, it's been almost eight months since you left and you're still depressed."

Shanti smiled wryly, setting down her paintbrush. "I am not depressed, Sum, just because I wouldn't go water skiing at the lake with you guys-"

"It's not like you not to want to spend time with Drew and Candy and our nieces. Especially to enjoy one of the last days on the lake before the cooler weather starts creeping in. And tell me you're not sad-" she pointed at the painting Shanti was currently working on.

It was of three people, tourists she'd seen around the town probably, but their faces were drawn very sad, almost in tears.

"You never paint sad people. You need to forget about the Lawtons and move on," she advised her sister.

"Actually Sum, I just got a letter from Chloe and she says her grandfather has been slowly recovering. And the last letter from

Serafina sounded very hopeful. I think I should be hearing from them soon."

Summer clicked her tongue against her teeth. "Eternally optimistic, that's you." She shook her head. "Anyway, shouldn't you be getting ready for your date with Marc? It's nearly six you know," she reminded her sister, pointedly looking down at her watch.

Shanti sighed heavily. "Yeah, you're right, I need to get going. I just feel like I have an unfinished job, you know? I pictured the Manor in my head how it would look on canvas, completed, and…well I just feel incomplete, lacking. You know what I mean?" She turned questioning eyes to her sister, asking her to understand what she was feeling.

Summer crossed her arms in front of her chest and leaned back against a table. She nodded her head slightly. "I guess I understand, a job started but not finished. You have too much of Daddy in you. He would always complete a project no matter how tough, remember?"

Shanti smiled at her sister's words, remembering her father instilling in them, a job well done is a job well doing, or something like that.

"Anyway, put your stuff away and get ready. Maybe Marc is going to pop the question tonight! You never know!"

Shanti laughed then shrugged. She plunked her brushes into a jar of turpentine and put away the paints she'd been using. She smiled crookedly at the painting she'd been working on.

It looked pretty depressing. Summer was right, as usual. She stood up, stretching her arms over her head, she'd been sitting and painting for hours.

"I don't know if I want him to pop the question, Sum. I like Marc okay, but, I don't know, sometimes I feel something missing…but I don't know what it is." She looked at her sister, her shoulders drew up, her lips pulled in.

Summer placed her hands on her slim hips. "You never get serious with any guy you go out with, Shanti. You're always looking for that something special, that extra…oh I don't know, like you're still waiting for that knight in shining armor. Honey, you're getting too old to believe in that stuff anymore, you know?"

Shanti shrugged again. Walking to the door, she said, "I don't have to give up my dreams just because they seem unrealistic, or because some old fuddy duddy said it can't happen. Look at you and Jason. He's a doll and you know it!"

Summer laughed, following her sister out of the studio.

Shanti turned off the lights as they entered the shop. They closed up the small store, locking the door behind them. They stood in the parking lot, each ready to get in her car and go home. Summer had plans herself with Jason.

"Yeah, I got lucky with Jason. I wish he had a brother for you! You go have fun now and forget about unfinished business for a while, you hear me?" She gave her sister a light shove towards her car.

"Fine, I will. Say hi to Jason for me," Shanti called just as she closed the door to her car.

Summer nodded and waved as the sisters drove off in different directions.

A couple of hours later, Shanti unlocked the door to her small house and turned on the lights. Marc followed her inside. "Make yourself comfortable, Marc, I'll get us something to drink."

"Okay hon." The young man went to the overstuffed couch decorated with pastel blue, yellow and white flowers and sank into it. He looked around while he waited.

Fresh flowers were placed around the room wherever there was a table with space to set them on. He couldn't see Shanti in the kitchen but he could hear her moving around. Suddenly, a bundle of fur jumped in his lap, startling him.

"Hey!" he exclaimed, shoving the cat off his lap. "Shoo!" Sneezing three times, he pushed the cat away with his foot.

"Damned feline," he muttered under his breath. He could see having a dog, but didn't see any point in having a furball roaming round your house, staring at you with unblinking slitty eyes.

Princess stared at him briefly then haughtily marched over to Grace, Summer's other Persian that was sitting by the kitchen door. Shanti was cat sitting for the weekend.

The cats sat silently, licking their paws, occasionally looking contemptuously over at Marc. At least that's what he was thinking. *How am I supposed to make a move on Shanti with those two watching us?* he thought to himself. He looked around for a closet to stuff them into.

"Here." Shanti came into the room carrying two sodas, she handed one to Marc.

He took the glass from her. "Don't you have anything stronger?" he asked as she gracefully sat down next to him.

"I had enough to drink at dinner, Marc. We had almost three glasses of wine and I must say, I'm feeling a little fuzzy and sleepy as it is. And you have to drive home. I don't want to be the one responsible for you getting in an accident."

"Hmm," Marc grunted. He gulped his soda quickly, setting the empty glass on a coaster on the coffee table. He leaned back and studied Shanti.

Her hair was up in a twist, loose tendrils swirled around her heart-shaped face. She had the prettiest eyes, he thought, heavily fringed lashes encircled blue eyes that could compete with the sky.

Her pretty lips smiled at him, begging to be kissed. He took the glass from her hand and set it on the table. Reaching over her, he picked up Princess and set her on the floor, again nudging her away with his foot. He struggled to smother a sneeze.

Marc cupped Shanti's head with one hand, drawing her to him. Holding her chin lightly with the other, leaning in, he kissed her. She responded, her petal soft lips pressed against his.

Still tenderly holding the back of her head, his other arm slid down to the small of her back, pulling her close to him. The short skirt of her pale yellow dress rode up her thighs.

As the kiss became more intense, Marc reached up with one hand and plucked the pins from her hair. Blonde curls sprung loose, tumbling over her shoulders. He pushed the locks back with both hands.

Cupping her face again, his mouth urgently sought hers. Separating her lips with his tongue, he gently probed her mouth, running his tongue slickly over her smooth teeth.

His ardor increasing, he pushed her back against the couch. As soon as he pressed his chest against her supple body he could feel fire start coursing through his veins.

Pulling his head back to catch his breath, he gazed down at her.

Her eyes were half closed, her mouth parted, she was breathing heavily. She looked up at him, blinking. Before she could say anything, he covered her mouth again with his, stilling her words.

Suddenly he was kissing her almost roughly now, she put up one hand against his chest. He took her hand and held it back against the couch. With his other hand, he pulled at the top button of her dress until it came open. He continued prying open the next three buttons.

Shanti brought up her other hand to stop him. He pushed her hand away, working now on the last button. He started to push the material apart, his hand stroking her neck and then moving down, inside the bodice of her dress.

She put both hands against his chest and pushed him away as hard as she could. He barely budged an inch. She tore her mouth from his.

"Marc! Stop! Marc!" She kept pushing his hands until he stopped groping her.

He sat back, puzzled. "What? You want me as much as I want you, I know you do," he muttered, reaching for her again. She held up a hand, holding him away.

"No Marc, I...I'm not ready yet. I told you that last week." She held her hand against his chest, panting from the exertion of holding him at bay. Her dress was open nearly to the waist, the skirt was pushed way up her thighs.

Marc first stared at her shapely thighs, then, slowly raised his eyes until he was looking at her bosom. She followed his glance, looking down she realized her breasts were in danger of being fully exposed.

She hadn't felt Marc's hands at her dress buttons at first, he had been kissing her so ardently. Quickly, she pulled her dress together and stood up. He stared at her, stunned that she was rejecting him.

"I invited you in because you swore to me you'd be a gentleman and not try anything," she accused him, rapidly buttoning her dress.

Marc ran a shaking hand through his hair. His eyes raked her length- he had been sure tonight would be the night. Shaking his head to clear it, *I guess not*, he thought to himself.

"Listen, Shanti, we're adults. How long do you think I can hold off? We've been dating for a couple of weeks now and I'm a red-blooded male you know."

He tucked in his shirt that had loosened during their embrace. "Besides, you were just as eagerly returning my kisses."

"No, I wasn't. You chose to ignore my protests, you wanted to believe I was participating. What's wrong with us being friends first, Marc? Can't we get to know each other, have fun, and then…you know…later." Shanti tried to twist her hair back up but it wouldn't cooperate.

Marc stood up, Shanti took a step back.

He laughed mirthlessly. Holding up a hand, he said snarky, "Please, I'm not going to throw you to the floor and rape you, for Pete's sake. I can get a willing girl you know, anytime I want. I might just go ahead and do that, if you're going to play the Ice Queen routine."

Sneering somewhat, he told her, "You know Trisha Vanderpelt has been after me all summer, but I've wanted to be with you. Every time she's around she's rubbing herself all over me, you've seen her."

Shanti shrugged. What he said was true. Trisha's family moved in at the beginning of summer. Being quite wealthy, they belong to the country club, as does Marc. She's seen the way

Trisha looks at Marc. Shanti was pretty sure they've already been together, for all his denying.

"Listen Marc, if you want Trisha, go ahead. Heaven forbid I would keep you from something you really want. We aren't going steady. If you prefer her to me, gee, go on, ask her out." Shanti moved to the door. She reached for the knob.

"I think you need to leave now." She pulled the door open.

Marc quickly stepped in front of her, pushing the door closed.

"Come on Shanti, I was just mad for a second. I have no interest in Trisha. She's pretty but she doesn't hold a candle to you."

Shanti smiled sadly. Looking at Marc she shook her head.

He was quite attractive himself. Almost purely black hair with equally dark eyes. She could see her own miniature reflection in them. Bedroom eyes, they were so sultry.

The way his intoxicating gaze traveled slowly down then up her body the first time they met at a dance at the country club.

She seldom went to the country club. But, her girlfriend, Jannell, had a thing for a musician playing in the band there and had begged her to go with her. Marc asked her to dance and they danced every dance until the band quit.

Jannell left with her boyfriend. Shanti and Marc talked for hours while walking along the beach in the summer night's balmy air. They had walked arm in arm, carrying their shoes in their hands, oblivious to other lovers sharing the sand.

"That's my point, Marc." She pulled the door open, standing aside for him to leave. "All you're interested in, in a woman, is her looks. I want a man to be interested in me as well. Thank you for a nice evening, I had a good time. Goodnight."

She gently prodded him out the door, closing the door quickly as he opened his mouth to argue.

He stood for a second, getting angry, then turned and hopped into his Mercedes, burning rubber as he tore down the road.

Sighing, Shanti turned off the lights and took the glasses into the kitchen. Her house was small, just two bedrooms a living room and a tiny kitchen. She used the second bedroom as a greenhouse and extra paint studio. Although she did most of her work at her shop Fleurtique, sometimes she liked to do a little jewelry making at home.

Shanti decided to take a quick shower before hopping into bed.

Feeling refreshed from her shower, she climbed between the cool sheets and reached for the book on the nightstand. She turned on the lamp next to the bed and settled back with her book. The phone suddenly rang, jarring her.

Before it could ring a second time, she snatched the white phone quickly off the table, and answered, "Hello?"

"Shanti? Hi...um...it's Marc. Are you in bed? I hope I didn't waken you."

"No, I was just reading," Shanti replied, figuring he was calling her to maybe apologize. "Where are you?" She could hear music and voices in the background.

"Oh...uh...I'm uh at the Club. I thought I'd stop on the way home, have a drink you know, settle myself...um..." Realizing he was stammering like a schoolboy, he took a deep breath.

"Listen Shanti, I want to apologize...um...I mean I'm not apologizing for my behavior, because I don't think I did anything wrong. I mean...you are a beautiful, sexy chick-...um...woman, and there'd be something wrong with me if I wasn't attracted to you, you know? Anyway, I got a little piss- um...ticked off and I know you didn't like that..." He hesitated but she didn't say anything.

"Anyway, I think we have something special going on, Shanti, I hope we're okay?" he ended in question, waiting for her to respond.

After a beat, Shanti replied, "It's okay, Marc, I'm not mad. I just want to be friends first, then...well then we'll see from there."

His voice lightened. "Hey, that's great Shanti! How about next Saturday, there's a concert at the Stranton Playhouse, do you want to go?"

Now Shanti hesitated. "Um...I guess that sounds nice...sure."

Marc awkwardly cleared his throat. "Okay then, I'll pick you up around-"

Shanti could hear a voice near Marc- "Come on handsome, let's go! Hang up, I wanna boogieee-"

Shanti recognized the voice, Trisha Vanderpelt. She heard Marc's loud whisper, "Shhh, cut it out, I'm almost done, go wait for me. Ahem, um, okay Shanti, I'll pick you up at seven, okay?"

Shanti sighed, what was she getting herself into? Well, it's not like they had declared they were exclusive. "Fine, that's okay, I'll see you at seven, goodbye." She abruptly hung up, not sure she even wanted to see him again.

Shanti reached for her book- again the phone rang, startling her. Feeling a little peeved now and not too friendly she said, "Listen Marc, about Saturday night I-"

"Shanti? Hi, it's Chloe," a timid voice said.

Breathing a happy sigh of relief, Shanti said brightly, "Chloe? Is that you? Hi, how are you? Is everything all right?" Suddenly she was concerned, it was pretty late for anyone to be calling.

Chloe laughed. "Everything's great, Shanti! I just couldn't wait to call you with the good news!"

"What good news, is it your grandfather?"

"Actually, yes, Grandfather is doing really well. He's been up and around a little, and he asks about you almost every day! Grandmother thought it might help him recover more quickly if you come back, that's why I'm calling. Will two weeks from today be too soon?" Her voice trailed off, afraid that Shanti may not want to come back to Idaho.

"Too soon? Tonight would be too soon, Two weeks would be fabulous!" Shanti exclaimed happily.

Chloe laughed. "Great! We'll overnight your ticket and Montgomery will be there, waiting for you just like last time, okay?"

"Better than okay, Chloe, I can't wait!"

The women talked for a few more minutes, then Shanti hung up and turned off the light, eager now to go to sleep. As her eyes drifted closed she remembered she needed to call Marc to cancel their date for the weekend.

Chapter Fourteen

$\mathscr{I}$t was dark, the night air crisp with an early autumn snap. The person deliberately dressed completely in black to blend into the night, hurried along the well-worn path to the barn. The moon was only a tiny crescent sliver in the sky.

With clouds covering most of the stars, there was very little light. The two dogs came out of nowhere, running right up to the person.

"Stay." The command was barely heard, but firm. The dogs stopped, recognizing the voice. "Go back," the order was barely a whisper, but enough for the dogs to hear. Immediately, they turned and rushed off back to the house.

The figure walked quickly but as quietly as possible. It was very late, everyone should be sleeping, but just in case, the person stayed in the shadows as much as possible.

Reaching the barn, the prowler slipped around to a small, side door, knowing the large door would creak and squeak, possibly drawing attention.

Stopping next to the door, the person quickly looked around to make sure they hadn't been seen. The wind was blowing cool air. Dried leaves blowing in the wind scraped over the ground and against the barn.

Shadows made by trees loomed sinister along the grass drawing ugly caricatures crawling up the red barn. A weaker person would be nervous in the eeriness of the cold, black night, generally quiet but still alive with night noises.

Secure that they hadn't been followed or seen, the person slowly pried open the wooden door, pulling it carefully so it wouldn't creak or grind loudly along the hard ground, then stepped inside, closing the door behind.

Looking around, the figure adjusted eyes to the even darker barn. Strong odors of hay and wet dirt assailed, twitching nostrils, horses snorted and stomped in their sleep.

The prowler moved over to the one tiny window emitting the barest of light. Standing with hands tucked deeply in pockets, they waited impatiently.

A noise in the corner caught attention. The head cocked, listening. Hearing footsteps, the person turned towards the sound.

A body separated itself from the darkness emerging cautiously.

"Is that you?" the question was hushed against the insulation of the hay-stuffed barn.

"Shh, why did you call me out here, what couldn't wait?" The two people stood close, whispering.

"Harvest time is here, I'm worried about those damned potatoes. What if there's something wrong again this time?"

"You worry too much. That infection was an unusual occurrence, you know that. It's rare. They cleaned and sanitized the storage area and all of the cultivation and handling equipment and burned the spoiled potatoes. The farm-hands applied Vapam, the nematicide, you were there, you saw."

"But... the agents might still be called in, what if-"

"Because the old man was so sick, the Vaughns were so concerned, everyone thought he was dying so no one got around to calling in the agents. The family kept it to themselves and the servants were threatened they could lose their jobs if they told. The Vaughns hoped it was a one shot deal."

"It's not like them to do something against the law-"

"I know. Like I said, they hoped it was a freak accident and they cleaned up really well. If it happens again, they'll be ruined, they know that. So they took a gamble keeping it quiet."

"Well, do you think we should take a chance? Maybe we need to skip this time, maybe we-"

"Are you insane- you idiot?" the voice whispered sharply. "Do you want to tell 'them' that we're going to just 'skip' this year?" The shorter of the two laughed harshly, mimicking the other person's fearful voice. "Do you want to find yourself swimming headless in the river?"

The taller person shook their head; shoulders slumped. "I'm just...I want out. This is too dangerous-"

"You should have thought of that before, it's too late now."

"But...but what about all those people, thousands can be hurt...killed..." The voice shook with fear. "I've been thinking, I can't sleep at night..." The taller person stood still, hands still deep in their pockets as it was damp and cold in the barn. They could hear occasional rustling. *I hope that's the cats chasing rats, ha, we're the rats being chased.*

Shortie walked a few steps from the other, head down.

Tall person was silent, watching the compatriot move around the barn.

Suddenly the shorter person swung around and stepped close to the still one. "You listen to me. You wanted in, in the beginning, remember? You needed the money for those gambling debts. They were going to break your legs, remember?" The person pointed a rigid, gloved finger at the other.

"Well, these people will do a hell of a lot worse, you know that. Just do as you're told and keep your mouth shut. Do you hear me?" The unsaid threat was still explicit.

Reluctantly, the taller person nodded their head. They both knew they were in deep. There would be no getting out of doing business with these people. Taller shrugged reluctantly. Oh well.

"Fine. I'll be ready." Taller's deeply held breath was harshly expelled a deeply held breath, trying to lose the fear along with it.

"Of course you will. As soon as it's here, I'll get word to you. Until then, stay away from me. Don't call, don't send messages, stay the hell away and keep your mouth shut." The severe voice ground the words out in a harsh whisper.

Taller's nod of submission was semi-sheepish.

"Now, wait until I've been gone for ten minutes before you leave, just in case someone has insomnia and takes to looking out windows like that Lane girl has occasion to do."

"Speaking of her, what about her? Maybe she's like a spy or something sent to-"

"Will you cut it out? She's just a harmless girl come to paint the house. Forget about her, she'll probably be gone soon after harvest. She's just a pretty head with no brain, you know?"

Then the short person moved quietly to the door they'd come in, and opened it carefully. "All right. I'm leaving. You wait, ten minutes, got it? And stay away from me."

Glaring a warning at the other, Shortie poked their head out the door and cautiously looked around. Seeing no one, they stepped out the door without even glancing back at the person still standing inside and closed the door behind them.

The person left inside could barely hear the other's footsteps moving rapidly away from the barn. *Damn. Why did I have to be the one left here alone in the dark? What's that?* The head snapped up at a sudden noise.

A cat bounded out from behind a stack of hay with a flailing mouse in its mouth.

"Whew, just a cat." Then, another noise, a twig snapping.

Jumpy already, the person hurried to the door.

"Screw 'em, I'm not standing here in this dank, dark old barn," and opened the door, not hearing the noise that was now right behind them.

Chapter Fifteen

Shanti was so excited to be back she could hardly sleep even though the luxurious Rose Room was so comfortable.

She'd gotten in late last night. Sharing a quick, but hot dinner of spicy chili and crusty bread with the family, they all went to bed soon after dessert and sipping comforting brandy in the den.

Langston looked older, frailer. His eyes drooped, but he smiled brightly at Shanti's return. He looked so fragile, his voice quavered as he told Shanti he couldn't wait to see the finished painting of the manor.

Shanti had smiled warmly at him, he was so endearing, the same white hair fell over still vibrant blue eyes.

It was very early, Shanti figured no one else would be up yet. Swinging her legs over the side of the bed, she slipped her feet into snuggly slippers and grabbed the terry cloth robe off the foot of the bed. Not hesitating, she hurried into the bathroom for a quick shower.

Emerging moments later, she blow dried her hair, then quickly stepped into jeans. Pulling open a dresser drawer, she blessed Serafina. Her clothes were all neatly folded and placed inside the lovely dresser.

A finger to her lips, she glanced over her array of colorful sweaters before choosing a pale blue with tiny snowflakes embroidered on it. She pulled the thick sweater on, savoring the warmth and softness. With practiced fingers, she easily tied her hair back into one thick braid.

Yanking the down-filled jacket off a hanger, she pulled it on as she was leaving the room. Flipping off the lights, she quietly closed the door and tip toed down the carpeted stairs, holding her boots in her hands.

Seems she was the only early bird. Pulling her hat and gloves out of her pockets she tiptoed across the marble floor, down the hall to the kitchen. Putting a gloved hand against the wooden café door, she slowly pushed the door to the kitchen open.

Peeking inside, she could see it was unoccupied and as dark as the rest of the sleeping house. Moving quietly across the room, she headed for the door leading outside to the back of the house.

Stepping outside, the brisk autumn air was cold but without the bitterness of winter, brushed her face.

Stars twinkled in the inky heavens, the sun was still sleeping too. Shanti's footsteps thumping across the hardened earth were the only sounds in the still night.

Across the yard, a glow emanated from the direction of the stables and barns. The light drew her. Quickening her pace, she moved purposefully towards the stables, she could hear noises now.

The rustling of hay, whimpering horses, and a male voice, low and gentle came from inside the first stable. The man sounded like he was talking to the horses. She stopped just outside stable. The large doors were wide open.

"Hello?" Shanti called softly, she didn't want to startle the man inside.

"Who's there?" A deep voice questioned. It was wary, but not unfriendly.

Shanti stepped into the doorway, into the brighter light and surprising warmth. The Lawton's foreman, Graham Duncan, was standing in front of the first stall. In his early thirties, his face was unshaven. The early morning whiskers sparkled in the light from just inside the door.

He was wearing faded jeans that were long enough to almost cover his mud-coated boots. His leather jacket with a warm looking furry collar covered most of a brown plaid, flannel shirt. His thick head of hair and callused hands were bare.

It appeared he was brushing a bay that stood patiently, never taking its large, languid eyes off Graham.

"Hi, I'm Shanti. Do you remember me?" Shanti grinned, holding out a gloved hand.

The foreman wiped his hand on the side of his jeans before shaking hands with her. "Sure," he said, motioning for her to come inside. "Of course I remember you."

The further inside she moved, the warmer it was. She unzipped her jacket and took off her hat and gloves, holding them loosely in her hands.

"He's beautiful," she admired. Coming closer she reached out and stroked the horse's long nose. The horse snorted, shaking his head. He stepped closer to Shanti, shoving his nose into her chest, asking for more. She giggled, rubbing his light brown ears.

Graham watched her for a minute. "It's nice to see you back here. What are you doing out so early, or is it so late?"

Shanti smoothed the huge animal's straw like mane then ran her hand down his neck, stroking the short rough hairs. She smiled at Graham.

"I'm happy to be back, Mr. Duncan. I hate leaving a job unfinished. And I was just getting to know the family. I like Chloe and Mr. Lawton a lot and I'd love to get to know them better."

Graham realized he was staring at her beautiful teeth. She had such a gorgeous smile it mesmerized him. He blinked, then coughed.

"Ahem...um," not sure what to say or do, he grabbed an iron rake that was leaning against a wooden wall and absently raked at the loose hay that was scattered across the hard mud floor.

Still petting the horse, Shanti gazed around the stable. "I didn't get to see that much of the estate before I left, Mr. Duncan. I didn't want to get in the way or be any trouble when Mr. Lawton was so sick. My curiosity and love of exploration have hit me. I just couldn't sleep."

Graham cleared his throat. "Aye, well Miss, um...Shantilly... I'd be more'n happy to show you around." He looked so serious, Shanti didn't know if he really meant his offer.

"Oh, that would be great. But, I don't want to be any trouble. I don't want to take you away from your work or anything, Mr. Duncan." The bay nudged her shoulder with his nose. He nudged her again before she noticed and stroked his ears again.

Graham set the rake back against the wall. He grinned mildly at her. "It's certainly no trouble at all, Miss. I've been here a number of years and know the place like the back of my hand. Of course I've ridden over every square inch of the property.

"You know we grow beets, but as you'll see, besides them and the horses, we also have chickens and a lot of land. The woods have to be constantly searched for squatters, poachers and predators. We don't need a fox in the hen house." He looked up in surprise at Shanti's laugh.

"No pun intended I guess, Mr. Duncan?"

He hadn't meant to be funny, but a corner of his mouth turned up in a crooked grin. "Here, let me show you the inside of the stables," he said, motioning for her to follow him.

"And please," he turned, serious again, "call me Graham. I keep lookin' around for me Da' every time you say Mr. Duncan." His Scottish burr tagged onto every word, but Shanti could easily understand him.

She followed him through the stable. He stopped at each stall and introduced her to each horse. The horses came right up to the bottom Dutch door of their stall, poking out their massive heads, eagerly seeking the attention of the pair.

Chapter Sixteen

Cook covered her yellow teeth and hideous breath with a man sized hand. She yawned loudly into a moist palm as she shoved the kitchen door open. Daisy and Libby were already inside.

Libby was mixing ingredients together in a large bowl and Daisy was taking the everyday flatware out of the dishwasher. They were engaging in typical servant gossip about the members of the manor.

"Where's that foreign bitch?" Cook growled at the maids. She stood with her fat hands balled into fists on her huge hips.

Daisy sniffed, saying nothing to Cook's inquiry of Serafina's whereabouts. The last thing she wanted was Cook's cruel attention on her. She had enough problems. Her boyfriend, Liam Gleason, a boy from town, hadn't called her for the past three weeks. She didn't get a lot of dates like Libby.

Libby was pretty when she put a lot of makeup on, and she was friendly and outgoing. She'd go right up to a man in a bar and start talking to him. Daisy didn't have the nerve.

She knew she was overweight and you'd think since she was given no brains she'd at least have some beauty, but no. Actually, when she looked at her reflection in the mirror, she thought she was pretty hot. But she'd overheard boys in school make fun of her fuzzy brown hair and plump figure.

One night Daisy had gone to the local pub with Libby. Not used to drinking hard liquor, she was feeling dizzy soon after Libby introduced her to bourbon and water.

Wearing a tiny dress and a ton of makeup, Libby quickly got asked to dance, leaving Daisy alone with her drink. The maid's eyes had traveled around the small cheap bar. The music was loud and the flashing neon lights were garish.

She didn't care. She didn't go out often. She'd jumped at the chance when Libby invited her to go to the pub with her. Dressed carefully in her frilliest blouse and flounciest skirt, she fluffed her hair and tried to look approachable.

She made nervous eye contact with several men, but they quickly looked down or away. Libby was way over on the other side of the bar shimmying and dancing with a young man.

Bored, Daisy drank her bourbon, then seeing Libby dancing with yet another boy, she replaced Libby's full glass with her empty one, downing her drink as well. She felt something bump her arm.

Turning blurry eyes to the stool next to her, she saw a cute boy lighting a cigarette. The alcohol gave her false bravery.

"'Lo there, honey, how 'bout giving me a cig?" Daisy asked, grinning her idea of a beguiling smile. Tilting her head back, she half closed her eyes, looking down her snub nose in what she hoped was a seductive look.

The boy, so drunk himself he could hardly stay on the stool without sliding off onto the floor, peered through a messy tousle of greasy brown hair. He blinked, pretty sure there should be only one, not two, girls perched on the stool next to him.

"Wha'?" he slurred, narrowing his almond colored eyes at Daisy. Squinting, he brought the two figures together until they blended into one person. Through his drunken gaze, he decided he was looking at one foxy lady.

Realizing he was attending to her, if somewhat confusedly, Daisy excitedly leaned towards him. "I asked yer if yer had a cigarette, handsome." Daisy batted her eyelashes at the young man the way she'd seen Dawn do to men. Males always seemed to melt under Dawn's coy green gaze and fluttering red eyelashes.

He blinked again, then patted his shirt pockets for his pack of cigarettes. Daisy giggled, pointing at the pack lying on the bar next to his beer.

"Oh." His shrug made him wobble. Picking up the pack, he patted one end until a cigarette popped half way out. He held the pack out to Daisy. She licked her lips and reached for the cigarette, awkwardly placing it between her two fingers.

He stared at her, not moving. She still looked blurry to him. The features of her face were fuzzy. She looked blondish, that was cool, he really dug blondes. In his drunken stupor, her hair looked like a glorious halo, sort of like Marilyn Monroe's. His gaze traveled down her body. The alcohol he drank made her body look wavy. Her plumpness turned into curvaceous in his watery mind.

"Um, can I have a light, then?" Daisy asked.

The boy looked up. "Oh," he said again. He looked down at the bar. Spotting his lighter, he picked it up and cupping it, he held it unsteadily to the end of Daisy's cigarette.

He turned in his stool until he was fully facing her. Following suit, Daisy giggled again, and awkwardly squirming her body, she turned towards him. Holding her stool, he pulled her closer to him, spreading his legs so hers would fit between his.

"So then, darlin' give us yer name," Daisy simpered. She managed to open several buttons of her blouse, spreading the bodice as far open as she could. Libby had instructed her not to wear a bra, said she'd look sexier that way.

Daisy leaned in when the boy lit her cigarette and now was watching him stare down her blouse. He was practically drooling.

She stifled a laugh. She clamped the cigarette tightly between her lips and drew heavily through her two large gaping front teeth. Coughing immediately, a huge cloud of smoke burst from her mouth. The boy laughed, leaning back.

Daisy coughed for several minutes, wiping her wet eyes.

"You okay?" the boy asked, still laughing.

Daisy glared at him. "*Hack*, I'm fine, *cough*, stop, *cough*, laughing at me."

The boy suddenly reached over and grabbed Daisy's thick neck, pulling her close he mashed his lips against hers. Daisy quickly forgot about her burning throat. They parted after a lengthy kiss.

"Well then," Daisy said, the room was spinning.

"Hey, who drank my drink?"

Daisy looked sheepishly up at Libby. "Uh…I …don't know what happened to it…" she lied, fearing Libby's wrath.

Libby just shrugged. Oh well, she'd just order another one. "Hey Daze, who's your fella?" Libby winked and nodded at the boy Daisy had been kissing.

Daisy smiled, embarrassed. Lifting one shoulder slightly she turned her palms up. "Well, uh, actually we didn't quite get to introductions, did we, ducky?"

Not commenting, he silently drank his beer.

"C'mon babe, let's go!" An impatient young man was tugging at Libby's arm.

She smiled, patting his hand. "Okay sweetie, I'll be right there." She looked at Daisy then at the sullen boy sitting next to her. "I think I've got a ride home, Daisy, what about you, will you be okay?" She nodded again towards the boy.

They'd taken the bus there. Daisy looked unsure. The boy didn't look in her direction. He sat with his shoulders hunched, elbows on the bar, his head sunk almost into his beer glass.

"I'll be all right, you go on ahead." Daisy reached out and grabbed Libby's arm as she turned away. "But wait…um, do yer got any money? I'm plum out."

Libby rolled her eyes, but she stopped and pulled a few dollars out of her purse and laid them down on the bar.

"That should cover you. There's enough if you need the bus, but" she winked conspiratorially. "I think you're covered." She dipped her head towards the boy.

Daisy grinned crookedly and set a hand on the boy's arm. He looked down at her hand then up at her chest. He didn't move his eyes from her partially exposed bosom.

Satisfied, Libby thrust her hand through her new beaux's arm and they returned to the dance floor. Daisy watched them dancing for a minute. She was hazy from the alcohol. She felt a touch on her leg.

Looking down, without moving her head, she saw the boy next to her had set his hand on her knee. When she didn't move it away, he boldly ran it up her leg and under her skirt, squeezing her thigh. She giggled.

"C'mon, let's get outta here-" The boy grabbed her hand and pulled her off her barstool.

She stood, trying to gain her balance. He put an arm around her chubby waist and led her through the smoky crowded bar. The pair stumbled past tables, uncaring that they bumped chairs and people until they finally staggered outside.

The air was fresh and cool, the last few days of summer still clung in leaves just beginning to turn colors.

It was quieter, but they could still hear the noise from inside the bar. Silently, the boy pulled Daisy across the parking lot, she allowed herself to be dragged over the stony driveway.

He stopped suddenly. "This'n's mine," he mumbled stopping at a rusting, beat up, old beige Chrysler convertible. He shoved Daisy against the door and immediately leaned against her.

Holding her head with his hand, he roughly kissed her parted lips. She eagerly accepted his tongue when he thrust it in her mouth. He grabbed both sides of her blouse, yanking them hard apart.

Daisy could hear the last three buttons she hadn't undone bouncing on the ground. She tilted her head back. Moaning, she relished the rush of cool air against her bare skin.

Feeling his own skin suddenly heat up- burning with desire, he covered her wet mouth again with his. Burying his face in her neck, he groaned, one hand clutched her hair, pulling it taught, his other hand was on her thigh again, moving slowly up under her full skirt.

"Hey, get a room!" someone yelled.

Embarrassed, Daisy pulled the front of her blouse together and tried to smooth her tangle of curly hair. She winced when the boy yelled out an expletive retort.

'C'mon." He opened the door of the car and pushed Daisy inside. She fell ungracefully onto the front seat.

"Git in the back," he ordered.

Dutifully, Daisy ungainly struggled into the back seat. The boy climbed into the car and closed the door. He turned the car on, then, pulled the old torn canvas top up and over them, locking it in place.

He twiddled with the knobs on the radio, settling on a country western station. Leaning over, he opened the glove box and pulled out a bottle of whiskey. Twisting off the cap, he took a healthy swig and then passed the bottle back to Daisy.

Unsure of herself, sitting in the back, she pulled her skirt down over her knees. She took the bottle from the boy's outstretched hand and put it to her fat lips.

Taking a short pull from the bottle, she winced, more used to beer than hard liquor. Coughing loudly again whiskey spurted out of her mouth.

"Hey!" the boy admonished. "Don't waste it!" He had turned in the driver's seat and was leaning an arm over the back, watching her.

"Hey," he said again, more gently this time. "Yer looked purtier a minute ago, ya know." He stared pointedly at her now covered up chest.

Daisy fuzzily followed his gaze down, giggling at her blouse, all mismatched buttoned. She sipped more whiskey

"Fix it the way it was," he insisted.

Daisy blinked at him. She handed the bottle back to him. He immediately drank heartily from it. She tried to pry the buttons open with her pudgy fingers, but the liquor was doing its work and she couldn't manage to get them apart.

The boy shook his head. "Here, I'll do it." He pushed her fumbling hands away. He wasn't much steadier than Daisy, but he managed to get the buttons open and pushed the white cotton material apart.

"Wowee!" He whistled when Daisy's plump, bare breasts came into full view again. Feeling exposed, Daisy modestly put her hands up in front of her chest.

"Tsk tsk," the boy clicked with his tongue, shaking his head. He reached over the back of the seat and pushed Daisy's hands aside. "'Ere," he muttered. "Move over."

Pushing the front seats apart, he climbed through, falling on top of a giggling, half naked Daisy. He pushed the blouse off her broad shoulders at the same time he reached to undue his belt. Daisy held up a shaking hand.

"Wait sugar," she slurred. "What's yer name?"

He laughed, pulling open the snap of his jeans. "Liam. Liam Gleason." His eyes closed as his head came close to hers.

Later he had driven her home. She barely remembered the drive home. Which was probably good as drunk as Liam was. He'd narrowly missed trees and mailboxes as he tried to keep the car on the road.

He stopped at the gate, waiting while Daisy swiped her card to release the lock. The gate swung open and they drove through, up the winding driveway to the front of the estate. Liam stopped the car, his eyes opened wide. He whistled when he saw how big the house was.

"Holy moly," he spluttered, his mouth dropped open.

Daisy laughed. "I told yer I'm a maid in a mansion, silly." She was wearing a jacket she found in his car to cover her damaged blouse.

"Huh." He said, "Here," and handed her a soiled, torn piece of paper. "Write yer name and number." He smirked guiltily when she looked sharply at him.

"It's Daisy, for Pete's sake, Liam." She scowled at him. After all, they'd just made love together, he could at least remember her name.

"Whatever babe, I been drinking, remember? If ya want me ta call ya, write it down." He handed her the paper and a pen, not caring whether she did or not. He was getting sleepy, and hungry. Sex always did that to him.

"Harrumph." Daisy let out a disgusted breath as she wrote her information down. "Fine. When're ya gonna call me, honey? I'm free Friday night." She handed him the paper and pen and he tossed them indifferently into the back seat.

He was cute even if he had dirty nails and his stringy hair flopped in his eyes. He was on the skinny side, worn black jeans hung on thin hips. But he had an arrogant swagger and was a great if sloppy, kisser.

Daisy rubbed the side of her plump face. His rough five o'clock shadow had scratched her cheeks. She knew come morning she's be wearing a turtleneck sweater under her white maid's uniform, she had a lot of purple marks on her neck to hide, also a few elsewhere that no one but she would be seeing!

She giggled at the thought of that priss, Mrs. Li taking a gander at her neck. The old bat would probably have a jealous snit. It's not like anyone ever jumps that bag of Asian bones. They'd be scared she'd give them the 'evil eye' and work her voodoo on them.

"Give us a goodbye kiss, then," she said, offering him her pursed lips through the window. He obliged, then threw the car into gear and took off down the circular driveway.

Sighing, she zipped up the jacket; he'd have to see her again to get it back. She hoped when he was sober he'd remember her!

Liam did call again and they went out that Friday night. But that was three weeks ago. She didn't know, but he had been shocked when he saw her.

Wow, he'd thought when she came out from the back of the house and jumped into his car. *Eek!* He practically gagged, suppressing a curse. *Uglier than I thought. Geesh, next time I gotta have a friend give a look when I'm that sloshed.*

Daisy grinned her big, gaping, buckteeth at him. Her hair clumped in an unruly frizzy mess around her round face. The mess of pale brown hair did little to hide the zits that covered three quarters of her homely face.

Yuk, I kissed that? He drew back, barely disguising his horror.

She never noticed. She was so excited she wiggled in her seat. "Where we going then?" she asked, putting her hand boldly on his knee.

Ugh. Where can I take this hideous creature where no one I know will see us? He remembered a dimly lit bar way on the other side of town and headed there. Once there, he found the darkest booth available and pushed her in against the wall. He sat next to her. Last thing he wanted was to be sitting opposite her having to look at her. That would spoil his appetite.

They had a lot to drink again, and after a couple of well-done burgers and fries, Liam was just drunk enough to not care what she looked like. Afterwards, they had sex again in the backseat of his car.

That was three weeks ago, and she hadn't heard from him. She was also a week late with her period. She wiped the sweat from her brow. She had stared all morning at her phone in the tiny room she and Libby and Serafina shared, willing it to ring. But it hadn't.

"I haven't seen Serafina since we got up this morning," Libby answered the cook's question, bringing Daisy's attention back to the kitchen.

Serafina had risen earlier than any of them. The last sound they heard was the bedroom door shutting. That was a couple of hours ago and they hadn't seen her since.

"Damn foreigners," Cook cursed. Picking up a paring knife, she plodded over to the sink. "Can't trust the bastards, tol' 'em not to hire the black-eyed bitch, but no, no one ever listens to me. Thieven' pack a' gypsies they are…" her grumbling trailed off.

Chapter Seventeen

"This is good soil to grow sugar beets in, Miss. Tis not the regular rich volcanic soil, but tis filled with nitrogen and the warm sunny days and cool nights are conducive to a good strong crop." Graham gestured to the fields of sugar beets as he spoke.

Trucks, tractors and pilers were out in the field ready to use.

"We irrigate from the river. Farther north the clear clean water comes from snow in the mountains. It melts and collects in large reservoirs above and below ground and eventually runs into the river."

They strode along the field's edge. Graham said, "Tis an ugly crop to the outsider."

Shanti nodded her head, agreeing with him He had a nice voice, and she was getting used to his rough Scottish accent.

The best looking part of the vegetable had been lopped off, leaving brown mounds of beets looking better with a shiny layer of dew covering them.

They strolled in companionable silence for a while. The sun was starting to rise. The east side of the pastures was slightly pink.

"We've already completed the vine-killing, we have to do that three or so weeks before the harvest."

Shanti nodded like she knew what he was talking about.

"During harvest, when we pull those 'spinning top' looking vegetables out of the ground and clean them up a bit, the ruby red orbs glisten richly, like gems. They're worth as much as real jewels to us!"

Shanti snapped her fingers and stopped. "Oh, now I get it, **Red Gem Farm**! I couldn't figure out why they named it that. How clever!" She smiled.

Graham chuckled. "Yup. They are expensive rubies to us. We usually complete harvest around mid to the end of October. They have to be out of the ground before the greatest risk of freeze damage can occur.

"Then we store 'em until after January, then truck 'em down to the distillery the other side of town and they turn 'em into sugar products, you know, molasses and such. They get about 300 hundred pounds of sugar per one ton of beets."

"My goodness, I didn't realize there was such a huge volume of beets and it involves so much timing. I thought you just tossed in the seeds and when they were ripe you pulled them out and that was it!" Shanti said.

They continued strolling the length of the field.

"My family grows a lot of different kinds of veggies, you know, like tomatoes, cucumbers, broccoli and varieties of squash, but I don't really have much to do with the gardens myself, I'm more into painting and stuff."

"Well, the sugar beets do get somewhat involved, but not as much as the potatoes. There's a 10 cent tax on every hundred pounds of potatoes that goes to the Idaho Potato Commission, which is used for research and advertisement to promote the potato. Beets aren't quite up to that level, but we're getting there.

The sun was creeping up the sky and now it was ablaze in streaks of reds and oranges.

Graham had seemed like an extremely quiet man, keeping mostly to himself. But when he talked about the beets, his face glowed and his voice surged with excitement. He sounded like a proud parent.

Graham tilted his head up, the sun reflected brightly off his weathered face. "Tis getting late, we'd better go. They'll be worried about you. There's the Idaho Potato Harvest Festival tonight. The whole family will be there. You should go, you'll enjoy it and get to see some of the country folk. You'll see how much they love this land of theirs."

Tiny white lines crinkled around his eyes in the tanned skin when he smiled. He gallantly took her elbow and steered her back towards the house.

When they reached the barns, Graham stopped and dropped her arm.

"You go on," he said. "I've got some work to finish up. Breakfast will be waiting for you." He turned abruptly and disappeared into the barn.

Puzzled at first, Shanti stood frowning at the empty doorway. Then she realized she was the 'guest' he was the 'help'. He wouldn't be invited to breakfast inside the big house.

She knew it was not something she could change. Suppressing the urge to skip along, the day was so beautiful it lifted her heart and gave her a strange feeling of energy, putting a bounce in her step.

She hurried back to the walk that led to the kitchen door. She didn't see a face in an upstairs window watching her. The curtain fluttered as it fell back in place.

Cook looked up when Shanti pushed open the door.

"Miss?" Cook said, confused and surprised to see her. She was alone in the kitchen.

"I'm sorry to disturb you, Miss...um, Cook. I just wanted to tell you how much I've enjoyed your cooking. You are absolutely superb!" Shanti took long strides to reach the portly cook. She reached out and grabbed her heavy arm, pumping her thick hand heartily.

Cook had an astonished look on her face. No one had ever complimented her cooking before. They just all took it for granted because, after all, it was her job to prepare tasty food.

"Why, why thank you Miss Shantilly, thank you very much, how kind of you to say so!" Cook grinned her crooked brown teeth happily at Shanti.

"I'm looking forward to more of it, Mrs., um, Cook. I'd better go now, I've been outside for ever so long this morning. What a breathtaking day, don't you think?" Shanti tossed her words over her shoulder as she exited the kitchen.

Cook stood shaking her head, she watched Shanti leave. The door swung closed behind her, Cook's capacious mouth was still open in a stunned smile.

Shanti trod softly down the hall, humming. The hallways in the huge manor were wide, the carpet plushly powder blue. Portraits of unknown Lawtons hung in rows on the walls.

Strolling by slowly, Shanti paused at every other painting that caught her eye. She stopped in front of a sweet picture of a young woman holding a toddler on her lap. The toddler was giggling and reaching up to touch the woman's golden hair.

She was looking down at him, a tender smile tugged at her rosebud lips. The style of their dress and her upswept hair held back by two tortoise shell combs led Shanti to believe the painting was at least 80 or more years old. It was encased in an intricately carved gold frame. A viewing light illuminated the painting.

"That was my mother and me, when I was around three."

Shanti turned, a smile ready. The smile quickly turned to a frown.

"Mr. Lawton! Are you all right?" Shanti rushed to the elderly man's side.

He was leaning against a wall. He had been watching her, now he was staring up at the portrait. His face was ashen and his hands clutched together in front of his chest were shaking.

Shanti touched his arm. "Mr. Lawton?"

He turned slowly, his weary eyes settled on her young face. A weak smile creased the wrinkled skin.

"Mr. Lawton, you don't look...um...very well. Are you all right? Shall I get someone? Mrs. Law-"

"No." He held up a quivering hand to stop her as she took a step away. "Please, get no one. I'll...I'll be okay. I'm...I can't believe that- I just can't believe...capable of such a...what will I do?" His words wheezed out with despair and confusion, he shook his head. Bringing a hand up to his face, he reached under his glasses and pinched his eyes.

Shanti didn't know what to do, he was obviously very distressed. His stricken face was almost as white as his hair. His head now buried in shaking hands.

"Mr. Lawton, are you ill? Please let me help you. Let me get you some water, maybe-"

"No, no Shantilly, I'll...just..." he turned, his shoulders slumped, he slowly moved down the hall, putting one foot painstakingly in front of the other. He looked very old, broken somehow. The spry step in his walk was gone. He held the wall as he shuffled along.

Not knowing what to do, Shanti followed alongside him. He stopped at the library, seeming to have forgotten she was there. He stood silently staring into the room, blinking.

"Mr. Lawton?" Shanti stood wavering. Maybe she should just go and get Maeve or Mr. Li or Chloe or anybody.

He turned and looked vacantly at her, then, remembering who she was, he patted her shoulder. "I'm okay, honey. I'm going to rest in here for a while, you run along now, they'll be looking for you. I'll make everything all right after the festival tonight..."

He dropped his head, shaking it. "No, I don't think things will ever be all right ever again...I need to...I'll call Jarrett, it's the only thing to do..." his quivering voice trailed off.

She stood unsure, but he stepped into the library and gently closed the door.

Shanti waited unmoving for a minute, wondering if she should knock and make sure he was all right. But, clearly he didn't want to be bothered. Hesitating, she finally turned, her step less bouncy now, she headed for the big dining room.

Everyone looked up when she entered the room.

"Miss Lane, we had grown concerned." Maeve motioned to the empty seat next to her and rang the bell by her plate.

Shanti slid into the seat. With her head down, she pulled the ring holder off her napkin and placed the starched white linen across her lap.

Serafina appeared by Maeve's side waiting for instructions.

Maeve nodded towards the table. "Please take everyone's fruit plate and bring the eggs, and Miss Lane's fruit."

Serafina nodded silently. She peeped at Shanti.

Shanti smiled brightly at her, but the maid didn't return the smile.

Serafina's eyes were puffy, like she'd either been crying or hadn't gotten enough sleep. She quickly left the room to do the missus' bidding. Shanti stared puzzled at the swinging kitchen door.

"We have been wondering where you've been, Miss Lane."

Shanti folded her hands in her lap and looked at Maeve.

Jaime, Dawn, Chloe and even Camelia and Logan Thayne were present. Jaime and Dawn were in conversation and had only looked up briefly at Shanti's entrance.

Chloe's smile was welcoming, then she looked down. Her dark hair hid her face as she studied the picture book next to her place setting. It was a book of local birds.

Camelia and Logan paid no attention to anyone but themselves. They were nuzzling each other's necks. Camelia was wearing a fuchsia silk blouse. The blouse had a wide, draped neckline. Camelia's lips were close to Logan's ear.

He was smiling, His finger was running along the inside of the scooped neck of his wife's blouse. They were oblivious to the rest of the room.

"I'm sorry to have kept you waiting, Mrs. Lawton. I rose early and Graham Duncan was kind enough to show me the stable and the fields. I got a healthy lesson in sugar beet farming!"

"Eyew." Dawn wrinkled her nose at Shanti. "What's the interest? They grow, they lop off their heads, they rip them out of the ground and they become sugar. The only interesting part is the sugar. Especially when it's wrapped in chocolate!"

The redhead, covered to the neck for a change in a tight green turtleneck sweater, licked her silky lips. Her orange hair was neatly tied back into a ponytail with a matching green bow. She chuckled and elbowed Jaime, expecting him to laugh with her.

He curled a lip and picked up his fork.

Serafina and Libby had come in and started serving eggs, bacon, toast, grits, and home fries.

"Actually," Shanti dug into the melon Libby set in front of her. "I found the procedure the beets go through quite interesting. Red gems, Graham called them-" She looked up at the sound Serafina made, sounded like a snort, not at all in her character.

As soon as she realized Shanti was staring at her, Serafina dropped her eyes and ran off to the kitchen.

"Well! What's gotten into her I wonder?" Maeve murmured, helping herself to the platter of bacon Libby was holding.

"Who cares, she's just the help for crying out loud," Dawn said, bored. She picked up a piece of unbuttered toast and nibbled absently at a pointed end.

Shanti cleared her throat. "Um...Mrs. Lawton, I was just in the hall by the den, looking at paintings and-"

"How nice for you dear, just a lot of ancient ancestors you know, Jaime, please pass me the marmalade, thank you dear." Maeve took the jar from her grandson.

Chloe continued to flip through her bird book.

Jaime opened the morning newspaper, separated the sports page then folding it neatly he laid it next to his plate. Ignoring the rest of the table, he perused the scores of last night's games. Digital appliances weren't allowed at the table.

His waves of brown hair with reddish highlights, still slightly damp from his shower, were moussed and combed back to tame the curls. He also had on a turtleneck, but it was white and cotton with long sleeves. A blue blazer with gold buttons, his initials engraved on them, was slung over the back of his chair.

Shanti cleared her throat. "Ahem, um...I mean, Mrs. Lawton, when I was in the hall I saw Mr. Lawton, and he was, he was..."

Maeve never looked up from her plate. Now she was running a piece of plain toast across the plate, sopping up the poached eggs.

"Speak up, dear, I do hate it when you young people mumble, what about Mr. Lawton?" She finally looked at Shanti, peering at her over the rims of her glasses.

Shanti pulled her lips in. "He didn't look very well, Mrs. Lawton. I asked him what was wrong, I mean he was white as a sheet and kind of trembling. He looked…well, frightened. I-"

Mrs. Lawton set her cup down, clinking it onto the china saucer. She dabbed at her lips with her napkin, then folded and set the napkin on the table next to her now empty plate.

"I'm sure he is quite all right, dear. I'll go check on him. Chloe, I'm going to Catherine Scott's this afternoon for tea, I'll be taking Serafina with me. While I'm gone, I would like you to see that the rest of the house gets ready for tonight's festivities. Please inform Miss Lane about the harvest festival and find her something appropriate to wear."

She smiled coolly at Shanti. "It's the biggest party of the year. Everyone wears costumes and masks for disguise. Chloe will help you choose something. She'll have to work to hide that glorious hair and toothsome smile you have."

Shanti didn't know what to say, so she said nothing, just smiled politely.

Maeve picked up the bell and gave it a light shake. Libby came quickly through the door at its tinkle.

"I'm finished, dear." The old woman stood and excused herself.

Shanti watched her leave the room. She was worried about Mr. Lawton. He was old, but he had looked really shaken.

More like it was something he had heard or seen that distressed him, not like he was actually sick.

Chapter Eighteen

*T*here was electricity in the air.

Excited chattering could be heard throughout the big house. The servants as well as the Lawtons were busy preparing for the big party.

The Lawtons purchased their outfits, but the servants had sewn and saved and worked on their costumes all summer. This was one night everyone could pretend to be someone else for a few hours. There would be few people in church tomorrow. Most would be home nursing hangovers.

Out in front of the manor were four horses. Attached to the back of pairs of the horses were wagons strewn with hay and straw.

The Vaughns were already there. The two families would be riding to the hoedown together. Eager to get moving, the horses occasionally stomped and whinnied in the balmy early evening air.

Mr. and Mrs. Lawton will be riding in the front of one of the wagons. Mrs. Lawton wouldn't get caught dead wallowing like a peasant in the hay in the back of a wagon normally used to haul beets.

The elderly Magnus Vaughn, and his son Tobias will be sitting in the front of the other wagon. Wooden seats lined the backs of the wagons. Pablo the groundskeeper and Dario the chauffer had hammered them in earlier. They would remove them after the party.

Dolly Vaughn loved to be in the heart of the action. She was thrilled with the anticipation of riding in the back of a wagon stuffed with straw and haystacks on the way to a costume party, where for an evening, she didn't have to be a matriarch and watch her manners.

She could play dress up and dance with whomever she wanted, and maybe, just maybe, a dark stranger would steal a kiss, neither of them knowing whom the other was.

Her husband, stodgy old Tobias will be blindly unaware as he always is. He hates parties and will be stowed away in a corner somewhere all night. He'll find some old codgers he knows and sit with them.

Tobias hadn't attempted dancing since college and that was only a square dance. But, others would be eagerly dancing and drinking and boldly stealing kisses well into the night.

Tomorrow, everyone would be looking at each other, shy, suspicious, thinking, 'are those the lips that touched mine in the dark, under a veil of stars?'

Whispering, "Ooh, it's so romantic," frumpy Dolly was practically swooning, she fanned her face, giggling like a young girl. Just a harmless little flirtation once a year never hurt anyone.

Slowly, the members of the house were gathering in the drawing room, while the servants were assembling in the kitchen.

They were all given the night off except for Montgomery and Dario. They would be in charge of the wagons. They weren't to drink, although they could join in the dancing if they desired.

Dario will be drinking anyway, he always did. He will be hanging out with his friends, hiding in the shadows alongside the main building commenting lewdly on the girls. He also will be in costume. Usually he dresses as an outlaw like Jesse James, his hero.

Montgomery would never lower himself to 'dress-up' like a character in a book. And, he would never get intoxicated. His duty was to care for the Lawtons and he would never do anything that could endanger them.

There are several rooms off the kitchen where supplies are kept and laundry is done. A small door at the back of the large kitchen leads to the basement. Vegetables and canned goods are stored in the cool basement.

To the left of the stairs at the bottom of the basement is a wine cellar. Dario was coming up the stairs, two at a time with a bottle of red wine clutched in each hand. The group was going to have a traditional glass or two before they were on their way, it's considered good luck.

The servants will be passing around a cheaper version. Dario hit the light switch with his elbow and pushed the door closed with his foot.

Whistling tunelessly, he moved quickly down the hall to the drawing room. He wanted time to get into his own costume and toss back a few with the farm hands already rallying behind the big house out back.

"My gawd Maeve, you look imperious!" Dolly gushed, accepting a glass of deep red sparkling wine. She took several quick gulps trying to quell the nervous knot that was in her stomach.

She felt a premonition that something exciting was going to happen tonight. Maybe it was just the fun of a party. They hadn't had one since the 4th of July picnic.

Maeve nodded solemnly. Even she liked being someone else once in a blue moon. She had gone to great expense to look exactly like Queen Victoria. Her white hair was swept dramatically high atop her head.

A jeweled crown was pinned tightly around the severe knot of hair. She wasn't wearing a mask, she felt it was sufficient to hold an eye-mask on a stick over her eyes. She was too old to engage in secret fiddle faddle.

Maeve's heavily outlined eyes took in Dolly's outfit. "Darling, I'm sorry, but I just can't figure out who you-"

"Oh Mrs. Lawton, of course she's Marie Antoinette! Look at that great pouf of hair- it must weigh ten pounds, we had a terrible time trying to get it not to tilt, didn't we Mother?" Tori laughed. She was quite fetching herself as Mary Poppins.

Her dark brown hair piled loosely into a chignon, she was wearing a red and white striped suit with a shin-length full skirt, a white crinoline peeked out all along the rim of the dress. She had an umbrella draped over her arm and a floppy hat on her head.

"This is so much fun, I just love it!" Dolly squealed, fanning herself with an antique fan. She was getting warm under the immense costume with the full skirt and thick petticoats.

Her husband, Tobias, was dressed as a Federal Marshal. He'd gone to the police store in the city and purchased a real gold badge.

His father Magnus was wearing what he always wore to every outdoor party, a black jacket with a white ruffled shirt and a bolero with a huge turquoise at his throat. His belt buckle, twice as large as the one Logan Thayne sometimes sported, had a picture of a bison etched in the silver. The tips of his boots were silver as well.

"Look at Jaime! Isn't he darling!"

All eyes turned to the young man as he entered the room.

Dressed as a swashbuckler, Jaime did a twirl for the group. Then his sword tangled in his legs and he almost tumbled. Quickly catching his balance, he stuck out one leotard covered leg, pulled off his huge hat with the feather plume and bowing deeply, he swept the hat across the front of him pretending his clumsiness was all an act.

Dolly and Tori clapped effusively, laughing gaily at his antics. They turned at more clapping from the doorway. Dawn was costumed as a dance hall girl.

"Quite appropriate, sister dear. But, I daresay you're going to freeze," Jaime said sarcastically. He put his huge hat back on his head and pulled out a mask and covered his face.

"Well, brother dear, I must say that is quite a big improvement!" Dawn laughed at her brother as he stuck his tongue out at her through a mouth hole in the mask. She wrapped a feathered boa around her neck, which was about the most covering she had.

The tightly corseted dress pushed her breasts up and almost out of the frilled scoop neck, and the thickly ruffled petticoat barely covered her bottom.

At every saucy step, her frilly underwear was revealed. Fishnet stockings webbed long slim legs that flowed into black stilettos. Her orange-sherbet hair was also piled high, she'd had Libby tie flowers throughout the curly locks.

There would be no way people would not recognize her even with a mask covering her face. Her flaming hair was a beacon. If she wanted to be disguised, she would need to totally hide her hair.

"I don't need mere clothing to keep me warm, there're other ways," Dawn sneered wickedly, ignoring the frown her grandmother tossed her way.

"Great disguise, sis, it's not like every guy in town won't recognize your half-naked body!" Laughing rudely, Jaime snaked out and arm and grabbed Dario as he passed by. "Hey old man, I need one for the road." He yanked a glass off the tray the chauffeur was carrying.

"That's enough, Jaime. You will behave yourself tonight. Please don't embarrass the family. Oh there you are dear," Maeve strode to the door.

Holding her voluminous skirts in one hand, she held the other out to her husband. Langston was tweedily attired as Sherlock Holmes, all the way from the plaid hat to the large curving pipe. He looked confused, dazed.

"Are you all right, Langston?" Maeve asked him, concern etched her face. She took his hand and pulled him gently into the room. "Dario-" she called the chauffeur.

He came immediately to her side. She plucked a wineglass off the tray and thrust it into Langston's shaking hands.

"This will help steady you, darling. You'll feel better once you get outside and into the fresh air. Let's get going, shall we? The girls can meet us out front, I can't think what's keeping them."

Maeve led Langston out of the room, the others followed chattering like magpies. The excitement was catching.

They pretended they didn't see various servants peeking out from doorways to see what they were wearing. They ignored the gasps and oohs and ahs.

The sun was setting but it was still light.

Maeve led Langston to one of the wagons and waited for Montgomery and Dario to help the old man up into the front.

Montgomery caught Langston's expression for the first time. His brows rose in alarm. The old man looked scared to death!

As soon as they were alone, Montgomery was determined he'd ferret out what was going on. In all the years he'd known Langston Lawton, he'd never seen such terror in the elderly eyes.

Langston kept blinking rapidly, like he was trying to dispel an image, or remember one. His mouth drooped open like a person suffering a stroke.

Montgomery helped Maeve climb up beside her husband and settle in. There wasn't going to be much room for the butler and her skirts.

Before he got in, Montgomery went over the Vaughns and helped them in as well. The two gentlemen climbed in the front.

Dolly was trying to climb up the back into the wagon, but the step was too high and she couldn't get her girth up and into the back. Matthew, dressed as Doc Holliday, was pulling her but she was yelling at him that he was hurting her and she couldn't get up the step.

Montgomery moved behind Dolly, looked around, shrugged, then put both large hands on Dolly's equally large bottom and with Matthew still pulling, he gave her a good hard push.

"Oh Montgomery!" Dolly squealed as she hurled face first onto the floor of wagon. She fell sprawling across the wooden floor, sending straw and hay flying in all directions. Her face red, she giggled, pulling her huge skirts quickly over her splayed plump legs.

"Oh Montgomery" she giggled again. "I didn't know you cared!"

Montgomery winked at the flushed lady and returned to the Lawtons.

Chloe and Shanti exited the house at that moment.

Chloe was perfect as Annie Oakley. She even looked like she had real guns in the holsters at her hips. A cowboy hat was pulled way down over her face and she carried her mask in one hand.

Her mahogany hair tied in one thick braid hung like a rope just an inch past her shoulders. She wore a fringed suede jacket and matching pants with brown boots with the tops folded over.

In contrast, Shanti looked every inch the Helen of Troy she was dressed to represent. Her golden hair in a twist high on her head, had one long, loose curl that came from behind and curled around her neck then draped over her breastbone.

The mint green silk dress, looped over one shoulder leaving the other bare, looked transparent, but was not quite, clung to her lovely figure, revealing every curve.

Dual armbands designed as serpents ran up both arms. Gold slippers and a gold band wrapped around her forehead finished the simple yet elegantly sexy outfit.

Shanti was a little embarrassed. It was not something she would have chosen. But there was nothing else. Dawn had bought it originally but had changed her mind for the dance hall girl. She said she didn't want to be a stately queen, she wanted to be someone looking for fun!

Shanti had grabbed a silky wrap on her way out the door. It was the third week in October. So far it was unseasonably warm during the sunny days, but she knew once the sun was fully gone the chill would set in quickly.

Montgomery was at her elbow helping her and Chloe easily up the steps and into the wagon. They settled in next to Matthew and Tori Vaughn. Dawn and Jaime were sitting on the opposite side. Jaime was smoking one of his small cheroots.

"You put that out, Jaime, for crying out loud, you want to light us on fire? We're surrounded by hay and straw you idiot!" Dawn chastised her brother.

He looked at her calmly, his large hat rested on his lap. He continued toking on the cigar.

Knowing she'd get nowhere, Dawn huffed and turned her attention to Matthew who was sitting next to her. Laughing, they made fun of each other's outfits. Camelia and Logan would have to ride in the Vaughns' wagon with Dolly.

Just as Maeve was about to order Dario to go fetch the missing members of the household, the Thaynes came stumbling down the marble steps.

As always, Camelia was clinging to Logan's arm. He was a suave Wyatt Earp and Camelia typically as a harem girl.

A sheer veil covered the lower half of her face, but you could tell she was whispering in his ear. As always, a sly smirk distorted his swarthy face, and as always, they were already drunk.

He too looked like he was holstering real guns. He had Earp's swagger down pat. The pair finally climbed into the Vaughns' wagon and the group started off.

The horses clip-clopped down the street. The sun sank into the horizon, taking its warmth with it. Shanti shivered. Unfolding the silk wrap, she drew it across her shoulders.

They traveled down tree-lined streets under a tapestry awning of colored autumn leaves. The leaves that had fallen and blanketed the street were kicked out of the way, sweeping back and forth as the horses trod along.

Soon they met neighbors as they came out of a side street to join in a caravan moving slowly down the middle of Main Street. Gay hellos and excited giggles echoed throughout the rapidly darkening evening.

Soon, an enormous harvest moon rose. Full and golden amber, it cast a brilliant glow all around it in the sky. Emerging stars basked in the moon's light.

The chattering grew louder as more wagons joined and they came closer to the area where the festivities would be held.

"Look! How beautiful!" Tori pointed to a stories tall bonfire that came into view as they turned a corner. Every head turned in awe, the orange fire reflected and lit up their faces.

The bonfire was built in an open area adjacent to a huge hall the town used for dances and concerts. The entire scene looked ready for Halloween, still a month away.

Scarecrows and all sizes of pumpkins galore, wagons stuffed with green and gold gourds and loose straw, tiny lights covered and draping from tree to tree, gave the area a marvelous mysteriously festive air.

A crowd had already gathered around the crackling bonfire. Hosts of characters, mostly western related, moved in a steady stream from the bonfire to the hall. Whoops and laughter reverberated throughout the night.

The cavernous hall was lit up like a Christmas tree. White icicle lights hung all around the double front doors and music blared from within.

A circle of young men mostly garbed as cowboys, marshals, and outlaws were hovering to one side of the hall smoking.

As soon as the Lawton's wagon stopped, Jaime hopped out. He waited long enough to help the women exit, then tipping his large, feathered hat adieu, he melted into the circle of smoking men gathered in the semi-darkness. The circle opened briefly to allow him in then quickly closed again.

"We shan't see him the rest of the evening, I'm sure." Maeve sighed.

"Don't worry Grandmother, Jaime is resourceful and has a lot of friends, he won't have a problem finding his way home," Dawn dryly reassured the elderly lady.

"And, speaking of a lot of friends, I'll see you around," Dawn added. She gave her grandmother a quick kiss on her rouged cheek. Tossing her boa around her neck, she moved from the group with saucy long-legged strides quickly vanishing into the huge crowded hall.

"Well! So much for a family event!" Annoyed with her wayward grandchildren, Maeve turned to Langston.

Montgomery had already helped the old man down from the wagon. The valet/butler, unable to hide his concern for his employer's obvious distress, tried to gently pull Langston to the side and slightly away from the group to question him. But the old man, in a severely confused state, resisted.

Chapter Nineteen

"I say, we as well shall be on our way." Logan grinned down at his platinum blonde harem wife.

Her childish giggle was incongruent with the almost fully transparent, psychedelic-colored outfit that displayed her womanly curves to their fullest advantage.

Logan took her hand, leading her up the steps into the hall. She was tugging at the low slung, hip-hugging sheer pants that were in danger of exposing her matronly hips.

In her late forties, Camelia still was a good-looking woman, but her body was starting to show her age. With surgery and her girlish affectations, people were always surprised when they got close enough to see she wasn't the young ingénue she played.

Logan Thayne had first noticed her blonde prettiness across a candlelit, hazy bar.

Towards the front of the dusky room, a girl in a slip dress tinkled light jazz on a piano. People sat around the piano, their drinks wetting circles on cocktail napkins, singing along when they recognized a tune.

To the right of the piano, couples listed gently. Their bodies barely touching, they swayed to the lazy jazz, moving torpidly across the small dance floor.

He had been sitting bored at the piano, thinking he had a shot with the piano player until he noticed the coquettish sly glances Camelia frequently slid over to a group of tables. The room was shrouded in a smoky haze as it was a semi-privately owned lounge and not serving food smoking was permitted.

Dismissing the singer, his eyes like hot, gleaming black coals, traveled seemingly randomly around the room. But, his experienced eyes knew what he was looking for. He hid his search with a benign placid expression, puffing on a cigarette. He knew the second he saw her.

She'd been out on the town with a couple of girlfriends and in-between husbands. She easily returned his bold look. Her head tilted back, her tongue circling parted crimson lips, she gazed steadily back at him through heavily mascaraed eyes. Puffing daintily on her cigarette, she listened to the blowzy woman next to her yakking in her ear.

Occasionally sipping at her drink, Camelia never took her eyes off of Logan.

He knew she was ripe for the taking. One polite drink to exchange names and he could probably leave right away with her. Her look was direct, inviting, but she was unsteady on her barstool. That usually meant the less work he'd have to do to get her to his car.

He could instantly tell she did okay in the money department. The jewelry, clothes and hairstyle were purchased from the chicest shops in the city.

He figured she was good for a quick one-night stand, maybe a slightly longer dalliance. With the looks of the ring on one finger alone, he'd probably only have to spring for the initial drink, and after that, everything else would be on her. He might even get some new clothes out of the deal.

Getting up there in age himself, he was starting to find the pickings amongst the wealthy widow set starting to become scarce. He needed to start looking for something more permanent before his age caught up with him.

He could still pass for early forties, but years of smoking, drinking and sometimes other ills of living life on the darker side were beginning to take their toll. Not above a little surgery himself, he kept his Grecian Formula hidden in his bathroom, and he'd just had some liposuction on his love handles to make them a little less lovable

As soon as he saw her buy another drink, he threw a dollar tip on the bar, picked up his own glass, and tucking one hand nonchalantly into a trouser pocket, he sauntered over to her.

As soon as she noticed him coming, she turned her full attention to the girlfriend blabbing in her ear. Pretending surprise when he nestled next to her at the bar, she opened her brown eyes wide, smiling innocently.

There were no open stools, so Thayne shouldered the guy sitting next to Camelia until he moved over a few inches. Leaning one elbow on the bar, he took a few small sips before he spoke. He wanted her to be waiting for him to say something.

After briefly smiling coyly at him, she had turned back to her friend.

"Every time you move your beautiful head," Logan whispered in Camelia's ear, "it looks like a thousand fireflies in the night flickering tantalizing shades of yellow and gold."

Camelia giggled her girlie giggle.

Logan wondered how long he'd be able to take that stupid giggle before he'd have to strangle her.

"My, you are a smooth poetic one," Camelia drawled. She reached for her drink. Her friend Sherry was still trying to talk to her.

In mid-word Sherry caught Logan's glare, warning her off. Hiding how scary she found him, shrugging coolly, she turned and starting talking to their other friend that was sitting on her other side.

"Can I buy you a drink?" Logan flashed his dazzling crowns at Camelia, nodding at her still full drink.

Camelia shook her head, staring boldly at him again. "Later, maybe." She looked him up and down, coming to rest on his full lips.

"Like what you see?" The smirk covered his artificially bright white teeth.

A seductive smile curved her lips, her eyes moved up to his. Camelia's own eyes were a light honey brown.

Logan's were as dark as his black hair. Camelia liked dark men, Italian, Latin, Black, whatever, the darker the better. They seemed so dangerous to her. And danger was exciting!

Just as Logan had planned, they finished the drinks they'd been drinking, then ordered another. Half way through the second drink Logan had Camelia already talked into leaving with him. It hadn't taken much.

He stared at her mouth when she talked knowing it would titillate her. He leaned in close, whispering nonsense things. He never touched her, but that only made her wish he would. She would lean towards him, but he would move back, just an inch, and pretend interest in his drink.

Hopping off her stool, Camelia picked up her purse, swinging it happily. "See ya later, girls," she giggled to her friends.

Sherry and Marla tried to hide their envy by sniffing indifferently. Logan Thayne looked a bit base to them; swarthy, something dark, shady, they couldn't quite put their finger on lurked in his eyes.

But still, he was a man, and they were at the age where that was about the only prerequisite they required.

Logan had a rental car. He told Camelia his Jaguar was in the shop. "They break down a lot." He'd sighed. There hadn't been much to choose from at the rental agency, he'd said, with it being summer and all, people were visiting and all the good cars had been rented.

Camelia didn't care. She knew it was a line. She was used to being wealthier than most of the men she dated when she stepped outside her family's circle. She allowed Logan to help her into the passenger side of the Saturn, giving him a chance at a long glance at her shapely legs as she pulled them one at a time into the car.

Her dress hiked up her thighs, she didn't pull it back down. He closed her door then ran around the car and climbed into the driver's side. Camelia had dropped her purse on the floor next to her feet and turned in her seat to face him.

Logan put the key in the ignition but didn't turn the car on. He leaned in towards Camelia. He put one finger under her chin and drew her to him. At first, the kiss was gentle, sweet, then it grew lusty, bold, soon their lips ground hard together. Their breathing became louder, heavier.

Logan pulled back first. He stared at Camelia. Her mouth was open, wet, her eyes provocative, begging. He grabbed the back of her head, tangling his fingers in her hair, he pulled her hard against his waiting mouth.

Camelia ran her hands through his hair, tugging, pulling the slick locks. Without breaking off the kiss, she reached down to his belt.

"Ow!" He pulled back abruptly, a hand to his lips. She'd bit him- there was blood on the tips of his fingers.

She chuckled at him.

Dragging a hand raggedly through his hair, he looked at her.

Defiantly, she returned his glare, running her tongue around her mouth. Her lips curved in a wicked smile. Her hand was still at his belt.

He promised himself she'd pay for that nip later. Not returning her smile, his face a mask, he turned the key in the ignition. The radio screamed hard metal music.

"We can go to my favorite hotel," she whispered.

"Which way?"

"Darling, I would never go anywhere but the Ritz. Do you need directions there?" She didn't even try to hide the patronizing sneer designed to put him in his place.

More payback later he thought to himself at her insinuation that he wouldn't know where the Ritz was. He jerked the wheel hard, pulling the car out into the main street without looking, he stomped the gas pedal to the floor, burning rubber, the car screeched down the road. Camelia's laugh danced in the wind.

As soon as she opened the door to the hotel room, he grabbed her shoulder, twirling her around to face him. He snatched her purse and tossed it inside. Snagging the back of her neck, he kissed her with a viciousness. Holding her body to his, he walked her backwards until they were just inside the door.

He closed the door behind him with a kick of his foot, never taking his mouth from hers. Eagerly, they ripped at each other's clothes, tossing them aside as they stumbled to the bed, still never separating their lips.

Logan Thayne was a dangerous man, including in bed. Camelia fully participated in the wild, dark, scary night.

She should have felt sick, used, guilty, over the things they had done, but no, every night she was alone after that first night together, she shivered, goose bumps rising along her arms she relived every second of the exciting, edge of the cliff he'd brought her to, all night long. They did things she never would have dared before.

She spent considerable time later hiding her bruises. Logan was a brutal, frightening lover. He'd had to hold his hand over her mouth to stifle her screams. But now, it was all she could think about. She knew what he was, but she didn't care. When she suggested marriage, he jumped at it.

Against all her lawyer's strong objections, she refused a pre-nuptial. She knew he wouldn't have gone for it. She was well aware that her money was her charm for him, and she was willing to live with the knowledge if it meant having him.

They lived in a suite of rooms in the mansion that were the farthest from everyone so no one could hear their games. The servants probably knew what went on, they cleaned the rooms and more than likely have seen their toys.

Someday she may tire of him, and if he didn't kill her, she'd find a way out of the marriage without giving up half her inheritance to him. She may be a ditzy flake, but she had damn good attorneys and she knew it.

And, Grandmother would never let a gigolo like Thayne get away with anything. She'd seen the two of them shoot sparks at each other. Camelia pretended to laugh and act like all the world was a game, but she knew her grandmother was planning and plotting how to get rid of Thayne when the time came.

For now, the time wasn't right. For now, she looked forward to the dark, lubricious nights they shared, sometimes with others, that part she hoped her grandmother would never find out about.

For now, she accepted her sick addiction to her husband.

After saying their polite good-byes for the evening to her parents, Camelia knew they wouldn't be going back with them, she and Thayne took off to meet a few other couples they knew were going to be there. After a few drinks and dances, the couples would meet at a pre-designated place for some adult games.

"Well then, let's see what's going on inside, shall we?" Maeve motioned for the rest of the group to follow her into the hall. She held Langston's arm while they imperiously strode up the steps.

Shanti and Chloe were elbowing each other discreetly, covering their giggles with their hands. The hall's doors were open wide, people were standing outside and inside, waiting to greet newcomers.

"Maeve dear, Langston," Several ladies dressed in flowery cotton dresses with matching bonnets welcomed them. "I recognize Chloe, but who's this beautiful child?" Maeve's friend took Shanti's hand, pulling her forward.

"This is Miss Shantilly Lane, Catherine. Shantilly, Catherine Scott is one of my oldest and dearest friends. Catherine, Miss Lane is an artist, you must see her work, she is quite talented. Langston has hired her to paint the estate. We are so looking forward to the completed product," Maeve told her.

"How do you like our little Idaho, dear?" The elderly Catherine smiled in question to Shanti.

Shanti stepped to the side so the Vaughns could come inside. They were being greeted by neighbors they hadn't seen since summer activities.

"It's different than what I'm used to, Mrs. Scott, but quite pretty and unique in its own way. You have lovely forests and fields that go on forever. Red Gem Farm is one of the most beautiful places I've ever seen!"

Catherine was taken aback. "Oh? Oh really...hmm...well my dear, I guess you're right. I am so used to seeing the estate, one quite gets used to its grandeur I suppose." She winked at Maeve.

"She is quite charming, and if her work is half as good as she is pretty, you'll certainly get your money's worth, Maeve!"

Maeve slightly bobbed her head in agreement.

Catherine pointed an age-spotted hand, numerous rings covered fingers made lumpy from arthritis.

"There's Beatrice over there. The dancing is inside, but the food is out on the lawn. Langston dear, are you...all right?" Catherine just noticed Langston who had been standing behind Tobias Vaughn.

Unconsciously, Catherine put a hand to her lips in shock when she took in Langston's gaunt face.

He looked ill; his hands were shaking. He lifted pain filled eyes to the elderly lady. Smiling weakly, he said, "Just a touch of the flu, I expect. I...I think some food will help." He looked at Maeve, then, his eyes fell to the floor.

"Yes darling, of course. We can visit later. Let's go on outside and get you something warm to drink. Chloe, why don't you take Shantilly around and introduce her to your friends? We'll meet you later for dinner." A suggestion from Maeve was really an order.

"Sure Grandmother." Chloe kissed both her grandparents on the cheeks. "Hey Tori, do you want to come with us?" she asked the young Mary Poppins.

Tori was standing awkwardly with her parents, not sure what to do. Then she leaned over and whispered in Chloe's ear. "I think I'm going to go hunt down your brother."

Tori grinned, embarrassed. "Mom keeps telling me I need to act and stop expecting him to come to me, so, I guess tonight's the night! I feel brave swathed in a costume." She twirled her white parasol cheekily in the air. The three young women giggled.

"I say go for it! You know I'd like nothing better than to have you as a sister in law!" Chloe patted her friend on the shoulder.

Tori tucked some escaping curls of hair back in her chignon and straightened her hat.

"You know, Chloe, you and Mat-"

"Don't go there, Tori, we're like brother and sister. I love Matthew like a brother and that's all that will ever be. Plus, you see the way he looks at Dawn-"

Tori held up a hand with a shudder and twisted lips. "Stop that thought! Wash your mouth out with soap! Heaven forbid that vamp and my poor brother, uh, I mean no offense Chloe-"

Chloe laughed. "Please, I know my sister better than anyone, I wouldn't wish her on my worst enemy-"

"Chloe!" Maeve's voice broke in, her face looked shocked.

Chloe looked immediately sheepish. "I'm sorry Grandmother. Um, we'll see you all later, come on Shanti." She winked at Tori and mouthed 'good luck!' to her friend.

Tori gave a little wave to the pair and slipped her mask on.

The girls weaved their way through the crowd. The cavernous hall was stuffed to the walls with costumed people. Dim lights projected shadows constantly moving across the walls.

Everything looked mysterious and magical to Shanti. Chloe took Shanti's hand and pulled her through the crowd. In the center of the room, the throng had pulled back in a circle and people were dancing in the middle.

Chloe drew Shanti up to a small group of young people gathered in a tight circle near the front of the dance floor.

"I want you to meet my friends, Shanti." Chloe introduced her to all sorts of costumed characters, princesses and pirates and judges giggled and teased each other.

Chloe and Shanti were boisterously welcomed and almost immediately they were dancing with cowboys and preachers.

Every few minutes of dancing with one person, before she could even strike up a conversation with her partner, another masked hombre would pull Shanti into his arms and off they'd go!

Bits of square dancing, country western hoofing and just plain whirling and twirling- they did it all! Every once in a while Shanti would try to peer over her partner's shoulder as she skipped back and forth in a Virginia Reel and look around for someone she knew. She hadn't seen Chloe for at least an hour.

Stopping to catch her breath, Shanti held up a hand, warding off a matador. He bowed politely then grabbed another girl and twirled away.

It was quite warm in the huge hall with all the bodies hopping around so close together. Shanti ran her fingers through her hair, trying to pin the loose strands back up where they belonged.

Chapter Twenty

After hours of dancing and twirling and bouncing off people, Shanti pushed her way through the mob of costumed strangers, making her way to a wall.

Finding herself a small pocket of space, she started to lean against the wall, when suddenly, something was against the back of her knees.

Losing her balance, she started falling backwards, her arms flailed out as she tried to stop herself from falling. A hand whipped out, quickly gripped her arm and held her until she regained her balance.

Twisting about, Shanti pushed her loosened hair out of her eyes and looked down. A poodle was sitting on the floor, tongue lagging out, haughtily staring at Shanti like *she'd* done something wrong!

The hand still gripped her arm like a vise. Automatically, she pulled at the fingers, trying to pry them off.

"Young ladies that aren't used to drinking alcoholic beverages should watch what they do, Miss," an authoritative deep voice spoke to the top of her head.

"What? I...how dare you!" Affronted, Shanti tried to snatch her arm out of the man's tight hold. He didn't let go.

She pushed a lock of gold hair out of one eye and glared up, way up, at the man who not only dared to chastise her as if she was a child, but now that she was safely steady on her own two sandaled feet, refused to release the iron grip he had on her slender arm. Shanti struggled, trying to pull her arm away.

A man dressed as a marshal with a gold badge hooked to the front of his belt, was glaring down at her. He looked the part of a policeman.

Shanti took in the neatly combed short brown hair and blue eyes. Her eyes drifted from the strong jaw down to a well-muscled chest and broad shoulders. One very real looking gun was in a holster at his slim hip, and a walkie-talkie was strapped to his shoulder.

"Do you mind?" Shanti pointed at her imprisoned arm.

He looked down at the arm he held tightly. He seemed surprised that he still held her. Abruptly, he released her. She immediately rubbed her arm. A band of red wrapped around it from his fingers.

"Apologies," he said stiffly. "You appeared to be about to fall off your jeweled slippers and land in a drunken heap on the floor."

"Huh! Well! I am certainly not intoxicated you- you-ruffian!" Shanti spluttered. Her mind blanked on something more disparaging to say to this man who was so arrogantly insulting her.

"Oh, pardon me for saving you from a broken neck- you're welcome," he responded sarcastically. Clipping a hand smartly to his brow in a salute, he turned and quickly strode off through the dense crowd.

Well! Shanti thought. *How dare he- the - the ruffian! Ruffian*? She giggled to herself. Where'd she come up with that word? He must think her quite the staid librarian!

And, yes, she had been a bit ungrateful. After all, he did stop her from falling and maybe seriously hurting herself. She decided she should thank him. She scanned the crowded room, but he had already blended in.

From her spot against the wall, she could see at least five other men dressed like him. Some short, some fat, some tall and thin, but none were just like the dark-haired marshal. Oh well.

Oh! She spotted Graham Duncan, the Lawton's foreman. He looked quite cozy with the girl he was dancing with.

He was dressed as Snidely Whiplash and he was either talking very closely to his partner, or they were kissing! The shapely woman he held so tightly appeared to be costumed as Natasha from the cartoon Bullwinkle. Bright pink nails stood out against Graham's black coat with long tails.

Shanti must have been staring, because Graham looked in her direction. He suddenly dropped his hands from his partner's waist then with a quick word gave her a gentle push away.

Shanti couldn't see the woman's expression because her entire face was hidden behind a mask. But her manner seemed peeved. She hesitated, her hands on her hips, she stood and watched Graham make his way over to Shanti.

When the woman saw Graham approach Shanti, she turned and stalked off, disappearing into the crowd.

"Miss Lane!" His greeting was warm and effusive. He grasped her hand and swept her into his arms.

Surprised, Shanti automatically put her hands up against his chest. His chest was like a rock. The music changed from an energetic line dance to a slow, romantic song.

Graham pulled her close. He took one of her small hands in his and placed the other lightly on her waist. They swayed rhythmically together.

"Are you having a good time?" he asked, his lips near her ear.

She pulled back slightly and smiled up at him. "Oh, Mr. Duncan, I'm having a wonderful time! I haven't stopped dancing for hours!"

He grinned at her. "Please call me Graham. Remember, I feel ancient with that 'Mr.' stuff." He spun her in a slow circle.

Shyly, she peered at him through long lashes. "Right. And please call me Shanti. When you say Miss Lane I feel like an old schoolmarm!" Or prim librarian.

He laughed. "I've got to tell you, Mis- um, Shanti, we field hands discussed what we thought you'd look like before you came here, and…well..." He stopped, his neck turned red.

Shanti cocked her head at him with a tiny grin.

"Well, let's just say, it wasn't really flattering…uh…I guess I shouldn't have told you that. I mean, well you are a beautiful young woman…I mean…well you know that I'm sure…uh…" he trailed off, totally embarrassed, his whole face was red as a cardinal in the winter snow.

Shanti giggled at his obvious discomfort. She decided to save him by changing the subject.

"Graham, your town has a charm all its own. But you know that, I've seen you in the fields, your face glows with a parent-like pride. No really, it does!" she insisted when he ducked his head to hide his discomfiture.

"Anyway," she continued, "everyone is just so nice here, well, almost everyone." She frowned remembering the rude marshal that had saved her from certain injury but insinuated she was too drunk to stand on her own.

Graham looked instantly concerned. "Did someone hurt you then? What happened?" He pulled back and stopped. She almost tripped he stopped so fast. He studied her face, his brows scrunched together in anger.

Shanti shook her head. Strands of long hair that had escaped from her energetic dancing now curled along her face and around her neck and shoulders. She held a hand up, smiling wryly.

"Please Graham, it was nothing. Just a rude guest dressed as a marshal or ranger or something." She explained what happened.

"See, it was no big deal, he just kind of hurt my feelings. I guess it bothers me that someone would think I'd get so intoxicated at a public place that I'd be stumbling all over the floor."

Graham put a hand on her shoulder. "He was probably just some ignorant farm hand feeling his oats all dressed up as a law enforcement officer and trying to play a big man. Do you see him now?" Graham looked all around them, searching for anyone dressed as a policeman.

"Please forget about it, Graham, there's like a hundred men dressed as cops here. And, well he really did do me a favor. If he hadn't caught me I could have been seriously injured. He just wasn't exactly gentlemanly about it. Come on, let's finish our dance." She smiled at him, her fingers lightly touched his arm.

He looked down at her returning her shy smile. "Okay, let's do-" as soon as they went back into each other's arms the music stopped.

They looked over at the band, they were setting down their instruments. They announced they were taking a break.

The pair stood looking at each other, not sure what to do next.

"Gray! Hey buddy, how ya doin'?" A voice called out. They turned and a big, burly man with a large red nose clapped Graham on the shoulder.

"Stuart! Hey, how's it going? Where's Lynn?" Graham introduced Shanti to his friend. The beefy man gave her hand a powerful shake.

"Welcome little missy," he said with a big grin. He was costumed as a bartender from the old western days. Thin hair was plastered straight back, and he had little, round wire rimmed glasses perched on the tip of his red nose. He fit the part perfectly. He turned to Graham.

"Lynn's here, she's outside I think with the girls. Hey, the guys have a quick game goin' over back in the barn next door, we need a sixth, whadya say?"

Stuart Jameson watched Graham expectantly. He'd been sent on a mission from his buddies to get a sixth player for their card game and Graham Duncan was usually an eager participant. But now...

"Oh go on, Graham, please. I'm fine. I haven't eaten yet. I think I'll see what's happening outside and if I can find Chloe," Shanti quickly assured him. Stuart winked at her.

"You're sure you're okay then?" Graham asked, eager to go but he didn't want to leave her stranded alone. As if she could be alone in a giant room stuffed to the gills with people.

At her assurance, "Okay, we'll see ya later then," Graham said and he and his friend moved easily through the crowd. People moved out of the way of the extra large Stuart Jameson.

Shanti watched them until she no longer could see the back of Graham's black jacket and hat.

She looked around for a familiar face. She didn't see Chloe anywhere, nor any of the other Lawtons or Vaughns either for that matter. She did think at one point she spotted Dolly Vaughn.

But it couldn't be the pleasant, matronly next-door neighbor, because the Marie Antoinette she was looking at was busily canoodling with a young prince near a small group of tables at the back of the big hall.

Shanti remembered Tobias Vaughn, Dolly's husband, was not dressed as a prince. And his heavy legs wouldn't look as trim as this man's did in tight leotards.

Both parties' faces were disguised behind masks that were only partially shoved up off the lower part of the faces. Before Shanti could get a better look, the crowd closed in again and she lost sight of the plump woman.

Deciding it was time for some food and fresh air, slowly and as politely as she could, Shanti pushed through the crowd until she made her way to the front doors.

She stepped out onto the porch made of sturdy wooden planks that curved in a semi-circle around most of the building. Huge baskets filled with colorful autumn leaves and scarecrows with happy faces sat on rattan tables between rocking chairs.

Older people not interested in dancing or eating rocked peacefully on the wide verandah, chatting easily with friends and drinking red punch. The cool evening air smelled of burning leaves, joyous shouts and laughter sprang through the night.

It was very dark outside now, several hours had passed since they'd arrived by wagon. Light emanating from the still raging bonfire was enough to brighten the entire park. Lanterns lined the walk, guiding the way to the hall.

When she stood still and looked straight up, clouds passed just in time for Shanti to see a shooting star streak across the velvet sky. Oh! She didn't have time to make a wish!

There were just as many people outside as there were inside. Shanti wandered towards the long tables where people were sitting on benches at long picnic tables eating.

Nearby, cooks dressed in white were laughing and chatting, waving tongs and forks in the air. Several barbecue pits were roaring with flames and all kinds of meat; hamburgers, ribs, hot dogs, sausages, enough food was roasting to feed an army.

A good thing, because there was an army of people there. She got herself a hamburger and some creamy potato salad, a brownie and a soda and found a spot at one of the long tables covered with blue and white plaid tablecloths.

Quickly gobbling her hamburger, Shanti sipped her soda and took the time to take in her surroundings. Wow, what a party! Kings and queens and sailors traipsed all around the park. It looked like New Orleans or something during Mardi Gras!

"I wonder what they do for Halloween!" Shanti thought, chuckling at a cute Raggedy Ann and Andy arguing over in a corner. Stifling a yawn, she searched the costumed people for a Lawton or a Vaughn. It was late and she was getting tired.

A little sore from all that dancing, she stood up slowly and made her way to a trashcan where she tossed out her paper plate and empty cup.

Feeling the chill in the air, she pulled her silk wrap tightly around her shoulders. It only helped a little. Her outfit was pretty sheer. She sure had no business judging Dawn or Camelia's slinky outfits.

Oh! There! That looked like Annie Oakley moving towards the back of the hall. Shanti ran lightly so she wouldn't trip, as quickly as she could towards the direction she saw Annie, who she hoped was Chloe, heading.

It was darker the further she ventured through the thick grove of trees and bushes. She could barely make out figures that were wandering around in the back of the midnight blackened park.

There were no lanterns or lit torches to guide her. She felt foolish yelling out Chloe's name so she just kept moving to the back of the building. She could feel the cold from the damp grass starting to permeate her thin slippers.

There. There she is. Shanti smiled in relief. She could make out the fringe on her buckskin jacket. She was near to a couple that looked like they were pressed against each other and the cement wall of the building.

Chloe was just standing there, watching the couple making out. It was so dark, Shanti couldn't even tell what anyone's costume looked like. She hurried up to the girl before she could take off again and tapped her sharply on the shoulder.

"Chloe! I'm so glad I found you I was starting to think-"

The Annie Oakley turned around, her expression surprised.

"Oh my gosh- I'm- I'm so sorry, I thought you were my friend." When the girl turned, Shanti could see she obviously was not Chloe.

But the couple making out looked up too and Shanti just about melted into the earth, or wished desperately she could.

The couple making out that looked up annoyed at her shout was the Lawtons' grandson Jaime and another man. They were still holding onto each other.

If only the ground would open up and swallow her, please! she begged.

As soon as he recognized her, Jaime just smirked and whipped out his mask, placing it over his face. He bowed. His partner sniffed, annoyed at the interruption.

Mortified, Shanti didn't know what to do, so she turned and ran. She ran as quickly as she could, no longer caring if she scuffed her sandals. She was slipping and sliding as she ran.

Shanti hurried from behind the building then along the side, ignoring well-wishers and people screaming and whooping as she kept running.

She came tearing around a dark corner so quickly she stopped just in time, just before she would have careened smack into Maeve Lawton.

Chapter Twenty-One

Strutting as imperiously as always, Maeve was holding two piled high dinner plates, one in each hand.

"Shantilly dear, it really is quite improper to hurtle oneself about at a public function," she scolded the young woman.

Shanti stood panting, trying to catch her breath and her decorum.

Maeve stared down her aristocratic nose at Shanti. Noticing the girl's shocked expression, her eyebrows arched. "What is it? What's the matter?"

Shanti didn't dare tell the old woman what she'd seen. Maeve spoke often of when Jaime gets married and has children. A joining with the Vaughns' farm is what everyone wished for. They had pushed Tori and Jaime together since they were babies.

Maeve was very vocal about her hopes that one of the grandchildren may show interest in the farm and she and Langston could rest easy that when they passed on, no stranger would have the farm that has been in their family for generations.

Chloe herself told stories of Jaime's hot dates he goes on. It was obvious the family didn't know about Jaime's sexual predilections. He was clearly still in the closet. And Shanti wasn't going to be the one that opens the door.

"Uh...I...it's nothing...I...just...an owl swooped out of nowhere- scared me...I-"

Maeve rolled her eyes, smiling indulgently. "You poor city girl, so unused to the wilderness. It's all right dear, it's just a big bird, nothing to be frightened over. We were just about to eat, come and join us." She motioned with her head for Shanti to come with her.

Shanti followed Maeve through a maze of tables still stock piled with people heartily and noisily eating.

"Here were are. Look who I found, Langston. She was running scared, the poor thing, hell for leather from behind the hall. Out of the dark like a frightened angel she almost knocked me over." Maeve set the two plates down.

The older woman gestured at two men sitting on one side of Langston, and to a woman on the other side of him. They looked out of place. All three wore dark suits, no costumes and no masks. They looked uncomfortable and awkward.

"Shantilly dear, these are business associates of Magnus and Tobias Vaughn. Miss Teresa Vaquera from Venezuela, Antonio Ciccocia from Italy, and Trihn Nu from Thailand."

Each person nodded as they were introduced.

"They purchase about 40 percent of the Vaughns' potatoes and ship them to their countries. They're only in town for two days then they're off to Washington to see farms there. They thought they could catch Tobias here. They...um...were unaware the type of event this is. They thought they could stop in and visit and be on their way." Maude chuckled dryly.

The two men tugged at their ties and sleeves, twiddled buttons and looked around. Mr. Ciccocia impatiently pulled at a short and neatly trimmed black goatee that matched his slick black hair. It appeared he had purchased his dark expensive suit in Rome

Trihn Nu in a dark blue suit with a red tie stared down at the table. The woman watched Mr. Ciccocia continue to tweak his beard. She looked impatient as well. Short dark hair curled prettily around her round face

She was very attractive with snapping almond shaped eyes and deep red bow lips. Her suit was distinguished and expensive and feminine. A gold necklace curled around her slim throat. A diamond in the center of the necklace matched the simple diamond earrings. The trio clearly knew they stood out like three sore thumbs.

Shanti nodded to each person in greeting then slid onto a seat across from Langston.

The old man barely seemed to have the strength to smile at her. He still looked shaken and unwell. Shanti felt something clutch at her heart, but she couldn't pinpoint exactly what she was feeling, some type of impending doom, or free-floating anxiety. Maeve shook her out of her dark musings.

"Have you had anything to eat, dear?" The older woman questioned as she sat herself next to Shanti. She pushed one of the plates she'd brought over in front of Langston. There, barbecued ribs, macaroni salad and green beans coupled on the paper plate.

Langston looked down at the plate. He didn't move.

"Go on Langston, eat. You'll feel better, it'll build up your strength. Go on." Maeve motioned to her husband to eat. He looked at her blinking then down at his fork. With a trembling hand he picked up his fork and stabbed three green beans.

"I've eaten, thank you Mrs. Lawton. It...um...it was delicious." Shanti felt ridiculous now, running like a scared sheep after seeing Jaime and almost slamming into Maeve. She'd acted like an adolescent schoolgirl. She knew people had different ideas of love, she hadn't just fallen off the turnip truck for heaven's sake.

Her sister Summer would laugh her out of town if she'd seen how goofy she'd acted. Poor Jaime, he must think her the perfect idiot. She started to relax a little.

"Have you been having a nice time Shantilly?" Maeve asked between bites of succulent ribs. She looked over at her husband like a mother hen. "Really, Langston, try some ribs, the protein will give you energy."

Langston was only eating the beans and some macaroni salad. He hadn't touched the ribs. He set down his fork and just stared in bewilderment at her.

The three business people had been drinking coffee. Their cups were empty. They surreptitiously looked at each other, then, as if on signal they rose in unison.

Antonio Ciccocia cleared his throat and held his hand out to Langston who shook it, his smile weak. "We've got to get along, Mr. Lawton. We'll stop by the house again and see if we can catch Tobias Vaughn. They should be home by now, it's too bad we missed them here. It was nice to see you and Mrs. Lawton again."

He nodded to Maeve and Shanti. "A pleasure to meet you. Good day." The other two nodded as well, but said nothing.

The three moved away towards the front of the park as quickly as they could. They disappeared immediately into the crowd that still filled the yard.

Suddenly there was a piercing scream!

Shanti's head shot up, she looked around wide-eyed.

Maeve and Langston didn't even stop eating.

More screams.

Then Shanti saw a bunch of teenagers running around the fire. Boys in costumes had girls perched on their shoulders. They were playing chicken, trying to knock each other to the ground. A pig-tailed Pippi Longstocking was the one shrieking. They were perilously close to the fire.

Adult cowboys were still adding wood to the bonfire. It raged and crackled and shot sparks and flames as much as it had when they'd arrived. The adults shooed away the screaming teenagers. The group, girls still atop boys, giggling and screaming moved away towards the more wooded area in the back of the park.

"I think as soon as we're done we should find Montgomery and head for home," Maeve said. "It's late, the others, what's left of them, will find the Vaughns' wagon. Dario left a while ago and retrieved the car to bring Magnus home. The festivities are really too much for him these days." She picked at her ribs with a fork.

Shanti smiled gratefully. "I've had quite a wonderful time, magical actually, thank you Mrs. Lawton for including me."

Langston looked positively green. Maeve set down her knife and fork. "Shantilly, would you please dispose of our plates and meet us at the front? I'm going to get Langston out of here, he doesn't look at all well. I hope I have no trouble finding Montgomery." Concern wavered in her voice.

Urgently, she stood up and hurried around the table to where Langston was struggling to rise.

Shanti got up as well and followed Maeve around the table. She got on the other side of Langston and helped Maeve pull him to his feet. As soon as he was up, Maeve led him across the lawn,

Shanti grabbed their plates and looked around frantically for somewhere to throw them.

"The can is right over there, dear. Aren't you that artist visiting the Lawtons?" A friendly helpful voice questioned Shanti.

Shanti hesitated, her hands filled with paper plates and soda cans.

An elderly woman with white hair and a kind smile stood calmly next to her. Her arm was pointed towards a trashcan a few yards from the tables.

"Thank you. Yes, my name is Shantilly Lane. I'm painting a picture of the estate. But I-"

"Well you are very lovely dear. It's nice to meet you. Where are Maeve and Langston?" Before Shanti could answer, the kindly blue eyes widened behind thick round eyeglasses.

"I'm sorry dear, how rude of me. My name is Beatrice Canton. I'm a longtime friend of Maeve and Langston's, I've known them since, oh let me see now, forty...um...no fifty...let's see, Camelia is around fifty I believe, and my Billy is in his late forties...and, well we-"

"I am so sorry to cut you off Mrs. Canton, but- but Mr. and Mrs. Lawton are waiting out front for me, you see he, Mr. Lawton I mean, he's very ill, I mean he looks unwell and we're going home-"

Mrs. Canton looked stunned and concerned. She put up both hands and waved them at Shanti. "You run along dear, it's okay, imagine my rattling on like a parrot when they're waiting for you! You hurry now, please tell Maeve to call me in the morning and let me know how Langston is."

Shanti smiled her thanks and scurried over to the trashcan, quickly dumped the plates and cans in and wiped her hands on a napkin then threw that in as well.

She pushed her hair back with the backs of her hands, most of it had fallen out of the bun and was in her face as usual. Her sandals were wet with green stains. She bent down and removed them, they only slowed her down.

When she stood back up, her eyebrows shot up in surprise. Standing a short distance in front of her, she thought but wasn't sure, was Mrs. Li.

A tiny Asian woman was in a heated discussion with an equally small pirate. The woman was wearing a red kimono and a half-face mask. Her pencil sharp eyebrows moved rapidly up and down above the mask.

Shanti couldn't see the eyes, they were either too black to be seen through the red mask or the mask just obscured them. Her oil-black hair was in one long braid down her back.

"Maybe that isn't her after all," Shanti murmured to herself. She'd never seen the housekeeper with her hair down. She couldn't picture the severe Mrs. Li with hair that long.

Suddenly the Asian's head turned and she caught Shanti staring, holding her wet shoes in her hands. The woman grabbed the pirate's arm roughly and pushed him towards the back of the park. They disappeared behind some broad Maple trees.

There I go again, Shanti thought, *scaring people off. What is it with me? Do I have a third eye or something?* She shook her head, then, remembering the Lawtons, she ran barefoot to the front of the hall.

The Rolls was there and Montgomery had already put Langston inside and he was helping Maeve when Shanti approached.

"Oh good, you're here Shantilly, hurry, get in," Maeve ordered as she climbed into the back of the Rolls. Langston was in the front, his head drooped practically onto his chest.

Montgomery made good time getting to the mansion. He pulled the car up front and stopped at the top of the driveway. He ran around the front of the car and helped Langston out. The old man shuffled to the steps, holding his stomach.

Maeve, not waiting for Montgomery, climbed out of the back and hurried over to Langston.

"Shall I call the doctor, Madam? Perhaps we should take him directly to the hospital?" Montgomery couldn't hide his concern.

"No, no, Montgomery. I'll take him to his room. You put the car in the garage. Shantilly, perhaps you could find Mrs. Li and send her to our rooms?" Not waiting for Shanti's response, she helped Langston slowly up the steps to the mansion.

"But- but-" Shanti tried to tell her she didn't think the housekeeper was home, but the Lawtons had already entered the house. She turned to tell Montgomery, but he'd already gotten back into the car and was driving the midnight blue car down the winding driveway towards the garages.

Still holding her shoes in her hand, Shanti ran lightly up the cold stone steps to the house relishing the warmth of the immense building as soon as she stepped through the doorway. Her bare footsteps flip flapping on the floor echoed through the large foyer.

Maeve hadn't turned any lights on so the mansion was dark. Maybe all the servants were still at the festival. She wasn't sure where to look.

She hadn't been shown the help's quarters and she wasn't sure if she should even go there. Their rooms were in the middle of the mansion but on the third floor. She decided to check the kitchen and pantry areas first.

She ran in the direction of the kitchen, careful not to slip and fall. "Hello?" she called out timidly. "Um, hel- hello- is anyone here?" she called more loudly, but was met with silence.

Then, she heard a noise. Her head jerked. What was that?

"Hello? Who's there?" she asked. Not normally afraid of the dark, she did feel a little nervous alone in the big empty house.

"Well of course it isn't empty, silly," she chided herself, "the Lawtons are home."

Squeak

What the- Are those footsteps? No one had answered her when she called out. *What the heck is going on?*

Hearing another squeak and then another indistinguishable sound, she silently tiptoed down a carpeted narrow hallway.

Shanti had never been here before. It was part of the pantry area and storerooms. Maybe the noise is from Cook bumbling around.

She crept down the dark hall keeping next to the wall. With no lights she could barely see one foot in front of the other. She ran her hand along the wall using it to guide her.

Another squeak.

It sounded like someone stepping on creaking stair steps. Her hand her mouth, she chewed on a nail anxiously. *Where was everyone? Who was creeping about in the storerooms at night?*

Squeak

She was getting closer to the sound. She stopped in front of an open door and peered around the corner. It was pitch black inside.

Without making a sound, she stepped past the doorway and kept walking down the hall. Her bare feet padded silently on the carpet. Hesitating again, she listened for another sound to guide her. Nothing. The big house was still.

In front of her were two more doors.

She stood for a minute, listening. Nothing.

One of the doors was wide open. Her head swiveled back and forth, looking up and down the hall, then, she crept over to the open door and looked inside. Stairs.

She realized they must lead to the basement and wine cellar. She stood at the top of the stairs and looked down, it was so dark she couldn't see the bottom.

"Uhmph!" Two hands shoved her hard in the back- Shanti felt herself fall- tumbling end over end, clunking, smashing all the way down the hard wooden stairs until she landed head first with a loud thump on the cement floor.

All went black.

Chapter Twenty-Two

"Miss? Can you hear me?"

Garbled words drifted in from the back of her mind. Shanti could hear someone calling to her. She couldn't answer. She couldn't open her eyes. Her head hurt, she couldn't feel the rest of her body.

Then, she could feel her body being lifted off the cold, hard cement floor. Through cobwebs in her brain, it felt like someone was holding her in sturdy arms, cradling her.

She couldn't keep her head from lolling, falling back. She could feel her hair flopping, swaying as the person carrying her moved.

"Uhnn…" Shanti moaned, trying to open her eyes.

"Don't move," a male voice ordered.

It felt like she was being carried upstairs, then, her brain went spinning and she blacked out again.

There was murmuring, mumbling. People were talking, she tried to force her eyes open. She was still being held in strong arms.

"Shanti! Oh my God! Is she- is she dead?" Chloe's voice, fear in her words.

"No." The male voice again, stern.

She struggled, he held her tighter. Finally, she opened her eyes a shade. Unbelievably long lashes framed eyes the color of turquoise that were looking down at her. They were horribly familiar.

Oh my gosh. Shanti slammed her eyes shut. Hearing a chuckle, she peered at him again.

He was looking at her; a half-smile tugged his lips. *It can't be, no, not the ruffian. Oh no.*

"I warned you about drinking young lady-"

"Oh!" Her eyes flew open in swift indignation. He was laughing at her! How dare the man! "You put me down this instant!" she demanded. Her own yelling hurt her head. She winced in pain.

"Hush, Shanti, you're okay, you're safe now. Whatever were you doing in the wine cellar?" Chloe was standing next to her. Her pretty face was all screwed up with worry, her eyes heavy with tears.

Shanti felt foolish still being held in this horrid man's arms. She struggled in vain.

"Jarrett, you may put Miss Lane on the couch." Maeve, authoritative as always, no longer in her costume and her make-up redone, was pointing to a couch in the parlor.

When he didn't move, Shanti glared up at him. He was looking at the body he held so tightly in his arms.

Shanti followed the direction of his gaze. *Oh my gosh!* Shanti's mind shrieked in mortification! Her silk dress was practically in tatters! Rips and dirt smudges destroyed so much of the upper part half her chest was exposed. And he wasn't being careful about the bottom of the dress exposing her legs either!

"Put me down!" she insisted.

"Of course, Miss, your wish is my command." He smiled at her as if she was a small child. But, he did move over to the couch and very gently set her down on the plump cushions. His smile vanished when he saw her face contort with pain as soon as she touched the couch.

"You better call Doc Baker back, Mrs. Lawton," the man, still wearing his marshal's costume said to Maeve.

Groaning, Shanti looked at Maeve.

Her face was drawn and pale. Something was terribly wrong.

"What is it?" Shanti asked, more anxious now. Her eyes ran around the group staring at her.

Chloe was crying. Montgomery looked extremely distressed. Dario was wiping his eyes, even Jaime looked on the verge of tears. The Logans were the only family members not present.

No one answered her question. She could hear sniffing around the room. "What happened? What is it?" she repeated, becoming more frightened. She looked up at the marshal. He dropped his eyes.

"Langston is dead." Maeve's words were stoic, but anguish marred her face. She looked down at the floor as well, not making eye contact with Shanti. Chloe was crying loudly now.

"What? I don't understand, where is he, I don't..." Shanti didn't know what to say. "How?"

"That's exactly what we want to know, Miss, um, what were you doing downstairs?"

Shanti's eyes flew open again, her mouth dropped in anger. Who did this guy think he was for heaven's sake, asking her questions like she was a criminal or something! "Listen Mr. uh...whoever you are, I don't see why you-"

"I am Marshal Jarrett Chase, I am employed by the Sheriff's Office of Mooserock County." He tucked his thumbs in his belt and glared down at her.

She shrank back against the sofa cushions.

"The question is, and I'll be asking the questions, the question is, what were you doing in the wine cellar in the dark?"

Shanti struggled to sit up. Every bone in her body ached and her brain felt as if it was banging against the inside of her head trying to get out. She put a bruised hand to her head.

What was left of her tattered dress was slipping dangerously low. She was unaware she was about to expose herself to a roomful of people.

The strange man, who called himself a marshal, leaned over her. He pulled off his jacket and dropped it over her shoulders.

Surprised, Shanti was about to refuse it, when she looked down and realized there really wasn't much of her dress left.

Cheeks flaming, "Thank you," she mumbled, not wanting to be grateful to this obviously delusional person who thought he was a policeman. She decided it would be best to humor him.

"Sir, I came home with Maeve and-" Suddenly she remembered what Maeve had said and she started to get up and go to the elder woman's side.

The marshal leaned over again and gingerly pushed her back against the cushions. "You've obviously been injured Miss, please don't move until the doctor returns. Just sit still and answer my questions."

If Shanti had a weapon she'd shoot the fire in her eyes right at the rude man. *How dare he order her about*? She started to move again when she realized he blocked her. He apparently wasn't going to let her leave the couch.

She didn't want to embarrass herself further by getting into a wrestling match with the man. Heavens, she couldn't understand why Maeve and the others, even Montgomery standing silently next to the door, didn't run the man off. How could they let this looney toon treat her this way?

"I...I came in after Mr. and Mrs. Lawton. I was to look for Mrs. Li. I didn't think she was home because I thought I'd seen her still at the party just before we left..." Her voice trailed off when she realized the diminutive housekeeper was in the room.

Half hidden over in a corner, she stood rock still, staring impassively at Shanti with big blank black eyes.

"Yes, what then, Miss Lane, why did you go down to the cellar?" the man asked more harshly, prodding her to stay focused.

She swung her gaze up at him. She realized for the first time what a handsome man he was. In a tough kind of way. Not a pretty handsome, more of a rough handsome.

Then her eyes narrowed. The uniform, costume, whatever it was, it looked familiar, she thought she remembered the same color, khaki, or brown, a flash just before she was shoved down the stairs.

She blinked. She wished Graham were there. His strong presence would comfort her, make her feel safe.

"Um...I went first to the kitchen to see if Mrs. Li, might be there. It was dark, no one was in the kitchen. I was going to go upstairs to the servants' quarters to see if anyone was there, when..." she closed her eyes painfully, trying to remember her steps.

"When what, Miss Lane?" he prodded.

She glared at the man. "When I heard something. Yes, that was it, a sound, a creak I think, or a squeak. It sounded like when you step on a creaky stair. I followed the sound down the hall to I guess...I guess it was the door to the cellar. I've never been there before." She looked up at Jarrett Chase again.

He nodded, encouraging her to go on.

"I...I saw the door was open..." she closed her eyes, picturing her movements. "I looked down, there were stairs, it was pitch-black, then-" She put her hands to her face but the tears slipped out and rolled down her cheeks.

The man sat down on the couch next to her and surprisingly put his arm around her shoulders. He didn't say anything, just waited for her to continue.

Swiping hard at her wet eyes, she took a deep breath. "That's all I remember. Hands at my back, pushing me, I was falling, head first down the-" she couldn't go on. Big gulping sobs hit her, she was unable to continue.

The man patted her on the back. Drawing her head to his chest, he stroked her hair gently and murmured in her ear, "It's okay, it's all right, you're okay now. Breathe deeply, slowly, you're okay..."

Sniffing, Shanti got a hold of herself and sat up. The front of the man's shirt was wet with her tears.

"But how did you get into the wine cellar?" Chloe asked. Her eyes were big and round and red and circled in dark shadows.

Shanti looked at her, confused. "But...but I didn't go into the wine cellar. I was unconscious, I think, before I hit the last stair."

"That means someone put you in the wine cellar," Montgomery said. All eyes turned to him. He shrugged. They looked back at Shanti.

Blinking back the tears and fright, Shanti said, "But what happened to Mr. Lawton-" she heard a pained gasp, it was Chloe.

Maeve stepped forward. She'd been standing quietly near the door. She looked sadly down at Shanti.

"I took Langston to his bed and then went to call the doctor. I realized when the house was dark that Mrs. Li wasn't home. Chloe came right in behind us. When she couldn't find us at the party she got worried and hitched a ride with some friends. She followed us up the stairs. By the time I got off the phone with the doctor and went back to Langston...he was...gone..." Her voice dropped to a whisper.

Chloe was sobbing. Even Mrs. Li looked sad.

"The doctor came with the ambulance. After some time...he um...he- they took Langston...we-" the old lady put a hand to her head, Montgomery hurried over and helped her to a chair. He continued for her.

"After things settled down, Maeve remembered you. No one had seen you for a couple of hours. Marshal Chase was here because of the...death...he and some of his officers searched the estate for you. The Marshal found you in the cellar."

Shanti's mouth dropped- *oh no, the lout is a **real** sheriff- you've got to be kidding-* She looked suspiciously at the marshal. "What made you think to look in the cellar, Mr. Chase?"

"Just the luck of the draw, Miss," he replied with a slight twitch to his lips.

Libby poked her head in the door. Tears streaked through the thick makeup on her face. "Mrs. Lawton, the doctor's back."

"Show him in." Maeve sighed, standing up, she moved to the doorway. Libby left.

Jaime stood, stretching and yawning. "I'm going to bed, grandmother. I don't want to be present for the scene when mother comes home. I haven't the strength for the histrionics we're surely in store for."

Maeve was so drained herself she didn't respond to her grandson's lack of respect for his mother. As soon as Jaime left, the doctor entered the room.

"This is Doctor Baker, Shantilly," the elder lady introduced them. "She's had a bit of a spill, Doctor, we'd like you to check her out."

The doctor smiled benignly at Shanti and shook her hand. "So you're the missing artist then," he commented, looking her over. "You've had the family in quite a tizzy over your disappearance, that with Langston's-" he stopped when he heard moans in the room.

"Terribly sorry Maeve, how indelicate of me, I apologize. Now then, is there some place a little more private where I can check this young lady out?"

"Certainly doctor. Montgomery, perhaps you can help Shantilly to her room." It was obvious that Shanti wouldn't be moving too well on her own. The girl was covered head to toe in cuts and bruises.

"Of course Mada-"

"That's okay old man," Jarrett Chase cut off Montgomery, holding up one hand. "I've got her."

Shanti's eyes opened wide in alarm. *Oh no! Not again!* She struggled to sit up.

"No, I'm quite able to get to my room on my-" stabbing pain hit her entire body at once, she doubled over, one hand to her stomach the other to her head. There was a bleeding gash across her cheek.

Suddenly, the marshal with one movement swept her into his arms as he stood up. The move jolted Shanti just enough to distract her from her pain. Her eyes fluttered shut as her head lolled dizzily against the officer's broad shoulder.

"I'll take her upstairs, Maeve. You get yourself to bed, you're going to need your rest," Jarrett Chase quietly instructed the elderly matron. "Chloe honey, show me where Miss Lane's room is, okay?"

He smiled gently at the young woman that was still dabbing at her eyes. She'd already changed out of her costume and had washed up then had helped in the search for Shanti.

"Of course, Jarrett, follow me." Chloe left the room. Jarrett followed her carrying Shanti.

The doctor handed Maeve a bottle containing pills. "Here Maeve. There's enough for you and Chloe, and Camelia and Dawn too if they need some. They're just a light sleeping pill to get you ladies through the next few days."

Maeve accepted the bottle, sliding it into her pocket.

"Call me when you rise tomorrow, the autopsy should be completed later in the week." He patted her arm then followed Jarrett out the door.

The policeman easily carried Shanti up the long flight of stairs and down the hall to her room. Chloe opened the door and flicked on the light. Jarrett entered the room and laid Shanti gently on her bed. She groaned and opened her eyes.

The tall marshal was smiling sympathetically now at her. He plumped pillows behind her head and helped her to sit up.

"You do as the doctor tells you, Miss Lane. I'll be back tomorrow with more questions, so get some rest." He turned to Chloe.

"I know how distraught you are, Chloe, but can you help Miss Lane clean up? And, do you remember where I left my hat? I know where my jacket is." He nodded pointedly at Shanti.

She looked down. She was still wearing his leather jacket. She hated to give up the warmth, but she hated more to be beholden to him. She tried to get it off, but every move she made hurt.

The officer helped her remove his jacket, carefully averting his eyes from her exposed flesh. Chloe hurried over with Shanti's robe and gave it to her.

Jarrett shrugged into his jacket. He shook hands with the doctor. "Sorry to see you under these circumstances, Doc. You should have been at the festival it was great fun while it lasted. I pulled extra duty for Pete, his wife was having their third child last night. Anyway, good thing some people didn't drink and drive or I'd have been busier," he looked pointedly over at Shanti who was glaring at him.

"I was not-"

"See you all later. Night Doc, Chloe. Miss Lane, I hope there's no broken bones after *any* of your falls tonight- bye." He hurried out before Shanti could disclaim any of her falls this evening were of her own doing, or throw something handy at him.

"That- that ogre!" she growled, holding her arm out so the doctor could take her blood pressure.

Chloe laughed. "Oh Shanti, Jarrett Chase is a really nice guy. He moved here a few years ago from Colorado, he's a great sheriff. Come on, tell me you don't think he's the handsomest-"

"Harrumph!" Shanti cut Chloe off. "He is rude and mean, and I can't tell which bruises I have are from when I fell down the stairs or when he so boorishly mashed my arm at the party!"

"What? You two already met? He manhandled you? Oh Shanti," Chloe excitedly sat on the other side of the bed next to her friend. "You've got to tell me all about it! Did you guys dance, or...kiss?"

"What! We most certainly did not do either! I would rather kiss a hungry piranha than that boor!" Shanti was beside herself to make Chloe understand there was nothing between her and the man she thought was playing dress-up as a cop at the party.

Darn the man, how embarrassing for her that he was really a policeman. No wonder he was such a bully and aggravating about thinking she was a lush.

She'd have to see him again just to explain to him that she hadn't even had one drink when she tripped over that dog. The marshal must not have seen the poodle behind her. No wonder he keeps talking down to her like she was a child or a disgusting drunk.

"Oh Chloe..." Shanti sighed and leaned back into the pillows.

"All right now ladies, let's settle down. You seem to have no broken bones or any serious damage, maybe a slight concussion.

I don't think there's any internal bleeding. But you must stay in bed, I'd say for at least a week. No getting up except to use the restroom. Do you understand young lady?" Doctor Baker sternly instructed Shanti after a quick examination.

Shanti was at this point trying to keep her eyes open and listen to the doctor. He was a kindly looking elderly man with such thick eyeglasses his watery eyes looked positively huge in his wrinkly face. Balding on top, the sides of his white hair were uncombed, messed by the wind outside.

"Chloe, do you think you can help Miss Lane clean up a bit? Then you need to get yourself to bed and get some rest as well. I am so sorry dear for your loss." He patted her shoulder then turned and put his stethoscope and other tools into his black bag, snapped it closed and stood up.

Chloe wiped away a tear and walked him to the door. "I'll see to Shanti, Doctor, can you find your way out?"

The doctor chuckled. "I've know you children since you were small, I've been in these bedrooms more times than I can count. I'm sure I can find my way out of this rambling cave you call a house." Carrying his bag he left the girls.

Chloe helped Shanti clean up, saw her safely tucked into bed then made her way wearily to her own room. She winced when she heard a harrowing wail- *Mother's home.* She hurried to her room and quickly closed her door.

The next morning, Montgomery opened the front door to the loud insistent knocking. Whoever was last in last night must have left the gate open. Impatiently he swung the door open. Didn't they know the house was in mourning for Pete's sake? His face widened in surprise- then confusion.

"Miss Shantilly, whatever are you doing out of bed? How did you get outside- and...where are your bruises...what the..." he broke off, totally bewildered.

"Where is my sister!?" an incredibly angry voice demanded.

Montgomery's jaw dropped, his hand fell off the doorknob.

"Who the hell are-"

The exact mirror image of Shantilly Lane was standing on the doorstep, and by the looks of her, she was steaming mad.

She pushed Montgomery to the side and stepped over the threshold. Her eyes widened as she took in the vast, opulent foyer.

"Well, Shanti sure was telling the truth when she described this museum. Now," she turned, pulling off her hat, blonde hair tumbled to her shoulders.

Sapphire blue eyes, identical to Shanti's turned to Montgomery, threatening as she repeated, "Where is my sister?"

Chapter Twenty-Three

"Madam, the doctor is on the phone." Serafina poked her tear stained face into the drawing room where Maeve was sipping tea with Dolly Vaughn, Catherine Scott, and Beatrice Canton. They were in the process of planning Langston's funeral.

"Thank you Serafina, I'll take it in here."

Serafina nodded. She dabbed a tissue to her exotic luminous eyes. She didn't look at the other ladies, just left. They could hear her sobbing down the hall.

Maeve shook her head. "She loved Langston, you know. He's the one that insisted on hiring her. I was totally against it. With her mother working in the same neighborhood, servants sharing our secrets and all, well, that's just never a good idea. However," she sighed, standing up she walked over to a telephone on a table next to the chair Dolly Vaughn was seated in.

Dolly was also periodically dabbing her eyes. Everyone loved Langston. Even though he'd been sick recently, he'd always been so spry and full of life, his death really was so unexpected. She sniffed then blew her nose so loudly, the other two ladies turned towards her to console her.

Maeve picked up the phone and held it to her ear. "Yes?" she said. Her mouth was a straight thin line as she listened. Her brows drew down then shot up.

"What? Are you serious?" she almost yelled into the receiver.

The ladies' heads whipped around to stare at Maeve. She looked shocked, her face was white as a sheet.

Dolly stood up quickly and went to her friend.

"Maeve?"

Maeve ignored her, still intent on what the doctor was telling her. "I don't really understand, Doctor, it's impossible-" she stopped mid word and listened. "No, that is utterly impossible-" her mouth still open, she paused as she listened.

Nodding absently, she muttered, "Fine then, fine, I'm sure Jarrett will be here soon. He'll explain I suppose. All right, yes, goodbye." She hung up the phone, but stood there silently staring at it.

"Maeve?" Dolly lightly touched her shoulder, her voice timid. "Maeve, what is it?"

Maeve turned slowly and looked down at the concerned plump matron at her side. She smiled vaguely, not really seeing her friend. She looked up at the open door to the drawing room, one thin hand to her chest.

"Doctor Baker says..." she drew in a wretched breath, "he claims...that Langston was...poisoned."

All three women gasped, their hands flew to their mouths.

Catherine Scott stood up, indignant. "That is totally ridiculous. Who is the brainless idiot that worked on Langston?" She set her teacup down so hard on the table some amber liquid spilled over into the saucer.

Beatrice sat with her mouth and eyes wide open.

"That's exactly what *I* said, Catherine. However, he was quite insistent. At first they thought it was a virus or flu or something or possibly his heart, you know at his age..." Maeve turned back to the other women.

"But he was quite adamant it's poison. They don't know what kind yet. Heavens," she laughed wryly. "I hope it's not arsenic or rat poison, they'll come straight for me, that's how it goes in the movies. Old women are always poisoning their husbands with arsenic. I must remember to ask Mrs. Li if we have any in the house."

"Now stop that, Maeve, you're being silly." Catherine went to Maeve and put an arm around the taller woman's shoulders.

"There has obviously been a mistake made. Langston's been sick for a while, he must have picked up some bug, gotten pneumonia, a virus. At his age and all, yes of course, they've made a horrible mistake." She gently squeezed Maeve's shoulders.

Maeve blinked rapidly, trying to hold back the tears. She was a matriarch after all, she couldn't be seen weeping like a peasant into her soup as it were.

"Madam," a shy voice on the edge of tears was in the doorway again. Serafina's lustrous black hair was pulled back severely into a tight ponytail. Even with no makeup, her lovely eyes were onyx pools of tears.

Maeve turned to the young maid. "Yes Serafina?"

The maid looked down, tears fell, splashing in tiny puddles on her red cheeks. Quickly she wiped her eyes with the already sodden tissue being torn apart in her nervous fingers. "Ma-Madam... the sheriff...he...he is here..." she stammered.

"Thank you dear, please have Libby see him in. And ask Mrs. Li to come here, then go to your room and wash your face and lie down for a bit."

Serafina looked in surprise at her mistress. Never had Mrs. Lawton ever spoken so kindly to her before. In fact, she only ever gave her orders, she had never spoken on a personal level with her. Ducking her head, she nodded her silent thanks and quickly left before the elder woman changed her mind.

The maid hurried down the hall to retrieve Libby. The mistress would prefer Libby because of her normal stoic manner. Yet today, even the normally non-flappable Libby was wiping tears careful not to disturb her plastered on makeup.

Serafina went to the kitchen and told Mrs. Li the mistress wanted her in the drawing room. Then she looked for Libby.

Once she found Libby and told her the mistress wanted her to show Jarrett Chase to the drawing room, she hurried off in the opposite direction of her own bedroom. She went elsewhere to find consolation.

Libby put away the crystal she was wiping and headed to the front foyer.

Jarrett Chase was standing patiently waiting in the foyer, his hat in his hand.

"'Lor, gi' me yer hat and jacket then, Rett." Libby had danced a few at the local pubs with Jarrett and knew him and his friends pretty well. He could fill out a pair of jeans nicely, and flannel shirts looked made special for his broad shoulders. She'd boldly thrown herself numerous times at the handsome officer.

But alas, he always nicely set her from him. She looked attractive in cropped tee shirts and mini denim skirts, her thin fine hair pulled back off her face with barrettes, but she wasn't his type. She was too easy. She never left a pub alone.

Single, Jarrett dating infrequently because his job with Mooserock County was pretty demanding, taking up a lot of his time. There was little real crime in the rural town of Brimstone Glen where their main office was. However, they were low on men and long on wide-open spaces.

They had to cover not only the town, but also the entire county of Mooserock. Plus, there were vast forests and fields to constantly patrol for poachers and people growing marijuana under the cover of heavy trees and foliage.

Another girl in town, Mary Jane Peltham, has her sights set on Jarrett Chase. They'd gone out a few times, set up by mutual friends. Jarrett had broken so many dates with her she'd lost count, but that didn't put her off.

Mary Jane does nails at the 'Strong as Nails' beauty shop in town. Whenever she sees another woman getting too close to Jarrett, she finds a way to warn her off. She considers the cop with the blue-green eyes that makes her think of the sea to be her property.

Unfortunately, he doesn't seem quite as serious about her. That just means she has to work that much harder. She'd gotten her breasts done last year, and this year she had collagen injected into her lips to make them puffier in hopes of snagging his complete attention.

"I don't plan on being too long, Lib, I'll hold on to them for now. How's the Lane girl?" Jarrett asked, following the sashaying hips of the earthy maid.

She peeked coquettishly over her shoulder at him. "I don't know. But wait'll you get a look at our new guest, yer eyeball's pop right outta yer head!" She laughed wickedly.

Summer Lane's unexpected visit had shocked the entire household. Who would have ever guessed Shanti had an identical twin sister just as strikingly gorgeous as the blonde artist?

If Libby herself had a twin and they looked like the Lane sisters, well, she'd call Playboy magazine so fast-

"What do you mean, who's here?" Puzzled, Jarrett stayed close to Libby's heels. He had an apparent murder on his hands and already there were too many people that could be suspects.

Libby just laughed. "Oh, you'll see soon enough. First, I'll take ya to Miz Lawton, she's in the drawing room with her old fogey friends, c'mon."

As he followed her, "You seem to be holding up okay, Lib." Jarrett said politely, making small talk.

Libby's face fell. Her normally placid face turned sad. She stopped, Jarrett stopped too.

"Listen Rett, I loved that old guy. I mean, he was always great to me and the others...sniff." She wiped angrily at a tear that slipped out of one eye. "He always stood up for me and the others against Miz Lawton and that Chinese bitch."

Her eyes slid back and forth, making sure neither the housekeeper nor some other person that could carry tales could hear her. She looked back at the policeman.

"You find out who killed him, you hear?" She stuck a finger in his face. "I wanna see him fry, whoever the bastard is." Clamping her thickly painted lips together, she turned. Her face placid once again, she blinked back her tears and cleared her throat.

"Marshal Chase, Ma'am," she announced. She winked at Jarrett then hurried away down the hall.

Maeve stepped to the door. "Come in, Jarrett." The matriarch greeted the young man, ushering him into the small room.

The ladies, still consternated at the information Maeve had shared with them, were standing awkwardly in the middle of the room.

Dolly spoke up first. "Hi Jarrett...um, I think I'll be off now, Catherine do you need a ride home?" She turned to her friend with the white hair and blue eyes softened by her thick glasses.

Catherine Scott shook her head. "No dear, thank you. Bea brought me. We're going to stop at the nursery on the way home. I need fertilizer for the orchids."

Catherine Scott had her own greenhouse in the back of her home where she spends a great deal of her time. "I'll call you later, Maeve. Please let me know if I can be of help and when the, uh, funeral is. Will you still come to tea next week?" She smiled kindly.

"Maybe the young artist will be better and you can bring her along. Fresh flowers will help cheer her up. I have the loveliest Lonicera giving off the most delicious fragrance-"

"Yes Catherine, of course. I will call you later. Perhaps Miss Lane would enjoy seeing your greenhouse. Actually she has a rather stunning visitor right now. I will tell you about it later. I'll have Serafina stop by this afternoon, Montgomery will bring her by for some of that green tea you're growing, it'll help us I think."

Catherine nodded in agreement, her wrinkled face gently sad.

Maeve walked all three ladies to the door and said goodbye.

She rejoined a patient Jarrett Chase who was still standing, holding his hat in his hands in the drawing room.

She motioned to a chair. "Please have a seat, Jarrett."

He acquiesced, sitting in the chair she pointed to. He set his hat on his knee and leaned back in the chair and softly uttered his condolences.

She sat on a loveseat with a modern design of mixed squares of burgundy and beige cushions. The heavy dress she wore had lace up to her neck and long sleeves. The full dark blue skirt covered her completely to her black-heeled shoes. Her ankles

184

were crossed and her hands folded primly in her lap. She nodded her thanks at Jarrett's offering of sympathy.

He leaned forward, first looking at the floor then up at the elderly matron. "Well, Mrs. Lawton, I spoke with the coroner, you know..." he hesitated, it was a delicate subject discussing the demise of a woman's partner of over fifty years.

Thank goodness she was made of stern stuff. He was never any good with boo-hooing females. And she certainly was not the kind he could pat on the back and comfort with meaningless words. And she sure wouldn't look as gorgeous as the artist with tears falling from those blue- he cleared his throat.

"Um...well, the results as they said point to poison."

"I know that, Sheriff, Doctor Baker told me earlier on the phone. I can guarantee you, there is no arsenic here. I just advised Mrs. Li to have the help scour the house, stables, barns, and all of the storage sheds.

"Other than basic herbicides, sulfuric acid, Paraquat, Diquat, Endothall herbicides and the like used in the fields, she said she found nothing. So, they must be mistaken." She looked at him calmly, sure of herself, her bearing stiff.

Jarrett Chase sighed inwardly, grumbling to himself, *Where the hell were the CSI folks- the entire mansion and grounds have been compromised-* he cleared his throat. "Ahem, well, Mrs. Lawton, apparently it isn't your garden variety poison. It's um..." He patted the pockets of his leather jacket.

Reaching inside, he pulled out a notebook and flipped it open. He leafed through several pages before he stopped. "Here it is. The poison is from...rosary pea seeds." He lifted his eyes up at her.

Maeve looked quite taken aback. "What? Rosary beads? I don't understand- he didn't choke on a bead...did he?" Two grey brows drew down like knives between her green eyes.

Jarrett shook his head. "No, Mrs. Lawton, not rosary *beads*, rosary *pea seeds*. They're some kind of plant or bush or something. Not even native to Idaho, they're from a tropical, humid kind of place, like, I guess Florida or something."

"Florida? We haven't been anywhere south in ages, Jarrett. This is unbelievable!" She stood up agitated. Pacing back and forth in front of the sheriff, her hands were clasped tightly behind her back. She stopped in front of him, her palms held out in question.

"What on earth is going on?" she asked in perturbed puzzlement.

Jarrett shook his head, looking up at her earnestly. "I just don't know, Mrs. Lawton, it's the weirdest thing I've ever heard of. But, we need to do some more investigation. Officers Johnson and Small will be searching the grounds, and Officer Mills will check out the interior. Is that all right with you? We need your permission, we don't have a warrant." He left off the 'yet' part.

He didn't want to piss off the pillars of the community, he'd have the governor and mayor all over his butt, and he sure didn't need that aggravation.

She sighed, giving up. "Of course, do what you must. This is all so insane, I can hardly think. Do you need me any longer? I believe I'll rest for a while. I must meet with Mr. Rogers the funeral director at four."

"No, no Mrs. Lawton. But I do have questions for your guest, that Lane girl. May I see her?"

Maeve shrugged, whatever. "Of course Jarrett, but I don't see what else she can tell you she didn't say last night. However, do you remember the way? If not I can have one of the girls-"

"No." He held up a hand as he stood. He still held his hat in the other. Regulation uniform, it was a heavy Stetson.

"I can find my way, thanks." He followed her out the door and down the long hall to the main staircase. They walked together to the second floor.

When they reached the landing, Maeve nodded and went off to the right, Jarrett turned to the left.

Chapter Twenty-Four

Jarrett counted the doors, hers was pretty far down, pink room if he recollected from taking her there last night. When he reached the room he could hear talking inside.

One voice was loud, almost yelling, the other was hushed, pleading. It sounded like someone was giving the poor injured young woman a hard time. *Not on my shift*, he thought.

Without knocking, he turned the knob and threw the door open. It banged against the wall then ricocheted back and hit the hand he held up to stop it.

"Who the hell do you-" he ground out angrily, ready to chew out whatever ignorant slob was yelling at the bruised and battered girl he'd carried up the stairs late last night.

He stopped, his words ringing through the room. His mouth dropped nearly to the floor, his eyes bugged out of his head. There were two of them!

Shanti and her obvious twin were in deep argument. They turned at the abrupt interruption from the angry sheriff.

The twin looked in interest at the young man with the cowboy hat in his hand, attractive in a tough very masculine way even though he looked mad as hell.

Shanti, on the other hand was glaring at him.

Jarrett could only tell the difference between them because of the bruises on Shanti. Both girls were so striking it took his breath away. Yet, something about Shanti punched him in his craw.

Last night with everyone in costume, he thought she was just a drunk looking for some place to fall. Still, he'd felt a tightening in his body as they shared insults. And when he'd found her crumpled on the floor of the wine cellar in the dark and carried her up the stairs, her face was so dirty and bruised he couldn't tell she was so pretty.

He also had been distracted by so much of her body being revealed from her tattered dress.

"What do you want?" Shanti ungraciously asked him.

He was standing like the village idiot looking from one to the other.

The twin's eyes widened, aghast at her sister's rudeness. "Shanti! Your manners!" She slid off the bed, her slim hand held out in greeting. "Hi, I'm Summer Lane."

They shook hands. Jarrett finally closed his mouth and regained his composure. He's seen twins before of course, it just took him by surprise, and they were so striking.

"How do you do, Miss, uh, Lane. I'm Marshal Jarrett Chase. I'm ah, investigating the murder of Langston Law...ton...ah," he straggled off at the look of pain in Shanti's face.

Her eyes immediately welled up. Summer noticed as well and swiftly sat back down on the bed and put her arm around her sister.

The thought of identical roses on the same vine came to Jarrett's mind as he stared at them. *Oh my God*, Jarrett thought, *I've turned into a freakin' poet*. He shook his head, *get a grip old man*, he told himself.

"It's a pleasure meeting you, Miss um, Lane. I'm sorry to intrude. I burst in because it sounded like someone was giving Miss uh, your sister a hard time, and after last night, I mean, she was pretty roughed up and...I...thought-"

Summer laughed, looking slightly ashamed. "Yeah, well, that was me yelling at my poor sister, Mr. Chase. You see," she turned and frowned at Shanti, "I want her to come home with me immediately. I feel she's in danger, I mean, just look at her!"

Summer pointed at her sister who had a determined look on her face.

"Don't be ridiculous Sum, I'm not going anywhere, it was just a silly acci-" she broke off her words when she looked at her sister. Summer was vehemently shaking her head.

"Come on Shanti, you didn't trip and fall down those stairs, you told me yourself someone pushed you. You are to come home with me as soon as you can walk. Maybe sooner. You're lucky the boys didn't come with me. It was all I could do to hold back our brothers Dan and Drew. They were ready to charge down here like the darn cavalry all ready to swoop you up and drag you home.

"But, Daniel has a big project at work lined up, and Drew needs to tend the garden, it's ending harvest time for some of the vegetables. Anyway," she reached out and stroked her sister's soft hair.

"I told them I was quite capable of bringing you home. You're not going to make a liar out of me are you?" she gently cajoled her sister.

Still trying to get used to the pair, Jarrett stood quietly watching the sisters. Pretty as shiny new pennies, the girls were obviously very fond of each other. Shanti looked mad, but she was more angry at being told what to do than who was telling her.

"Summer, I appreciate you coming out here to get me, and I know I must look a fright-"

"Huh, fright indeed!" Summer snorted. "You want a mirror?"

Shanti frowned at her sister, then smiled. "We've never needed a mirror before, have we Sum?" The girls laughed at shared memories and pranks.

"But," Shanti said, her voice serious, brooking no argument, "I am not going home. I have to attend Mr. Lawton's funeral," she held back the waver in her voice. "And I have a painting to finish. I'm going to do it for him, it's what he would have wanted." She looked so determined, Summer gave up with tightlipped shrug.

She said to Shanti, "I'm going to go clean up. That nice Chloe showed me a room. They've invited me to stay the night in this- this-" she looked around the room, "castle." Standing up, she murmured, "I'll be leaving in the morning. It's nice meeting you, Marshall."

"Ah, that's Marshal Chase, Ma'am, Marshal as in Sheriff. I'm the local law. First name is Jarrett."

"Oh," Summer's cheeks turned slightly pink. "Anyway, Marshal, maybe you can talk some sense into her, but I doubt it. I'll see you in a few, sis." She leaned over, her hair swung across her face as she gave her sister a kiss on her forehead. She smiled at Jarrett and left the room.

The marshal and the injured woman stared silently at each other. She was resentful at the things he'd said to her yesterday, and he was suspicious of her.

He moved to the bed, she cringed. That bothered him. He wasn't used to people being afraid of him, especially beautiful young women. He didn't come any closer.

"I don't think you should go home just yet, Miss Lane. Not until we've cleared up this mystery." He ignored her glower.

Glancing around the room, he went over and picked up a chair and brought it back to the bed. Setting it down, he sat in it and silently studied the girl in the bed.

"You're looking better today, I guess washing off a layer of dirt helps, huh?" he said.

Shanti's mouth dropped open in dismay. Why, the absolute boorishness of the man! She'd be darned if she was going to be baited by him. Closing her mouth she continued to glare at him.

"Do you have anything to add to your story of falling down the stairs yesterday?" he asked. He sounded like she wasn't telling the full truth about her fall.

She sat up straighter, pulling her sheet with tiny roses on it up to her chin. Her face fierce, her eyes spitting blue fire just like they did last night, she said her words slowly, carefully, as if to a dimwitted child.

"I was pushed, Marshal, I did not just fall. I am not in the habit of lying and I'd appreciate it if you'd stop insinuating that I am."

Chase leaned back calmly. "Anyway, where are you from? Chloe tells me Langston hired you to do a painting of the estate. However, everyone I've talked to so far have said they've not seen a lick of paint in the vicinity."

Angrier than she's been in a very long time, Shanti pulled herself up as straight as her sore back would let her. "Listen Mr.-ah," she stumbled for his name, she couldn't remember it. Must have been the knock to her head. "Uh, Marshal, I am an artist, I have my own studio back home. I can certainly prove it, I-"

He cut her off, "Don't get yourself in a flap, honey, I didn't say you couldn't paint, I just said there's no evidence of it. And," his dark brows rose, "suddenly you have a sister here you never told anyone about. Who knows if the two of you are in cahoots to cheat the family out of-"

"How dare you! Get out of here! Get out!" Shanti who never loses her temper screamed at the officer.

He looked slightly ashamed. He was just trying to get down to the bottom of Lawton's murder, he didn't want to upset a sick girl, at least until she was better. It was kind of fun snapping angry sparks off her.

He held up both hands, but he didn't move off his chair. "All right, all right, simmer down, you're going to hurt yourself. I have to ask questions, I'm a cop you know. It's my job."

"Harrumph!" Shanti fell back against the pillows. Cop indeed. She felt like such an idiot thinking all last night he was just some goofball dressed in a policeman's costume.

"So…" he pulled out his notebook and flipped it open. "What sorts of chemicals do you have in this workroom of yours?" He nodded towards her studio.

Shanti rolled her eyes. Again, speaking slowly, as if to a very young child, she said, "Marshal, I have no poisons if that's what you're asking. Chloe told me they think Mr. Lawton was poisoned. I have just cleaning solutions like turpentine."

She looked at him, suddenly worried. "Oh my gosh, it wasn't turpentine was it?"

He shook his head and looked down at his notes. He crossed one leg over the other and sat his hat on his knee. "Nope. Rosary pea seeds."

Her head shot up. "Excuse me? Seeds?"

"Yup. Rosary pea seeds. Highly toxic according to the coroner. He had to consult an agriculturist. He didn't know what he'd found. Ripe, they're red seeds, unripe they look sort of like," he referred to his notes, "string beans." He raised his eyes from the notebook to her.

"Apparently, normally they can kill almost immediately after ingestion, but for some reason we don't think they got Mr. Lawton right away. According to Mrs. Lawton, her husband had nothing to eat once he got home. He was already too sick. She just put him into bed and called for the doctor.

"Chloe was right at her heels. In fact," he looked down at his notes again, flipping a few pages. "Yup, in fact, Chloe was by his bedside when he died. She didn't know it though, not until Mrs. Lawton returned. The old lady's the one that noticed he wasn't breathing."

Shanti brought her hands up to her face. "I didn't know. Poor Chloe, she loved her grandfather so much." She cried softly.

Chase didn't know what to do. He was gut smacked at her tears. He looked around, then got up and went into the bathroom where he found a box of tissues. He brought them out and set them on the bed.

Shanti didn't notice. She kept crying into her hands. Jarrett pulled a tissue out and shoved it into one of her hands. She took it and dried her eyes.

"Thank you. I'm s…sorry…sniff…I didn't know. All I cared about was me. I was so hurt and scared. Heavens, I'm so selfish! I need to go to her-" she moved to climb off the bed.

Jarrett put both hands on her shoulders and gently held her for a few heartbeats, then pushed her back.

"You need to stay here. You have a right to be a little selfish, you had a rough night yourself. Besides, I ran into Chloe outside, she said she was going out for a ride to clear her head."

"Oh. That's good, that'll help." Shanti wished she was well enough herself to go riding too, but she knew better. The doctor said she was lucky she hadn't broken any bones, especially her neck. But, she might have a slight concussion and was supposed to be still for a few days.

"Anyway," Jarrett sat back down, "where'd you say you're from?"

Pulled from her thoughts, Shanti turned wet eyes to the marshal. She sniffed, then, wiped her nose with the tissue. "I...I'm from California."

He looked at her with interest and took a pen out of an inside pocket and wrote something in his notebook. "California? Near the coast? LA?"

Shanti shook her head. "No, in a valley near the mountains, more northwest." Why was he asking her, couldn't he easily just run a record on her?

"Hmm." He wrote in his book. Nonchalantly, he looked her in the eye. "It's warmer and more humid there than here, isn't it?"

She looked puzzled. "Not really, maybe a little, warmer I mean. It's dry air, not humid. Why do you say that?"

"Hmmm, um, no reason, no reason." He smiled genially. "So, uh, how did you meet the Lawtons? How long have you known them, and how long are you staying?"

Shanti frowned and crossed her arms in front of her chest. Her eyes narrowed in anger. "You suspect me for some reason, don't you?"

He just smiled, not answering her.

She rolled her eyes. "Actually, they, the Lawtons, came to *my* state, *my* store, and solicited *me*. *I* did not search *them* out. And, for your information, Chloe knows all about my sister Summer, we've spoken at length about our families. As far as my plans," she shrugged.

"My sister is leaving tomorrow now that she has seen that I am fine. Then, well, I need to go to the...the funeral. And I will complete the painting. Chloe has asked me to stay until it's done.

She says she wants to hang it in the main hall to honor her grandfather. I only hope it's good enough to...to be there."

"Oh, I'm sure you'll do just fine, Miss Lane. Well, I'll let you rest now. I need to question the servants. Someone had to have seen or heard something. The house is big, but it has ears, they all do." He stood up.

"I don't think you'll find out much, Marshal. When I got home that night there was no one else around except Mr. and Mrs. Lawton and they were upstairs, and I guess Chloe who came in right behind me. I went through a good deal of the house and there wasn't anyone else here." She watched the big man walk to the door.

He stopped. He put his hat on his head, his hand hesitated on the doorknob. "If no one was in the house Miss Lane, who pushed you down the stairs?" One eyebrow rose and a corner of his mouth pulled in.

Before she could answer, he stepped outside and closed the door behind him. He didn't hear her response, but he did hear the pillow hit the door.

Chuckling, he headed for the staircase.

Chapter Twenty-Five

Once outside in the chill of late autumn Jarrett Chase met with his fellow officers.

Huddling in a tight circle, they shared notes. No one had found any kind of bush the rosary pea seeds could have come from.

They'd gathered examples of the toxins used on the farm to take to the lab for analyzing, but they knew herbicides weren't what they were looking for.

Jarrett decided to wander around the grounds and storage sheds and go over some of the already searched area. He told the others to head back to the station, he'd meet up with them later.

The two policemen and one policewoman climbed into two of the marked police cars parked along the winding driveway.

Jarrett had parked his Bronco truck further down, nearer the gate. He waited for them to drive off before he moved.

He zipped up his jacket and pulled his hat down over his forehead. Tucking his hands into the pockets of his jacket, he followed the walk around the estate to the back.

When he reached the area behind the huge house, the sparkling water of the rapidly moving river caught his eye. He walked over the hard earth. Winter was fast arriving, fewer and fewer hardy leaves clung to the half bare branches.

The wind was picking up, it had a sharp bite to it. The sun struggled to emit its weak rays through the heavy clouds. Jarrett pulled his head down and his furry collar up around his ears.

It took him almost ten minutes to get to the river. He passed the barns and stables. He had expected to see a farmhand or two, but not a soul was in sight. Even the horses were all snug in their stalls in the stables.

He could hear whinnies and snorts and an intermittent stomp as he neared the stables. Already some of the wild animals were preparing to hibernate. It was October and this far north, winter could happen overnight.

He stopped beside the riverbank and watched the rushing dark blue water hurtle by. The deep blue, almost purple water reminded him of that artist girl's eyes.

He shook his head. Spoiled little flaky artist, he thought. Pretty, but probably doesn't know how to work a real job and drinks too much. Too bad. His brain thought negatively of her but against his will, his body reacted to his thoughts of her.

Damn. Just what he didn't need was some physical attraction to a nutty girl that he considered a possible suspect in a murder case. And not just some murder case either. Langston Lawton was a well-known aristocrat and deeply loved and respected member of the community.

The entire county will be up in arms to have the head of his killer on a silver platter. If he was killed. It was undetermined yet if he ingested the poison by mistake or if it was a deliberate act.

Jarrett stared down at the ground along the river. There must be a hundred footprints there. *That's odd*. His eyes followed the path of the footprints.

They went to and from the river and the storage sheds, and then to and from the direction of the Vaughns' neighboring farm a couple of miles or so to the west. He decided to trace the prints and see if they did indeed lead to the Vaughns' farm.

He'd only gone a few yards when he saw someone exiting from one of the stables. It was a female, one of the maids by the look of her white uniform and shoes. She had on a pink sweater and scarf on her head. Her arms were tight across her chest and her head was bent against the cold. She hurried along a well-worn path from the stables towards the back of the big house.

Jarrett decided he should ask her some questions. He changed direction and jogged after the woman.

Quickly catching up to her, he startled her when he called out, just feet from behind her.

She jumped, her hand to her throat. "Marshal! You scared the feathers out of me!" Serafina cried. She knew the policeman, everyone in Brimstone Glen knew him. But, she always felt guilty for some reason and avoided him.

Her mother was an undocumented immigrant, everyone knew it, but they looked the other way. They knew the country she came from was extremely poor. She left her family because there were too many children to feed and she would soon have to work the streets as a prostitute to help support them.

Pregnant at 14, Serafina's mother escaped on a fishing boat with others like her and was working in an overcrowded filthy sweatshop in a neighboring city sewing dresses.

She was indigent and in a hospital giving birth to Serafina when Dolly Vaughn's church heard of her. Ever charitable, Dolly brought her and the baby home and gave her a job.

When Serafina was old enough to work, Dolly talked Maeve into hiring her as a maid. Being born in America automatically made Serafina a citizen. But, she still always felt guilty and ashamed that her mother was not.

"I'm sorry, Serafina." Jarrett didn't look the least bit ashamed for frightening her. Catching people unaware, he realized a long time ago, they were more apt to speak honestly when they didn't have time to make up a lie.

The young maid didn't make eye contact with the sheriff. She looked everywhere but at him. The wind was threatening to blow her scarf off her head, much of her glossy black hair was flying about her face. She clutched her sweater tightly, it was really too little protection against the cold. She started to shiver.

"So, where're ya hurrying off to?" Jarrett asked, staring her straight in the eye.

Nervously, she looked away again, trying to tuck her hair back into the scarf. Beautiful exotic eyes, the iris's so dark it was hard to tell where they ended and the pupils began, darted anxiously back and forth like blackbirds dancing.

"No- nowhere...Marshal Chase, I was going nowhere," the anxious maid stammered. She kept looking back at the stable she'd just left like she was looking to see if anyone was watching.

Jarrett followed her eyes to see what she was looking at. He still didn't see anyone.

"Just out for a walk, then, all alone, in the cold?" he asked her, pushing the brim of his hat back off the front of his head so he could get a good look at her. The blustery wind even blew his short brown hair around.

She obviously was not just out for a walk, she wasn't dressed properly for the chilly air. She stared down at her feet. The white shoes were caked in mud. Bits of straw stuck out from the bottoms.

She'd have to sneak quickly up the back stairs to her room to clean them before either Mrs. Li or the madam saw her. And the sheriff was holding her back. The longer she was out here, the better the chance of someone noticing she was missing.

"I...uh...I ...was out to get some...some...fresh mint from the gardens for the...tea...Mrs. Lawton. She loves mint in her tea...you know..."

She glanced at the marshal then quickly away. He was a policeman, she thought, they can see right through people's lies, they were trained to do that.

"Tea? My mother puts mint in her iced tea in the summer, Serafina, but it's cold now, I doubt Mrs. Lawton is drinking iced tea. Besides," he looked towards the fields and gardens that spread to the west, not east, where the stables she came from were. He looked down at her shoes.

She obviously had been in the stables or barns, the straw on her shoes betrayed her whereabouts. He wondered about the mud.

All around the area they were standing in was already hardened by the frigid nights.

"It's well past the prime season for mint, don't you think?" He stared at her, willing her to look at him.

She refused, speaking to her feet, "I...uh...that is why I do not have any, it is all dead now, you know..." Her voice grew quiet as her words dropped off again.

She had a slight accent, probably from living in such close quarters with her mother when she was growing up. Her mother spoke little English, she spoke only her native language of Spanish to Serafina.

"Listen, Serafina, I need for you to tell me-" suddenly the walkie-talkie at his shoulder started squawking. Metallic chatter burst from it.

Serafina couldn't understand a word, but Jarrett leaned his head in towards the machine and said a few words. All she caught was that he'd be right there. *Thank God*, she thought, *I can go*.

"You can go," Jarrett said her thoughts out loud. "I have an emergency to attend to. But I need to speak with you, I have some questions. I'll be back this evening. Be around- do you understand?"

He held one hand to the speaker at his shoulder, the other motioned to her as he spoke. He looked her squarely in the eye. He wasn't smiling, he was dead serious and he expected her to follow his orders.

Her lips pulled in, dark eyes lowered as she nodded.

He pushed his hat back down over his head and jogged to the house.

Serafina let out a big sigh and briskly followed him. She didn't see the window in the stable close behind her.

Chapter Twenty-Six

Hundreds of people crowded into the church for Langston Lawton's funeral. The family sat up front, Shanti sat with them.

Dressed completely in black with a large picture hat, Maeve sat stiffly, dry eyed and stoic as ever.

On one side of her, Chloe sobbed into a tissue, and Jaime sniffled on the other of Chloe. Dawn sat next to her brother, dabbing at her eyes with a Kleenex.

Camelia, drugged to the teeth, rested her fluffy blonde head on her husband's shoulder. Logan Thayne tried to keep the smile off his face. He was counting dollars in his head. One down, one to go, he was thinking.

Maeve would still have control of the estate and all of the money at this point, but she was getting on in years, it was only a matter of time. Camelia should be in control when Maeve passed on. He doubted the grandchildren would be given free reign yet. He wished he could get a peek at the damned will.

Next to Thayne Logan, Shanti cried quietly, trying to ignore his leg pressed against hers. He knew she couldn't move away, there was no room on the cramped pew.

Her eyes sought the casket at the front of the room, *sniff*, she already missed the dear old man. She wished she'd finished the painting before he died. Now he'll never get to see it. She now also wished that Summer could have stayed at least to support her through the funeral. But she was needed back home at the family restaurant. Life does go on, albeit jagged with grief.

The servants lined the seats directly behind the family. Because they lived in the house they were all considered family as well. Sobbing and sniffles could be heard all along the row.

Montgomery sat iron-faced, a few more grey hairs laced his temples. He stared unblinking at the coffin up front. A vein pounded hard in his temple.

Next to him, Serafina wriggled nervously. She held hands with Libby. Libby wasn't holding back her tears or her sobbing. Her loud cries rebounded off the high arches of the wood-beamed ceiling. Beside Libby, Daisy blew her red nose in a sodden tissue.

Serafina could hardly see through the steady stream of tears that coursed down her face. But she also couldn't stop from turning around periodically and looking towards the back of the church.

Standing near the oaken doors was Jarrett Chase. She felt like he was staring holes in the back of her head. She was unaware another pair of eyes watched her as well.

Jarrett leaned one shoulder against the wall by the front doors. He crossed his ankles, his hands held his big hat in front of him. Rainbows from the lovely stained glass windows streaked over his hair and uniform.

It was a struggle to hold back his own sorrow for the old man. He'd known Langston for a while now. Langston Lawton was a fine old gentleman. They'd played cards and chess together. Lately, he hadn't much time to visit. The last time he saw Langston was at the festival.

The old guy hinted he had something dire to tell the sheriff. Jarrett had tried to get him to spill his problem at the time, but Langston refused. He had kept looking all around, like he was going to get caught at something. He told Jarrett he would ring him up in the morning and make plans to meet.

Jarrett quelled the guilt that rose up his throat. If only he'd forced the old man to talk he might still be alive. If only. The marshal blinked back tears that threatened to well up in his blue-green eyes. It wouldn't look right if the sheriff was crying like a baby. The town looked to him to be strong and supportive, not whiny and weepy.

Buck up, he told himself. He stood a little straighter. He noticed Serafina kept turning her head and looking back at him. She looked as guilty as a hit and run driver with blood on her bumper.

Considering her ancestry, chances were good that she was Catholic. Maybe rosary beads held rosary pea seeds. He needed to speak to that black-haired little temptress, and soon. She obviously knows something.

The parson was also in the back of the room, opposite to Jarrett. He was in quiet yet serious conversation with Graham Duncan and Miguel Perez and two other Vaughn farmhands.

Although they all had their heads together, occasionally one of the five men would look up, his eyes would flick around the room then he would drop his head and rejoin the conversation.

The organ music playing softly in the background, suddenly grew louder.

The parson looked up and around. He patted both Graham and Miguel on their shoulders. Nodding to each of the men, he left the group and moved down the aisle to the front of the church.

The service was long. A great many people wanted to get up and say some words about one of the most beloved patriarchs of the community. None of the family members spoke.

As soon as the eulogy ended, the mourners rose and left the church to gather outside. Coats were buttoned up and hats pulled on against the ferocious wind and icy air that hit them the second they left the building.

Most of the men wouldn't dawdle at the cemetery. They were in the process of clearing their fields and adding nitrogen and potassium and other elements to the soil and cleaning out barns to prepare for next seasons growing. They needed to get all of the remaining crops in storage before the first real frost hit. Judging by the coldness of the air, that would be soon.

People visited with each other on their way to their cars. The Lawtons climbed into limousines parked in front of the church. The sounds of church bells ringing and organ music ushered the grieving people out to the parking lot.

It was a long drive to the cemetery, everything stretched for miles and miles in the rural county of Mooserock. People huddled together against the vicious cold and wind at the bottom of the small hill where Langston was being laid to rest.

Bagpipes cried in the distance, their wailing song carried by the wind over the hilltops and down the valleys, mourning the loss of a great man. The vicar spoke briefly amidst the crying and moaning group gathered around the coffin.

The hole was already dug out, the pile of dirt sitting, waiting for the coffin to be lowered in. As soon as the vicar finished, the Lawton women tossed single red roses in on top of the descending coffin. There wasn't a dry eye in the crowd.

The parson shook Maeve's hand and offered her meager comfort. She thanked him for the service. People came up to Maeve and her daughter and grandchildren to offer their sympathies.

Shanti stood off to the side, not knowing exactly where she fit in. She didn't want to be in the way. Something blocked the weak sun. She looked up. *Oh, the ruffian.*

The marshal was standing next to her, one hand in his pocket, the other holding his hat in respect for the ceremony. The wind ruffled his hair. Turquoise eyes seemed to drill right through her.

Shanti had her blue knit hat on and her hair tied back tightly. Still, wisps of blonde curls sailed around her face bouncing off round cheeks made rosy from the wind. Her eyes glowed from the cold air. She tucked gloved hands deep into her coat pockets.

"Miss Lane. You seem to be faring better. Is your sister still here?" Jarrett inquired politely. He put his hat back on, his head was freezing.

The swelling and darkness of Shanti's bruises had diminished quite a bit. Jarrett had stopped by frequently to question people, but he'd gotten nowhere. The house was in mourning and the servants never seemed to be available.

He'd particularly been looking for Serafina, but she was nowhere to be found. Today was the first time he'd even seen her since they met out in the fields. He'd returned that night as he'd promised, but Montgomery had asked that he come back later, the house was too distressed right then to be questioned.

"I'm healing well and quickly. My sister left last week. She realized it was useless to try to convince me to leave until my work is done. And she needs to be there to run the restaurant."

Shanti tried to hide her annoyance at the policeman. She knew he suspected her and that aggravated her. *The nerve of him*, she thought. She tried to smile politely, but not one normally good at hiding her feelings, especially if she disliked someone, her annoyance was clear on her face.

Jarrett smiled broadly at her. He knew she didn't like him and he found it amusing she was unable to disguise her feelings though she tried to. He wished he had the time to play around, tease her into spitting blue fire at him like she did the other night, but he had work to do.

He had more important things to do than hang around riling up pretty, vacuous alcoholic blondes.

Jarrett offered Shanti a big smile. "Well, I'm glad to hear you're getting back to normal. I've got to get to work, I'll see you again after I've questioned some other people."

"Gee thanks for keeping me in mind, Marshal." Shanti was uncharacteristically sarcastic. He made it sound as if everyone else was more important than her to question- well, really that was good she told herself, she was slipping down the list of suspects- and that's as it should be!

Still, for some reason she was annoyed that he hadn't more questions to ask her, like he couldn't wait to get away- she returned his smile, actually her lips pulled back into more of a grimace than a smile.

Jarrett chuckled to himself knowing he irritated her. He watched her stalk off.

She strode over to Chloe, the two young women hugged each other. Chloe was drying her eyes. She pointed to the limousine Maeve was getting into. They followed her into the big car.

Serafina was first on the policeman's list to question. He looked around. A group of the servants stood to the side and a bit back from the gravesite.

The servants huddled together, sharing their grief and fears. They didn't know if there would be any big changes now that the beloved master was gone. There would be no buffer between them and Maeve and Mrs. Li.

Just about everyone that worked at the Red Gem Farm was there. Except Serafina.

Damn. Jarrett should have grabbed her at the church. But that had seemed too intrusive. Now he'd have to drive to the estate.

His shoulder crackled. The voice coming from it advised there was an emergency and he was needed. He'll have to hit the mansion tomorrow.

Striding quickly across the hard ground, he could see his breath in puffs, it was getting colder.

Chapter Twenty-Seven

*H*ordes of people stopped by the mansion to pay their respect.

Maeve had food catered, she knew the help wouldn't feel like cooking and serving. And it was hardly calming to have a weeping Serafina and sniveling Libby serving guests. Most of the Lawtons upon arriving home had gone to their rooms to change.

Shanti did as well. She removed and hung up the black dress she'd worn to the funeral. She frowned at the dress hanging on a hanger in her closet. She'd never be able to wear that dress again without thinking of Mr. Lawton. Tears welled up. She didn't want to start crying all over again. Wiping her eyes, she went into the bathroom to wash her face.

Feeling refreshed after washing her face and hands, she changed into a white sweater and blue jeans and clipped a banana barrette in her hair. The barrette forced the golden locks to swirl in big curls down her back. She hurried downstairs to help with the visitors.

People came and went in bunches well into the evening. There was plenty of casseroles, pasta dishes, sandwiches, chips, cookies and cakes, and fruits and vegetables with dip to last for days. Coffee, tea, punch and sodas were set out.

After several hours of mingling and making small talk, Shanti was exhausted and had a mild headache from trying to make conversation with people she didn't know. She needed to sneak away for a few minutes and rest. The den was one of the rooms furthest to the back of the house; she headed there.

She slowly opened the door, it was dark inside. Slipping inside, she closed the door, breathing a sigh of relief. Remembering a lamp was over by the sofa, she trod carefully across the carpet lest she trip over a piece of furniture she couldn't see in the dark.

Plopping down on the couch, she sank luxuriously into the soft thick cushions. Ahhh, this is great, she thought. She leaned back, letting her head fall back against the fluffy pillows. Her eyes drifted closed.

She couldn't breathe! A heavy weight was pressing against her, suffocating her! Her eyes flew open- she looked right into the oily black eyes of Logan Thayne. He had climbed on top of her, his lips were mashing hers.

Thrashing her head from side-to-side, Shanti tried to get away from his mouth and scream- but he covered her mouth with one hand and tried to hold her head still with the other. Kicking up at him, Shanti bashed at him with her fists- but her small fists didn't faze him.

Thayne had been prowling the house knowing everyone would be in the great room with the guests. He saw his chance to explore a little without anyone seeing him. He wanted to get into the old man's desk and go through his papers before they were removed.

He figured the den would be the best place to start. Imagine his pleasant surprise when he opened the door and saw the blonde beauty snoozing alone on the couch. He couldn't resist. She wasn't family, so to whom would she complain? The old man, her protector was gone.

She wouldn't want to be thrown out, so he surmised she'd keep anything they did together to herself. What he hadn't reckoned on was her struggling as hard as she was. A little she-lion with tiny claws he was thinking as he grabbed her fists in one hand and held them.

"Come on little kitten, we both know what you want, and I'm here to give it to you. Let's make it pleasant, eh?" Holding her hands with one hand, he grabbed the back of her neck with the other to hold her still while he quickly pressed his lips against hers before she could cry out.

Shanti squirmed like mad- trying to yank her hands out from his grip, her frantic screams muffled against his fist. Thayne straddled her, then still holding both her hands with one of his, he held her arms up over her head. Still kissing her, he pushed her sweater up.

"What the hell is going on in here?! Dammit Logan! Stop it!" a furious voice exploded from the doorway.

Thayne pulled his head up immediately, but didn't let go of Shanti. As soon as he moved his head, Shanti screamed.

"Shh, you'll bring the whole house in here, you want that girlie?" Thayne quickly covered her mouth again with his hand.

Her blue eyes were wide in disbelief and anger, she tried to buck him off of her but he settled more of his weight on her so she couldn't move.

He'd pushed between her legs, but was now kneeling to address his infuriated wife.

Camelia stormed over to the couch, her hands on her hips. Madder than a wet hen she started screaming at her husband. "Damn you Logan, get the hell off of her! What are you doing- you son ofa-"

Logan let go of Shanti's hands to put a finger to his lips to hush his raging wife. "Be quiet Camelia, it's not what you think. She wanted-"

"What do you mean it's not what I think? What else can I think with you climbing all over that young girl like a dog in heat? Get off of her, get off before I scream this house down!"

Thayne scrambled off Shanti, quickly getting to his feet. He held his hands out to his wife, palms down.

"Okay, okay honey, shh, calm down now." He tried to quiet her.

She was fuming. It looked like steam was about to pour out her ears.

Behind him, Shanti sat up quickly, pulling her sweater down. She jumped to her feet and rushed from behind Thayne and towards the door.

Camelia crossed her arms in front of her heaving chest and stamped her foot several times. "You'd better explain fast, mister, I'm waiting."

Thayne smiled his most charismatic smile and rolled his arm around his furious wife. "Listen baby, I snuck in here to grab a quick snooze and that little floozy was all over me while I was sleeping. I woke up and she was on top of me, I swear!" he exclaimed at the look of disbelief on Camelia's face.

"What?! I never-" appalled, Shanti's denial burst from the safety of the doorway.

"Really honey, that little whore was crawling all over me. Just before you came in I had flipped her over and was trying to climb off and get away, she was holding on to me, she wouldn't let me go! Seriously, I swear baby..." Thayne tried to cajole the look of skepticism from his wife's face.

"I didn't-" Shanti started, but Camelia flounced over to her, a finger waving at the young artist's face.

"You stay away from my husband you- you slut! Keep your claws to yourself honey, or I'll get you thrown out of here so fast your head'll spin! Come on Logan." She grabbed her husband's hand and pulled him out the door.

They left so fast, Shanti just stood there with her mouth open. She snapped it shut. It's time she finished her picture and got out of this looney-toon house.

Running her fingers through her hair, she leaned over and turned off the light. Her banana clip lay forgotten, wedged in the couch cushions.

Chapter Twenty-Eight

*F*irst thing in the morning, Jarrett Chase drove up the winding driveway and parked his white Bronco at the top of the circle.

He left the truck and walked up the stone steps to the mansion. The report he received earlier confirmed the seed poisoning. The coroner said the reason Langston hadn't died immediately after eating the seeds was he'd apparently been ingesting minute amounts of herbicide poisons over a period of time.

That's why he'd been so sick for so long. He hadn't had enough to kill him, just slow him down and make him extremely ill. When he'd eaten the seeds that night of the festival they adversely reacted with the herbicides. The herbicides actually caused the rosary pea seeds to work more slowly through the evening.

However, they eventually did work, and Langston died. When Langston had first gotten sick six months ago, his quack of a doctor just assumed the old guy had picked up a stomach flu a while back and hadn't bothered to test for anything, not even a virus. He told Maeve that her husband would mend in time. His body just had to fight through the 'bug'.

The botanist Jarrett had consulted said it was unlikely that Langston had just happened to ingest the pea seeds that were not only not a native plant grown locally, but they had been unable to locate any plants or bushes anywhere. The autopsy revealed there was a bit of partially digested ribs, macaroni salad, green beans and the seeds in his gut.

It was concluded that someone had deliberately put the seeds in with the beans where they wouldn't have been easily noticed. Therefore, the coroner declared the death a homicide.

Jarrett rang the bell. Montgomery opened the door, one eyebrow arched quizzically.

"Hi Montgomery, I need to speak with Serafina." He moved to enter the house.

Montgomery stood still, he shook his head. "She's not here. No one has seen her since the funeral. We've called her mother at the Vaughns', but she hasn't heard from her either."

"What? Is this normal for her?" Jarrett asked, frowning. He wondered if people were covering for her, it was so difficult lately for him to be able to get to the maid.

Montgomery looked slightly concerned. He shook his head again. "Maybe for one of the other maids, but not this one. Some of the other girls stay over at their boyfriend's when they have a day off, but Serafina has never done that. No one thinks she even has a beau."

Jarrett raised an eyebrow in surprise. The voluptuous body of the young maid screamed sexuality. Though her exotic eyes reflected her innocence there was no way that girl wasn't involved with a man. Yes, the maid was sizzling hot, but for some reason a small blonde pushed away the image of the sensual Latina.

"Do you know who was the last to see her?" Jarrett pushed his hat back off his forehead. Short hairs sprang out when he moved his hat back. He set one boot on a step and crossed his arms.

"When we noticed she was missing, Mrs. Li questioned the staff regarding her disappearance. Apparently Serafina had never returned from the funeral, and no one saw how she left. In other words, we don't know if she left alone or with someone. She doesn't drive, you know, so she doesn't have a car."

"Obviously she left with someone. The cemetery is miles from here and it's damned cold out." Jarrett remembered the thin dress and high heels he'd seen her wearing at the funeral.

Outside at the gravesite she'd pulled on the little pink sweater that matched her shivering pink painted lips. She sure as hell didn't walk home. He drew his hat back down over his forehead and took his keys back out of his pockets.

"I'm going to issue a missing person report. We don't normally do that for an adult unless they've been missing for 48 hours, but because of Langston's death and all-"

"We were going to call you this morning, Marshal. We'd hoped she'd show up. We'll let you know if we hear anything."

"Okay. I'll be in touch." Jarrett waved and headed back to his car. He hopped in and turned it on.

The driveway was long and curved all the way to the street. When he reached the gate, Jarrett saw someone sitting out in front of the house on a chair. It was the little artist.

He stopped the car and got out. He strolled over to her.

She had seen his car coming down the drive, but she pretended not to see him coming towards her. She had set up her easel and was pulling out her paints. A canvas was on the easel.

Jarrett stopped just behind her and looked at the canvas. The painting was half done. "Wow," he said, awe in his voice. He stepped closer. "Wow," he repeated.

Shanti ignored him, continuing to set up her gear.

"You did that?" he asked foolishly, stunned. Her work was absolutely amazing. He couldn't believe a human being had such talent to make a picture come so alive.

The painting looked more like the house than the house itself did! He felt it could breathe.

Shanti glared at him as she squeezed some paint onto a tray, but she didn't answer his redundant question.

"Ahem. Um, I mean of course you did it…it's…incredible. It's so beautiful…it takes my breath away!" he babbled, searching for words to describe the feelings the painting elicited in him. He was at a loss for words.

Shanti shot him a brief smile of thanks at his praise then continued opening her paints.

Shifting his feet, Jarrett coughed then said, "Listen, uh, Miss Lane, have you seen or heard from Serafina?" He decided to change the subject before he made a total fool out of himself.

Shanti looked directly at him, her yellow brows drawn in a V. Concern was evident in her expression. She set her paints and brushes down.

"No, Mr. Chase, I haven't heard from her nor have I seen her since the funeral. We seemed to be growing close as friends, albeit I know she's a servant...I mean...I don't look down on her...or anything..." She felt stupid. He probably thinks she's such a snob! First a drunk and now a snob. Great.

He smiled at her. "It's okay, I understand what you're saying. You didn't grow up in the lap of luxury, you probably can't quite understand the space between the help and the family. Chloe's probably the closest to the servants, but still, she knows her place. And so, I'm afraid, does Serafina."

Shanti nodded. "What I was trying to say was, we were sort of close at first, but then something must have happened, because she withdrew from me. She wouldn't make eye contact, but I could tell she was staring at me sometimes when she didn't think I could see her. I don't know what I did..." her voice diminished, unsure of where she was going.

Jarrett put his foot up on one of the large boulders that was decorating the lawn and leaned forward, setting his forearm on his knee. He studied the artist's pretty face. Maybe there was more going on inside there than he originally thought.

"It's hard to know what sets someone off sometimes, especially with a girl like Serafina. She never has felt like she fit in anywhere because of her mother."

Shanti nodded in agreement with him. "Yes, Chloe told me her gloomy story."

"Anyway," Jarrett stood up, brushing off an imagined piece of dirt from his trousers. "If you see or hear from her, or remember anything that can help, please don't hesitate to call." He started to turn to walk away back to his car.

Shanti was smiling for real now. *Hey*, she was thinking, *he's not so bad after all*!

Then he turned back and called over his shoulder, "It's amazing what one can accomplish when one isn't drinking, isn't it?" He walked quickly up the lawn and jumped in his car.

"What? You- you-" Shanti sputtered angrily at him. But he was already driving away through the gate. "Darn that man!" she yelled, throwing her brush to the ground.

She would have been even madder if she could hear him laughing at her as he drove down the street lined with arching oak trees.

Chapter Twenty-Nine

The following weekend was Dawn's birthday.

A huge extravagant party seemed inappropriate since the house was in mourning, but Maeve didn't want Dawn's birthday to pass by without any acknowledgment. She told Dawn to invite just a few close friends for a quiet dinner party.

Her granddaughter hated the stuffiness of the formal dining room, so Maeve ordered heating units to be placed every five feet or so outside around the pool area.

The metal containers with electric heaters would warm people if they were within a few feet of them.

Excited, brightly dressed guests started arriving around seven. Montgomery showed the chattering young people to the patio off the rear of the house. Newly arriving guests headed immediately to the outside bar.

Dawn, dressed in a body hugging, iridescent green dress shimmered in the middle of a clutch of people most in their twenties. Colorful Chinese lanterns hanging in the trees reflected off the shiny stone patio.

Candles placed strategically in the grass and on small round tables offered diffused lighting. A three-piece band played music in one corner of the deck with a tiny dance floor partitioned directly in front of them. Only one couple was dancing so far.

Two long tables lined one side of the deck laden with food drew people looking for easy to eat finger food. Platters of chicken wings, shrimp with cocktail sauce, pigs-in-blankets, meatballs, cheeses, chips and raw veggies were rapidly disappearing.

Family members wandered out occasionally, but they knew Dawn wanted to be alone with her friends so they visited briefly then went back inside.

As more people arrived and drank, the noisier the patio became. Sound echoed off the pool making the non-enclosed area even louder. A small quiet dinner gathering was quickly turning into a loud boisterous party.

Fortunately, knowing Dawn and her propensity for inviting hordes of people to her fetes, Maeve had ensured there was plenty of food and drinks to feed an army. A big army.

The unheated aquamarine pool looked inviting, but it was too cold for swimming. Plastic swans and colored balloons in honor of Dawn floated lazily around on the water. Trees surrounding the area blocked the wind but did nothing to diminish the noise.

Dawn could be heard above the din of the crowd. By the sound of her voice, she was smashed. She had one arm around the neck of a young man with a lemon-drop martini clutched in her hand that dribbled drops of yellow vodka down his lapel.

She alternated between squealing and giggling. Every few minutes she would stand up straight and kiss the man she was clinging to. He happily obliged her with an arm around her waist and his own drink in his other hand.

He looked like he was enjoying the flame-haired birthday girl's attention. A group of young people gathered around Dawn and her flavor of the week. The sky had long gone dark and stars poked holes in the heavens.

Guests greedily stuffed themselves on food and drink then worked off the excess calories by frenetic dancing.

Dawn suddenly grabbed her suitor's hand and pulled him to the dance floor. Pressing her lithe body tightly against his, they danced, barely moving to the sultry song the band was now playing.

An occasional loud laugh could be heard from somewhere out in the dark spacious grounds from couples seeking shadowed privacy.

Growing amorous, Dawn's dance partner ran his palms up and down the curved sides of her waist, then against her back, pressing her harder against his starched white shirt.

The iridescent dress was like a second skin. Even in matching green four inch spiked high heels she had to stretch to meet his lips. Her hands clasped behind his neck, she suddenly tossed her head back- her hair fluttered around her head, she laughed, taunting and teasing the young man.

He was more than willing to take her up on the invitation in her emerald eyes. She reminded him of Hawaii; all different shades of green and blazing orange, like the lichen covered mossy mountains with peaks of fiery orange volcanoes erupting, spewing thrilling energy and fear.

He whispered in her ear, "Let's get a blanket and go outside to the back…"

Still holding the back of his neck with one hand so she could lean back and look up at him, she put a finger to his lips. Her mouth curved up in an enticing smile.

Abruptly, Dawn let go of him, stumbling backward. He whipped out an arm and grabbed her wrist, just catching her before she fell. Pulling her back up, he gripped her arms tightly above the elbows to keep her steady.

She twisted back and forth, shaking her head madly; her laugh was so loud and outrageous it pierced his ears. He stared at her with puzzled pale blue eyes, trying to laugh with her, but he couldn't figure out what the heck she was doing.

Suddenly, she twisted out of his hold and giggling, she danced away from him, twirling then skipping backwards. She tossed her empty glass into the pool, ignoring the small splash it made.

Still dancing small steps backwards, she beckoned to him with one blood red tipped finger. Dragging her long, tapered fingers through her hair, she drew the locks up onto the top of her tilted head, smiling sensuously as the curls tumbled back down springing all over her shoulders.

Her cat's eyes purred an invitation. Skimming her hands along the sides of her waist reminiscent of his earlier caresses, Dawn continued dancing backwards, calling to him to follow her.

"Look out!" the young man yelled, but not soon enough.

Dawn barely had time to glance over her shoulder before she accidentally stepped off the side of the pool and plunged into the freezing water. Sinking like a rock, she quickly submerged to the bottom.

Her shoes had flown off as soon as she hit the water. When her bare feet touched the tile at the bottom of the pool, she bent her knees and pushed off, popping out of the pool like a champagne cork, springing at least a foot into the air. She fell back into the pool with a splash and a screaming laugh.

"Dawn! Are you insane? Get the hell out of there!" Her bewildered young man stood at the edge of the pool yelling at her.

"Jeremy darling, come in and join me, the water is fabulously refreshing!" She kicked away from him when he kneeled down and reached for her. He stood back up and looked down at his black trousers, soaking wet at the knees.

"Damn you Dawn, I'm not coming in after you, it's freezing for crying out loud. C'mon, get out before you get sick!" Stepping away from the pool, he looked at her, shaking his head.

Other people were gathering around the pool, pointing and laughing at Dawn's drunken antics. She swam around the pool, laughing and waving at them.

Suddenly, her eyes widened, she looked strangely stricken. Her fingers went to her throat. Her laughing friends didn't realize she was in trouble.

The freezing water had finally gotten to her. Hypothermia quickly sapped her strength, she couldn't call for help. Slowly, she fell back on the water, her legs bobbed to the surface, her body floated listlessly.

The people around the pool thinking she was faking kept laughing and drinking. Her boyfriend, Jeremy, had turned away in disgust.

Dawn was starting to sink, just a few locks of her orange hair were still above water.

A body had separated from the crowd and ran to the pool.

Splash!

Graham Duncan had stopped by to wish Dawn a happy birthday. He'd cut himself a piece of a cake and the bartender gave him a beer. He took swigs at the beer as he meandered through the throng looking for Dawn when he saw the people gathered around the pool, pointing.

Some were screaming in terror now as they realized the birthday girl was really drowning! Graham didn't hesitate diving into the freezing water.

Swimming effortlessly, the foreman moved quickly to get to the unconscious girl. He reached through the freezing liquid and grabbed a handful of her swirling hair.

Pulling her to him, he put an arm strengthened from years of hard farm work around her ribs and swam to the edge of the pool.

By then, Montgomery was at the side. Shanti and Chloe were next to him, their faces reflecting dual horror. Graham held Dawn up in the water and Montgomery, with the girls' help, grabbed Dawn's freckled arms and pulled her out. Montgomery laid her down alongside the pool.

"Oh my gosh, Montgomery, save her!" Chloe screamed, kneeling down beside the prone girl.

All the color had drained out of Dawn's face, her freckles stood out like sprinkles of brown sand on a white sidewalk. She lay still, her wet hair splayed around her head, her sodden iridescent dress had become transparent.

Montgomery rolled her on her side and patted her back. A tiny pool of water poured out of her mouth, she started coughing. The butler rolled her back and helped her sit up. She was shivering uncontrollably.

"Miss Lane, run to my room in the bunkhouse, you know, in front of the stables." Shanti nodded as Graham pointed to the back yard. "Get some wool blankets. There's a bunch in the top of the closet."

Shanti wasn't exactly sure which room was Graham's. She did know that the farmhands lived in the bunkhouse and Graham had his own room separate from the hands', it was connected, but separate. She ran as fast as she could.

Out of breath by time she got to the bunkhouse, Shanti ran around the building, not sure where his door was. Then she recognized a pair of his work boots that he usually wore every day, outside a closed door.

She ran up to the door and turned the knob. It was unlocked. Pushing the door open, she stepped inside. It was dark, but with several windows letting in light it wasn't pitch black.

She felt the wall next to the door for a light-switch. Quickly spotting the closet, she hurried over and opened it. She immediately saw blankets stacked on a shelf. Pulling at them haphazardly, they all fell, first hitting her on the head then landing in heaps on the floor.

Darn. Feeling clumsy and worrying about Dawn freezing to death, she dropped to her knees to gather up the blankets. A glass was lying on the floor. The blankets must have knocked it off the desk that was next to the closet.

The room was sparse, containing only a bed, a table, four chairs and a desk, and a tiny bathroom. The desk was piled with papers and an overflowing ashtray. She'd never seen Graham smoking, but the hands played a lot of cards during slow times, they probably gathered in here for privacy.

Shanti reached for the glass. A pool of pinkish liquid was next to the glass. It looked like it was already drying. *Oh great, I've ruined the carpet*, she thought.

There was a towel on the chair at the desk. She grabbed the towel; it was damp from his shower, and tried to rub off the liquid. It only made it lighter, a pale bubblegum color.

"I'll have to tell Graham I've gotten a pink stain on his carpet, I hope he's not mad," Shanti muttered.

She gathered three blankets in her arms and tossed the remaining onto the chair. She was sure the foreman would understand her not taking the time to return them to the closet.

Quickly, she turned off the light and closed the door to the small room. She ran across the lawn back to the patio.

By the time she reached the pool, the lights were all turned up. The patio was so brightly lit in such severe contrast to the nighttime, Shanti had to squint as she approached the building.

Dawn was sitting in a chair, Graham was rubbing her hands and feet. Shanti hurried to him and handed him a blanket.

Taking the plaid wool blanket from her, he draped it around the shivering girl. She was still white as a sheet, her lips blue. Her hair was plastered in wet red ringlets to her head. The partygoers not knowing what to do shifted about restlessly.

Mrs. Li suddenly emerged from the house with a steaming cup of tea in her hand.

The guests stepped back and let the tiny woman through like the parting of the red sea. No one wanted to block the housekeeper's path. The entire town always gave her a wide birth. They didn't really believe she did voodoo, but it didn't hurt to be careful.

The tiny woman stood in front of Dawn and handed her the tea. Gratefully, Dawn took the china cup and saucer, immediately taking small sips of the hot brew.

Indiscernible oo's and ah's were heard, and quickly hushed, as Mrs. Li pulled a miniature metal box out of her pocket. Ignoring the sounds of the audience, she took out two pills and gave them to Dawn.

Without hesitation, Dawn popped them into her mouth. Over the years, Dawn had seen the Asian lady commit many miracles, instantly curing her and her brother and sister of childhood illnesses. She totally trusted the woman.

Within minutes, the color flowed back into her face and she sat up straighter. The oo's and ah's grew louder. The guests gawked in awe at the housekeeper, each stepping back a foot or two.

"I believe the birthday girl should go to bed now, you all must leave." A steely voice cut through the crowd. Maeve stood in the doorway.

Disappointed moans and groans ran through the crowd. After all, it was still relatively early, and Dawn hadn't even opened her presents yet. Maeve clapped her hands for their attention. Dawn stood up on wobbly legs, the blanket still wrapped around her.

"But Grandmother, I'm-" she started to say. Maeve silenced her with a look.

"Go to your room and dry your hair. Take a hot bath and then get into warm clothes," Maeve instructed her sodden granddaughter.

Dawn slapped the blanket tightly around her wet body. "Fine," she snapped, angry. She knew there was never any arguing with Maeve. Her orders were law.

The sopping redhead strode to front of the patio and addressed her friends.

"I'm sorry gang." She smiled weakly at more moans and groans her words brought. "But I guess we hafta call it a night. I want to thank you all for your attendance and well wishes, and-" she motioned to a table piled high with gifts. "I'll have to open your treasures tomorrow, when I'm all alone..." her sad smile turned pleadingly at her grandmother.

Maeve stood staunch. Tears and begging never had any impression on her. She did what she thought best and expected everyone else to do as she ordered without argument.

"You may have just a few of your girlfriends over tomorrow after luncheon, Dawn, to watch you open your presents. But-" the iron-haired old woman held up a hand at her granddaughter's quickly brightening smile.

"You will go to bed right now and stay there until lunch tomorrow, and only three of your friends may attend you when you open your gifts. Do you understand me?"

Slightly giving in was unusual for the matriarch, but Dawn wasn't giving her a chance to change her mind.

"Okay, I agree. Chloe, be a dear and help me get up the stairs," she said to her sister. Chloe immediately nodded her acquiescence and stepped to Dawn's side.

Satisfied as some of the guests started heading to the door, Maeve turned and went back inside the house.

Dawn waited until her grandmother was gone, then she turned back to her friends. "Hell of a party, huh guys?" She laughed heartily.

Holding her blanket brazenly wide open, she laughed at her friends' gasps of dismay- her dress was totally see-through. The chlorine in the water had stripped the material of its color. It looked as if Dawn was standing naked but for a few sequins and twinklings of material here and there.

Chloe put a hand to her mouth, shocked at her sister's total lack of modesty.

Graham chuckled, shaking his head. Montgomery swiftly stood in front of the young woman, dropping a second blanket over her completely covering her nudity.

"Get inside now, Miss Dawn, goodnight everyone," Montgomery ordered the girl, gently pushing her into the house.

Her laughter reverberated out the door.

Montgomery and Chloe followed her inside.

Mrs. Li handled herding the guests out and calling Libby and Daisy to come out and clean up the patio.

Graham left through the patio striding off in the dark towards the direction of the bunkhouse.

Flabbergasted at the shocking events of the evening, Shanti shook her head and hurried to her own room.

Chapter Thirty

In the shadow of the night, Jarrett Chase drove his white Bronco through the thousands of acres of woods.

The uneven rocky ground jostled him but he kept the truck on the winding path. He tried to keep his head down to prevent it from hitting the roof every time he ran over a large rock, but never took his eyes off the half-hidden trail.

Horses and wild animals, not cars had beaten down the trail. Finally he left the woods and entered open fields. The moon silvery bright in a cloudless sky was enough light for him to see his way.

The marshal drove slowly over the rough ground keeping a watch out for any flickering light that might betray poachers. The crop fields eventually turned into pastures, the brown grass two or three feet high made viewing more difficult.

Through his open window, Jarrett could hear a plane in the distance. He came to a stop in a patch of trees and stuck his head out of the window. He could hear the plane, but he couldn't yet see it.

Reaching behind his seat, he felt around on the floor. Recognizing the feel of his binoculars, he grabbed the glasses, turned off the engine and got out of the truck. He walked around to the front of the truck, stopped, and leaning back against the warm engine he drew the field glasses up to his eyes.

At first scanning the sky, he saw nothing. But then peripherally, something caught his eye. He moved away from the truck. Bringing the glasses lower, he swept them across the pasture until-

There. A flicker of light. Hundreds of yards away, he could see what was maybe a flashlight blinking in the dark. Peering through the glasses he looked for the location of the light.

Because of the darkness and distance, Jarrett couldn't make out anything except a few tiny flashes of light. *Huh.* Those weren't just random flickers, he suddenly realized, they were signals.

He heard the plane returning. Stepping back in the shadows of the trees, he put the glasses back to his eyes and searched the sky. He spotted it.

A small private plane emerged from the darkness, it was circling the area. It slowed over the flashing light hovering momentarily, then a tiny parachute tied to a package hurled out the door and the plane roared off, quickly disappearing in the horizon.

The beacon of light on the ground suddenly went out.

Smugglers or drug runners Jarrett thought. He tossed the binoculars onto the passenger seat and quickly climbed in. Without taking his eyes off of where he saw the signal light, he turned on the truck, slammed it into gear and tore out of the patch of trees and through the pasture.

He drove as fast as possible over the bumpy tall grass. His head banged against the roof every time he ran over a hidden rock or dipped in an unseen hole. His body bounced in the seat, but clutching the wheel tightly he never veered from his course.

The light was long gone before he reached the other side of the pasture. It was hard to tell where the light had been. He could hear the river. He was probably five or so miles from the Lawton farm.

The land here was extremely uneven and rocky and covered with scrub bushes. He doubted any of the Lawtons ventured in the area. He knew Chloe usually went the direction of the covered bridge because she preferred the forests to the pastures.

What was that? He thought he saw a light!

He took off his hat and set it on the seat next to him. Reaching blindly for the glasses again, he put them to his eyes while trying to hold the truck as steady as possible.

There. He could see people in the dark. Three or four it looked like. They were putting several kayaks into the river, a difficult feat in the rushing waters.

"They've got to be insane," Jarrett muttered. He knew he was too far away, they'd be gone before he could get to them. He set the binoculars down and continued driving towards the river, thinking hard.

Throughout the past few years, the young sheriff had driven all around the county, including these woods and pastures. He knew where every road and trail led and also where the river curved and wound, pulsating and charging like a race horse to the north.

Suddenly, he yanked the wheel hard, turning the truck away from the men with the kayaks and back towards the woods. He knew the clearing along the river where the smugglers were wouldn't last. The river at some points had very steep sides. He wouldn't be able to drive alongside it.

But he did know where the river hit a huge turn. The water narrowed and slowed down greatly at that point. If he could outrun the kayakers he might have a chance to catch them. He reached the cover of the woods quickly.

Without slowing down, he searched for the trail that was a hundred or so yards from the river but basically ran parallel to it. Within seconds he found it.

Jarrett drove as fast as the truck would allow- bumping erratically all over the jagged rough-hewn path his body jarred with every rock, hole and tree stump he ran over.

He hurtled through the thick woods scraping trees and boulders yet never slowing. He was in a race and he knew he had only a slight chance of getting to the bend before the kayaks did.

Twenty minutes later of hard, body beating driving, Jarrett could finally see the woods were thinning. He knew in only moments he'd exit the forest and be out in the open again without the protection of the trees to hide him.

He'd have to take the chance of the men not being able to hear or see his white truck approaching in the dark. *Fat chance of that*, he thought. But he wasn't a man to back down from his duty, even as dangerous as this most certainly was.

He left the safety of the forest behind and ventured across the open fields aiming for the bend in the river. He had no way of knowing if the kayakers had already gone by or not.

There was a small shed near the river. It was built there long ago for the farmhands when they were out all day repairing fences, searching for runaway horses, or just looking for a private place to fish.

Only about six feet by twelve, there was no food, electric, or running water in it. It stood out too much like a sore thumb for him to hide in, but he thought he should check it out and make sure no one else was hiding in it to jump out and surprise him.

At least he could hide his truck behind the rotting old wood, then the smugglers wouldn't be able to see the vehicle from the river.

Jarrett drove the Bronco more slowly now, veering off the path and through the tall grass again, heading for the shed. It stood in the dark veil of night looming innocuously like an enormous, ancient tree stump.

He pulled up behind it and killed the engine. Sitting perfectly still, he listened. Hearing only familiar sounds of the night, a hoot owl, the rustle of a startled hare moving away in the grass, he climbed quietly out of the Bronco.

Creeping stealthily around the shed, he made his way to the front. He opened the door, it creaked loudly like a crying child in the still of the night. He stuck his head in and looked around.

Empty except for one broken chair and a table with mismatched legs.

Closing the door to keep the animals out, Jarrett moved quietly around the shed where he could easily see the river. It ran slightly uphill here causing it to slow quite a bit. That's what made it a particularly good spot to fish.

The grass was stomped down all around the bank of the river. Someone must have been here earlier fishing. Jarrett stood under the awning of the shed, his hands on his slim hips and waited.

He hadn't waited five minutes when he heard something. Voices. Voices coming down the river.

Gotcha. They'd have to slow to almost stopping to circumvent the steep turn of the river. The water was shallow here as well as slower.

Jarrett pulled his gun out of his holster and ran towards the bank of the river. He leaned over as he ran, trying to keep hidden in the tall grass.

He'd left his hat in the car, he had no desire to be any bigger a target than he already was. Well over 6' with broad shoulders, he wouldn't be hard to miss.

The kayaks pulled up to bank. It appeared that the kayaks were stopping and the occupants were going to get out.

Seeing his chance, Jarrett stopped a few feet from the river and held his arms straight out with the gun pointing at the kayaks.

Just as he opened his mouth to call out to the men, something hit him hard in the back of the head.

And the world went black.

Chapter Thirty-One

He wasn't totally unconscious when he landed facedown, but almost.

Hazily, Jarrett heard a voice from behind as he lay flat on the cold hard ground.

"Dammit you idiots, didn't you see the ranger following you in the woods?" The voice was gruff and belligerent.

Jarrett could barely make out other mumbling voices further away. The others were exiting the kayaks. He could hear the small boats scraping against the riverbank as they were pulled up and out of the water.

His head was swimming, he tried to move but couldn't.

"Listen, don't yell at us, it's dark for cryin' out loud. Who would expect some hero to be out wandering around this far in the woods at night anyway? If I hadn't spotted his truck we'd all be under arrest right now."

Jarrett could hear numerous footsteps approaching him. He couldn't move and when he tried to open his eyes, only blackness filled them. One of them gave him a savage kick in the side, he grunted.

"Well, he ain't dead. We gonna shoot him?" a heavily accented voice sounded near his head.

Jarrett could feel, and smell, the man that had knelt next to him. The man gave him a push then tried to pry open one of

Jarrett's eyes. He grabbed a handful of Jarrett's hair and pulled his head up.

The marshal couldn't hold back a groan. The man abruptly let go and Jarrett's head bumped back on the hard ground.

"I'll shoot him Da-"

"No names, you idiot, you know that. Leave 'im alone, gunshots can be heard for miles. Get the boats unloaded. You," the speaker said, "hold a gun on 'im while we clear the boats. We'll take 'im to the well, dump 'im there."

Jarrett heard chuckles as the footsteps receded. He heard the men making jokes about the well keeping their secrets as they moved away from him. Gingerly moving his head, he tried again to open his eyes. He got another vicious kick in the side for his trouble.

"Don't move, Ranger. I'd shoot ya as soon as look at ya," the kicker warned.

Jarrett knew he'd have to bide his time and wait for his brain to clear and strength to return before attempting an escape. Right now, he couldn't see and he had less strength than a newborn.

He must have passed out, because what seemed like only seconds, the men returned.

"He try anything?" an authoritative voice sounded from a few feet away. Jarrett assumed he must be the one in charge.

"Nah. He's been out the whole time you was gone." The man gave Jarrett several more harsh kicks to the ribs.

The marshal stifled a groan, keeping his eyes closed. His only chance, he thought, was if he pretended to be unconscious and wait for an opportunity to escape. He knew the chance of overpowering four or five armed men while injured would be close to impossible.

"All right. I got the product. You two, carry the ranger over to the well and get rid of him. Hit him or knife him if he wakes up. I don't want no gunshots telling our whereabouts. We don't need no one tracing us by fingerprints on bullets or some crap like that neither. We'll meet ya back at the warehouse."

One man grabbed Jarrett's arms and another his legs. They half carried, half dragged him some distance before he was suddenly dropped.

He could hear boots thumping on a hard surface. Some of the men must be getting back into the kayaks. The boats scraped back down the bank and the water splashed as they walked through the river, pulling the boats back into the water.

The sound of the splashing from the oars diminished as they moved away, down the river.

"Let's screw with 'em, Donny. When're we ever gonna have a chance to mess with a cop again, huh?" The eager voice was directly over Jarrett.

The young marshal winced when he received several brutally sadistic kicks to his legs and side. Then a swift kick to his chest knocked the air out of him. He hoped his painful ribs were only bruised, not broken.

"Cut it out, already. And quit sayin' my name, jackass. Let's just stick a blade in him then dump him and go. It's cold and dark and I wanna go. C'mon, help me."

Jarrett knew they were about to grab him- this was probably going to be his only chance.

Suddenly, the lawman rolled, and kept rolling. The two men were so surprised they didn't move.

When he was ten feet from the felons, Jarrett jumped to his feet and ran half bent over towards the woods, his hand was clamped to his side to keep his ribs together, something oozed in his eyes, blurring his vision.

"Don't!" One man shoved the other man's arm down as he raised it to shoot the fleeing officer. "He's hurt bad, we can catch him, c'mon." The shooter reluctantly stuffed the gun into his belt and the two ran after Jarrett.

The criminals underestimated the marshal. He knew the woods, they didn't. He made his way quickly to a small bank, and gritting his teeth so he wouldn't involuntarily cry out in pain, he jumped over a fallen tree limb and rolled down the bank.

At the bottom, he scurried on his hands and knees to a huge gnarly tree and squeezed into a hollow carved out at the bottom. Thick grass and the steep bank hid him pretty well.

He sat for a second, trying to quietly catch his breath, he could hear the two men running back and forth at the top of the bank calling to each other. There was no way they could find him in the dark.

He wanted to go after them but knew it would be foolish. They'd taken his gun, and he was beaten too badly for a physical fight with two psychopathic burly men. When in normal good form, the two wouldn't get a solid hit at him before he took them both down, but right now, he could barely suck in a scant breath or stand for more than a second.

Jarrett waited for an hour. He was sure the men had long since gone. He hadn't heard their voices in quite some time. And by the whiny sounds of them, they wouldn't be sticking around in the dark forest for long. He'd heard one of the thugs ask about bears.

Bruised and battered, the lawman squeezed out of the tree and slowly and painfully stood up. There wasn't one inch of him that didn't ache or hurt.

"Well," he muttered, "I can certainly empathize with blondie now." He was sure he felt the same way Shanti had when he'd found her at the bottom of the stairs.

He rubbed the ooze out of his eyes and looked at his hands. They were covered in blood. He wiped them on his filthy trousers already covered with dirt and blood and leaves.

Agonizingly slowly, he climbed, sometimes on all fours, back up the bank. He held on to grass and rocks to keep from falling back down the hill. His hands were scraped and bloodied.

When he finally reached the top, his legs were shaking. It was a long way back to his truck. He prayed they'd left it there untouched.

Another hour of slow, step-by-step tortured walking, he made it back to the shed. Unbelievably, the Bronco stood where he left it, the keys were still under the front seat. His wallet was in the glove box, the thugs had taken his gun and trashed his shoulder radio.

Cautiously, he looked around, but he knew the felons were gone. He opened the door and gingerly climbed in.

He laid his head gently on his steering wheel, trying to regain his strength. The stabbing pain in the back of his head where he'd been hit was excruciating and throbbing. It felt like darts were being thrown at his bare skull.

He reached for the car radio and put it to his ear. It was working. He called in to his dispatch and told them what happened. He told the dispatcher to have as many men as possible in cars and in boats, scour the area to try to find the smugglers.

Unfortunately, he knew it would be to no avail, they were long gone. And, since he never saw any of their faces he would be unable to describe them.

Before he hung up he asked the dispatcher to contact one of his deputies to meet him at the hospital.

Chapter Thirty-Two

Shanti was waiting for Maeve in the car. Montgomery was driving them to Catherine Scott's house for tea.

Normally Serafina would go with Maeve to carry back the fresh herbs for the cook, but the maid was still missing. No one, including her mother, had seen her since the funeral.

The police questioned everyone in the household but no one could even recall seeing her leave the cemetery. They searched her room, her clothes and personal things were there untouched.

Officers checked the hospital and morgue, but Serafina had simply vanished without a trace.

One theory was that somehow she'd fallen into the 'River of No Return' and her body had washed all the way to the main branch of the Snake River. It could travel all the way out of Idaho and to another state before someone found it, if it was ever found.

Yet, Libby and Daisy, her two closest friends, said since Serafina couldn't swim she never went anywhere near the river, or even the pool at the house.

When she was required to serve at pool parties she was always careful to steer clear of the sparkling water. Aware of her fear, Libby usually took care of the guests and family members that sat closest to the pool.

The servants and field hands of all of the mansions in the Brimstone Glen were whispering about the mysterious disappearance of the beautiful young woman.

The other maids of wealthy townsfolk made up fantasy stories that Serafina had met a rich, handsome young prince and he secretly swept her away to his kingdom in another land. They said this more to allay their own fears than an actual belief in their fairy tales.

Catherine Scott didn't live in a huge mansion, but her house was still pretty big. She was waiting at the front door herself for her guests. As soon as Maeve and Shanti arrived she ushered them into her parlor. Montgomery left, he would return in a couple of hours to bring them home.

Catherine had tea and cookies waiting for them in the pink and gold room. Just about every item that had material on it was covered in tiny flowers. Even the paintings on the walls were of flora.

Maeve and Shanti sank deeply into the plump cushions of the couch. Catherine seated herself in a chair opposite the pair.

Their hostess was elderly yet she still moved easily. After greeting her guests, she reached for the teapot covered in tiny yellow roses and poured them each a cup of tea. Sugar, lemon and cream were on the silver tray that was on the coffee table in front of the couch.

"Please ladies," the elderly woman said, "help yourselves to the cookies." She pointed a heavily age-spotted hand at the plate of tasty looking mixed assortment of cookies on the coffee table.

Maeve and Shanti both picked up a china plate and set a cookie on them. Shanti chose a chocolate chip and Maeve picked up a powdered lemon and a sugar cookie.

"How are you fairing, Maeve?" The old woman smiled gently at her friend. Pure white hair pouffed in a cloud around her head. Watery blue eyes shone kindly from behind round glasses.

Maeve stirred her tea, setting the spoon on the saucer. She took a sip and set the cup down. "Oh, Catherine, it's difficult, you know, but…we're getting along." She sighed, missing Langston.

"The hardest part is harvest time, and that's the time of the year he loved the best. Even at his advanced age, he was right out there with the hands helping, instructing with tilling the land-" there was a catch in her voice, she took a sip of tea.

"I miss him terribly, Catherine." Maeve reached for her purse on the couch next to her, pulled out a tissue and dabbed at her eyes.

Shanti sat still, not knowing what to do. Maeve wasn't the kind you could pat on the shoulder and murmur sympathetic words to.

"I know, dear. When Stephen passed, I was beside myself for a long time, you remember." She smiled at her friend. "You were here with me constantly trying to raise my spirits. You really helped me tremendously, you know."

Maeve put her tissue back in purse and set it down next to her. She smiled back at Catherine. "That's what friends are for, Catherine, to help us through the rough times. The harvesting is still going on, it'll be better when it's completely over. Then there'll be Christmas to get through…" she sighed again.

Catherine stood up. "Let's go into the nursery, dear, the lovely flowers always raise one's spirits. Come along. You'll love my greenhouse, Miss Lane. I have a huge variety of flowers. Do you like orchids?"

Shanti set down her empty teacup and stood up. She smiled at the perky old lady. "I love flowers, Mrs. Scott. I have looked forward to seeing your greenhouse ever since you told me about it at the harvest festival. Chloe says your orchids are absolutely spectacular. She's quite jealous, you know, she told me she wishes she could have a greenhouse too."

Shanti slid a look in Maeve's direction. The older woman was nibbling on a sugar cookie. She didn't look at Shanti.

"Anyway," Shanti looked back at her hostess. "I can't wait to see your exotic plants and flowers."

Catherine waited for Maeve to join them, then she led the two women through her house, stopping occasionally so she could show Shanti a room or two.

Most of the rooms in the house were decorated in Victorian style. Everything was neat as a pin. Shanti looked for servants, she knew the old lady had no one living with her, but she didn't see anyone else as they made their way through the big house and out to the greenhouse.

Montgomery arrived precisely two hours later and drove Maeve and Shanti home. The two women sat in the back of the blue Rolls chatting contentedly about their hostess and pleasant visit. The butler let the ladies out at the front door then left to put the car in the garage.

"I'd really love to go for a horseback ride before lunch, Mrs. Lawton, do you think that would be okay?" Shanti asked as they entered the house.

"Certainly dear, of course you may. You needn't ask permission. However," Maeve hesitated.

"I believe Chloe is down at the public library today, I think that's where she said she was going at breakfast. And when that girl gets around books, well, she'll be there all day. So, I don't know how well you know your way around the land. I'd hate for you to get lost..."

Shanti headed for the stairs to change into jeans and a flannel shirt. "Oh don't worry, Mrs. Lawton, if I stay on this side of the river I don't think I'll have a problem. I'll stay near the open fields, away from the woods."

Maeve smiled at the young woman going up the stairs, obviously eager to get on a horse.

"Fine then, dear. Have fun, but be careful. Just tell Graham or a farmhand which horse you want, they'll saddle it for you."

The elderly lady went in the direction of the kitchen to speak with Mrs. Li.

Shanti spotted Graham Duncan walking by one of the windows. She hurried to the front door to catch the foreman.

******

In the hospital, the doctor checked to make sure Jarrett didn't have a concussion. The nurses had cleaned him up, wiping away the mud and blood.

The doctor stitched up some of the deeper cuts and bandaged his ribs. Thankfully, his ribs were only badly bruised, not broken. After the doctor gave him a couple of shots of tetanus and penicillin he gave Jarrett a few instructions such as complete rest for at least a week then he left the room.

As soon as the doctor left, Jarrett opened the side table drawer next to the bed and pulled out his cell phone. He called one of his deputies to come and meet with him.

When Jarrett first made his way to the hospital several of his officers had shown up, but the doctor had run them off telling them he needed care and rest.

Within twenty minutes, Deputy Bill Johnson opened the door to the hospital room slowly, and stuck his head in.

Jarrett was still sitting on the side of the bed wearing a green hospital gown. He was writing in the small notebook he always carried with him. Thankfully the thugs hadn't taken the time to search his truck or worse, take or destroy it.

He looked up when he heard the door open and saw the deputy peering at him. "Come in, Bill." Jarrett motioned for the officer to come into the room.

Deputy Johnson cautiously approached his boss. "Man, Rett, you look like the devil rode over you on his motorcycle with spiked wheels."

Jarrett hadn't looked in a mirror yet. He didn't need to. He could see and feel his arms and legs. They looked bad enough, scraped and badly bruised, he had no desire to see what damage had been done to his face.

"I know, Bill, it isn't as bad as it looks. I won't be winning any beauty contests for a while, but I'll heal. Come in and sit down, I have some stuff to tell you." He pointed to a chair by the window.

The deputy obliged him and went to the chair, picked it up and brought it to Jarrett's bedside. A brawny young man, Bill sat down straddling the chair. Dragging his fingers through his short sandy hair, he grimly eyed Jarrett's wounds.

Resting his forearms on the back of the chair, he leaned over and sat his jaw on an arm. Deputy Johnson couldn't take his eyes off his boss' face. Besides being beaten pretty savagely, rolling down the rocky bank hadn't helped.

"We're gonna catch those sons of bitches, Rett, and I'll take care of them. I can't believe what those bastar-" the young officer angrily spat out his words. Jarrett Chase was a greatly respected and admired boss and friend, and Bill Johnson wanted to avenge him.

"All in good time, Bill," Jarrett cut him off. "But right now we have to do some figuring. We need to find out as much about that little plane as we can. Where it came from, who owns it, where it was going, etc."

"What about those kayaks you told dispatch about? Can we trace them do ya think?" the deputy asked.

Jarrett shook his head. "I doubt it, Bill. Unless they purchased them around here, chances of us tying them to any of the smugglers will be minuscule."

"Hey, Boss, do you think these smugglers had anything to do with old man Lawton's murder?" Bill tipped his hat back, his sandy-colored eyebrows arched over blue eyes.

With his legs still hanging over the side of the bed, Jarrett leaned his torso against two pillows that were stacked against the bed frame and sighed heavily. He shrugged.

"I don't know Bill, maybe. We don't get that much major crime here, it would be pretty coincidental." His eyes drifted closed.

"Boss?" The deputy said quietly.

Jarrett didn't respond, he was asleep.

Bill Johnson stood up. He picked up Jarrett's legs and swung them onto the bed, then he covered the marshal with a blanket. He tiptoed out the door.

Stuffed full of painkillers and antibiotics, Jarrett slept for most of the afternoon.

He was sitting up eating a hamburger and fries one of his men had smuggled in when he heard a soft knock at the door.

Before he could call out for the person to come in, the door opened. The spitting image of the maid, Serafina, except about 15 years older was standing in the doorway.

"Mrs. Vesela, please come in." Jarrett set down his half eaten burger and motioned to the woman to join him.

She took a few steps towards the bed, her head was down. She stared shyly at the floor. She held a hat and mittens in her hands, her hair, as blackly lustrous as her daughter's was pinned on top of her head. She raised exotic sad eyes to the marshal.

"Please sit down, Mrs. Vesela," his voice kind, he pointed to the chair by the bed.

The maid shook her head. "No, thank you, sir, I be a minute," she said in broken English. She stood closer to him. Her eyes filled with tears. "Please sir, please find my Serafina..." she pleaded breathlessly. Her palms were pressed together, praying for him to help her.

Jarrett swung his legs to the side of the bed and slowly stood up. He was a little dizzy. He waited for his head to clear then he stood up. Gently, he set a hand on her shoulder.

The tears broke loose and ran down her face.

"I'm sorry, Mrs. Vesela, we're looking everywhere for her, we just don't-" he broke off. His hand went to his head. Frowning, he scratched the top of his head, trying to remember something one of the thugs that beat him said.

What the heck was it...*the well gives up it's- no, the well keeps their secrets, that's it, not **one** secret, meaning **his** body, but secrets, meaning more than one - oh my God.*

He moved as fast as he could to the closet. Yanking the door open, he started to take his clothes out.

"Mr. Marshal?" the maid's voice was timid.

He'd forgotten her. He turned slowly and looked at her.

She was puzzled by his behavior, but the sadness still shrouded her eyes.

His face fell, anguish dug lines around his eyes and mouth. He didn't know what or how much to tell the woman. Even she must realize at this point her daughter has been missing too long, chances of her being alive were thinner than an eyelash on a flea.

"I'm sorry, Mrs. Vesela, I've just, uh, thought of something I need to do. I've ah, got to go. I'll check with you later, okay?"

He pulled out the shirt and pants that Bill Johnson had brought him. Bill must have cleaned his boots for him too because they were on the floor of the closet, all black and shiny. Man deserved a raise.

"You, um, need to excuse me now, all right?" He paused with his clothes in his hands.

"Oh." She nodded. "You call later, me?" she asked quietly, her dark eyes swimming with tears.

Jarrett set his clothes on the bed then walked back over to her. He put a large hand on her shoulder again. "I won't forget you, don't worry." He smiled down at her and patted her shoulder.

"*Gracias*, Mr. Marshal." She tried to smile back at him, except her mouth turned into a sad crooked line instead of curving upwards. She left the room so he could get dressed.

As soon as he reached his car, Jarrett called dispatch and told them to have a couple of deputies meet him out by the old shed near the river. Everyone knew about the shed.

He drove as quickly as he could without jarring and jolting his healing body too much. It took him 45 minutes to get there. At two o'clock, the sun was high in the air.

Jarrett found the shed then drove another ½ mile to the south. He parked the truck, got out and went around to the back of the vehicle. Opening up the rear door, he pulled out a toolbox. Lifting the lid, he pushed some tools around until he found what he was looking for. A flashlight.

Leaving the box open, he stuck the flashlight in his back pocket and started walking. A few dozen feet from the truck he stopped and looked down at the hole in the ground. The old well.

A hundred years ago the Lawtons' ancestors had built their first homestead out here and they had dug out the well. No one has used it for years. There were some planks laid across it, old leaves and dirt covered the planks.

Jarrett stared down at the planks. At least the last time he remembered seeing the well the planks were covered with dirt and leaves. But they weren't now.

He bent over ignoring the pain in his ribs and pushed the planks one at a time off the opening of the well. When he removed the last plank he got down and lay on his stomach next to the well then pulled the flashlight out of his back pocket.

He shuffled his body forward on his elbows, moving as close to the opening as he could get.

Flipping the flashlight on, he peered down into the deep darkness. Aiming the light at the brick wall he followed it all the way to the bottom.

There. Damn.

Groaning out loud, he pulled his head out of the opening and rolled over on his back. He wiped his eyes with the heels of his palms.

"Marshal?"

He opened his eyes.

Two of his deputies were standing next to him, blocking the sun. He sat up. Then, slowly, with great effort he stood. His legs weren't as shaky as he had expected. His head down, he handed the flashlight to one of the men.

He said flatly, "The missing maid is in the well," and started to walk back to his truck. Then he stopped and turned back to the deputies. "I'm going to go call the fire department to get her out."

Jarrett sat in his truck while he waited for the fire truck to arrive. When he saw the red truck coming across the field he got out and went back over to where his men were standing near the well.

They had each looked down the well then sat down next to it without saying a word.

The firefighters tied a rope to a basket and another to one of the men and lowered him into the well. When he got to the bottom, he wrapped the body in a sheet then pulled it from the shallow dank water into the basket and secured it.

A somber group of men pulled the dead girl out of the well. She'd been there a couple of weeks and looked pretty bad. She'd been in about a foot of water and her body was partially decomposed. And the bugs were there.

She was quite unrecognizable. Would need DNA or prints to verify her identity.

The men slipped her in a body bag as fast as they could.

Jarrett followed the firetruck out of the fields and into the city. At the police station, he headed inside to make his report. Several deputies interrupted him with questions as he worked.

It was after he took a dinner break he received a call from the coroner, Jarrett made his way to the morgue where he went in search of the coroner.

The coroner, Jim Black, pushed his visor up and pulled off his rubber gloves. The gloves made snapping sounds as he removed them. They'd put a rush on the maid's autopsy.

The air smelled of blood, bleach and metal. It was a cold sterile room. The body was on a table. One hand hung over the edge. Her nails were broken, but what was left of them was still painted a dark pink.

"Very preliminary, Rett, her neck was broken. I'm not positive yet, but I think she's been in the well since she's been missing. I found this-" He reached over to a table and picked up an item with some tweezers. "Clutched tightly in one hand. She must have pulled it off the guy as he was killing her." He held the item out for Jarrett's inspection. It was a button.

Jarrett studied the button. "Can you bag it, Jim? Of course it needs go to forensics."

"Sure." The coroner went to a drawer and pulled out a small plastic bag and dropped the button in it. He came back over to Jarrett and handed the button to him. Jarrett shoved it into a pocket.

"Okay, well thanks Jim, I guess that's all I need for now. Call me with the rest of your results, all right?" He headed for the door.

The coroner nodded and turned back to the body of the once beautiful, now unrecognizable dead girl.

With the white uniform and work shoes and long black hair, Jarrett was pretty sure it was Serafina, but Jim Black will check her teeth or prints for full identification.

When he climbed in his car, Jarrett called dispatch to have them find out where Serafina's mother was. He didn't want her to hear the inevitable news over the radio.

Chapter Thirty-Three

*T*he dispatch told Jarrett he could find Mrs. Vesela at Red Gem Farm. He drove straight there. It was about six o'clock, he hoped the family wasn't eating dinner.

Montgomery opened the door to his knock. He had been there waiting for the marshal. Jarrett had called while on his way.

"Come in, Marshal. Please wait in the drawing room, I'll get Mrs. Vesela," Montgomery said, his tone tight and formal. Then he stopped and looked at the officer. His face fell.

"You found her." It was more of a statement than a question.

His lips pressed, Jarrett nodded wordlessly.

The butler sighed, running a suddenly shaking hand through his greying hair. Without saying another word he left to find Serafina's mother.

Mrs. Vesela's wail was so loud it brought half the household into the small room.

When Maeve, Chloe, Dawn and Mrs. Li arrived, the maid had her face buried in the sheriff's broad chest and was sobbing.

Jarrett patted her head softly, there was nothing he could say to ease a mother's pain of finding out she would never see her only child again.

Not working today, Mrs. Vesela had been waiting at the Lawtons' house. They'd heard word that something had happened regarding the missing girl.

The women hovered uncertainly in the doorway. Chloe's hands were in front of her mouth. Dawn stood chewing on a nail, and Mrs. Li turned quickly and left.

Maeve entered the room, her head high and her back rigid. "Marshal?" She spoke quietly, one brow rose quizzically, but she already knew. Mrs. Vesela's wail was that of a mother learning her child was dead.

Jarrett looked over the maid's head to Maeve. The coroner had called him just as he was parking with the confirmation. "We found Serafina."

He waited, as Mrs. Vesela's cries grew loud again then quieted into heaving sobs.

"She…ah…we…found her out a mile or so by the shed. You know, the fishing shed by the river. She was, ah, in the old well."

The maid broke out in fresh cries.

"Oh my God," Dawn gasped. Her hand quickly covered her mouth. "The…the old well in the south fields?" she asked, her eyes wide in horror. "Is she- is she…" she didn't want to say the words, not with the girl's mother weeping in front of her.

Jarrett nodded affirmatively. He continued stroking Mrs. Vesela's hair. The coroner had called a few moments ago confirming it was Serafina. He already had her dental records to match.

Maeve turned to Chloe, whose eyes were as wide in horror as her sister's. "Chloe, please take Mrs. Vesela to the gold guest room. Mrs. Li is probably already preparing something for her."

Chloe quickly wiped her eyes that were already springing with tears. Serafina was very well liked in the household. She and Chloe had gotten as close as a servant and a family member could get.

She hurried over to the maid and Jarrett. Gently Chloe pulled Mrs. Vesela from Jarrett and put her arm around her shoulders.

The weeping woman, at least a foot shorter than the tall willowy Chloe, laid her head against the girl's shoulder. The bereaved occupants of the room could hear her sobbing retreating down the hall.

"Jarrett?" Maeve looked at the marshal.

He ran the back of his hand across his forehead and sighed deeply. Dawn and Maeve waited for him to compose himself. He pushed his fingers through his short hair. He only confirmed again that the body was found in the well and that it was Seraphina.

"Oh God-" Dawn sobbed and ran out of the room. Maeve stepped near the young marshal and laid a hand on his arm.

"Let me get you something to drink, Jarrett, you look pale. You should probably be home in bed, you look like hell." Not one to candy coat her words, Maeve always said what she was thinking. However, she didn't point out that he had clearly suffered a terrible beating.

"Sit down," she ordered, pointing to a loveseat. He happily obliged. Before she left the room, she could tell he was asleep.

When Jarrett opened his eyes, he saw a tray on the table in front of him with coffee, water and a sandwich. It was dark outside but someone had slipped in and turned on a small lamp next to him.

Picking up the sandwich piled high with roast beef, lettuce and a juicy tomato, he chomped it down quickly. He was sipping the coffee when Maeve came back into the room. Worry lines marred her forehead.

"What's wrong?" Jarrett could tell there was something wrong by the look on her face.

"It's the Lane girl, Jarrett. She left hours ago to go horseback riding. It's dark, she should have been back long before now. Graham and Dario have been looking for her. Her horse just came back to the stable without her."

"What?!" Jarrett jumped to his feet. "Have someone saddle a horse for me, I'll meet them at the stables. I've got to call the station." Without waiting for her response, he ran out of the room and out to his car.

Within minutes he was out at the stable, a huge horse was being saddled. He zipped up his jacket, pulled his hat down tight on his head and tugged on leather gloves.

Jarrett stepped one boot into a stirrup and heaved himself easily onto the big horse.

"Thisn's Silver Bullet," the farmhand informed him. "He's one'a the largest horses on the farm." He squinted an eye at Jarrett. Jarrett was such a big man the farmhand knew to give him a sturdy animal.

Jarrett could see the Palomino the artist girl had been riding tied in a corner. He had his big head in a bucket and was greedily slurping the water. The saddle was still on his back.

"Which way did she head out?" Jarrett asked.

"Uh, she'd a told the missus she was goin' along the river, prolly headin' south to keep the west sun outta her eyes. The fellas headed out south an' east."

Jarret dug his heels into Silver Bullet's side and snapped the reins. The horse threw his head back, whinnied, and then took off out of the stable like a bullet.

Horse and man hurtled across the fields as one. It was dark and freezing. Jarrett gripped the reins tightly and hunkered down on the horse. His knees pressed against the horse's belly as they whipped through the grass. He grit his teeth against the pain of his injuries.

The full golden moon shone down on them as they approached the covered bridge. Jarrett decided not to cross it. The girl wasn't familiar with the area, it was doubtful she would have ventured into the woods.

He slowed when he reached the river. Looking down, he searched for hoof prints. The farmhand had told him the area Graham and Dario had already searched.

Jarrett headed in the opposite direction. He was actually only about two miles from the house when he found the prints. Jarrett pulled on the reins until the horse stopped.

Sliding off the animal, he knelt next to the prints. He touched them with two fingers. The prints were going and returning, but the returning prints were shallower. That meant no rider. Jarrett hopped back on Silver Bullet. He kept the horse's pace at a canter so he could follow the prints.

Another seven miles or so, and Jarrett could now make out a tiny figure in the dark walking towards him.

He called out. "Miss Lane!" Cupping his ear, he kneed the horse to move slightly faster. He could just make out the sound of her voice, but he couldn't tell what she was saying, she was still too far away.

Jarrett made a call on his cell advising he'd found Shantilly. Within a few minutes he met her. Her arms were scraped and her hair was a mess but she didn't appear seriously injured. She looked wearily elated.

"Thank heavens, Marshal. I've been walking for hours. I could sure use a cup of tea and a ride." Her smile was tired but grateful.

The tall man grinned down at her. He leaned over and reached down to her. They grabbed each other's arms and he easily pulled her up onto the big horse. "The ride I can provide, the tea will be up shortly."

Jarrett sat her in front of him and rubbed her arms. She felt like ice. He pulled off his jacket and ignoring her protests that he'll freeze, he dropped it over her shoulders. She pulled it on and snuggled into it. It went almost to her knees.

It had been sunny out when she had left and a lot warmer, so she hadn't worn anything over her flannel shirt. It was at least 20 to 30 degrees colder now.

Without realizing it, Shanti leaned back against Jarrett's chest. He put one arm around her and held the reins with the other. He didn't know how injured she was so he didn't dare gallop but he kept the horse moving quickly.

He gave Shanti a few moments to relax and collect herself before he asked her what happened.

"Miss Lane, I need you to tell me exactly what happened and what and who you may have seen today, all day."

He lowered his head. His lips brushed her ear, her hair muffled his voice. His tone was low and serious. Damn but the girl smelled good. Faintly flowery.

Chapter Thirty-four

"Maybe my sister was right, Marshal, maybe I should go home." Shanti sounded like she wasn't sure what to do. She stared straight ahead looking over and past the horse's head. It was around 7 or so, and she'd now been out in the cold for over 5 hours.

The last 3 hours she'd been walking in around 30 degree weather. The whole way she'd been wishing she hadn't traveled so far. But the ride was so wonderful she'd lost track of time and distance.

"What are you doing out here, Marshal?" She didn't yet realize he'd come for her. She thought he was investigating something else, the murder maybe, or poachers.

"I need to know, Miss Lane, what happened." His voice suddenly gruff, brooked no digressed discussion. It was not a friendly question- he wanted her to answer him.

Shanti heard the urgency in his voice, and the order. She twisted around to face him.

Huh, she thought. *Chloe was right; the guy had gorgeous eyes. Kind of the color of the sea just after a storm, a melding of blue and green. And lashes a man should be embarrassed to own*!

When she turned, she hadn't realized how close their faces were. They were mere inches apart. She could feel his warm breath on her face. Her eyes narrowed on his battered face. "Heavens, what happened to you?"

"Nothing, just a day's work," he grumbled, his own eyes roved her soft face.

Their lips were almost touching, they were gazing steadily right into each other's eyes. Embarrassed, her cheeks quickly stained pink, Shanti blinked and turned away.

Clearing her throat, she said, "Honestly Marshal, I really can't tell you much. I didn't see anything." Thinking back, she tried hard to remember. Her forehead wrinkled, she pushed her hair back out of her eyes tucking it behind her ears.

"I was out maybe seven or eight miles or so, I stayed along the river so I wouldn't get lost. It was so beautiful, crisp, clear, the sky was deep blue, not a cloud in it. I could feel the wind gently tossing my hair, cleaning out my brain. Then I heard some birds chirp-"

"Miss Lane, I know what it's like out here in the fields on a nice day, I don't need a rendition, I need to know what happened."

She could hear the impatience in his voice. She sat up straight, away from the comfort and warmth of his hard body.

"I was getting to that, I was telling you, gee. Anyway, I heard a flock of birds take off, like something suddenly spooked them. It wasn't us, we were too far away. The birds made a tremendous racket suddenly bursting out of the woods across the river.

"Seconds after the birds flew away I heard a gunshot. The horse reared, his front legs came right off the ground and he threw me off. Frightened, the poor thing ran away and left me. I hope he's okay?" She had been worried about the beautiful horse.

"Yeah, he returned to the stable none the worse for wear. Were you injured when you fell? You seem all right?" He was colder now that she pulled her warmth from him.

Finicky woman, he thought. She had felt good nestled up next to him, all soft and feminine. He could still smell the faint flowery shampoo in her hair.

"I'm so glad he's okay, I was so worried. I'm fine, a little bruised again, that's all. The grass pretty much broke my fall,

252

thank goodness." Sighing, she was so exhausted she didn't realize she'd leaned back again against Jarrett's broad chest.

He didn't say anything. He didn't want to spook her. Women were like horses sometimes, he thought, one minute they're all friendly, their noses in your hand and the next they're skittish.

"Anyway," she continued, "I didn't see anything or anyone except for the birds. By the time I'd gotten back up and brushed myself off, it was quiet again. I started walking back."

She twisted and looked at him again, but kept more of a distance between them. "So, why were you out here?" she repeated.

Jarrett's eyes never stopped sweeping the area. If someone was out here taking potshots at the girl they might still be around. And two people on a horse were definitely a big target. Likely, whoever it was by now the chances of them still lurking around would be slim.

After two murders, and it wasn't quite hunting season yet, Jarrett was pretty much assuming the gunshot had been for the girl, and she was very lucky someone wasn't the greatest shot. Of course it was quite windy. Bullet could have missed her by inches if pushed by a suddenly heavy gust.

The girl had been walking for hours. He wondered why they hadn't finished her off. She was a sitting duck hiking across the open fields. Maybe they were stuck on the other side of the river and didn't want to take a chance shooting at her from there in case they missed and then draw attention to them.

If they shot at her and missed, and she saw them then ran into the woods and hid, she could possibly ID them.

He decided not to tell her he had come looking for her. He didn't want her to get any ideas. She was beautiful and all that, in fact he was having a hard time trying to control the effect her proximity had on his body.

A red-blooded healthy male, it would be perfectly normal for Jarrett to react to a gorgeous, sexy woman snuggled tightly against his body. Normally he had better control of himself. What was it about her that- he cleared his throat.

"Um, Miss Lane, there's something you should know before we get back to the house…"

She turned again, her sapphire eyes sparkling in the moonlight.

Jarrett quickly shifted his head away pretending to study the sky, so black now it looked like someone had taken a brush and tarred it.

The wind picked up, it was harsher and colder. It struck their faces and whipped her hair. He tried to brush the tendrils down with one hand to keep them from tickling his face.

"What? Is everyone okay?" Suddenly fear grabbed her. What else could have happened? Was someone else she had grown to love hurt- or worse?

Jarrett looked down at her, then away. He didn't want to burst out the news about Serafina insensitively. "Well, I…we found Serafina…but," An owl hooted in the distance causing a fox to wail its scream.

The fox shrieked for a moment then hushed. The night was quiet and still again, except for the occasional howl of the wind streaking through the bare trees far off in the woods. Even the constantly flowing river was unusually quiet.

At first, Shanti's face lit up, her pristine teeth glistened as her mouth widened in joy. Then she saw his expression. Her face instantly fell. "Oh my gosh, Marshal…she isn't-" she didn't want to say the words, but his face told it all.

Jarrett shook his head sadly. "I'm sorry, Miss Lane, we didn't find her alive." He waited for her reaction. Holding the reins with one hand, he pulled off his cowboy hat and ran a tired hand through his short hair.

He put his hat back on and yawned lightly, he was growing weary. It'd been a long day, and he was still recuperating from his own ordeal at the river.

Shanti put a hand up and covered her mouth. Her eyes immediately filled with tears. There was silence for several long minutes.

"How?" Her voice shook with emotion, tears slid down her cheeks reddened from the cold. Her full lips trembled with the energy she used to try not to weep out loud.

Jarrett wrapped one arm around her, holding her tightly. He didn't want to tell her the gory details, but he knew someone else would and he didn't want her to be taken by surprise.

"We... uh...I found her in an old well around 6 or 7 miles down the river to the north."

Her gasp was painful and full of shock. "A...a...w...well? How...how..." she bit her lip not knowing what to say. She pictured poor Serafina so young and beautiful, her hair a black cloud and exotic eyes so dark they looked all shiny pupil, lying alone and broken at the bottom of a cold dark well.

Shanti started sobbing. Jarrett gently pulled her head onto his chest and caressed her hair.

He let her cry for a minute, continuing to run his hands down her long hair. The locks were so silky. He went from comfortingly petting and stroking her head to feeling each individual fat lock of blonde hair.

Twisting a lock between his fingers, Jarrett marveled how soft it was.

After a moment, her sobs subsided, she sniffed. He remembered his handkerchief in his pocket. He pulled it out and handed it to her. She accepted it with murmured thanks.

"I...I don't understand, Marshal...how did she get there? Was she riding and the horse threw her, or she slipped?" Shanti asked, wiping her eyes.

"Ah...no, we think it was foul play, Miss Lane." Jarrett stopped smoothing her hair. He took the reins with both hands, they were nearing the farm.

As they approached the stables, Graham and another man ran up and grabbed the reins as Jarrett tossed them to him.

"Miss Lane! I am so relieved to see you! Are you all right?" Graham cried, his expression alarmed at seeing her sitting up in front of the Marshal. When he saw her move, her eyes open and bright, his face relaxed realizing she was not seriously injured.

"What happened?" he asked. His question was directed at the big man holding the missing woman.

She had been leaning back against him as they neared the stables, her hair splayed across the front of the lawman's brown uniform. They sure looked pretty cozy, the foreman's eyes narrowed.

Shanti leaned forward, out of Jarrett's embrace. She smiled weakly at Graham. He looked so worried.

"I'm fine, Mr.- um…Graham, I just got thrown, that's all. No broken bones, I'll live." She tried to sound cheerful, but as she said the words, *I'll live,* a picture of Serafina lying in the bottom of a fusty old well took her cheerfulness and smile away.

She could almost smell the odor of wet cement and stagnant water. Her lovely eyes saddened and refilled with tears, her lush lips turned down at the corners.

Jarrett still had one arm wrapped around her. He hugged her gently.

She sat up quickly, moving away from the security of his muscled body.

Graham held the horse still as Jarrett swung one leg around behind him and jumped off the tall horse. He stood with his arms held up to help Shanti.

Normally she'd jump right down herself, but this was an enormous horse. She knew she'd hit the ground hard if she dismounted alone and she was already bruised again from head to toe.

Shanti reached down and put her arms around Jarrett's neck. Since she was sitting up above his head, he reached up and grasped her around her slim waist and easily lifted her up and off the horse.

Briefly, he held her in the air, then his hands moved up until they were just below her breasts, he brought her to his chest and hesitated.

Their eyes close, lips a breath apart, he hesitated, then let her slowly slide down the length of him until her feet gently touched the ground. He didn't even feel the stitch and pain in his ribs or other bruising around his body.

"Miss Lane-" Graham's curt voice broke between the two, quickly dispelling whatever emotions may be running high. "They will be worried about you up at the house. Chloe was beside herself, I think you should-"

Shanti stepped back from Jarrett. He stood silently watching her. His eyes were hooded, she couldn't tell what he was thinking. She turned and looked at the foreman. Her lips curved into a soft smile.

Graham was so strong and it was comforting to see his concerned face. Actually, he looked a little angry. Maybe he was jealous. *That's kind of sweet*, she thought.

Shanti took in Graham Duncan's handsome weathered face. He was dressed in faded worn jeans, a flannel shirt covered by an old leather jacket and boots, dusty and worn that had seen better days. A red bandanna was tied in a square knot around his throat.

She could just see his chest hairs exposed from the top open buttons of his shirt, brown mixed with a few strands of grey. He stood sturdy and strong and safe. Shanti looked back at Jarrett. He was still standing quietly watching her, his expression unfathomable.

"Run along, Miss Lane, let them know you're all right," Jarrett said, dismissing her.

Well! Shanti furrowed her brow, her hands on her hips. The nerve of him, always ordering her about like she was a child. And just when she was starting to think he was human and had some compassion and a tiny bid of kindness-

The two men turned to each other talking, totally disregarding her presence.

Fine. She turned and stalked off towards the house fuming. At least she stalked until she was some distance from the men. She was way too tired and sore to continue walking fast. Her pace slowed and she tried hard not to limp.

Suddenly, she heard footsteps pounding the earth, running up right behind her! Her hand to her throat, a large hand fell on her shoulder- she turned in terror-

"Miss Lane! Wait!" It was the marshal.

She breathed a deep sigh of relief, and then she frowned at him. "Marshal Chase! You scared the daylights out of me! You shouldn't come sneaking up on a person in the darkness!" she angrily scolded him.

He laughed and took her by her arm, guiding her to the house. "Don't get your feathers ruffled, honey, I was hardly 'sneaking up on you' the horses could hear me coming a mile away." He looked at her, his expression extremely serious.

"I do not want you to be alone until I find out exactly what's going on around here, do you hear me?" He pointed a finger in her face, instructing her like she was a baby.

She scowled at him and tried to jerk her hand from his grasp but he didn't let go. She'd be darned if he was going to manhandle her like he had at the festival and try to give her orders. Who did he think he was after all, he had no right-

As if he read her mind, he said calmly, "I have every right to tell you what to do if you want to remain free. I can arrest you and hold you right now as a suspect in either Langston Lawton's or Serafina's murders."

"What?!" Shocked, she struggled to make him let go of her.

His grip only became more like an iron band. He pulled her towards the house. She tried to dig her heels into the hard ground, but he easily dragged her along.

"Come on, Miss Lane, don't make me toss you over my shoulder. I can and will." His voice lowered in warning. He'd had enough of this little spitfire getting in trouble, endangering herself and fighting him at every turn.

Abruptly, he stopped. She banged right into him. She would have fallen if he didn't still hold her tightly. He jerked her around to stand in front of him. She struggled to regain her balance.

Pushing her hair out of her face, she was outraged. Her mouth opened to tell him where he could go-

He gripped both of her arms above her elbows and shook her.

Stunned, her mouth and her eyes widened.

He looked furious. His brows were drawn down hard. His mouth matched his brows, his turquoise eyes darkened like thunderclouds. She tried to draw away, he suddenly frightened her, he looked mad enough to do her serious harm.

He shook her again. "Listen to me, Miss Lane," he hissed roughly through clenched teeth, trying to control his temper. "You have been near death twice now, and I have two dead bodies on my hands. You are either a suspect, a victim, or a witness, and to the best of me, I can't figure out which.

"None of this murder and mayhem was going on until you arrived on the scene. I should arrest you right now and toss your shapely butt in jail, throw away the key and forget all about you."

He let go of her with one hand, but held her tightly with the other. He ran the back of his hand over his brow, breathing deeply to get a grip. He didn't know whether to spank her or kiss her.

She stood looking at him, her big eyes all wide and innocent. The stubborn pain in the- either she was a great actress or-

She tried to pull his fingers off from around her arm. Handcuffs would have been softer than his steel grip. He ignored her struggles.

"I'm not going to tell you again, you do exactly as I say, when I say it, with no smart remarks, or I swear to God, I'll drive you myself straight to jail."

She had turned away, searching behind them for Graham. Why didn't he come and rescue her from this big ruffian?

Jarrett swung her around hard to face him. She blinked through the hair in her eyes. Suddenly, she was so tired she could hardly stand.

"Fine, big bad Marshal, whatever, I'll do whatever you say. Please just let me go home and go to sleep. I'm so tired, so hungry..." She swayed slightly, her hand over her eyes.

"Swear to me you'll give me no more trouble? Swear you'll not be alone, ever, and you'll tell me anything strange that happens to you, or any strange people you see." He shook her as he said the demanding words.

"I...I swear. Please, Jarrett, please, I want to go home..."

Her use of his first name got his attention. He looked down at her. Slumped shoulders, her head was down, her hair almost covered her face but it didn't hide her extreme exhaustion.

Damn. What a barbarian I am, he thought, *the poor thing had been out in the cold for hours, walking for miles, bruised and sore, and here I am like a big lug, threatening and accusing her, what a jerk.*

His urge was to swing her up in his arms and carry her to the house but he knew she'd object, she probably already thought he was the meanest man on the earth. Besides, his ribs were killing him.

He let go of her wrist, but gently dropped his arm around her shoulders to help her get to the house. She was practically asleep on her feet.

By the time they reached the manor it was lit up like a showboat.

Chloe and Maeve came running out of the house to help Jarrett get Shanti inside.

She was barely aware of the attention they gave her. As soon as they got in the door, Maeve grabbed Jarrett's arm to usher him into the drawing room where he could answer her questions.

Just as they disappeared around the corner, Shanti caught a glimpse of something that was familiar. The pants and the shoes. She remembered before thinking they were identical to what she saw seconds before she was pushed down the stairs.

She'd forgotten until just now. "Oh my gosh," she whispered, "was it him? Why would the marshal want me dead? He could have killed me tonight, no one would have ever known. Maybe he thought Graham or someone else might have been out in the fields too near us."

She shook her exhausted head in confusion and consternation. She must be mistaken.

Chloe helped her get cleaned up and put into bed.

Shanti didn't say anything to Chloe about her suspicions, she'd never believe her.

She was asleep before her head hit the pillow.

Chapter Thirty-Five

Montgomery pushed the release button for the security gate at the front of the long drive.

Someone had been urgently and unceasingly pushing the button on the box by the closed gate. Montgomery figured it was the police, those ham-fisted young bucks never knew patience or their own strength.

The butler swung the door open just as a fist was about to strike it.

"Matthew! What on earth is the matter, boy? Where are your manners-" Shocked at the young Vaughn standing there, breathless, obviously upset, his eyes glazed and his mouth open wide, Montgomery grabbed the young man's arm and pulled him inside.

All of a sudden, Matthew lost all his energy and stood mute, frozen as still as a statue.

"What is it boy? Speak up!" the butler loudly ordered. He could hear footsteps coming behind him clicking across the marble foyer floor.

"What's going on, Montgomery? What is it?" Maeve stopped next to the butler and looked quizzically at Matthew Vaughn.

The young man looked petrified, his lips had clamped together, but his eyes were wide and staring.

"Matthew?" Maeve spoke firmly, tugging at his arm.

Matthew swung his eyes around at her. He pulled his hand over his dry mouth, licking his lips to moisten them. He dragged his hand through his dark brown hair. Scared brown eyes suddenly dropped and looked down at his feet.

"Tell us boy, speak up," his voice gruff but now gentle, Montgomery tried to coax the young man to talk.

Matthew shrugged, then chuckled mirthlessly. He was wearing blue jeans and a navy jacket. A white, long sleeved button down shirt was exposed from the half-zipped jacket.

His skin was still tanned. Long hours in the sun in the summer and fall, and equally long hours outside on horseback in the winter kept his skin dark.

"We're in big trouble, finished, destroyed," Matthew announce in a harsh blurt. He smiled wryly, shaking his head as if he couldn't believe it but knew it was true. Wringing his hands he ran them raggedly through his hair again.

"Matthew…" Maeve warned.

He looked around the vast grandiose room. Fresh flowers were as always in the gold urn on the marble stand in the middle of the blue and white marble foyer. The crushed velvet blue curtains were pulled back and held by sashes letting in the winter sun. The house was quiet. It was early still.

"Matthew Vaughn, you tell me this instant what the hell is going on," Maeve spoke sharply, imperious. She shook his arm, dropped it, and then stood back from him.

He looked at her, his hands shoved deep into his jean's pockets. His shoulders hunched. He looked like he had the weight of the world on his young shoulders.

Almost painfully shy, Matthew was a hardworking, good looking young man. His family and their farm were the most important things in the world to him. He let out a shuddering sigh.

"We're almost through with the harvest. We were suspicious, but no one wanted to confirm it" He took a deep breath.

"The rot is back. The entire harvest is infested. The County Extension Agent just left. Both the Idaho's and the Ranger

Russets…all spoiled… We weren't sure until we got them into storage."

Controlling her shock with a stiff expression, "Ditylenchus Destructor?" Maeve asked.

Even Montgomery who never worked the fields had been around long enough to learn all the names of fungus and potato rots and diseases that could wipe out a farm in one foul sweep.

Matthew shrugged morosely again, nodding. "Yup. We're out for four to six years. We can't plant a thing in the fields- we're screwed. If we don't come up with a crop for the exporting this year the other countries will drop us like hot potatoes, pun intended," he added with chagrin.

"We will never be able to get them back again. Thailand and Venezuela are our biggest buyers. They'd quickly find another farm to buy from. Grandpa Magnus is so…so…devastated. He's taken to his bed. Mom is worried to death about him."

Matthew looked close to tears. He choked back a sniffle.

At his dire words, Maeve made a strangled sound in her throat. Her hands flew to her mouth, her eyes looked like two green rocks suddenly thrown into a turbulent lake.

She patted the young man's arm to console him. "Poor, poor Magnus…" she hummed in distress.

Montgomery stood like a third hump on a camel. He didn't know what to say.

"What is it, Grandmother?" A timid voice spoke from behind. The three turned and looked at Chloe.

She was almost getting used to horrible happenings around the manor. She dreaded to hear the news. Her expression indicated she knew it was bad, they all looked like the wind had been slammed out of them.

Crossing her long slender arms protectively in front of her chest, she slowly came to stand with them. Her mahogany hair was pulled back in a ponytail. She hadn't bothered with makeup. She just kept crying it right off. The whites of her cherry brown eyes were red from crying all night over their loss of Serafina as it was.

Maeve took in her granddaughter's almost resigned bearing. Slim and pretty as always, she wore jeans and her favorite yellow sweater. Clips decorated with yellow butterflies held up the hair that tried to escape from the ponytail.

"Close the door, Montgomery, we're not in a barn," Queen Maeve directed the butler.

Montgomery wordlessly did as she ordered. He left the room. Just as he was closing the door, he almost jumped finding the housekeeper standing there with a glass in her hand.

Montgomery quickly hid his surprise- he should be used to it by now, Mrs. Li always had the uncanny ability to know when something was wrong, and usually appeared as if by magic holding the exact medicine or drink that was needed.

Chloe hurried to Matthew's side. She had to stretch to reach an arm around his shoulders. She was tall, but he was still at least six inches taller than she.

"I'm so sorry, Matt..." She didn't know what else to say to comfort him. Not being able to plant anything for a number of years would totally ruin any farm, no matter how wealthy.

And there's all the employees to think of as well. A few new people drifted in and out of a farm but most of the workers and servants had been with the families in the county for years.

"But...Matthew, you have the cattle and bulls and other things your dad has been diversifying in. What about them? This doesn't affect them does it?" Chloe asked, her tone tinged with hope.

He shrugged. Letting Chloe pat him on the shoulder, he looked at her face.

Clear innocent eyes the color of a freshly brushed russet horse, she had the purest skin he'd ever seen. Not a blemish on her, and to top it, she was just the nicest girl around.

Tall and graceful and slender, shyly pretty, he wished it'd been her he'd been smitten with instead of her tramp of a sister. But unfortunately, there was nothing he could do about it.

His heart beat faster, his palms were damp and his jeans grew tight every time the striking redhead came into a room. Dawn only had to look in his direction with those flashing green eyes and he was a goner.

He knew he was a fool over her. He also knew she was well aware of his feelings for her. She laughs right in his face as she rubs her svelte body against his in pretense of a hug of welcome whenever the Vaughn family came to visit.

As soon as she's aware he's aroused, she dances off, knowing he's totally under her power. He shook his head to get the picture of the flame-haired vixen out of his mind.

"But, Matthew, I've heard nothing but amazing things about the diversifying your dad's been into," Chloe frowned at him. "It sounded to me like he's making profits out the kazoo."

"You're always so good to us Chloe, you're a true friend," he said to her. She rewarded him with a big toothsome smile. Patting his shoulder again, she dropped her arm and stood back.

Matthew still had his hands tucked into his jean's pockets. He considered her words. "You know, being away at school the last few semesters, I'd almost forgotten, you know, about the animals. Daddy pretty much takes care of that side of the farm." Blinking hard for a second, he brightened.

"Actually, thinking about it, he's probably got close to a thousand head by now out in the east pasture. Hmm." He clasped his chin between two fingers, deep in thought. His gaze cut to Maeve.

"No wonder Daddy wasn't as distraught as the rest of us. His bulls and cows might just pull us through. Plus, he's got a couple of big plots of corn and soy he seeded last year going along the river, and we still have the honey bees. According to Tori, the bees are her babies and she's tearing up the market with her local honey." Matthew turned and hugged Chloe tightly.

The girl's russet eyes widened in surprise.

"Thanks, Chloe!" Matthew crowed with glee. "Thanks! I knew coming here was the right thing to do! We're like family, cheering each other up, looking for alternatives!"

Shaking his head, the corner of his mouth curved up. "Look at me going off all half-blast with my distress over the rotted fields. I didn't give the rest of the farm half a mind. What a dim-witted brain I had for the moment! I just panicked and ran."

He grinned at Maeve. "Thanks for being our friends, Mrs. Lawton. I've gotta go, I've gotta go talk to Granddaddy."

Maeve's brows arched and her body became rigid, not sure if he was going to hug her or not. He didn't.

He grabbed her hand and pumped it. "I'm so relieved, no wonder Daddy was calling to me as I rode over here in haste, he was trying to tell me!" Like a whirlwind, the young man yanked the front door open and ran down the steps to his car. He was gone in a flash.

Mrs. Li was gone. Chloe chuckled slightly shaking her head at the disappearing young man as she closed the door. Maeve stood stoic and silent.

Chapter Thirty-Six

*T*he family returned from Serafina's funeral.

The vision of the young maid lying so peacefully in the coffin with her mother's sobs filling the church was still in Shanti's mind. She was sitting in a chair out in the front lawn bundled up to the neck.

She hadn't started painting yet. Leaving the Lawtons to their sorrow inside, she had come outside to clear her head. She was still picturing the dead girl as she had been described when found. Decomposing.

There had been pictures placed around the coffin of the lovely maid attired in her favorite pink, her lips and nails always matching.

According to the police, someone had snapped her neck like a dead rose on a dry stem and then tossed her into the grave of a well. Shanti angrily swiped at the tears that were slipping out of her eyes and reached for her paints.

The young artist worked steadily, ignoring the cars that drove up and down the driveway. People were coming and going, paying their respect for the deceased maid. The painting was almost done. She sighed deeply, if only Mr. Lawton could see it.

"What the hell are you doing out here?!" a furious voice bellowed, shocking her.

Her head jerked up, the brush fell from her startled fingers.

Jarrett Chase stood behind her, his hands balled into fists slammed on his hips, he stood solid with strong legs harshly akimbo. The glower on his face was so menacing it would scare the most hardened of dockworkers away.

Shanti reached down on the brown grass and picked up her brush. She glowered right back at him.

The marshal stepped in front of her stopping next to the easel, his fists still on his hips. He pointed a finger at her.

"I thought I instructed you to never be alone. What the hell is wrong with you? Do you want to get killed? Do you have a suicide desire?" His voice thundered, his brows drew down so hard his eyes were barely visible.

Shanti stood up fuming. Her hands went right to her hips, mirroring him. She leaned her upper torso forward, her face in his.

"Listen buddy, I don't need to worry about a murderer if you're going to continue to sneak up on me and give me a heart attack all the time! Besides, half the county has been in and out of here all day, I'm hardly alone, and out here in the middle of the lawn I'm hardly hidden from view! Now, you need to get off my case!"

He crossed huge arms that were obviously well accustomed to lifting barbells, in front of his chest, his expression calmed. One chestnut brown eyebrow raised up over one turquoise eye. "I see. I thought you were a woman of your word, apparently I have been vastly mistaken." He sniffed condescendingly, his nose in the air.

"What?" Shanti's mouth dropped open, her eyes puzzled. "What are you talking about 'my word' I didn't give you my word on anything-"

He nodded his head, looking coolly down at her. "Yes you did. Have you already forgotten last night? When I brought you back here, you promised you'd do exactly as I said, and without sassing me or back talking. Remember?"

Shanti was bewildered. She frowned, thinking back last night. She was so tired and hungry and sore...it's amazing how well she felt this morning when she got up. She raised her blue eyes up and gazed at him.

Smug arrogance was written all over his face. The man was just too attractive for his own good. She had always distrusted his kind, thought the world was there to do their beckoning-

She looked away, her gaze followed still more cars traipsing up and down the winding drive. Twiddling with the buttons on her powder blue jacket, she suddenly felt warm.

"I uh..." She didn't know what to say. She didn't want to give in and confirm what he was saying about last night. She didn't want to give him the satisfaction.

Boy, he sure irritated the heck out of her, rubbing her the wrong way like a bad case of poison ivy. Darn the man.

He smirked at her. "Come on, I can tell by your face that you remember you promised me last night that you'd do what I say without argument. Give it up, Miss Lane."

She speared him with narrowed eyes. "That's not fair, Marshal, I was in a tremendously weakened condition. You took unfair advantage of me."

Crossing her arms in front of her chest again, she snipped, "You are hardly a gentleman." Now she turned her small nose up in the air and sniffed indignantly.

"Listen lady, you have no idea how 'gentlemanly' I have been to you. There's been plenty of times I could have easily wrung your lovely neck."

He didn't mention it took a lot of control not to drag her off the horse last night and ravish her on the hard ground every time she wriggled that shapely butt of hers against him.

He couldn't help but feel her breasts rub against the arm he held around her to keep her from falling off the horse.

Shanti's eyes shot up to his, her fear was very apparent. He frowned. *Damn*.

"I'm sorry Miss Lane, that was a really poor choice of words, considering Serafina and all..." His words choked off, the picture of the firemen pulling the dead maid, her head lolling unnaturally, up out of the well sprang into his mind.

He shook his head and took a step towards her, his arm out. "Nonetheless, put your stuff away and come with me back up to the house."

She cringed and backed up, staring at his arm, it was obvious she was terrified of him. His brows knit together. Why was she afraid of him for heaven's sake?

"What's the matter with you?" he asked, scowling at her. He sure wasn't used to women being afraid of him, this was ridiculous.

She just stared at him, eyes wide like a baby bird staring at a python.

Losing his patience, he barked at her, "Don't make me tell you again, get your stuff and let's go, now." He turned to her easel, and without taking in the striking painting, he flipped the white material that was hanging off the back of the easel forward over the painting, covering it.

Shanti blinked. *Well*, she thought, *at least he couldn't kill her out here in broad daylight...could he?* Carefully skirting him, she gathered her paints and brushes, tossing them haphazardly into a paint box.

She wiped her stained fingers on a towel, tossed that into the box as well and snapped the lid closed. She picked up the box and mockingly saluted the marshal.

"Yes sir, whatever you say, sir, I'm ready!"

Jarrett Chase shook his head and rolled his eyes skyward. Why was he blessed with the care of this woman? He picked up the easel and started up the small grassy hill to the house.

"You can leave the sarcasm here, Miss Lane, I don't need it. I thought you were a lady and stood by your word not to give me a hard time, forgive me if I was misled." He stalked up the hill away from her.

Shanti felt small. He was right. She'd given her word, and she'd also given him nothing but trouble. After all, twice now he'd rescued her. Not that in either circumstances someone else wouldn't have found her, but still...

She made a pact with herself to resolutely do as he asked, or actually in his case, ordered, without smart-mouthing back to him. It was surely unlikely that it was the marshal's clothes that she'd caught a glimpse of before she was flung down the staircase. She ran lightly up the hill to catch up with him.

She got to the door first and held it open for him.

Slowing his pace, his stern look turned suspicious. What was the spitfire up to? Glaring down at Shanti, he judiciously slipped past her through the doorway.

As soon as the couple entered the manor, warmth hit them.

Jarrett set her easel down by the door and she set her paint box next to it. He unzipped his leather jacket with the furry collar and pulled it off. Surreptitiously he watched Shanti.

She walked over to a chair by the door and pulled off her gloves and knit hat. Her saffron hair tumbled out, falling in loose curls around her shoulders.

Setting the gloves and hat on the chair, she unzipped her jacket and pulled it off. The jacket joined the hat and gloves and she smoothed her tousled hair, running her fingers through the locks. She was wearing a white knit body suit under an open flannel shirt. Jarrett's hooded eyes followed her every move.

Shanti lifted her hands up to untangle her hair, her shoulders pulled back and the flannel shirt spread open, exposing the tight shirt. The knit shirt grew taught over her chest.

Jarrett couldn't help but stare at her rounded breasts that jutted out every time she pulled her fingers back through her hair. Shanti appeared to be deep in thought.

Hearing Jarrett cough, she suddenly remembered he was there. She'd been daydreaming, thinking maybe she and Chloe could get in a ride later. She turned to him and smiled. His expression was blank.

"I'm going to take my things upstairs, Marshal, I guess I'll see you later," she said, bending to pick up her paint box and her discarded outerwear.

He cleared his throat. His Adam's apple was in danger of choking him. The damned woman had such an effect on him, he needed to get a grip and keep his head clear. He was here investigating a murder, not gawking like a teen-aged boy at a voluptuous young woman! He shook his head to clear it of sensuous thoughts.

Jarrett told her, "I need to see everyone in the family. I came by because I knew the Vaughns and most other folks in town would be here and I could save time questioning people. I know it's lousy timing, the funeral just over and all, but I can't let the trail get cold." He nodded to her paint box.

"So, put your stuff away and come back down and join the others." It wasn't a request, it was an order as usual. It instantly got Shanti's ire up. She started to scowl.

"Listen Marshal, you-" then she remembered her promise. Her face cleared, she smiled politely. "Of course, as you wish. I just want to clean up a little and I'll be down."

He looked slightly taken aback. He expected her to argue with him, spit blue fire as she usually does. But, she turned and calmly headed for the stairs carrying her box and clothes. She'd get the easel later. Sometimes Montgomery brings it up for her.

Jarrett stood astonished, watching her jog up the stairs. He couldn't take his eyes off her derriere swaying back and forth as she ran lightly up the steps. He was still gawking when he heard a voice at his back.

"Jarrett?" Chloe was standing there, pretty as a buttercup all in yellow.

He turned to her, blinking.

"Are you waiting for someone?" she asked, following his gaze up the steps, but the stairs were empty.

He coughed then swallowed awkwardly. "Uh no, Chloe...I ah, thought I heard something...someone...I mean...Miss Lane just went up and I..." He ran a finger under the collar of his uniform that was buttoned at the neck.

"I mean...I don't like her being alone, you know, the danger. Ah, where's your grandmother, I need to speak with her and some other people?" He quickly changed the subject before she realized how red his face was becoming. Damn, what was he, 14?

Chloe smiled. "I understand, Rett, so many things going on lately, and for some reason, it looks like someone has it out for Shanti too." She sighed, worry lines crossed her forehead.

Then she brightened again. "But you needn't worry about Shanti, Graham is keeping an eye out. I think he's kinda sweet on her, you know?"

Jarrett frowned at Chloe. Then he quickly smoothed out his expression. "Oh yeah? The foreman and the artist?" His mouth curled drolly. But he wasn't smiling.

Chloe giggled. "Yeah, isn't it cute, Rett? Maybe they'll fall in love and marry and she'll have to stay here, wouldn't that be great?" She walked over to the easel leaning against the wall and lifted the sheet covering it.

"Yeah, great." Jarrett frowned again. He hadn't thought about the artist completing her work and leaving. He was sort of getting used to seeing her here, even if she might be a killer. Although, he truly doubted that the girl had murder lurking behind those stunning sapphire eyes.

He visualized Shanti and Graham kissing, walking arm and arm down the aisle - ick. The Scotsman was way too old for her.

Jarrett firmed his lips and crunched his eyes to get the unpleasant vision of the burly foreman with his muscled arms and big hands pawing all over the curvy blonde out of his mind.

He followed Chloe to the easel and looked at the painting. Chloe lifted the sheet over it.

"Wow."

Chloe grinned. "She's incredible, isn't she?"

"Yeah, incredible."

Chapter Thirty-Seven

*C*hloe and Jarrett found a group of people gathered in the Great Room. As large as it was, the room was still crowded. The townspeople came to pay their respect to Maeve and the Vaughns.

The servants for a change were allowed to mingle in the manor with the upper crust. Serafina was one of their own, she had been deeply loved and respected. Even as shy as she was, she was well known in the neighborhood, most of them had grown up together.

The rich kids went to private schools, they didn't mix with the servants' children that attended public school. But, Serafina had been hard to miss with that lush black hair and exotic eyes, only her extreme shyness kept people at arm's length.

Even though they were welcome, the servants huddled together in a corner of the room speaking in hushed tones.

A line of people wandered along the tables filled with food. There were no casseroles here. The tables were filled with salmon, caviar, cheeses and wine.

Anyone wanting something stronger could go over by the front window where Montgomery was bartending at the pocket bar and get just about any kind of liquor.

Siblings Jaime and Dawn sat next to each other on the couch. Jaime was trying to hide a bored yawn behind one hand.

Dawn was pretending not to notice Matthew and practically every other man in the room stare at her bosom. She'd worn a black dress, thank God she looked fabulous in black, the darkness was such a good foil for her brilliant hair.

When she swept down the stairs earlier, Maeve had stopped her, shaking her head disgustedly at her granddaughter.

"Dawn, you are a disgrace. You are attending a gathering in respect of the death of one of our servants. You are not on your way to a sleazy bar. Get upstairs and either change that outrageous dress or put something over it." Maeve pointed a rigid arm back up the stairs.

Dawn sighed so loudly Maeve took a step closer to her.

Hating herself for not being able to hold back a cringe, Dawn thought her grandmother was going to strike her- she turned quickly and ran back up the stairs. She didn't dare look back down at her grandmother, the queen had spoken, "Long live the queen," she growled. Old bag.

She pulled a black sweater on over her dress, but left it wide open. Her décolletage was so daringly low her breasts were practically bare. She knew every man in the room was ogling her. Every time she looked over at Matthew or any of the other men, they quickly averted their eyes, pretending they were looking elsewhere.

Jaime yawned again. He leaned back, not caring if he wrinkled his black suit. He was tired of black already, and he couldn't wait to pull the noose of a tie off and toss it in his closet. He crossed one leg over the other and glanced at his sister.

"Geez Dawn, why don't you give Matt a break for Pete's sake? Why don't you just spread your legs for him once and get it over with. The game you play is getting tedious. He looks like a lost little puppy for crying out loud."

Dawn sniggered. She was fidgeting with a teardrop diamond earring dangling from one lobe. She glanced back over at Matthew.

He looked pathetic with big sad eyes and his tongue practically hanging out. Although he stood chatting with a group of men his own age, he couldn't keep his eyes from drifting over to the couch.

She preened, fluffing her hair. "Please Jaime, if I did it once with that boy he'd never leave me alone. He would considered us married. End of story."

Jaime glanced around the crowded room. He nodded across the chatting people towards Jarrett.

The marshal was standing off to the side talking with a small group of people. He and two maids, a butler and Jarrett's girlfriend, or wannabe girlfriend, Mary Jane Peltham, were deeply engaged in conversation. Mary Jane was hanging onto Jarrett's arm so tightly it looked like she was about to pull him over.

"Okay," Jaime said. "So you're bored with the baby meat in town so…what about our handsome sheriff?"

Dawn followed the direction of her brother's inclined head across the room. She grimaced. Huffing, she crossed her arms in front of her chest. Half a dozen men in the room turned their heads in a different direction. She peered at the marshal through a fringe of red lashes. Her lips pursed.

Seeing his sister obviously annoyed, Jaime said, "What puts you off about him? The lean hips, muscular arms, those broad shoulders that span a doorway, or-" He nudged his sister with his elbow, watching her stare at the marshal with greedy eyes.

"Is it those gorgeous turquoise eyes framed in mile long lashes, or maybe it's his easy smile and gallant manners that turns you off?"

Dawn shrugged, pulling her gaze away from the young sheriff. She patted her hair then uncrossed her arms and pulled the sweater back away from her breasts.

She crossed one leg over the other, pretending she didn't notice her skirt slip up well past her thighs. A dozen eyes turned back in her direction.

"I tried hitting on him a couple of times," she said indifferently. "He wouldn't give me the time of day. He's really finicky. You can tell he only tolerates Mary Jane because there's not that many pretty townies here to interest him. I hear he goes over to that little town over the hill, you know, Gulleyridge, for his kicks and giggles."

"Hmmm, I see, well then…" Jaime snickered at her irritation at the marshal. His interest in his teasing game was increasing. Shifting in his seat, he scanned the room. He saw all the male eyes discreetly peering at his sister who was sitting so nonchalantly half-naked next to him.

"You better be careful, sis, yours may be the next dead body they find. You must be driving half the married men in this room crazy, and, if looks could kill, most of the women would have just murdered you!"

Dawn chuckled. "Don't be snide, Jaime dear, or are you jealous that the men are looking at me and not you?" She pretended she didn't see him jerk his head and glare at her.

"Anyway," he said, "speaking of married men and games, I've got it-" he snapped his fingers. Grinning, he searched the room. "How about going after that lascivious boor Mother married? Where is he anyway?"

He finally spotted their mother Camelia sitting alone on a barstool in a corner. She was staring down at her drink, her face was one big sour pout. She tipped her glass back and forth, watching the amber liquid swirl.

Montgomery had placed a lemon slice on the side of the glass to make it look like she was drinking iced tea, but no one was fooled. They knew it was three quarters bourbon and one quarter water. Besides, it was déclassé to drink ice tea in the winter.

Dawn gracefully lifted one leg and set it down then slowly lifted the other and crossed it over her knee. She knew many pairs of eyes were following her every move hoping for a peek under her dress. Most would be trying to see if she was wearing any panties or not. She was bored with Jaime's game.

"Didn't you know, Logan hasn't been home the last two nights? He made a brief appearance at the funeral. As soon as he and Mother got home they started bickering in the parlor, everyone could hear them. Mother was accusing him of seeing some tramp from town.

"They yelled at each other for a while then he slammed out the door and drove off in the Jag. Didn't you hear Mother wailing up the stairs? My God, the Vaughns could have heard her from their place miles down the road."

"I thought she was crying over Serafina," Jaime said.

Dawn sidled a cynical glance at her brother, one brow raised.

He laughed. "Oh. What was I thinking?" he slapped himself in the head. "That's our mother we're talking about, she wouldn't cry over anything that didn't have something to do with her, like a broken heel or nail or something, duh."

He shook his head. His brown hair was slicked stiff with mousse as always, it didn't move. The hair waved straight back like frozen ripples in an ocean. "Well? What about lusty Logan? It would be fun for you if only to tick off Mother."

Dawn held out a long arm that looked like it had been sprinkled with ginger. The freckles were showing up again, time for a new lemon treatment at the spa. She held her hand up and studied her manicure.

"Puleeze Jaime, bedding Logan Thayne would hardly be a challenge. He's already all over me whenever no one's around. My talents deserve more than that loser Lothario."

"Hey, check it out," Jaime whispered, nudging his sister in the side. He nodded towards the door.

Shanti had just stepped into the doorway. Hesitating just inside the threshold, she looked around. She didn't know where to start. She definitely wanted to speak with Serafina's mother. Craning her neck, her eyes scouted the room trying to find the petite maid in the crowd.

She knew she was drawing some frowns for the way she was dressed. But she didn't care. She'd worked hard on her hair to make it neat, finally managing to get it to come down in one wave, curling just below her shoulders.

She was wearing a pale pink angora sweater, black pants, hose and heels. She'd worn her black dress to the funeral out of respect for the family, but she knew Serafina better than that.

Serafina loved color. She hated to wear a plain black or white uniform all the time. She always had something pinned to her lapel, whether it was an animal, flower or butterfly, it didn't matter as long as it was colorful.

Her favorite colors were pink and red. They made her feel soft and feminine she confided once to Shanti when they were alone in the parlor.

Shanti was just about to make her way through the room when Dawn's movement caught her eye. Her head turned towards the couch where the Lawton grandchildren were lounging.

Something was nudging Shanti at the back of her head, there's something wrong, she thought, if only I could pin point it- something was bothering her, but she just couldn't put her finger on what it was. She stared at Dawn's outstretched arm-

"Miss Shantilly!"

Shanti jumped and turned around.

Libby grinned crooked teeth at her. She was holding a mug with steam pouring out of it. "Damn!" the maid cursed, looking down. Her cell was attached to her apron and apparently it was buzzing.

"Mrs. Li wants me immediately. Miss Shantilly, please do me a favor-" she thrust the mug into Shanti's unsuspecting hands and turned to run off.

"Please give this coffee to the marshal, I gotta go." She started to hurry away then turned back not seeing the reluctant look on Shanti's face. "Tell him I made it like he likes his women, hot and sweet!" Libby tossed a saucy wink and disappeared down the hall.

"No! But- Libby come back! I don't-" Shanti held the mug out in front of her. The last thing she wanted to do was wait on the arrogant bully standing in the middle of an adoring circle. Darn. The maid was gone. Sighing, Shanti carefully made her way through the sea of people, all dressed in black.

Jarrett was still talking to the two maids, butler and Mary Jane. Mary Jane was still clinging tightly to his arm. Shanti hesitantly approached, stopping an arm's length from the sheriff.

He knew she was there, he'd seen her the second she'd entered the room.

"Here," Shanti muttered, thrusting the hot coffee into his hand. Quickly, before he could acknowledge her, she turned to make her escape. She didn't need to stand around and listen to his war stories, he had plenty of people to do that already.

Just as she took a step away, his arm whipped out and he grabbed her wrist, stopping her. He pulled her into the group. Imperturbably he sipped his coffee.

"Miss Lane," he said, "please join us. I don't think you've met Melanie, Karen, Joe, and this is Mary Jane. Everyone, this is the Lawtons' artist." Jarrett smiled mockingly down at Shanti. It was so easy to ruffle her feathers. Bright rosy spots lit up on her cheeks in a skinny minute every time he teased her.

"I am not the Lawtons' art-" she objected but Jarrett cut her off. He still held her wrist with one hand while holding his mug with the other. He casually took sips of coffee like he wasn't holding her prisoner.

She knew better than to struggle. He'd let her go when he was ready. She'd only call attention to herself if she squirmed and tried to get loose. The girl, Mary Jane, however, was staring daggers at his hand grasping her wrist. He had shrugged away from her as soon as the blonde approached.

"We're going to be treated to a showing of her painting Saturday night, aren't we Miss Lane?" Jarrett's expression looked benign to everyone else but she knew he was smirking at her.

"How long are you staying here, Miss...uh...Lane?" Mary Jane dragged her eyes off their hands and looked at Shanti under disdainful lowered lids. She ran her eyes up and down Shanti's figure. She stared contemptuously at the artist's soft pink sweater.

Shanti tried to pretend Jarrett wasn't calmly holding her wrist. She smiled at the brunette that was glaring at her.

Mary Jane was very pretty and very petite. She was wearing six-inch heels to give her some height. Even so, her head was still below Jarrett's shoulder. Her short legs were rock hard, like an aerobic instructor's.

The girl trying so anxiously to clutch at Jarrett's arm and pull him back to her, away from the blonde artist, was wearing a black miniskirt and black blouse. Her dark brunette hair was very thick and curly. Dark brown eyes flashed a warning at Shanti to stay away.

Not a problem, Shanti would have liked to say out loud. Instead, she found herself awkwardly stuttering, "I...uh...will probably leave soon after Saturday, I expect...I-"

"I don't guess she'll be leaving until we have the murders solved. She could be a witness or more," Jarrett said, looking down at Shanti.

His words brought the pink blush back to her cheeks. He was practically calling her a suspect! Her eyes were spitting that familiar blue fire- he knew he was pushing her. Jarrett bit back his grin.

"So, I guess she'll be hanging around for a while, huh?" He now smiled broadly at the very angry woman at his side that he was still holding onto. He turned back to the group.

"Anyway, the reason why I'm here," he handed his half empty mug to Mary Jane and reached into his pants pocket and pulled out an item. He held it out in his open palm for everyone to see. It was a button.

"This was clutched in Serafina's hand. We're hoping it can help us find her killer." He waited while everyone nearby peered at the button. He ignored the gasps as he swept his arm slowly back and forth.

Others gathered around him to look at the button.

"Does anyone recognize it?" he asked.

Chapter Thirty-Eight

A timid voice came from beside him. "Um…actually I do."

Jarrett looked over at Daisy.

She nervously pulled at her stringy hair. A white barrette hung crooked on one side of her head. Jarrett held the button out in front of her. She stared down at it like it was a tarantula about to spring off his hand and bite her.

"You know whose this is?" he asked her, one eyebrow arched in surprised inquiry.

She nodded. The maid was sweating like a stuck pig. Even as chubby as she normally was, her jeans and white sweater were becoming even snugger. Her boyfriend Liam seemed to have fallen off the face of the earth.

She'd looked for him, but he never responded to the messages she left at the bar where they met. She didn't know where he lived or worked. She hadn't even told Libby, her closest friend about the baby

"Well?" Jarrett prompted.

Frightened, Daisy looked around the room. She kept tugging nervously at her hair. Suddenly, her eyes widened, she stepped closer to the marshal. "It's his-" she spouted, pointing.

A hundred eyes followed her plump finger straight to Tobias Vaughn.

He looked shocked. So did Dolly standing beside him.

"Me? It's mine?" Tobias pushed through the crowd, Dolly followed close to his heels.

Daisy quickly stepped behind Jarrett pushing Mary Jane aside. She nodded vigorously.

"Y...yes, sir, it be y- yours," Daisy's voice shook, her eyes bugged out in fear, the white barrette slipped to hang more crookedly.

Jarrett turned and looked at the frightened maid trying to hide behind him. He still held Shanti's wrist. He smiled kindly down at the homely maid thinking she might be a bit 'slow'.

"Daisy, how can you know that? You work here, not at the Vaughns'. Are you saying you recognize the button from seeing him wearing it before?"

She shook her head so vehemently the barrette almost made its escape. "No Marshal, sir, a few months ago the flu was going through the Vaughns' household and a bunch of the help was sick. Mrs. Lawton brought me over to help out. I did some darning."

Daisy pointed at Dolly who looked baffled. "She said it was the master's shirt, her husband's. I remember the button because it's such a funny color."

Everyone looked at the button again. It was an odd shade of red mixed with purple.

Tobias gulped so loudly heads turned. His friends were now glaring at him with suspicion. "Uh...that's...that is my button...I recognize it-"

"Shut up you big oaf! Do you want to be arrested!?" Dolly snapped at her husband.

His face screwed up in confusion. "But, but...I don't know how the little maid would have gotten ahold of it-" He looked around the room, his palms were raised as if he had nothing to hide.

"Don't you people look at my daddy like that! He didn't do anything wrong, tell them Daddy!" Tori had reached her father's side to offer her support.

Her daddy was the gentlest man in Mooserock County, he wouldn't hurt a fly, and everyone knew that! Accusing eyes swung from Tobias to his fuming daughter and back again.

Behind Jarrett, Daisy coughed. He turned again and stared at her. She looked peculiar, her face was greenish.

"What Daisy, some on girl, spit it out?" the marshal commanded.

She gulped now, loud. Keeping her head down, the pimply pudgy maid peeked up at Tobias. Her lips were trembling with fear. "I heard 'em arguing a few months ago, be- before the master was...kilt..."

"Heard who arguing, Daisy?" Jarrett asked.

All eyes were now on the untidy plain girl not used to being in the spotlight. She nodded at Tobias.

"Him. Him an' Mr. Lawton. Right after we was told to keep quiet about the first time they found the rotted potatoes. They didn't know I was outside the servants' door. I was waitin' to clear the room." Her lashes flew up and down rapidly in agitation.

"Mrs. Li sent me, but I had to wait until they left to go in. But I could hear 'em. They was angry. I only remember because it was so unusual to hear those two fighting. Mr. Vaughn left then, right away, Mrs. Lawton came in the room, she said-"

"Daisy!" Maeve's voice cut her off. No one had seen her join the group. "They were not arguing, dear," she tried to sound soothing, a difficult task for her. She clasped her hands benignly in front of her mid-length dress.

"They were discussing the potatoes. Langston, being such a strictly honorable man, wanted Tobias and Magnus to tell the County Agent about the potato rot. Tobias was trying to convince my husband that it was just a chance thing, that he wanted to wait until the next harvest to be sure." She turned to Jarrett.

"As soon as I saw Tobias leave, I came in to consult with my husband about how he wanted the household to behave during all this," she finished calmly, smiling at the hapless maid.

"But, Mrs. Lawton wasn't-" the girl started to say-

"Sir! Marshal Chase! We have something important to tell you!" Two policemen burst into the room and hurried over to the marshal. One of the men leaned near Jarrett's ear and whispered something.

Jarrett's eyebrows shot straight up. He turned to look at to Tobias.

Sweat dripped down Tobias' flaccid face, fear crept into his eyes. All of this drama was too much for the simple farmer to take in. He could hear his wife, Dolly, breathing heavily next to him. She was at a loss as well.

"Tobias, it appears that the County Agriculturists and the Extension Agent have been at your farm taking samples and studying the potato crops for the past week," Jarrett said.

Tobias nodded. "Yes, they've been all over the farm. They've taken several pounds of potatoes and dirt from the ground. Because of everything going on we've been late in our harvesting. We've only got about...uh...let me see..."

Tobias put a finger to his lips and looked up thinking, counting to himself. "We've only got about, I'd say, less than a quarter stored so far." He cocked his head at Jarrett, his expression serious, waiting to hear what this was all about.

Jarrett let go of Shanti. However, his look advised her to stick around as if he still didn't know what part she played in the murders or whatever else was going on in Brimstone Glen in the county of Mooserock.

Before she came around, it had been a peaceful wealthy farming district. People went about their business friendly, without fear.

Now, the townsfolk were coming and going in a steady stream in and out of the sheriff's station ordering him to do something about the local murders, to find the killer before it happened again. It could be one of them next they told him.

Jarrett's eyes narrowed in suspicion at Tobias. He took in the middle-aged man's plain face and flannel shirt stretched over his burgeoning belly. He'd known the gentleman farmer for years. It wasn't possible this kind, simple man could be guilty of anything nefarious.

"Apparently, Tobias," Jarrett said quietly, "the agents have found the potato rot nematode all throughout your crop." Jarrett could hear gasps from people reverberate all around him.

Tobias looked stricken, then he lowered his head and looked guiltily down at his feet. He nodded sadly.

Jarrett's eyes popped in surprise. "You knew about this?" He was astonished that the man would know about this dreaded disease and keep quiet about it absolutely stunned him. It could endanger the entire potato crops and livelihood of all of his neighbors.

Tobias continued to stare at his feet, but he nodded slightly.

Murmurings flew around the room, growing louder as the shocked townspeople took in what was being said. Accusing eyes stared at one of their own. They couldn't believe it of Tobias Vaughn.

Maeve and her people kept mum, they were aware of the rot due to Matthew's recent visit. They also knew the state agents were investigating. But the Lawtons didn't engage in scandalous gossip so tongues were held.

"I don't understand, Tobias, what the hell is going on?" Jarrett touched Tobias' arm lightly, his voice kind. This gentle bear of a man seemed incapable of any sort of deceit.

Tobias took a deep breath and tucked his hands into his pants pockets. He looked sadly around the room at his friends, then back at Jarrett. He could hear Dolly sniffing next to him.

"Yes, Marshal, I sorta knew about the rot." He cringed at the loud gasps that circled the room again. He raised his hands, palms up, pleading for his friends to understand. Then he put his hands back in his pockets, his shoulders slumped as he explained.

"Last February, we found some evidence of the rot in our storage. We destroyed the lot of it. We...uh...cleaned and disinfected the storage sheds and the cultivating and handling equipment. Then...you know...we applied a nematicide...um...it was Vapam, Telone II" He looked close to tears.

The room now was as silent as a cloud covering. Everyone craned their necks and cupped their ears to hear.

Jarrett tried to keep the shocked look off his face. The deputy next to him was furiously writing in a notebook.

When no one said anything, Tobias continued. He looked steadily into Jarrett's eyes, hoping the young Marshal would not condemn him. "I uh…I knew it was wrong," he ignored Dolly's intake of breath, "and I offer no excuse, except, well…you all know how sick my daddy has been," people nearby nodded, silently.

"And I knew it would break his heart if he heard about the rot. We asked everyone to keep it quiet for a while so we could see how ingrained it was. We'd hoped it was just a fluke, you know, just a onetime deal…" his voice faded as he spoke the truth.

Some people still nodded, agreeing with him, others shot accusing looks at the portly farmer.

"The uh…fields looked fine after the cleanup and disinfecting, we thought it was just a small singular patch. We kept the soil dry and we thought we could fix it…" His voice washed-out again as the murmuring in the room grew louder.

Jarrett shook his head and crossed his arms in front of his chest. "I'm not a farmer, Tobias, and even I know that an outbreak of the rot can occur even 30 years later in a previously infested crop. And it spreads like wildfire-"

Tobias nodded again, his face aging years in just minutes. "Yes, I know Jarrett. I…I…we took a chance…we'd so hoped we had eradicated it. The hands and I were out every day the past few months looking for evidence of it.

"But, so far, the spuds were hard, not soft or crumbling, we saw no larva, no holes, no decay…no surface cracks. I'd heard that with proper treatment, well, that sometimes it goes away…" He looked earnestly around the room seeking to ensure his friends he would never deliberately endanger their fields.

"Unfortunately, Tobias, you were wrong."

Tobias stared back down at his feet. Then he raised teary eyes to Jarrett.

The marshal sadly shook his head at the farmer. "The agents have brought us a report," he nodded to his deputy.

The deputy that wasn't writing held up a piece of paper, his face solemn. The deputy handed the report to Tobias.

The farmer took it with shaking hands and quietly read it.

Jarrett said, "The agent and agriculturists found evidence of the rot. Irrefutable evidence." He looked around the room, first at Shanti, then to Maeve who had moved back from the crowd.

She hovered unlike her normally queenly self, silent near the doorway to the great room.

Then, Jarrett looked over to the couch where even self-absorbed Jaime and Dawn Lawton were listening with rapt attention. He looked next to Chloe who appeared about to cry, then over to the bar where Camelia was totally ignoring the entire scene.

Montgomery stood with the group of servants gathered in a tightly knit group in the corner.

The only people Jarrett could detect missing from the household were Matthew Vaughn and Mrs. Li, the Lawton's housekeeper.

Jarrett knew where Matthew Vaughn was. The young man was at his home talking with the County Extension Agents discussing whether or not charges would be brought against the Vaughns.

He wondered where the Asian housekeeper was. She did have a peculiar habit of appearing and disappearing at opportune times. She was probably in a closet in the room somewhere listening.

Jarrett glanced at the deputy that had handed him the report. He'd also handed him another paper as well. Jarrett studied that while the room grew louder. He looked up and his eyes traveled around the room again.

"And that's not all they found…" He hesitated, his voice ominous. He had everyone's attention again, which is exactly what he wanted. He wanted to catch unprepared expressions.

Chapter Thirty-Nine

*F*rom across the room Maeve drawled, "Pray tell, Marshal, what other horror has befallen our heretofore undisturbed, innocent sleepy little village?"

The planes of her majestic face were hard, but her eyes seemed weary. Her back rigid as a rake, she made her way back through the throng until she reached the circle of people gathered around Jarrett and Tobias. One grey eyebrow rounded in question at Jarrett.

The marshal turned to the grand lady. He held the report up in one hand and skimmed it again before answering her. "The agents found something else inside the potatoes besides rot."

Tobias' head shot up, his expression surprised. The farmer's brows furrowed, he seemed totally taken aback.

Maeve looked on with interest. Jarrett scanned the room quickly, everyone appeared surprised and or curious.

"Hidden inside a few hundred potatoes, which isn't that many considering the tons that are harvested and stored- were vials of," he looked back at the paper in his hand, then directly at Tobias before saying, "nerve gas."

"What?!" Tobias exploded. He and half the room gaped open mouthed and bulge-eyed at Jarrett.

Sharp gasps and exclamations were heard before loud utterings and questions filled the room.

"Nerve gas?" Shanti shook her head. "How can nerve gas get into potatoes? Isn't that stuff deadly?"

Jarrett cut his glance at the blonde beauty then he turned back to Tobias who looked like he was about to have a heart attack. His face had been red with humiliation, now it was rapidly turning white and his brown eyes bugged with confusion and anguish.

"You're out of your mind, Marshal." Dolly's country voice stood out, angrily. She pushed Tobias aside and shook a furious finger at the sheriff.

"You government folk are just trying to get back at us for the rot. We didn't mean any harm, and you know it. We've been here for generations. I've worked for charities and the hospital volunteering my whole life. We...we wouldn't never, ever hurt any-" The matronly lady in her blue gingham dress became choked up, her words dissolved into sobs.

Tobias stared blankly at his wife. He had no idea what to do-this was so outside his small realm of experience, nothing horrible like this had ever happened to his family before. He just stood impotently staring at his sobbing wife. Their daughter Tori was speechless, she stood trembling, clutching her father's sleeve.

Maeve quickly stepped forward and put an arm around her old friend. She looked up angrily at Jarrett as she tried to console the weeping Dolly. "You'd better be damned sure of what you're saying, Jarrett Chase," she threatened the lawman.

One side of Jarrett's mouth pulled back into a crooked smile. He ignored Maeve and turned his attention to Shanti. He wished he could brush away the distressed look on her face. He'd rather have her spitting blue fire at him than see the dread in her eyes, waiting for what else he had to say.

He looked her in her baby blues, she came across so trusting and innocent. She couldn't have anything to do with the murders, he thought.

"Nerve gas is dangerous, Miss Lane," he answered her, "in fact it's deadly. A tiny bit can wipe out hundreds of people instantly. They think they narrowed down what kind it is..." he looked down at the paper in his hand.

"Ah...Amiton it's called. It's a second-generation nerve agent similar to VX-gas. Apparently it's 10 times more toxic than Sarin. Sarin is a more common form of gas. Americans call them..." he ran a finger across a line in the paper. "G-Agents."

While he was reading, the room was silent. Now it burst with nervous chatter.

Everyone in the room, fear and bewilderment in their faces and voices, questioned each other, what the heck was the lawman talking about?

Tobias, still looking sheepish, but rapidly becoming greatly disturbed, asked, "But Jarrett, doesn't that stuff kill people?" Others around the room murmured in agreement.

Jarrett responded, "It sure does, Tobias, it sure does. Like I said, it's deadly. A small amount is lethal. A person can carry it in a closed soda can into a room full of people, set the can down, pull off the lid and leave quickly of course." He paused, watching the group rigid with fright, eyes rounded wide in horror.

"Within seconds, people will drop like flies. Other people will wander in unaware and see the people lying on the floor. Before they can get to them to see what's wrong, they will succumb and collapse as well."

"I heard it's a nasty, painful way to die!" a man standing to the side exclaimed.

His expression solemn, Jarrett nodded. "It is. First a person can have eye pain and feel drowsy. Then convulsions, wheezing and sweating may come, headache, blurred vision, nausea, until finally, respiratory arrest."

Moans and mutterings roamed through the room. Some women looked on the edge of fainting. Abject fear distorted faces.

"But sir, isn't that...uh...Sarin gas stuff...isn't that foreign? I mean they don't make it here, do they?" a scared man asked, panic scrawled all over his face.

Jarrett nodded. "Yeah, they can make it here, John," he replied with a crooked smile, "But they think this strain is from maybe Japan, actually Tokyo. There's a cult called the Atara Shan that has previously been responsible for Sarin bombing, they may link this to them."

"But Marshal," Shanti said, her face still exhibiting confusion, "how did it get into the potatoes?"

Shrugging, the marshal folded up the paper and shoved it into his pocket. A foot away, his deputy continued to scribble in his notebook.

"That's a good question, Miss Lane." Jarrett gestured to Tobias. "Tobias, we were wondering if you could help us out in that direction."

"Me?! Me?!" Tobias pointed at his thick chest with his thumb. He shook his head urgently back and forth. "No, no Jarrett, never, I have never…I don't even know what the stuff is! I don't know what it looks like, or smells like…I mean, where would I get something like that?!" His voice grew shrill, mortified that anyone would think he would have anything to do with such a wretched, hideous thing like nerve gas.

He held his pudgy palms together, pleading, "Please Jarrett, you must believe me!"

The marshal looked at the country farmer sadly. "Tobias, frankly, I just don't know what to believe. We have two people murdered, you've got a deadly fungus growing in your fields that can destroy all the crops around you and you kept quiet about it knowing that was against the law, and now…something we never thought we'd hear about in our lifetime.

"Something left over from WWII, a horrendous, colorless, odorless gas, 26 times more lethal than cyanide. A pinprick can kill, quickly and with agonizing symptoms was found right in all our backyards."

The deputy that was writing suddenly flipped back a few pages. He read something that disturbed him. He handed the book to Jarrett to read. The marshal took the book and read the words. Then he looked at Tobias.

"What now?" The farmer shrank back, his hands came up as if warding off a threatened strike.

"It says here, Tobias, that over the years there have been attempts on your father's life."

Tobias looked even more confused. "I don't know what you mean by attempts, Jarrett?"

"Someone has tried to kill Magnus on several occasion," Jarrett responded with a narrowed glare.

Chapter Forty

*T*obias looked shocked again. "You...you mean those times he had those strange accidents? But- but those were just weird accidents...weren't they?"

Jarrett and the deputy both shook their heads. Gasps ricocheted in the room again at this latest information revealed. Jarrett nodded a cue at the deputy.

"Go ahead, Bill," he instructed the lawman.

Bill Johnson cleared his throat nervously, he wasn't used to a room full of people gawking at him. He sneaked a peek at Tori Vaughn. When he'd first come around to question people, he'd been quite taken with her quiet dark beauty.

He'd hoped after the investigation was over he might ask her out. But the way she was looking at him now, well, going out on a date looked like the last thing on the young woman's mind. He looked down at the notebook Jarrett had given back to him.

"Ahem...uh...it's noted here that...uh...six years ago Magnus Vaughn was accidentally shot while on a hunting trip in the woods."

The group's rapt attention was on the deputy, although glances slingshot from Bill to Jarrett to Tobias and back to Bill.

"Who shot him was never determined," Bill read. "It was recorded that another hunter that was not with the hunting party must have shot at something in the woods and was far enough away they didn't know Magnus and his party were there, missed the animal he was shooting at and the old man took the bullet in his leg."

"That's right, sir," Tobias cut in, "they examined all of our weapons, the bullet didn't come from me or anyone else in our group."

Bill kept reading his notes out loud, "And then, five years ago, Magnus' brakes failed when he took his Silverado truck down to the auction in Farnsworth. He was lucky, when he went over the cliff, it was in a low area and the truck eventually stopped without any harm coming to the old man. Then-"

Tobias tried to protest again, but Jarrett held up a hand silencing him. Tobias' mouth snapped shut, his jaw clenched.

"Around four years ago, a gunshot in the woods jolted Magnus Vaughn's horse and it tried to buck him. Luckily, he maintained control of his animal and again he was not injured."

"Now really, Marshal, there's always people sneaking about, hunting and poaching illegally in the forests and accidents-" Dolly Vaughn tried to intersperse her protests, but Jarrett held up a hand to her as well.

"And then," Bill continued speaking, "three years ago, Magnus went to the hospital with a terrible stomach ache. They were never sure, but the doctors believed it was some kind of poisoning. However, with all the toxins in the barns and stables, they let it go that it might have been an accidental ingestion. Two years ago, a bale of hay just missed his head when he was in the barn overseeing the harvest-"

Jarrett broke in, "Since he's become more feeble this last year, the 'accidents' have not happened. We believe that may be because he doesn't venture far out of the house anymore."

"But Sheriff-" Tobias started to say, then took a deep breath. "Listen Jarrett, those were all just accidents. That's what the police said every time they came and made a report. They weren't *attempts on his life.*"

"I'm sorry, Tobias, taken alone, they may seem like accidents, but put together, they look to me like someone sure wants Magnus Vaughn dead. And these are only the 'accidents' that we know about, there may be others that didn't get close enough to hurt him that no one even noticed."

Jarrett nodded to the two lawmen with him. Bill closed the notebook and tucked it into an inside jacket pocket. They both stepped closer.

"We did some hard thinking this morning when all of this was brought to us. I was here hoping I could get a clue or a handle to what's going on, but unfortunately, I just don't have an inkling. So we talked about motive...and...well gee, Tobias, you're the only one here that would have a motive to see your father dead."

Tobias slammed a hand to his chest, his eyes filled with tears. Dolly gasped and grabbed at his sleeve.

Tori grasped his other arm. "No Jarrett, no, you're wrong! My daddy would never hurt an ant, you know that, you don't know what you're talking about!" Tori screamed at Jarrett.

The marshal's face turned red. He knew how hard this was going to be. He nodded again at his deputies. Bill pulled a set of handcuffs from behind his back.

Tobias stood back, his eyes wide in fright.

"I'm sorry Tobias, I have to arrest you for the murder of Langston Lawton."

"What?! Langston-" Tobias cried. "I don't understand- it wasn't me!"

Bill pulled Tobias' hands behind the large man's back and snapped the handcuffs on his wrists then he held onto Tobias' beefy arm.

The other deputy held up both hands to hold off Dolly and Tori who were crying and yelling at Jarrett.

"We can only think, Tobias, that while you were trying to kill Magnus, that somehow, Langston found out, and maybe also Serafina, so you killed them to keep them quiet. It's a theory that you planted a contaminated mother tuber in the potato fields to destroy the crop deliberately to break your father, maybe give him a heart attack so you could inherit," the marshal explained.

"Take him, Bill," he told the deputy, inclining his head towards the door.

"You're insane, Jarrett! Absolutely insane! Help me Dolly, help me!" Tobias cried, as the two deputies led him outside to their patrol car.

The entire room stood stunned. The only sound was the sobbing of Dolly and Tori Vaughn.

Montgomery stood at the head of the room. "May I have your attention," he called out, his voice full of authority. The consternated group turned to him.

"I am very sorry for the events that have transpired. However, I'm sure you will all understand if we ask you to leave, now." He held his arms open then gently gestured to the door.

Talking amongst themselves, the people did as Montgomery asked, slowly leaving the room until it was empty, except for the Lawtons, Shanti, Jarrett, and Dolly and Tori Vaughn.

Maeve stood in front of Jarrett. Two vivid red spots were in the middle of her cheeks. She was enraged.

Pulling her shoulders back as straight as she could get them, "You better get ready for a fight, Jarrett Chase," she railed at him.

Her green eyes looked almost black from her fury. "You've made a big mistake today, a big mistake." Her voice was low but flooded with fury, slitted eyes burned with fierce fire.

"I'm sorry, Maeve, you know I truly am. The mayor has been at our door telling us to do something. Everything that has occurred has done so here, between yours and the Vaughns' farms," Jarrett said softly.

"This area is the vortex of whatever is going on. It was necessary for me to commit to some type of action." He turned to Dolly. "I suggest you contact an attorney."

Not sparing a glance at Shanti, he turned on his heel and headed for the door. Stopping at the door, he turned again and looked straight at Maeve.

"The agents are investigating Red Gem Farm next." He pivoted away before he could see the look on her face. It pained him to be hurting people he's known for years, people he'd considered his friends. He made his way quickly through the house before Maeve could gather her wits and come after him. She will be a hardy foe.

The patrol car containing Tobias was disappearing down the drive as he came outside and hopped into his Bronco. He followed the patrol car to the station.

Shanti didn't know what to do. Dolly and Tori had run to the window to watch the police car take their husband and father away to jail.

Montgomery had returned from seeing the guests out and into their cars. He came right up to Maeve.

She turned furiously on him.

"That- that whippersnapper!" she ground out. Her face contorted with rage. "He has the nerve to have his men inspecting our grounds and barns! I can't believe it, I just- I am beside myself, Montgomery, just beside myself!" She shook her head, wringing her hands, a decidedly 'unMaevelike' action.

"Is there anything I can do?" Shanti asked timidly. She feared Maeve's wrath just as much as the next guy.

Maeve ignored her at first. Then her head swiveled, stopping when she spotted Dolly and Tori at the window weeping.

"Yes, perhaps Shantilly dear, you could see to the Vaughns, get them some tea, or maybe find Mrs. Li, she'll know what to do…"

Maeve looked around absently, she was thinking of their recourse. First, she needed to call a lawyer for Tobias. Dolly was apparently going to be useless in this emergency.

Shanti hesitated, then she hurried over to Dolly and Tori. She took each of their arms and led them out of the room.

She looked around for Chloe, but she and the rest of the Lawtons had disappeared.

Chapter Forty-One

Jarrett needed to clear his head, so he turned off a fork in the road that led to a little lake on the way to the station. His truck bounced over the bumpy road before he came to a stop at the bank of the lake. He turned off the engine and got out of the truck.

Taking a few careful steps down the small bank he stood in front of the crystalline water. Looking down, he could see hundreds of minnows swimming near the water's edge.

His watery reflection echoed back up at him. He studied the reflection of the tall wavery lawman dressed in a khaki uniform, leather jacket with fur collar and black boots now covered with a bit of mud. He'd left his hat in the car, the winter sun highlighted his dark brown hair.

He was too far away to see the consternation in his blue-green eyes. Blinking hard, he knelt down by the water.

Thinking if he could just hold the water still for a second, the answers to all of the questions that had plagued him lately would be revealed.

Who killed Langston Lawton and Serafina? And why? Were the two murders even tied together? Most likely they were. There hadn't been a murder here in Brimstone Glen in over five years and that had been a murder/suicide between old man Simon and his sickly wife, Martha. There was no puzzle to that one, a suicide note was next to the bodies.

His brows drew down, full yet chiseled lips pulled in. He was totally perplexed. He tried hard to puzzle this one out, but there were just no clues.

Maybe Langston and Serafina were killed because they saw something, or knew something to do with the deadly toxin. And the smuggling from the airplane, was that any part of the killings? The men with the kayaks had tried to kill him without a second thought.

Jarrett leaned over and stuck a finger in the middle of his reflection. Silently, he watched the circle of ripples caused by his finger drift away until the lake was almost smooth again.

Standing up, he tugged his jacket back down to his hips and walked back to his car. He remembered the rest of what his men had told him when they first arrived at the Lawton's.

They told him they might have tracked down the kayakers. He jumped in his truck and hurried over to the station.

They were booking Tobias Vaughn when he got there.

Tobias, wiping the fingerprint ink off his fingers with a paper towel, looked back at Jarrett mournfully as the deputies led him to the back of the building where the cells were.

Jarrett felt bad. He was pretty sure Tobias wasn't the killer, or even one of the smugglers, but he had to do something, the Mayor was on his back to get this thing solved. He hoped making an arrest might make someone think the heat was off and do something stupid or rash to reveal themselves. Unfortunately, at the moment all the arrows pointed at Tobias Vaughn.

"Hey Peters," Jarrett walked over to a red-headed deputy sitting behind a typewriter.

Deputy Peters was pecking at the computer keyboard with two fingers, his tongue stuck out of one corner of his mouth to help him concentrate. He looked up at Jarrett.

"Sir?" he said, his brows cocked. He drew splayed fingers through his orange hair.

"Peters, Bill and Tom were telling me something about tracing the kayakers, what's the deal with that?" Jarrett leaned against the deputy's desk and crossed his arms in front of his chest and his legs at the ankles.

He looked down at the deputy and a lock of hair fell in front of one eye. He'd been so busy lately he hadn't had time for a haircut and his hair was getting long. He pushed the chestnut lock back off his forehead.

The freckled deputy put his hands down on the desk and leaned back in the chair.

"Well, sir, Bill said they questioned all the kayak rental shops here in the entire Mooserock County, with no luck. So they widened the search and put in some calls to surrounding counties. This morning they got a call from…"

His forehead wrinkled as he tried to remember. "Hold on a sec…" He pushed the chair back and stood up. Poking his fingers through his hair, he went over to another desk.

Jarrett watched him go to the desk. He could hear one of the dispatchers talking to someone on the radio.

Joellen Sanders was good at her job. She had earphones on and was speaking in abbreviations to someone over the radio. She had a husky voice for a female, but her voice matched her personality.

Around forty-five, she kept her greying hair in a short pageboy bob, the ends tucked behind her ears. She was also pretty muscular for a female. She had a no-nonsense approach to life.

Her tough exterior hid the soft as marshmallow inside that she displayed very infrequently. Only small children and women beaten by their husbands could bring out her soft side.

Joellen had looked up and given Jarrett a little salute when he'd first entered the station. She then frowned at him, nodding towards Tobias Vaughn.

Everyone in town knew the Vaughns. Everyone knew Tobias was just a simple country farmer that would never hurt a fly much less a good friend and neighbor, or an innocent little maid.

Jarrett had just shrugged at her and moved over to Peters' desk. She turned back to her radio.

Jarrett looked around the station while he waited for Peters to return. This was his home. He spent more time here than at his small cottage.

The station was paneled in amber colored wood with dark knots. The desks were old but functional. They did the best they could with their budget. They had pretty much the most up to date equipment. Radios, fax machines, computers and their own NCIC proxies for nationwide record checks.

Peters is a redheaded eighteen-year-old brought up poor and home-schooled. His family lived in an extremely rural section of the county.

Jarrett had detected a brightness in the boy's pale blue eyes, and an eagerness to please, so he'd taken a chance and hired him. The boy had worked out very well. Pleasant and easygoing, he was a pleasure to have around the station.

"Here, sir." Peters came back to Jarrett carrying a file. It was open and he was holding it carefully so the papers wouldn't fly out. He handed the file to Jarrett.

The marshal moved away from the desk. Standing with his boots planted firmly on the tiled floor, he held the file and flipped through the pages. He peered briefly over at Peters.

"Davey," he addressed the boy by his first name, "these papers need to be clipped in, you know." He looked back down at the file, not seeing the boy's nod.

He knew the kid would do as he asked as soon as he was done with the file. He skimmed the pages in the file.

So far they only recorded the events he already knew - *wait-here*, Deputy Johnson wrote they had picked up a lead in Sprucehill County, one of Mooserock's neighboring counties.

Jarrett took the file over to a huge map of Idaho pinned on a wall. He looked down at the address of the kayak rental store, then back up at the map. He quickly located Mooserock as it was already circled in red.

North of Mooserock, Sprucehill, a small county, barely registered on the vast map. Jarrett ran his finger up the map searching carefully for the address in the file. It took him a few minutes to find it.

The kayak store was as far to the north as it could get and still be in Idaho. The marshal reached over and took a pencil off a desk and circled the spot on the map he'd just located.

He wondered if the smugglers had ridden the kayaks clear up the Snake River to Sprucehill. But then, where had they begun?

"Marshal?"

Jarrett turned around. Deputy Bill Johnson was standing next to him. He hadn't heard him approach. "Hey Bill," Jarrett said. "How'd it go?"

Bill shook his head sadly. "Gee Boss, it was pretty rough. Mr. Vaughn is a great guy. I've known him ever since I was ankle-high to a cricket. He used to catch me and my brothers poaching rabbits in his woods. He'd always let us go with a warning." He paused and sucked in a sorrowful breath.

"You know, I just don't think he's guilty. I mean he's guilty of keeping quiet about the rot, yeah, but I don't think his intention was for anyone else to get harmed, you know?"

Jarrett nodded in agreement. He'd tucked the pencil behind his ear, it poked out just below his hat. He gestured to the open file in his hands. "What makes you think this is the place the boats were rented from?"

"We called every single boat rental place in Idaho, Boss. This'n came to our attention because the kayaks were rented with a stolen credit card. It didn't come up as stolen until after the sale.

"Deputy Parker over in Sprucehill told me they found the owner of the credit card in the hospital. Parker said the guy was carjacked at a gas station and taken to a dirt road in the woods where the jackers hit him over the head and tossed him down a gorge apparently thinking he was dead. The guy was out I guess for a while, then came to and managed to get back up to the road where he hitched a ride."

Jarrett nodded again. It was close to what happened to him a week ago. He felt his ribs twinge as Bill told what happened to the poor guy that was carjacked.

"The thing is, Boss, if you're gonna steal a credit card, kayaks seem the last thing on your mind to get, ya know? That's what made it stand out like a sore thumb to us."

"Has anyone gone out there for a description?" Jarrett asked.

"No sir, we just got the word and then went to the Lawtons 'cause we knew you wanted Mr. Vaughn arrested."

"Get your jacket, Bill, I'll meet you out by the truck."

Deputy Johnson barely had time to grab his hat and jacket, Jarrett was already out the door.

Chapter Forty-Two

It took the better part of the day for Jarrett and Bill to get to Sprucehill County.

Bill perused the map while Jarrett drove. They took the interstate as far as they could. Eventually they had to turn off and head on a two-lane road towards the hills. Bill folded the map as small as he could get it to pinpoint where they were going.

Jarrett had called Joellen to contact the store to get directions as GPS was terribly shaky through the very rural areas. Studying the map, it looked like it was a rental shop used by fishing cabins tucked deep into the woods.

After ten miles of the two-lane road they looked for a sign indicating Wood Road Joellen had told them was their turn off.

"There!" Bill said, pointing to an old weathered sign they would have missed if they had blinked. Fortunately, Jarrett was driving slowly so they wouldn't pass it.

The sign was half overgrown with tall grass and weeds. They turned off the two-lane road onto a dirt road. Bumping along for a mile or so, Bill kept looking down at the piece of paper where he'd written down dispatch's directions.

"She said it was about two miles down the dirt road, then look for a sign for 'Clemmet's Boat Rentals', we turn right at the sign." Bill craned his neck to spot the sign in the dense forest of trees that lined the road.

"I see it-" Jarrett said, pointing to right.

Bill put a hand over his eyes to stop the glare from the window so he could see better. "Wow, the way they hide signs around here you'd think they don't want any business!"

Jarrett turned the truck at the sign. As soon as they turned they could see a two-story high ramshackle building that had seen better days. Jarrett pulled up in front of the building that looked about to fall over and parked the truck.

They could make out a view of a part of the river running behind the structure.

The two lawmen zipped up their jackets and put their hats on as soon as they exited the truck. The wind was blowing so viciously both men pulled their collars up around their necks.

"At least it's not snowing," Bill remarked gratefully, the wind tearing away half his words. They moved quickly to the door of the old building.

The wood on the shack was so old and weather-beaten the brown was mostly grey and white now. The door slammed closed behind them as soon as they stepped inside.

A man behind the counter was talking to another man on this side of the counter. They didn't even look up when the door slammed. The two lawmen approached the counter.

The inside of the building didn't look much better than the outside. All kinds of small boats, rowboats, canoes and kayaks were hanging in the double-high rafters. Fishing poles, lure, chewed up dusty buoys, lifejackets and oars were on shelves and just lying on the floor.

Faded pictures of fish hung haphazardly on the paint peeling walls. It was dim inside, the tiny windows didn't let in much light. They were designed to keep the inside warm.

Cobwebs draped from window to rafter to window. Steel containers labeled 'bait' lined a wall. As soon as the lawmen reached the counter, the man behind it looked up.

"Howdy there, gentlemen. Your dispatch operator called and tol' us to expect you," the man behind the counter greeted Jarrett and Bill.

He was darkly tanned with deep laugh lines alongside his mouth. His hat had a picture of a bass on it, and his jeans and corduroy shirt looked like they could do with a wash. He looked about 45, but was probably in his mid-thirties. He obviously spent a lot of time outside. Two cans of beer and a pack of cigarettes were on the counter.

The man on the other side of the counter appeared to be a friend, not a customer. He looked more or less the same as the counterman.

Smiling broadly, Jarrett held out his hand. "Hello, I'm Marshal Chase and this is Deputy Johnson. We're hoping you can help us."

The man behind the counter reached over and shook Jarrett's and then Bill's hands.

"Pleasure boys." He smiled and nodded to his friend. "I'm Sam Griswald and thisn's my pal Joey Fairfield."

The other man nodded, but didn't offer to shake hands.

Griswald turned his back for a second and pulled a paper off a nail stuck into a block and handed it to Jarrett.

"Thisn's the credit card receipt. One of your deputies asked me ta find it and save it for ya."

Jarrett didn't take the receipt right away. He pulled a plastic bag out of his jacket and held it out. Griswald obliged and dropped the paper into the bag.

"Fingerprints, huh? Gee fellas, I'm sorry, we didn't think about touchin' it an' all," Griswald apologized. He looked sheepish but his eyes were bright with interest.

Being part of a murder investigation was the most exciting thing to happen in these parts. The only arrests made around here were for drunk and disorderly, hunting out of season or without a license and catching more than the legal limit of fish.

Jarrett nodded without saying anything. He sealed the bag and put it into his pocket. He leaned over and laid his forearms onto the glass countertop. Bill stood next to him and pulled out his notebook and pen.

Joey Fairfield moved slightly away from the lawmen.

"Sprucehill police will come by and take your prints and then fax them to us so we can eliminate them. Can you describe the renters, Mr. Griswald?" Jarrett asked the fisherman.

Griswald's forehead furrowed as he thought. He scratched an arm with dirty fingers.

"It was a couple a' weeks ago…let me think…" Griswald pulled the cap with the bass on it off his head exposing a crop of dirty blonde hair. He scratched his head.

Jarrett and Bill stood patiently. They unzipped their jackets and pushed their Stetsons back off their foreheads.

Bill was studying the fisherman, he'd always thought that would be the life, fishing all day, but looking at this untidy grubby fellow, he was having second thoughts.

Bill could see his reflection in the glass case behind the fisherman. Tall, not as tall as Jarrett Chase, but a good height, trim, in good shape, well, he'd be in better shape if he laid off the beer and wings on the weekends.

He pulled off his hat and ran his fingers through his own wheat colored hair. His hair color was almost the same as the fisherman's, only clean and shiny, and shorter and neater. He put his hat back on and dragged his eyes from his reflection and back to the man behind the counter.

"Only two of 'em came inside, Sheriff," Griswald stated. "I hardly remember the one 'cause he looked like a regular joe, you know? But ta other, he was foreign…you know, black hair, short, round face and darker skin," he shrugged.

Jarrett raised his eyebrows, his shoulders hunched as he leaned in further towards the shop owner. "Foreign? In what way?"

Griswald pulled his dirty cap off again and scratched his head leaving tufts stuck straight up. "Well, sir, like one of 'em there Mexicanas, I think. Wait!" He snapped his fingers.

"Ya know, I did catch one 'a ta dudes that stayed outside, he looked, ya know, like a Oriental kind. I woulda thought he was a Mex too, but his eyes, ya know, were like crescent moons, and his coloring was different from ta one in here, more yella."

Rolling his eyes at the offensive descriptions, Bill bit his tongue and wrote furiously.

Jarrett asked, "What were the chaps wearing, Griswald, do you remember?"

The fisherman grew deep in thought again, his brows hunkered down between his thoughtful eyes, his friend moved even further away.

Fairfield smoked pot on weekends and also when he was in his boat fishing, and he didn't need no cops nosing around. He discreetly shook his jacket trying to wave off any smoke that might be lingering.

"Overalls!" Griswald blurted, pleased with himself for remembering.

"Overalls?" Bill hesitated writing and looked up

"Sure dude, overalls like on a farm, ya know, on a tractor," Griswald answered.

"Was that the Mexican or the 'regular' guy?" Jarrett questioned.

"Oh, that'n was ta Mex. Like I said, ta regular guy just looked...um...regular...so I didn't pay him no attention." Griswald shrugged. He spread his arms out placing both hands on the glass counter, his fingers splayed and his shoulders hunched.

"Did you see the vehicle they came in?" Jarrett asked him.

Griswald closed his eyes, trying to remember. He shook his head. "Naw, didn't pay no attention."

"Sprucehill police told me it was stolen. It was a white Toyota pick-up. They found it stashed in the woods with two flat tires," Bill supplied.

Jarrett gave the deputy a look that said 'why didn't you tell me that before?'

Bill's mouth pushed out with a shoulder bump- oops. "Gee Boss, everything happened in a hurry. First arresting Mr. Vaughn and then trying to find our way out here..." his shoulders bumped again.

Jarrett wasn't looking at him anymore. "Did they put the kayaks in here or take them with them?"

Griswald's eyes shifted to the right as he tried to picture the event. "Ah, yeah, I remember. Could hear 'em cursing and arguing as they shoved the boats in the bed a' the truck. So, yeah, now I remember the white truck too. "

Jarret figured as much. It was too cold and too far of a haul to ride the kayaks from here to where he caught them. "Didn't bring them back I suppose?"

"Ha," Griswald chuckled. "Naw sir. Don't 'spect we'll be seein' the boats again. Prolly scuttled 'em in the river. Don't make sense crooks buying stuff with stolen credit cards and haulin' 'em in a stolen truck then kindly return them, hey?" He grinned at Joey.

"Is there anything else you remember? Anything else you can tell us?"

Pawing at scruff on his chin, Griswald shook his head. "Nah, they was just rentin' kayaks, ya know? We rent 'em all the time, who pays any mind to people? I mean 'ceptn' girls." He winked at Jarrett and Bill.

"If they was chicks, I could tell ya how many moles they had on their arms!" He chuckled.

Jarrett grinned at him. "Well thanks Mr. Griswald, you've been a tremendous help to us." He held his hand out again. Griswald shook it.

Bill snapped his notebook closed and shoved it in his pocket. He tipped his hat at the shop owner. He looked for the other man. But Joey had slipped away unnoticed.

Jarrett zipped up his jacket and pulled his collar back up around his neck. He clamped his hat down tight on his head. Bill followed suit.

The lawmen left the building, the door slamming closed by the wind behind them. They wasted no time getting to the truck. It was getting dark.

"What do you think, Boss?" Bill looked over at Jarrett.

Jarrett was quiet behind the wheel. They'd tossed their hats in the back seat as soon as they got into the truck. Jarrett's hair was growing over his back collar and a thick lock in the front kept falling over one eye. He impatiently shoved it back off his forehead.

Jarrett didn't look at Bill. He kept his eyes on the road. It was dark now and there were no streetlights on the dirt road. The trees blocked the moonlight. He hoped no animals took it in their minds to run across the road in front of the truck.

"I've got a good idea who at least one of the smugglers is," Jarrett said.

"What?" Bill was amazed. "You're kidding? How'd you figure that out?"

Jarrett pulled off the dark dirt road and onto the two-lane road. They had a long drive ahead of them.

"I'll tell you over a burger and a cup of coffee," the marshal said, speeding down the road heading back to Mooserock.

Chapter Forty-Three

$\mathcal{E}$very police car in Mooserock was pulling into the Vaughns' farm.

In the pre-dawn darkness, red and blue lights strobed for miles and the sirens wailed through the whole town.

Outside lights on the house were blaring brightly, lighting up the entire grounds. By the time Jarrett and Bill arrived the driveway was lined with police cars.

Armed deputies were running around the area in the dark. Jarrett could see the lights of flashlights funneling up and down the lawns. A uniformed man standing in the driveway holding a clipboard was pointing and giving orders.

Matthew Vaughn was standing near the front of the house. He had buttoned his wool coat up to the neck and a plaid scarf was wrapped around his neck. Hatless, his black hair blew around in the biting wind.

As soon as Matthew saw Jarrett pull up he rushed down the driveway and waited for the marshal to park the truck.

"Jarrett, man, what the heck is going on? You're scaring Ma and Tori to death!" Matthew yelled at the closed window. He grabbed the door handle of the Bronco and yanked Jarrett's door open.

The marshal turned off the blue dome light he'd placed on the dashboard so they would let him get past the roadblock the police set up at the entrance to the farm. Bill hopped out of the passenger side quickly pulling on his hat.

Jarrett stepped out into the freezing night air. "Calm down, Matthew, this has nothing to do with you-"

"Nothing to do with me?" Matthew's voice rose into a squeal. He followed Jarrett who was striding quickly over to the man that was giving orders.

"What do you mean 'nothing to do with me'? Heck Rett, you've arrested my father, the entire police department of Brimstone Glen and Quillshead and every other village in Mooserock County as well are here. They're tramping all over the place, in and out of the barns, up and down the lawn-"

Jarrett kept moving briskly towards the man standing in the middle of the driveway. With so many lights on, the Vaughns' house looked like a neon Las Vegas street.

He could see Dolly and Tori standing in the front doorway holding each other. He could also see curtains all throughout the house parted. Many pairs of servants' eyes were following the business going on outside.

"Rett-" Matthew couldn't keep the fear and anxiety out of his voice. His whole world was being flipped upside down.

Jarrett reached the man in charge. They shook hands. "Hey Sarg," the marshal greeted him. "Where are we at?"

The man, Don Maxwell, was second in command to Jarrett. He was a sergeant in the Mooserock Sheriff's Office. His leather jacket was zipped up to the neck like everyone else, but his head was bare. The wind rifled through his brown hair peppered with grey, blowing it almost straight up at times.

"Cold one, eh Rett?" The sergeant had a short cigar clamped between his teeth in one corner of his mouth. It wasn't lit. Jarrett waited without responding.

Sergeant Maxwell hunkered down into the collar of his jacket, his shoulders hunched against the harsh wind. Without taking the cigar from his mouth, he drew his arm in a semi-circle around the area.

"We have boys surrounding the entire grounds. We even have men in the woods. They're flushing out the stables and barns as we speak. I've sent Deputy Janey Lenders up to calm the women."

Jarrett looked over towards the front door again. The bitter wind screamed in his ears and tried to sweep his hat off his head. He reached up and pulled it down as tight as it would go.

A female officer was ushering Dolly and Tori into the house. Deputies were running all over the yard yelling back and forth to one another.

"Rett-" Matthew was at his elbow. His nose red from the wind and cold, the ends of his plaid scarf waved wildly about. He'd stuffed his gloved hands deep into his pockets.

Jarrett turned and offered Matthew a wan smile. He laid a hand on his friend's shoulder.

"Matthew, I'll tell you as soon as we have what we want." The marshal patted his shoulder and turned back to the sergeant.

Just as the sergeant opened his mouth to say something, they could hear a commotion coming down the hill behind the big house.

A crowd of policeman was bringing something down the hill.

The sergeant and Jarrett started walking towards the group of excitedly chattering men. Matthew followed close at their heels.

"What do we have here, boys?" the sergeant bellowed to the group of policemen.

Two of the men pulled someone forward and held a flashlight in his face.

"There ya go, sir, we got him!" one of the deputies cheerfully announced to Jarrett. The crowd of police stopped moving and waited.

The marshal stepped forward and looked at the man they held. His hands were handcuffed behind his back. He stared down at the ground. His face was dirty and he had a black eye. A bruise was already coming out on his forehead. He looked like he had resisted arrest.

"Tried to run, sir, we had to chase him down. Fast little bugger too!" the same deputy exclaimed, excited at his catch. "Took a swing at Officer Jasmine Wilks. She's the one who gave him the shiner!" He said it aiming a proud grin to the female officer who was glowering at the captive.

Jarrett took the flashlight from the officer and shined it directly in the prisoner's face.

The man looked up, squinting. Even through the dirt and his face all screwed up and shadowed from the light, Jarrett recognized him.

"Miguel Perez," Jarrett said, his voice smug.

The Vaughns' number one farmhand squinted at Jarrett through dirty hair, then his eyes dropped to the ground.

"Do you recognize these, Marshal Chase?" A man held up a blue quilted jacket and a pair of galoshes caked in mud.

Jarrett turned from Miguel and looked at the clothing. He smiled. "You bet I do, deputy, I surely do." He turned back to Miguel and said, "Take him, boys."

The deputies happily obliged, half pulling and half dragging the farmhand to a patrol car.

"Good work, Sarg, he was one of the men that tried to throw me in the well, I recognize the jacket and boots. The boots were eye level from my position on the ground, and I saw the blue jacket when I rolled and ran. Thanks for getting the job done so quickly," Jarrett said, shaking the other officer's hand.

"Any time, buddy. Your call to grab him was spot on. You said when you heard the description the shop owner offered, you got an inkling of who it was. His trying to run, and the jacket and boots confirm his culpable activity in the smuggling drop and your attempted murder. We'll clean up here and meet you back at the station, okay?" The older man spoke gruffly through the cigar still clamped in his teeth.

Jarrett stood for a moment, watching the officers put Miguel into the police car.

Someone on a bullhorn was calling everyone back to the front yard. Slowly, the officers climbed into cars and dispersed. A parade of blue lights could be seen twirling and flashing down the drive and out into the street.

"Rett." Matthew said, becoming impatient. "You owe me an explanation."

Jarrett turned to him and clipped his head. "Let's go up to the house, Matt. I need to do some paperwork and I'll come back later to talk."

Chapter Forty-Four

Shanti was in the kitchen visiting with Libby and Daisy.

Half the Lawtons' help were chattering like nervous parrots over Tobias Vaughn's arrest. The artist listened to everyone's fears and theories.

"I think ol' man Vaughn was doin' Serafina and the master found out and threatened to tell Mrs. Vaughn, so he had to kill them!" Libby shared her theory with everyone.

Daisy sighed wearily, her hand on her chubby belly. "Oh Lib, c'mon now, Serafina wouldn't ta been with an ol' geezer like Mr. Vaughn, he's like fifty. She hadda boyfriend, I know 'cause she told me."

Daisy sniffed, her nose up in the air, she felt special that the maid had confided in her and not anyone else.

Libby glared at Daisy. "Serafina didn't have no boyfriend, she'd a told me," Libby snarled, jabbing a thumb at her chest. "Yer lyin'!" she accused the homely maid.

Daisy sniffed again. "It's true. And that's not all I know. I heard-"

"What is going on here!" A voice barked from the doorway.

All three women's heads snapped to the door.

An iron-faced Mrs. Li was standing there, her hands on her hips. She was wearing a tunic styled suit. The knee-length silk jacket was white with flowing pastel green leaves decorating it, and the matching silk slacks were white.

The white silk slippers looked out of place in the pre-winter season. Her black hair was pulled back severely and pinned to the top of her head. The severity of the tightly pulled back hair made her eyes look like barely visible slits on her face. But, they could see the light glinting off the onyx orbs.

It was the first time Shanti saw the woman without her necklace on. Perhaps it was under her tunic. Libby and Daisy jumped up immediately.

"Uh excuse us, Miss Shantilly, we...uh...have to dust and...stuff..." Libby and Daisy scurried to the door.

Mrs. Li stepped aside to let them pass. They both hurried through the doorway with their heads down ducking like they were afraid she was going to hit them.

As soon as they left, Mrs. Li stared unblinking at Shanti for a second, then turned on her heel and was gone.

Well! Shanti thought. That woman has the entire household running around like scared blind mice! Shanti stood up and stretched. She left the kitchen and headed for the center staircase.

She peered in all the rooms along the way to see if anyone was about. Sighing at the empty rooms, she moved across the marble and tile foyer to the grand staircase. Maybe Chloe's upstairs in her room. The house was suddenly very quiet.

Silently, Shanti made her way up to the second floor. It was still early afternoon outside, but inside where the sun couldn't get to, was growing dark. She flipped on some lights as she walked down the hall to Chloe's room.

When she reached the lilac room, not closed all the way the door opened from her hand lightly hitting it. She stuck her head in. No Chloe.

She headed for her own room. Turning on the light to the rose room, she looked around. What to do until everyone comes home? The painting was done. She'd completed it yesterday. Maeve had ordered a frame made for it.

She moved over to the desk. A magazine she'd been reading earlier that morning lay on the desk. Sighing, she picked up the magazine and settled in the rocking chair. Flipping through the magazine she realized she was bored. It was an almost unrecognizable feeling. She was seldom bored.

Thinking about a walk around the grounds was quickly dispelled when she heard the wind beating against the sliding glass doors. She wandered into the little sitting room off her bedroom. Looking over at the television, she shrugged. Maybe the news was on.

Shanti picked up the remote and settled into the easy chair. Aiming the remote at the TV she turned it on and searched for the news. An anchorman was talking excitedly. She turned up the volume.

"The Sheriff's PR person told us they have captured one of the people that might have had something to do with the nerve gas being smuggled in the potatoes at the Vaughn Farm. As we reported earlier, Tobias Vaughn had been arrested on suspicion of murder, but we've been told he was released earlier this evening. Here we go-" The anchorman turned in his chair and looked at the screen behind him.

"Yes, we have it live...Sharon? Sharon are you there?" The anchorman held a finger to his ear as he called to his colleague.

The screen showed a newswoman clutching a microphone in a gloved hand standing in front of the Sheriff's station. The wind was tossing her hair violently, her coat kept blowing open. Her other hand was stuffed inside a pocket.

The mid-calf, woolen beige coat covered her almost to her ankles, but she still looked cold. She held the microphone to her mouth.

"Yes Mike, we're here in front of the Sheriff's station. The Sheriff declined to speak with us, but his spokesperson was here a few minutes ago." The camera zoomed in close to her face. Her nose and cheeks were red from the cold.

"According to a suspect arrested an hour ago, he said that a businessman from Thailand was smuggling nerve gas into this country. Allegedly, he would leave his country in a small business plane- the authorities in Thailand did not search his aircraft for contraband. They say he would enter the US then fly over the miles of thick forests in Brimstone Glen west of the river. Hidden deep within the woods he had confederates waiting."

Photos of small aircraft as well as pictures of Thailand flashed behind her.

"When the hiding men heard his plane they would flash a code at him with lights. The plane would slow, then a man would toss a parachute out the door with a bundle tied to the bottom. Then the plane would fly off to land innocently at an airport somewhere on American soil.

"When custom agents searched the plane they of course found nothing." The newswoman pushed her hair out of her eyes and turned to look at the building behind her. She pointed as she spoke.

"They were able to capture a farmhand, a...uh..." she looked down at an iPad she pulled from her pocket. She tried to hold it steady in the wind.

"A Miguel Perez. Allegedly, the smugglers hiding in the woods would take the package from the parachute then climb into kayaks and then float down the river until they reached the Vaughn farm. Then, Mr. Perez would meet them, and he and others would insert the vials of nerve gas into hundreds of the potatoes under the cloak of the dark night.

"The plan apparently was to at some point before the potatoes were disbursed to have the ones stuffed with the toxin be diverted to a warehouse."

The anchorwoman took a breath and glanced at the building behind her again.

"This scheme would never have some to light if not by a fluke. The Vaughns' potatoes were struck with a dreaded disease and the County Commission Agents and agriculturists from the University of Idaho came to investigate the disease, when low and behold- they found the vials!" The newswoman smiled brightly at the camera.

"Thanks to the ingenuity of our sheriff, Jarrett Chase, they were able to track the kayaks and locate a receipt one of the smugglers allegedly signed for the boats. It's been confirmed that Miguel Perez's fingerprints were found on the receipt." She took a much needed breath before continuing.

"Supposedly the police say they don't think any of the persons they've caught so far is the mastermind behind this whole scheme. And-"

"Sharon? I'm sorry, I hate to cut you off, but we have an aid to the Prime Minister of Thailand on Zoom. Hello? Sir" The camera panned to the anchorman in the station. He was tapping on his earpiece.

"**Yes? Hello? I am here,**" a voice came over the television.

"Yes, you are...uh...Sanga Tar of the Royal Tahi Supreme Command Headquarters?" the anchorman asked.

"**Yes, yes I am. We are broadcasting this to tell the American people that we abhor the events that have occurred and will do everything we can to cooperate with the United States in capturing all involved. We have already detained Mr. Trihn Nu.**"

"Yes, I understand Mr. Nu was the businessman that was flying the plane from Thailand to here with the vials of nerve gas, is that correct?" the newsman asked.

Sanga Tar nodded vigorously. "**Yes, yes, that is he. The suspect Miguel Perez gave him up. We understand Mr. Nu would fly the gas from Thailand to the states. The gas would then be hidden inside the potatoes and then eventually smuggled into Venezuela.**

"**Idaho exports many of their potatoes to Thailand and Venezuela, apparently that is how these people, as you say, 'hooked up.' They planned to give the rebels hiding in the hills in Venezuela the gas, then they would use it to overthrow the current government. Allegedly, they also had plans for harming America as well.**" A picture of Mr. Nu was displayed on the screen.

"Oh my gosh!" Shanti leaped to her feet. "I remember him!"

She stood gawking at the television her hands over her mouth. She couldn't believe it. That was the very man she'd been introduced to at the harvest festival.

They showed a picture of Mr. Nu's Venezuelan contact. Shanti moved closer to the television.

It was one of the other people that had been with Mr. Nu, the female, Teresa Vaquera.

The commander agent, Sanga Tar was standing in front of the Thailand ministry of defense building. The Thailand flag as well as others waved behind him. Shanti's eyes opened so wide she thought they'd pop right out of her head!

She grabbed up her cell but was dismayed to show she'd neglected to charge it.

Turning off the television, she ran down the stairs, remembering there was a landline in the library, she needed to call the marshal immediately! She hastened to the library.

Spotting the phone sitting on an end table, she ran over and picked it up. She didn't know the number to the police station, so she dialed 911. Finally reaching the station, she told the dispatcher she needed to speak immediately with Marshal Chase.

"I'm sorry, Miss, the marshal is not available right now," the dispatcher informed her.

Darn! Shanti drew a deep breath. "Please tell him that Shanti Lane called, from the...the Lawtons' place. Tell him I have urgent news! Urgent, do you understand?" Shanti cried into the phone.

"Yes, Miss, I understand." *Sure*, the dispatch said to herself, everything *is always an emergency. Her cat is probably stuck in a tree.* "I'll tell him as soon as he calls in. Goodbye." The phone clicked off.

Shanti stared at the receiver. "Maybe I should go to the police-"

"Miss Shantilly."

Shanti swung around from the doorway

Graham Duncan was standing there. "Is everything all right?" His forehead was bunched in concern. He walked towards her. He was as usual dressed in worn jeans and a flannel shirt with a black t-shirt beneath the blue plaid. His dark hair was slightly mussed, he was wiping his brawny hands on a red handkerchief

Shanti gulped and smiled. He looked so strong and capable, he would help her. She set the phone back into its cradle. "I- I need to speak with the marshal but he's not in."

Graham stopped bare inches from her. She could smell his cologne. Odd, she thought, an outdoorsy farmhand wearing cologne.

"Maybe I can help?" he offered. Reaching out, he grasped her hand.

She looked down as his large, darkly tanned callused hand enveloped hers. Then she looked up at him. He'd moved closer. His face was inches from hers.

"Um...no...uh...it's just something I think the marshal can...handle..." she stammered, suddenly feeling awkward.

Graham put a hand to the small of her back and gently pulled her forward. His lips touched hers lightly at first, then he opened his mouth and pressed his lips harder against hers.

"Ahem-"

They broke apart at the cough coming from the door. Libby was standing there, trying to stifle a giggle.

Shanti pressed the back of her hand to her mouth.

Graham looked like a boy caught with his hand in the cookie jar.

"The cow is calving, Graham, you're needed at the stables. They sent me to fetch you." Libby stared at the foreman with rounded eyes.

He looked at Shanti and back at Libby. "I'll uh, see you later, Miss...uh...Shantilly." He nodded and disappeared out the door.

Shanti turned when she heard Libby snickering.

The maid clamped a hand over her mouth, but her eyes peeking over her hand revealed the mirth she was trying to hide. She made an effort to look serious.

"Miss Shantilly, are you and…Graham, um, I mean it's none of my business, but…" Libby hesitated. She was vastly curious but she didn't want to overstep her bounds.

Shanti was embarrassed. To be caught smooching with the family's ranch hand was not high on her list of things to do. In fact, if Libby hadn't interrupted them, Shanti herself would have broken off the kiss.

Kissing the brawny foreman wasn't as exciting or even as pleasant as she had pictured it. Something seemed to push between them. She shook her head. There was no time to think about that now, she needed to find a way to get to the police station.

"Libby, where is everyone?" she asked the maid.

"Um…Mrs. Lawton and Chloe are at the Idaho Beet Sugar Cooperative. There's a ten-cent tax on every pound of beets that goes towards advertising and uh, research and promotion. Mrs. Lawton said she wanted to go over some promotional ideas she had.

"Then I think they're goin' to the distillery to see if the police found any…um…evidence, I think she said, of the nerve gas stuff in the Red Gem Farm jars. She said the molasses made from the beets could easily hide the gas and transporting them would be a snap."

Libby worked at Red Gem Farm long enough to have a good idea what went on with the harvesting and bottling the sugar beets.

She looked pretty proud of herself. Dropping out of high school usually had her at a disadvantage to other people. That's why she hung around with Daisy and Serafina. Daisy was dumb as a rock, and Serafina was so intensely shy people thought she was stupid too. They both made Libby look like a genius.

"I don't know where Master Jaime and Miss Dawn are. They usually leave the house pretty early on Saturday afternoons, and are gone most of the day, and evening too. Jaime goes to the club to play racquetball and Dawn is either shopping, lunching or at the salon.

"But I didn't see them leave so I don't really know. And Mrs. Thayne is probably down at the local...spa..." Libby winked conspiratorially at Shanti.

Shanti was puzzled.

Libby looked mischievous. Gossiping was one of her favorite pastimes. She looked around to see if anyone was about, then she leaned in near to Shanti and spoke in a low voice.

"Mr. Thayne, did ya know, well he ran off with some woman, a couple a' years younger than Mrs. Thayne, but a whole lot richer. Mrs. Thayne is very wealthy, but I guess this new babe has her beat."

"Uh, I don't think-"

"Anyway, Mrs. Thayne has been drowning her sorrows, if ya know what I mean, alone in her room. She refused to come out until this morning. Mrs. Lawton said leave her be, said this isn't the first time, nor the first husband to run out on her. Eventually Mrs. Thayne will be out to the nightclubs again and she'll find her fifth husband." Libby winked at Shanti.

"Oh dear, Libby, that's so sad." Shanti shook her head, but she didn't like to gossip. She started for the door, stopping in the threshold.

"What about Montgomery or Dario? Do you think I could possibly borrow one of the cars? I need to go into town."

Libby shrugged. She stuck a finger in the corner of one eye. She wore so much mascara some usually clumped in her eye sockets.

"I dunno, I don't see why not. But I don't rightly know where Mr. Montgomery or Dario are. I haven't seen 'em all morning. Dario is usually out by the garages takin' care of the cars. You can check out there if you want."

Shanti nodded with a tight smile. "I'll do that. Thanks Libby, I'll see you later." She headed back down the hall. Surprisingly, with so many people ensconced in the manor, she didn't run into a single soul on the way to her room.

Chapter Forty-Five

At the Vaughns' farmhouse, Jarrett Chase put a spoonful of sugar into his mug. He looked down into the dark brew, stirring the sugar around until it blended thoroughly. Setting the spoon on a napkin, he waited for Matthew Vaughn to sit in the other chair at the round table in the kitchen nook.

The young man looked almost haggard, not like his usual neat and proper self. His corduroy shirt was unbuttoned at the collar revealing the white tee shirt underneath. His black hair was tousled and he obviously hadn't shaved since yesterday. Things were taking a toll him.

Matthew set his mug on the table, pulled out a chair and sat down. He dragged a weary hand through his hair, smoothing it somewhat. He stared down at his coffee. He was so tired he could hardly think.

Jarrett was silent, letting the young man gather his thoughts.

Finally, Matthew looked up at Jarrett, his somber eyes relayed his exhaustion and confusion. "Okay, Rett, what in the hell is going on around here?" Not normally a man to curse, Matthew was at his wit's end and he didn't hide it.

Jarrett took a sip of his coffee and leaned back in the chair. The wooden chair squeaked from the weight of the tall, muscular marshal. "It's a long story, Matt, and we still don't know the whole lot of it."

It was late afternoon, the sun shining through the window was making long shadows out of the furniture in the small area they were sitting in.

They wanted some degree of privacy so they'd sought out the little nook where they were near the kitchen to get coffee, but were out of the mainstream of the house. They sat next to a large window where they had an extensive view of the grounds. Soon Matthew would need to turn a light on.

"You know part of it. I was in the west woods when I saw a parachute drop a package in the fields. I tracked it and followed some guys that retrieved the package and had hopped into some kayaks then made their way down river." Jarrett sipped some coffee.

Matthew was staring hard at him, the marshal had his full attention.

"So I followed them in my truck and waited at the bend. They took me by surprise and tried to dump me in the old well. I got away of course. Then, as you know, I realized maybe Serafina had also been thrown into the well. So we found her. She had one of your dad's buttons clasped tightly in her hand."

Matthew nodded, draining half his coffee in one swallow.

"Actually, now we think that was a deliberate plant to throw us off, to make us suspect your father and not look at anyone else as the perpetrator."

Jarrett pulled in the corner of his mouth, shaking his head. He gazed steadily at Matthew. "I'm real sorry about that Matt, you know, what we've done to your dad, but we really had no choice." Jarrett raised his brows at Matthew, hoping he'd understand their having to arrest his father.

Matthew dipped his head. "I know, Rett, I can see what you had to do. It was just so…heartbreaking. You know, poor Dad." He closed his eyes, holding back tears as the vision of his father behind bars sprang to his mind.

Jarrett nodded, commiserating. "I know, Matt, I'm really sorry."

Matthew wiped at a tear that escaped down his cheek. "Go on, I'm okay." He sniffed. He didn't want the rugged marshal to think he was a sissy by crying.

Jarrett looked away, giving Matt a chance to regroup. He wondered where Dolly and Tori were. He really didn't want to have to deal with weeping women too. His gaze swerved back to Matthew.

His eyes were red and shiny, his lips compressed together, but he gave Jarrett his full attention again.

"Okay, so anyway," Jarrett continued, "we managed to find the place where the smugglers rented the kayaks and the guy gave a description of two of the renters. One of them sounded familiar. You have some Mexican migrant workers here at the farm, but off-season you only have one permanent ranch hand, Miguel Perez."

"Yeah," Matthew acknowledged glumly.

"No one else in the county has a permanent Mexican employee. So I figured it was Miguel. The police found his jacket and boots I had described in his closet, He didn't know I was conscious half the time and had seen them. I recognized the clothes as one of the smuggler's and we arrested Miguel.

"Miguel was scared so he quickly pointed the finger at the Venezuelan. We also tested the receipt at the kayak shop for fingerprints. They had used a stolen credit card, but stupid Miguel left his print on the receipt."

Jarrett stood up and went around the corner to the kitchen and returned with the coffee pot. He filled up his mug then topped off Matthew's cup. Setting the pot on the counter, he returned to his chair.

"So, witnesses told us they had seen the Venezuelan girl and the guy from Thailand together at the harvest party. After arresting and interrogating them, that led us to discovering the nerve gas being smuggled out of Thailand and here to America, where it would travel on to Venezuela.

"There was a third guy at the party, an Italian. We looked into him, but he seemed an innocent dupe. The smugglers needed to look like serious business people, so they had drawn him in to buy exported potatoes with them. He was never with them on the trips when they dropped the vials into the woods."

Jarrett added more sugar to his mug, wincing when he sipped the boiling hot coffee.

"The potatoes were a good screen for the smuggled nerve gas. We were exporting to their countries and it gave them an opportunity to move the gas back and forth. It offered them a good reason to periodically fly over here without looking suspicious."

Matthew hung his head and chuckled wryly. "What a great gambit. Who knows how long it would have gone on without anyone finding out? Actually, our crop getting the disease may have in the long run saved lives!" Matthew grinned at Jarrett.

The marshal smiled back. "You know Matt, that is so true. Your family is really the ones that technically uncovered the plot. But..." his face grew serious. "I'm sorry about your quarantine, is it going to ruin your family business?"

Matthew's expression brightened for the first time since Jarrett had seen him out on the lawn this morning. He shook his head with a smile of relief.

"No, thank God my dad was so insistent about diversifying. Grandfather was against it, he's a purist, but Dad was interested in other things besides potatoes. We have the bulls and cows now, and we'll expand some other crops Dad had growing in the far fields. We have enough land not to use the diseased areas. Do uh..."

Matthew looked embarrassed and concerned, "Do you think charges will be brought against Dad because he kept quiet about the potato rot?"

Jarrett cupped his hands around the hot mug. It was warm in the nook but he could feel the chill from outdoors being so close to the window.

"I don't know, Matt. Anyone knowing your dad knows he's a standup guy and would never do anything that was against the law. I believe he had full intentions of telling the commission about the disease when he was positive the crop was infected."

"However," Jarrett sidled a glance at Matthew, "he'll probably face a hefty fine for keeping quiet as long as he did."

Matthew nodded bleakly. "I understand, he did put the county at jeopardy. I know he was worried, for the past year he was anxious all the time, and he wandered the fields constantly."

Matthew took a sip of coffee and looked at his friend across the round table. "So who, or why do you think Mr. Lawton and Serafina were killed?"

Jarrett shrugged, both hands wrapped around the warm mug.

"We haven't found any kind of tie in yet with the smugglers. There's no apparent reason for the killings, unless they heard or saw something. These guys have no problem killing people, I can tell you that from personal experience." Jarrett smiled ruefully.

Matthew reached over and patted Jarrett's arm. "I'm glad you weren't killed, Rett, what a horrible thing for you to go through! Were you scared? Did you think you were going to die?" Worry for his friend dug fret lines in his forehead.

"Well," Jarrett drank the rest of his coffee and set the empty mug down on the white and yellow plaid tablecloth. "Sure, I was scared, but I was concentrating more on how to get myself out of the situation.

"There were more of them than me, so I waited until some of them left. Then, I took the other two by surprise, I knew that was the only way. I was injured too badly for a fight with two husky and hostile men that were itching to kill me.

"One of them wanted to continue beating me before they stabbed me then tossed me in the well. Thank God the other one just wanted to get it over with and get out of the woods." Jarrett laughed, remembering the fear in one of the men's voices. He had kept asking about bears and other wild animals.

"How'd you get away, Rett?" Matthew asked, interested. His friend led a much more exciting life than he could ever imagine himself doing. However, he was perfectly happy to live vicariously through the lawman.

"Oh, they were carrying me to the old well. I knew they'd have to pass near the bank of the river, so I waited until they got as close as they were going to get and they set me down. I rolled hard away, then jumped up and ran, which wasn't easy with these bruised ribs.

"They thought they could easily catch me so they didn't run after me right away. But, I knew once I rolled down the bank there would be plenty of places to hide, especially if they didn't see me go over the bank, and as luck would have it, they didn't. I just hid in the hollow of an old tree until they left."

"Whew, Rett, that was damned close don't you think? What if they hadn't set you down until they got to the well? The well if I recall is a bit away from the riverbank."

Crossing his bulky arms over his chest, Jarrett shrugged. "I would have had to take my chances and fight them. Believe me, Matt, I wasn't giving up without a fight that's for damn sure." Jarrett's voice was hard and serious. "And if I didn't make it, I was sure gonna do some damage on the way out."

Matthew stared at awe of his friend. "You know Rett, you're so brave, I don't know what I would have done."

"Listen Matt, you never know how you'll react when you're facing the snapping jaws of death. Your mind goes a hundred miles a second trying to figure a way out. Patience is the big thing, really. You have to wait for the best opportunity and that's hard to do when people are trying to do their best to kill you!"

He chuckled. "But you do what you have to do. You'd probably be surprised at how ingenious you are at thinking up ways to escape. And, don't forget, you're not dealing with the sharpest darts in the box, you know."

Jarrett laughed, but Matthew still looked frightened. He had doubts about his ability to face danger and act bravely.

"Anyway, I-"

The radio at Jarrett's shoulder had periodically crackled and a staticy voice could occasionally be heard speaking in code, but this time Jarrett stopped talking and cocked his head to the radio and listened. The voice halted.

Jarrett pushed a button and spoke into the radio.

"Repeat that, Joellen."

Matthew could hear static and the voice crackling in code but he couldn't tell what was said. Jarrett's face though, caught his interest. The marshal suddenly looked alarmed.

"I'm on my way to the Lawtons, send backup," he ordered. Shutting off the radio, he stood up looking troubled. "I've got to go Matt."

Almost frantically, he searched the small area for his hat. Finding it on the kitchen counter, he slapped it on his head and grabbed his jacket off the back of his chair.

Matthew jumped up too. "What? What is it Rett? What's the matter?" He was concerned now by his friend's behavior. Jarrett didn't normally act panicky, he was as solid as they come.

Jarrett headed for the door, shrugging on his jacket as he walked. As he opened the kitchen door, he looked back at Matthew.

"Joellen told me Shanti Lane called saying she had something urgent to tell me. I used to think she was just a dumb blonde bimbo, but now, well, I think she's not one to take things lightly. If she called me, and I'm not her favorite person, to tell me that she had something urgent to tell me, well that worries me. There's too much going on, I'm afraid she might be in danger. I've got to get to her."

He zipped up his jacket and not waiting for a response from Matthew he hurried out to the front driveway where he'd left the Bronco.

Matthew grabbed his own jacket and ran after the marshal. He got around the side of the house just in time to see Jarrett go screeching down the driveway and onto the front street.

The Bronco quickly disappeared down the road.

Matthew could only hear the truck's engine barreling away in the distance. Standing in the cold, slowly buttoning his jacket, he wondered what else could happen in their small, quiet village?

Chapter Forty-Six

Shanti reached the top of the stairs and headed down the long carpeted hallway to her suite.

When she finally reached the rose room, she stopped outside the door. Frowning, she stared at the closed door. That's odd, she thought, I could have sworn I left the door ajar…she turned the knob and slowly pushed the door open.

Standing in the doorway, she looked around the room. All looked in order, just the way she left it. Hmm, she must have left in a hurry and only thought she'd left the door open. Still, as she entered the room, she kept looking around, waiting for something, or someone, to jump out at her.

Then she laughed, shaking her head. "You're acting silly," she chastised herself. "You're just a little edgy from everything that's happened. Get a grip," she instructed herself moving quickly to the closet on the other side of the room.

She decided to freshen up before she went to the police station. She didn't want to look like the harridan Jarrett Chase was always accusing her of! Shaking her head again, she thought, *why do I even care what that obnoxious, arrogant marshal thinks of me anyway*? She hurried into the bathroom.

Emerging some twenty minutes later, her hair was combed with two barrettes holding back the hair on either side of her heart shaped face. Standing in front of the armoire, the marshal's turquoise eyes, framed in those obscenely long lashes floated in front of her closed eyes.

Snapping her head hard side-to-side to dispel the vision, she yanked a drawer open and pulled out a pair of jeans and the first blouse she got to. The blouse was black with white satin buttons running all the way down the front, and probably too thin for the weather outside, but she didn't want to take any more time to choose something else.

She really needed to get moving. It was imperative she told the authorities what she remembered about the Thailand flag she'd seen on the newscast. She finally realized where she'd seen it before.

There still was something else though, that was just on the fringe of her memory that she still couldn't quite pinpoint. That was so aggravating. Oh well, it'll come to her, it's only a matter of time.

Grabbing her jacket off the bed, Shanti decided to take one last peek in the mirror over the dresser to make sure she looked all right. She hurried over to the mirror, then stopped abruptly.

Something was taped to the middle of the mirror. It was a note. She crept closer, puzzled, and read the note:

Dear Shantilly, I've thought of something terribly important. Please meet me out by the farthest barn, I don't want anyone to hear. And, please don't tell anyone- don't trust anyone. Come quickly! Bring this note with you.
Chloe.

Shanti stared at the note. "What on earth? What is it that Chloe couldn't just tell her here in the privacy of their rooms? I thought she was out with Mrs. Lawton. It sounds like she is scared of something. I'd better go right away, poor Chloe!" She ran out of the room without looking back.

Her footsteps thumped loudly as she ran down the plushly carpeted staircase. When she reached the bottom, she hesitated, looking around. Should she get someone? Maybe she should get Montgomery or look for Graham...no, Chloe said not to trust anyone.

She moved quickly through the estate to one of the back doors. She hadn't come across anyone. It was very unusual not to run into at least one person wandering around the immense manor. But then she remembered it was Saturday and there was normally a skeleton crew on, everyone fends for themselves on the weekends.

Most of the family members went out somewhere. Now that Langston was dead, Maeve couldn't stand to be alone so she did her visiting on Saturdays. According to Libby, today she was supposed to be at the Idaho Beet Sugar Cooperative with Chloe. But Chloe left a note so she, or they were back?

Shanti opened the back door, the brutal wind smacked her in the face. Quickly, she zipped up her jacket wishing she'd taken the time to grab her hat and gloves. But she didn't want to waste time going back to get them now.

The sky was rapidly darkening, Shanti could barely see the ground and she suddenly tripped over a tree root. Clamoring to her feet, she brushed her hands off.

The moon was just coming up but it was bright. She could see it shining huge and silvery behind the bare branches of the trees. The air was icy and cloudless.

Shanti hurried, but didn't run, she didn't need to fall again, she'd be no help to Chloe with a sprained ankle. As she passed the stables, she could hear the horses moving around but there were no lights coming from inside.

Her eyes looked longingly in the direction of the bunkhouse, searching for a tiny light, hoping Graham might be there. She hadn't seen anything going on as she passed the first barns, the cow must not have calved as they thought.

But then, she remembered Chloe's instructions to trust no one. Sighing, she persevered. Her breath puffed in front of her like white steam. It was freezing and the wind creaking through the trees was eerie.

She shivered, not from cold but from an ominous feeling. It was dark and cold and things just didn't seem right.

There, finally, she could make out the big looming barn in the darkness. The moon outlined the roof but the rest of the building was in shadows.

The winter grass crackled as she trod over it, she shoved her hands deep into the pockets of her down-filled jacket. The wind whipped her hair all over her head. She put her hand up to brush her hair out of her eyes and realized she'd lost one of her barrettes.

As she approached the barn, she noticed it wasn't kept as neatly as the others. Maybe because it was the farthest one out they didn't get to it often. The other barns were freshly painted red, but this one was weathered and peeling.

She stopped in front of the door. It was slightly ajar. It appeared to be dark inside.

Jarrett Chase drove to the police station.

At first he'd hesitated, trying to decide if he should go to the Lawtons' first to see if Shanti was there, he was only a few miles away. But, Joellen seemed to think the girl was coming to the station. He decided not to waste any time and drove to the station, away from the Lawtons' estate.

Pulling right in front, Jarrett turned off the engine and ran inside, not even taking the time to grab his hat off the seat next to him.

"Hey Joellen-" he started to greet the husky dispatcher as soon as he opened the door, but the woman wasn't there.

Davey Peters was on the radio. He turned grinning at the marshal, raising his hand in greeting. He was talking to someone over the radio.

Jarrett moved quickly to the radio station. Davey kept talking. Growing impatient, Jarrett drummed his fingers on the railing. He could tell the second he'd entered the room that the Lane girl wasn't there. Davey kept talking.

Finally Jarrett reached out and put his hand over the microphone and growled to the surprised boy, "Davey, where the hell is the Lane girl?"

The boy's eyes opened wide, the marshal was always the nicest most patient man he knew, this behavior was unlike him. He sat there speechless, with his mouth hanging open.

"Answer me, boy, where the hell is she?" Jarrett's voice was low, but intense. He didn't touch the young man, but Davey felt he'd been shaken.

"Uh...uh...gee Marshal Chase...I- I d- don't know where she is...I ain't seen her," Davey stuttered.

"What do you mean you haven't seen her? Wasn't she here?" Jarrett barked at the boy.

Davey leaned back in his chair, what the heck was wrong with the marshal? His head pulled back, he gazed up in confusion at Jarrett.

"M- Marshal Chase, she- she ain't been here. I've been here all day and I ain't seen her, sir," Davey sputtered, he didn't like the marshal like this, he was frightening in his growly intensity and impatience.

"What do you mean, are you saying she didn't come to the station? Were you here when she called? Where's Joellen?" Jarrett hammered out, his voice getting louder, his eyes narrowed in demand.

"Gosh Marshal, Joellen went home twenty minutes ago. Yeah, I was here when the girl called in. Joellen said she had something urgent to tell you, but Joellen thought her cat was just stuck up a tree or something, she said she'd send someone out to make a report. Joellen didn't want to bother you with something so...so...friver...friva-" Davey searched for the word Joellen had used.

"Frivolous," Jarrett supplied.

"Yeah, that." Davey snapped his head up and down. "So Stan went out there, but he couldn't get past the gate. He figured no one was home and it was a false alarm. The cat probably got out of the tree on his own."

337

Jarrett shook his head, running his hand through his hair. It was long enough now it kept flopping in his eyes. "Davey, the Lawtons don't have a damn cat. There's something wrong. Didn't you get my call to send backup?"

Davey looked nervous, he fiddled with a pencil on the desk. "Well...you know...Marshal, when Stan couldn't get in, we...uh...didn't send anyone else because we thought you didn't know the cat had gotten down...you know..." he sputtered off, seeing the thunder in Jarrett's blue-green eyes.

The marshal didn't let the boy finish, he turned and stalked to the door.

"I'm going out to the Lawtons, send the damned backup," he ordered over his shoulder. The door slammed behind him.

"Wow!" Davey spurted, letting out his held breath. He sure didn't ever want the marshal mad at him, he looked like the devil himself, ferocious and big and very intimidating.

He could hear Jarrett burning rubber all the way down the road.

Chapter Forty-Seven

"Hello? Chloe?" Shanti called timidly into the open crack of the door. Her call wasn't answered.

Carefully, she put her hand against the splintered wood and slowly pushed the door open. Poking her head in, she looked around.

It was incredibly dark inside, she could barely make out bundles of hay and loose straw strewn about. Only a few tools hung along the wall, spades and a rake and an old coiled hose.

Stepping just inside the door, she waited for her eyes to become accustomed to the dark. There was one tiny window way up about twenty feet in a far corner. A ladder was leaning against a loft.

"Hello?" she called again. "Chloe? Chloe are you here?"

No answer.

With trepidation she slowly moved into the barn, leaving the door open for the little light it gave. It was only slightly warmer inside, the walls blocked the worst of the wind.

The wood groaned and shook with every blast of the blustery wind. It howled through the tree limbs and around the barn. Shanti could hear the straw under her feet crunching with every step she made.

"Ow!" She banged right into a wheelbarrow she hadn't seen in the dark. Leaning over, she rubbed her knee. Something lying on the ground beside the wheelbarrow caught her eye. She knelt on the straw peering into the dark.

It looked like a body.

She screamed and lurched back falling onto the ground. She had looked right into the open, sightless eyes of Daisy, one of the housemaids.

Gasping, "Oh my gosh," Shanti scrambled to her feet. Heedless of the straw and hay that clung to her jeans, she took a shaking step nearer the body and knelt down again.

Daisy was on her back, staring blankly at the ceiling.

Clearly the maid was dead, yet Shanti still gingerly felt for a pulse. The flesh was cold and there was no pulse. Shanti snatched her hand back.

An iron garden claw was sticking out of Daisy's chest. Shanti clamped her hand over her mouth to hold back the nausea that threatened to hurl out of her throat.

Legs quivering, she stood back up, gulping for air, trying to keep her stomach from hurling. She put a palm to her own chest feeling her heart slamming away at her ribs.

Poor Daisy. Shanti didn't know her very well as she was kept hidden in the kitchen. She'd only seen the homely maid a few times.

Her eyes of their own volition crept back to the chubby body, trailing down the maid from her white bonnet over her chest with the awful weapon protruding from it, to her stomach…wait…oh dear, Shanti bit back a groan. She could tell by her enlarged belly that the girl was pregnant. "Poor thing. Wait!"

Shanti moved her hand to her head, pressing her fingers against her pounding temple, something just came to her. She didn't think of it at the time…but now…she pictured the note taped to her mirror.

That's it!

It had said 'Dear Shantilly' *Shantilly*. Chloe never called her that, only the servants and Mrs. Lawton. That meant…Chloe didn't write the note. That meant…she had been lured here-

Suddenly the door slammed closed with a loud bang!

Shanti's head whipped around, she could hardly see the door in the dark barn. She ran to the front praying it was only the wind that had shut the door.

As soon as she reached it, she pushed the door with her hands. It didn't move. *Oh no!* She put her shoulder to the door and pushed it, maybe it was just stuck a little... but it didn't budge.

Urgently, she stepped back and threw her shoulder against the door. It creaked and shook, but didn't open. Someone had deliberately closed and somehow locked the door. But there was no handle so they must have put something across the front of the door to keep it secured.

Shanti stood next to the door and tried to peak through a crack. She couldn't see anything.

"Help! Help me!" she yelled.

Waiting a second, she heard no response. She cupped her hands around her mouth and screamed- "Help me! Someone please help me!"

She was met with zero response. There appeared to be no one outside the door. She put her ear to the door, but the only thing she heard was the wind battling the trees.

Shanti rubbed her arms, it was freezing in the damp barn. Thinking there might be another way out, she slowly walked around the perimeter of the barn searching in the dark for another door. She avoided the spot where the dead maid was lying.

After a few minutes, she concluded the place was tight as a drum.

There was no other way out. She looked up- except for that window. But the window was at least 20 feet in the air, and there was nothing near it.

The hay, not even packed in bundles was loosely raked in the opposite side of the barn. Maybe there was a tool or something she could use to pry the barn door open.

Continuing her search, she peered in the dark looking for something, anything that could help her get out.

While she looked, she tried to figure out what was going on. Why had someone lured her out here? And poor Daisy...why kill her? The only possible reason could be that she and Daisy saw or knew something. What could it be?

She was completely on the other side of the barn when she heard something. She jerked around.

The door was open.

Quickly she ran towards the door. Something was tossed in then the door slammed closed again.

"No! No! Come back- wait!" Shanti yelled, still running to the door. Suddenly she stopped. She could now see what had been thrown inside.

A lit match. Already the floor directly in front of the door was ablaze. The dry hay was like kindling.

"Oh my gosh!" Shanti shrieked, hurrying to the flames.

Quickly she yanked off her jacket and dropping to her knees, she frantically tried to smother the fire. But the straw was too conducive to catching and quickly blazed.

Burning her hands, she jumped back leaving her jacket to burn along with the hay and straw. Gaping at the flaming ground, her eyes bulging in abject terror.

Blowing on her hands, she stepped backwards away from the rapidly spreading fire. In an utter panic she fled from the flames, looking around for something, anything to put out the fire or provide an escape.

She ran around the barn in a frenzy of panicked circles.

Jarrett pulled up to the closed gate and pushed the intercom button. Nothing happened, no one answered.

He pushed it again and again, harder and longer, but still nothing. Then he saw wires hanging from the intercom. Someone had disconnected them.

Damn! He punched the security box and threw the truck back into drive. Tearing down the road, he knew where the gate ended a few miles away, and the woods began.

As soon as he saw the end of the gate, he drove right off the road and into the woods. Bashing his head against the roof of the car was reminiscent of his chase through the woods after the smugglers.

Only this time, he felt a life was at stake. His heart was beating hard- he felt deep down there was something wrong.

First the Lane girl calls the station, he knew she thought he was a little less than the nearest savage in a cave, she always treated him like he was poison ivy, like a nasty itch.

And, he must admit his constant teasing caused her to treat him that way. He had been scared. He didn't like the feelings the blonde elicited in him. Not analyzing his feelings, he had suppressed them and behaved badly towards her to keep her at arm's length.

But now he had to admit thinking that she may be in some immediate danger just scared the life out of him. He had to breathe deeply and concentrate so he didn't get carried away with frightening thoughts of her in jeopardy.

Right now he needed to keep his wits about him, later he could sort out his feelings for the curvaceous artist.

Driving as fast as he could, the truck hurtled over rocks and craggy ground it was all he could do to keep the Bronco on a steady path. He needed to get through the woods and eventually come around the back of the Lawtons' estate.

The night black as coal, made it hard for the silver moonlight to make its way through the dense trees. He could barely see five feet in front of the truck.

He was straining so hard to see through the windshield he almost missed seeing the tree that suddenly loomed out in front of him. He yanked the wheel just in time to miss it and kept going.

Shanti tried to hold down the hysteria that threatened to overwhelm her. She needed to keep a clear head if she had any hope of escape.

The thickening smoke brought tears to her eyes and was clogging her throat, she tripped over uneven dirt and hay when her foot caught a rake someone had carelessly dropped and left. She hit the ground hard knocking the wind out of her lungs.

She lay on the ground gasping for air. The barn was filling up with thick black smoke. She could see it rising to the window. Panting, she wiped the tears and smoke from her eyes and struggled to her feet.

When she had fallen, the rough ground tore a big hole in one knee of her jeans. She couldn't even scream anymore, the smoke was burning her throat.

She grabbed one of the spades and went to chop at the door, but the entire ground in front of it was ablaze. The walls were too thick for her to chop through with a small garden spade. Dropping the spade she glanced at the hose, then quickly dismissed it, there was no water to hook it up to.

Maybe I can hide for a while in the loft, she thought.

Hurrying to the back of the barn, she turned and could see the whole front was engulfed in flames. Murmuring a prayer, she ran to the loft.

*7*he woods were becoming less dense. Jarrett knew he was coming near the end of the forest. He tried not to think of what kind of danger the girl might be in.

A picture of her lying on the ground, her beautiful sapphire eyes blank, dead - popped into his mind. *Damn*, the vision spurred him on to drive even faster and more recklessly.

Finally, he burst out of the woods and hit the fields. Glancing down at the speedometer, he was going 60 miles an hour, quite a feat on the thickly grass covered rocky ground and in the dark.

His hands, sweating from the exertion of keeping the truck from flipping over and staying on track were slipping on the wheel. He wiped one hand then the other on his pants. His mouth was dry with fear and apprehension.

There! He spotted the first of the barns way out in front of him, maybe a half a mile or so- he would skirt the barns and stables and drive right up to the-

"Holy mother of-" his eyebrows shot straight up, his mouth dropped. One of the damned barns was on fire! *What the*- he could

see the flames shooting up from the front of the barn, they dissipated as they shot up in the dark sky.

Sudden dread hit him like a punch in the stomach. An urgent call from Shanti, no one at the intercom, the lights all out in the big house, and a barn on fire- thinking the worst - the girl could be in the barn!

He slammed the pedal to the floor, heedless of the passing trees and boulders - he couldn't take his eyes off the burning barn- suddenly the truck hit something-

The Bronco flipped on its side and skidded along the ground where it came to a crashing stop against a sturdy oak tree.

Chapter Forty-Eight

Shanti stumbled in the thick smoke, holding her sleeve across her mouth to block some of the smoke from reaching her lungs.

Tripping and coughing, tears streaming down her face, she made it to the ladder leaning against the loft. Reaching for the ladder she set her foot on the first rung. She looked back.

The fire had reached Daisy. Her hair was already burning.

Shanti said a quick prayer for the poor maid, she'd never get to have her baby. Wiping at her eyes, she grabbed the sides of the ladder and started to climb.

In the dark, she couldn't see that halfway up, one of the rungs was broken. Her foot slipped right through the broken rung. She started to fall!

Frantically, she held on for dear life to the sides of the ladder, her legs kicked out into open space – she was dangling 20 feet in the air, her hands were bleeding and slippery and splintered from holding on to the ladder so tightly.

Flailing wildly, she felt for another rung with her feet. Clutching the ladder as tightly as she could, her heart pounding in her ears, she finally found a rung and stepped on it.

Hanging on for dear life, she stood still, sobbing in relief. Looking down to the ground, she realized she was far up enough if she'd fallen, she probably would have broken something.

Tipping her head back, she could barely make out the top of the loft through the haze caused by the smoke. She continued to climb.

*7*he Bronco lay on its side, the engine sputtered and died.

Smoke poured out from the hood. The sound of the wind and escaping steam seared the silence of the night.

Then a door on the side of the truck that faced up creaked open an inch. It was pushed open farther, then it fell, slamming back closed. The door was thrust open again, harder this time; it bounced against its hinges and then stayed open.

A head popped out.

Jarrett, a bruise turning purple on his forehead, looked around in a daze. He spotted the barn. The entire front was engulfed in flames furiously grabbing at the roof to catch and burn.

Placing his scraped and bloodied palms on either side of the car's doorway, he pushed himself up until he was sitting on the side of the car.

He sat for a second to catch his breath, and waited for the dizziness to pass. Even with the airbag and seatbelt his head had banged against the side window when the truck flipped.

Swinging his legs to the side, he slid down the truck until his feet hit the ground with a thud. He paused, apparently he hadn't broken any bones. There was pain but it was livable.

Jerking the truck keys out of his pocket, he went to the trunk and opened it. Pushing tools and equipment around, he found what he was looking for.

Not wasting time closing the trunk, he immediately ran towards the barn, now a bright orange beacon in the night.

*S*hanti struggled to climb from the ladder onto the loft.

Grunting, "Humph!" she fell onto the dirty hay that layered the floor of the wooden loft. As soon as she fell onto the loft, the ladder slipped - she reached out to grab it - but it fell - striking the ground with a barely heard thump.

Shanti's despairing gaze stared at the ladder lying on the barn floor, then over to the front of the barn.

The room was more than half filled with terrifying flames. She didn't have her jacket anymore but it was warm now. When she crawled onto the loft most of her blouse ripped apart. She couldn't take her eyes off the raging fire that was creeping closer and closer to her.

She scooted backwards, away from the front of the loft until she hit the back wall.

Drawing her knees up, she wrapped her arms around them and waited for the first flames that would peer greedily over the top of the loft.

Jarrett raced to the barn. Adrenaline was pumping through his veins- he could feel it coursing through his arms and legs. His heart was beating so hard he thought it was going to explode.

He could see the fire had already consumed a good portion of the barn. Fear gripped him, he just knew something was horribly wrong, he prayed that Shanti was not in the barn.

When he finally reached the barn, he dropped the ax he'd taken out of the truck on the ground and bent over with his hands on his knees to catch his breath. He could feel the heat from the fire even over here on the side of the barn.

Something glinting in the winter grass caught his eye. He picked it up. It was a barrette. It had a flower design on it and wasn't rusty so it was freshly dropped- was it a lure or a pointer? He slid it into his pocket.

Black smoke billowed in a huge cloud over the barn, the wind carried the smoke over the pasture towards the estate. He didn't bother running around to the front of the building to see if he could get in the door.

He could tell he would only be met with a wall of flames. The door was probably already dusty chars of black ash on the ground.

The marshal stood back from the barn and looked up at the window at the top. The small bit of glass that had been in it had blown out. Smoke poured out of it.

Jarrett cupped his hands around his mouth and yelled, "Hello! Hello! Is anybody in there!?" He waited, listening.

Did he hear something? It was hard to tell, the fire was making its own loud noise now- crackling and roaring, wood splintering and burning then crashing to the ground.

He yelled again, "Hello! Anybody in there!?"

Wait, he heard something.

*W*oozy from the smoke, Shanti lifted her head. What was that? Did she hear someone calling over the roar of the fire?

Crawling to the edge of the loft, she coughed, trying to clear her throat. She swallowed hard to moisten her mouth and throat so she could yell.

Putting her hands around her mouth she tried to scream. "Hel- *gasp, cough*, help! Help!" Her voice was weak and scratchy.

She covered her mouth again with her sleeve and breathed deeply. Swallowing again, she tried to make saliva to lubricate her throat.

*J*arrett looked up again at the window. He thought he heard something, but it could have been the wind or a bird in the distance. He yelled again, "Hello!! Is anybody in the barn!"

There was definitely someone out there. Shanti gathered up all the strength she had, closing her eyes tight, she clenched her fists and screamed as loud and as long as she could then broke into spasms of coughing.

Choking, she palmed her eyes to clear them and looked around the loft for something to throw out the tiny window to catch attention. But the loft was bereft of little but flammable straw and hay.

Jarrett was sure he heard a faint scream. He was right-someone was trapped in there. And if he didn't work damned fast, it would be too late to save them!

He grabbed the ax and holding it firmly in both hands, he whacked with all his might at the back wall of the barn. The ax stuck in the wood. He pulled it out, and struck the wall again, and again.

Shanti wiped her stinging eyes, the smoke was burning the hell out of them. She leaned over the edge of the loft.

Less than ten feet from the loft the flames raged- licking and spitting across the floor, the straw and hay making perfect kindling to feed the fire.

Burning beams in the rafters started falling, crashing onto the floor, sparks flew in all directions.

Shanti stared in horror at the inferno coming towards her. She tried to scream again, but her voice was totally hoarse, she could only make rasping whispers.

But she could hear something pounding below the loft. She scrambled on her stomach and looked down.

Directly under the loft she could see rays of light from outside streaking dimly through the smoke and across the floor.

Oh dear God- someone is breaking down the wall!

She hugged the edge, dropping her head over the side she tried to yell, but her voice only came out in hushed squeaks.

Jarrett could feel the heat hit his face as soon as he chopped a hole big enough for him to climb through.

He stuck his head in first and looked around. He could hardly make out anything, the room was so filled with thick black smoke.

He called out, "Hello? Hello? Shanti – are you in here?"

He tried to keep the panic out of his voice. He could see the inside was almost completely engulfed with flames. The fire burned and sparked and crackled, the heat was intense. He heard something.

A tiny sound.

He listened but he couldn't separate the sound from the roar of the fire and the crashing of beams hitting the ground. A shower of straw tumbled onto his head.

The marshal looked up. He could see Shanti's head hanging over the side of the loft.

Clinging to the edge with big terrified eyes and her face covered in black soot, she was pointing at something on the ground.

Jarrett looked down and saw the ladder. He ran to it and picked it up. Grunting, he slammed the ladder up against the loft. Immediately he started climbing. He could hear Shanti coughing.

His eyes watered, his lungs screamed. He heard something, a tiny squeak. He looked up, she was pointing again at the ladder.

Jarrett looked down just in time to see the broken rung. He stepped over it and safely onto the next rung.

Quickly climbing the ladder, he reached Shanti in seconds. She looked pitiful he thought when they were finally eye to eye.

Her golden hair and her face were covered in a layer of soot, her eyes stood out like blue sapphires on a black velvet cloth like they use in jewelry stores to display gems. She was the most beautiful thing he'd ever seen in his life.

Wordlessly, Jarrett held out his hand to her when he reached the top. The hand she held out to him was trembling. He grabbed it and pulled her none too gently to the ladder. They had no time to spare.

When he got her to the top of the ladder, he climbed on first then he put his hands under her arms and lifted her onto the rungs.

She was so weak she could hardly move. He took each of her hands and set them on the top rung of the ladder. Standing one rung below her, he tucked an arm tightly around her waist.

Step by quivering step they climbed backwards down the ladder. Sparks of fire and pieces of charred wood fell on their heads. They couldn't protect themselves, they had to hurry.

Jarrett's feet finally touched the ground. He put his hands around Shanti's waist and pulled her off the ladder and onto the dirt floor.

Shanti looked up and screamed.

Jarrett followed her gaze. His eyes widened in horror. The fire had crept along the ceiling, the entire roof was ablaze and the beams that were still there were on fire. The entire roof was caving in! Large planks and pieces of burning wood crashed all around them.

Jarrett wrapped both arms around Shanti and rolled them to the side narrowly escaping a crashing giant piece of burning lumber.

The marshal leapt to his feet and grabbed Shanti's hand, yanked her up and quickly pulled her towards the hole he'd made in the wall.

Suddenly, huge pieces of flaming wood hurtled towards them- the entire roof was coming down on top of them!

Jarrett stepped through the hole then reached back inside. Grasping Shanti's arms, he yanked her so hard through the hole she fell into him – the momentum knocked him flat on his back with Shanti landing on top of him.

Shanti's eyes were inches from Jarrett's. He smiled. She didn't.

Squawking rasps, Shanti said, "Jarrett, there were tanks of some kind in there-" she didn't get all the words out-

Jarrett shoved her off him, leaping up he pulled her to her feet again and he ran as fast as he could dragging her after him.

They were barely 50 feet away when they heard the explosions.

Jarrett threw Shanti to the ground and hurled his body on top of her.

The explosions were deafening. Jarrett protectively covered Shanti, hiding his face in her neck.

Flat on her stomach, her face pushed into the grass, Shanti stuck her fingers in her ears.

When he didn't feel any flying missiles hitting them, Jarrett rolled off Shanti and sat up. He pulled her up next to him.

They sat in silent awe watching pieces of wood still flying in the air from the explosions. Flames and smoke flew up to the heavens, the sky itself look on fire.

Behind the burning barn, black clouds covered the sky in puffy streaks.

Jarrett felt something strike his face. He brought his hand up and touched his cheek. It was a raindrop. He looked at Shanti.

Her eyes were so wide, he could see white all around her irises, she was mesmerized by the barn now fully engulfed in flames.

They watched for a few minutes, until with thunderous booming crashes, the entire barn finally came down. Soon, there was nothing left but a big pile of burning wood. It started raining.

Shanti looked at Jarrett. "Sure, now it rains!"

They laughed together, terribly relieved and breaking the tension after what they had just gone through.

Then, Shanti grew serious. She reached out a scraped-up soot covered arm, the sleeve hanging off in tatters, and lightly touched Jarrett's face. Her expression solemn, she took in his bruised and equally soot covered face.

He watched her, watching him.

"Marshal, I- I owe you my life. Thank you…I mean…how can I ever thank you?" She looked at him with big, wide teary eyes.

They were still close enough to the barn for the fire to reflect off their faces. The same recalcitrant lock of hair flopped over one blue-green eye. Shanti tenderly pushed the sooty lock back. Her brows drew down in an angle between her eyes, she tilted her head quizzically at him.

"How on earth did you know I was in there?" she asked, swallowing soot and coughing.

Jarrett chuckled, shaking his head. He had one knee bent up, his arm lay across it. The light rain was wetting his hair and spotting his shirt. He shrugged.

"I don't know. I just had this feeling. You called the station with urgent news, but then didn't call back. No one answered me, or the patrol car that came out to the house. Things didn't feel right.

"When I drove through the woods to come in the back way, I saw the barn on fire. Then I knew something was really wrong. I just...had... this ...this... feeling...that you were in there. I can't explain it." He smiled.

Lifting an arm, he also reached to her face and smoothed back her hair. A barrette with a dusty flower on it clung to a few wisps of straggly hair. He felt its twin in his pocket, but left it there, a souvenir.

"Well, whatever 'little voice' told you I was in trouble, I'm so very very grateful...Marshal..." Shanti smiled at him. Her lips quavered, she was shivering.

Jarrett looked down, there was very little left of her blouse. Raindrops ran in rivulets down her neck and then down between her breasts. The water left little trails in the soot on her skin.

Jarrett's gaze followed the trails- he suddenly felt warm even in the cold rain.

"Here-" he pulled off his jacket and swung it around her shoulders. He helped her shrug into it.

The leather was warm and comfy. Shanti smiled gratefully at him. "This is becoming a habit, Marshal," she said, her voice scratchy.

He grinned back. "Listen, we'll think of how you can thank me later." Laughing at her shocked expression, he stood up before she could respond. Leaning over, he grasped her hand and helped her up.

As soon as she stood, she swayed, her knees buckled, she started to collapse back onto the ground. Jarrett swiftly reached out and caught her. Her eyes rolled back in her head, she was losing consciousness.

The strapping marshal swung her up in his arms, her head dropped on his shoulder. He stood holding her. They were standing on a slight hill they'd run up to get away from the barn and stared at the burning embers that were left.

They sky darkened as the flames diminished. Jarrett looked down at the bundle he held tightly in his arms.

Shanti stirred slightly, her eyes fluttered open. She looked up at him.

Light rain sprinkled on her face, her eyelashes were spiking from the drops, and her lips parted. He leaned his head down and pressed his lips gently against hers.

The kiss was so exquisitely sweet it almost hurt. Jarrett realized he'd been waiting to kiss her since the very second he had first laid eyes on her.

Chapter Forty-Nine

Shanti understood now why Graham's kiss hadn't excited her. In fact, it repulsed her. She hadn't wanted to admit her intense attraction to the arrogant sheriff.

Forgetting his merciless teasing and insults, Shanti reveled in the joining of their lips. Her arms slid up around his neck. They didn't even feel the misty rain showering their skin, dampening their clothes.

Jarrett could feel his body stir in arousal, he reluctantly pulled his lips away and gazed tenderly down at her. It started raining harder.

"We've got to go," he gave her one last quick, light kiss then started walking towards the estate. He smiled at her.

She grinned brightly at him. "We have to stop meeting like this Marshal," her voice husky, she pretended to be stern. "I think I can walk now, you can set me down."

He kept striding, taking long steps, they moved quickly through the low fields.

Without looking at her, he said, "Maybe I like the way your arms cling so tightly around my neck."

Shanti frowned at him. She could now see the bruise on his head, the rain was washing away some of the soot. He was covered in bloody cuts and other burgeoning bruises.

"Jarrett, you're injured– what happened? Put me down, you must be in pain!" she insisted, concern written all over her pretty, albeit grimy, face.

He shrugged, but kept moving. "I'm fine, honey, just a minor car accident. We'll get there more quickly if I carry you. It'll be easier than dragging your beautiful butt through the fields."

He ignored her affronted gasp. Actually, she was fairly light and he made good time to the house.

Suddenly she remembered. "Jarrett, I remember now why I called you!" The urgency was back in her voice. She looked up at his rugged face, her eyes grew tender again. If she had thought Graham was strong and capable, this man was a bulwark.

Jarrett smiled down at her again. "I love it when you call me by my name."

Shanti shook her head impatiently. "Listen, Marsh…uh…Jarrett, when I was watching the news this evening, you know about the nerve gas and how you caught the perpetrators and-"

"Yeah, can you believe the Vaughns' farmhand Miguel Perez was involved in this? We never would have found out if not for the potato disease. We're pretty sure that we still don't have all of the offenders involved. They have hinted we didn't get the mastermind-"

"I know, Marshal, that's what I'm trying to tell you! I know who the leader is!" Shanti exclaimed, wriggling in his arms.

"Hold still, hold still, I don't want to drop you. Now, what the heck are you trying to say?" Jarrett's expression aimed at her was confused. Raindrops streamed down his face, his hair was dripping wet. He stopped and set her gently on her feet.

Shanti pushed her hair back and wiped her hand across her face. It was freezing, but the shower was starting to dissipate. She pulled the leather jacket more tightly closed. Her legs were shaky, but she fought to stand as steadily as she could.

"When I saw the representative from Thailand on television explaining how they wanted to help us, the Thailand flag was behind him. I recognized it." She stopped to take a breath and clear her parched throat. She was so weary she could hardly stand.

Realizing this, Jarrett wrapped his fingers around her arms to hold her steady. He waited for her to continue.

"You see, Mrs. Li, the Lawton's housekeeper had a necklace that she always wore, or actually she wore until all this nerve gas stuff hit the fan, then I didn't see it anymore. I remember when I first met her, I asked her what it represented. She told me it was the flag of her country. Jarrett," she touched his shoulder, enthralled with the thick strength of it gave her pause.

"Anyway, Jarrett, the flag on her necklace was the Thailand flag. Chloe had told me Li said she was from Viet Nam. There's something else I remember..." Shanti had the marshal's full attention. Not that his aroused eyes hadn't already been beamed in like a steady laser at her.

"I saw Mrs. Li talking often with Miguel. One morning, I saw three people way out by the river talking from my balcony. At the time I had thought they were Graham Duncan and a couple of hands, but now I recognize Miguel as one of the people, and the other was really tiny, it was Mrs. Li!

"I just always figured she was giving or getting information about the Vaughns for like dinner parties and stuff, but now I realize that's too coincidental. Besides, I can't see the stoic dragonlady being friendly with the likes of Miguel Perez.

"Plus, for dummies sake, there are phones they could have used if their contact was purely innocent. I think they didn't want anyone to have a trail of them by phone, email or text. Anyone else seeing them like I had would have assumed the same as I did, that they were discussing work. But in reality they felt safer being out in the open field where no one could hear them."

Jarrett was nodding as she talked, taking in everything. His face relaxed, then his mouth turned up in a wide smile. "I think you broke the rest of the case, Miss Shantilly Lane, private eye!" He saluted her, they laughed together.

"Miguel must have been too terrified of her to cough up her name. I'll call the boys to pick her up for questioning as soon as we get back. Come on, let's move, it's freezing out here!" He took her hand and they held hands all the way back to the estate.

By the time they reached the manor, the police were running towards them. It looked like every light in the house was on. There were people swarming all over the place.

A firetruck, siren screaming, streaked past them, racing out to the burned barn, just a little too late! Bill Johnson ran up to Jarrett, his face was pinched with worry.

"Marshal! Someone driving by called in and said one of the Lawtons' barns was on fire, and you told us you were on your way here, but then when we got here there was no sign of you! We were totally freaked- What the hell happened? Are you guys okay?"

"We're fine, Bill, just bruised and shaken, and real tired." The exhaustion was clear in Jarrett's voice and demeanor. He had his arm around Shanti's shoulder, her head rested against his chest. Their clothes were torn and covered in black soot.

Bill tried to keep the surprise of seeing them so obviously cozy off his face. Just this morning, the marshal was cursing the beautiful blonde, although, now that he thought about it, Jarrett hadn't really seemed all that angry...

"Bill-" Jarrett broke into the deputy's musings.

"Yes, sir?" He snapped to attention.

"Get some of the boys and go find the Lawtons' housekeeper, Mrs. Li, and take her to the station. I'll fill you in when I get there. Oh, and, see if someone can get my truck, I left it about a half a mile behind the barn. It's going to need a tow," Jarrett said wearily. His smile at Shanti was lopsided.

"Shall we go inside and rustle us up some grub?"

She giggled, rewarding him with a dazzling smile. They headed towards the house, leaving a bewildered deputy staring at their backs.

Chapter Fifty

After sharing her harrowing experience with the rest of the household and breaking the news of Daisy's murder, Shanti took a long, hot shower. It was hard to scrub the soot off her skin. She was pink and raw in spots by time she toweled off.

Taking only a few minutes to blow dry her hair, she couldn't resist lying down for a moment on the satiny bed. She was asleep before her eyes closed.

She didn't wake up again until nine the next morning. Yawning and stretching, she could smell hot coffee. Next to the bed on a nightstand, a cup of coffee, steam still pouring out, cream and sugar and a blueberry muffin, were nestled on a freshly polished silver tray.

Sipping the hot coffee, she carried the cup around while she gathered clothes to wear. Dressing in her usual jeans and sweater, she quickly combed her hair before going downstairs. She found the rest of the family in the dining room.

"Shanti, you don't look the worse for wear!" Chloe greeted her, and pointed at the chair next to her. "Come and sit next to me, I can't believe what's happened! I could hardly sleep all night!"

Shanti stopped next to Chloe. The girls hugged then Shanti pulled out a chair and sat down.

"I'm so glad you're okay, Shanti," Chloe said, with as much fear and sincerity Shanti's own sister would have. Her eyes grew sad. "I just can't believe it, you know, first Grandfather, then Serafina, now poor Daisy! What on earth is going on?"

"Chloe, please, let the girl catch her breath," Maeve said stiffly from the head of the table. The austere grey dress and the red hair streaked with white pulled back tightly in a bun, suited the somber mood of the house.

The lines in her face seemed to have deepened almost overnight. But her back was still rigid, her head high. Picking up the silver bell, she jerked it lightly twice then set it down.

After several minutes, Maeve turned and stared at the kitchen door. Her mouth turning down further and further with each moment that passed.

Finally, the kitchen door swung open. A different maid than any Shanti had ever seen before was in the doorway.

"Christine, you must attend to the bell immediately upon hearing it," Maeve said through tight lips. She frowned at the maid.

The maid looked about 24, with short brown hair, brown eyes, average height and weight albeit a bit lumpy, in fact she was so average she'd never get picked out of a lineup. Her brown eyes looked vacantly at Maeve. She shrugged like a bland pile of mashed potatoes slumping.

Maeve rolled her eyes. She needed to replace Mrs. Li as soon as possible. But good help was so hard to find in this small town. Christine and a few other servants worked at the mansion part time. She'd now have to enlist them for full time service.

"Please bring the eggs. And get Libby," Maeve told her.

The maid blinked at her mistress. "Miz Libby is gone, Missus, she left early this morning. Said she wanted out of this murderous manor. Are there ghosts about? Am I safe?" Her hands went to her throat, the brown eyes widened in sudden fear.

"Stop it this instant, Christine. There are no ghosts here. Just go get the eggs." Maeve's square shoulders now drooped slightly in exhaustion. She'd have to go out of town to hire help. No one was going to want to work in a house where three of the occupants had been murdered.

Christine stood for a second, her arms crossed in front of her. She looked in turn at everyone at the table.

Chloe and Shanti were talking quietly to each other. The blonde and russet heads so close single strands of their hair mixed together.

Dawn, bored as always when the attention was not on her, was staring out the front window, her mother, Camelia was studying her coffee, trying to figure out how to get the bourbon she had in her purse into her coffee cup without anyone seeing, and Jaime was reading the newspaper, ignoring everyone.

The longer the maid hesitated, the further down Maeve's mouth and eyebrows drew.

Finally, the girl shrugged negligently again, heaven knows, she really needed this job with three little kids, and her being a single mother and all, that no-good husband of hers running out on them – oh well, she turned and went back into the kitchen, the door swung closed behind her.

Maeve sighed, turning her attention to Shanti. "Shantilly dear, we are having a few people over this evening to view your painting. I had hoped for a bigger event, however," she sighed deeply again, "with everything concerned, it didn't seem proper. We'll have to cater it also, I suppose.

"I've only been able to get that Christine creature and another woman, Selma, another part timer, heavens, she's so old her bones creak worse than the stairs and it takes her forever to get the fires lit, and that ungrateful wretch, Libby, for heaven's sake. No notice, just up and left, she'll never work in this town again, you can count on that!" Maeve shook her head with annoyance and sipped her coffee.

"Grandmother, what...uh...do you know what happened with Mrs. Li?" Chloe asked timidly.

Maeve shrugged, continuing to drink her coffee. Her head turned. She stared impatiently at the kitchen door again after the maid- that insolent girl was fairly new and going to need a lot of work, and without Mrs. Li to train her, damn. She looked down her aristocratic nose at her granddaughter, her ancient face pinched.

"I don't know, Chloe, I suppose we'll hear when they've caught her. I don't want her name spoken in this house ever again, as far as I'm concerned, she is dead and gone, never worked here." Maeve sniffed, her nose in the air.

Dawn snickered. "Oh Grandmother, be realistic, it'll be all over the paper for crying out loud. Our housekeeper not only was smuggling nerve freaking gas from another country, but she kills our Granddad and two of our maids and you think you can sweep it under the carpet like it never happened?"

Laughing at her grandmother's absurdity, shaking her head drolly, Dawn crossed her arms in front of her chest and leaned back in her chair.

Maeve glared at her granddaughter, her lip curled but she said nothing.

"Why do you think it was Mrs. Li that killed Grandfather and Serafina and Daisy?" Chloe asked her sister.

Dawn turned to Chloe, smirking. Her elbows on the table, she twiddled with a forest green earring. Her ruffled green blouse slipped out a bit in the back where it was tucked into skin-tight black jeans when she leaned forward.

"Oh don't be so naïve little sister, who else around would have done it? She smuggled nerve gas for Pete's sake. Who else has those kinds of brass ball-"

"Dawn!" Maeve snapped, frowning at her granddaughter. "We don't use that sort of language in this house and you know it!"

Dawn lifted her chin in the air at the reprimand. She smoothed her flaming hair off her face and looked back at Chloe.

"At least the spooky witch had some nerve, nothing else has ever happened in this boring little town. Besides, people will look at us with interest now, espousing, 'There goes the family that harbored a voodoo, spell-making, murderous, terroristic poison smuggl-'"

"*That is enough, Dawn. Stop*." Maeve's voice grated through clenched teeth.

Dawn drew her shoulders up and down blithely. Her head turned back towards the window, she pretended to lose interest in the conversation.

"But Grandmother, why would Mrs. Li kill Granddaddy?" Chloe asked.

Maeve's lips pursed, her eyebrows rose. She didn't quite look at Chloe, but just past her shoulder. "Who knows dear, he must have heard or seen something, we may never know. These people are thugs and criminals that belong behind bars.

"I shudder to think if we have to go through some lengthy awful trial, the media following us about, people staring at us…" she trailed off, shivering slightly in distaste.

Dawn's lips drew up in a mischievous grin. "Great! Our own paparazzi! Gee Grandmother, that means we all need to go out and get a whole new wardrobe! Mother," she turned and said to Camelia, "I suggest black, you know the camera puts on a good ten pounds, and black you know is thinning…"

Camelia's mouth compressed in a thin line, her eyes hardened at her daughter's not so veiled jab about her weight. Since Logan left she'd done nothing except eat and drink, and it was starting to show. Her face and figure were rapidly bloating.

She leaned across the table at her daughter, pointed a finger at her and said viciously, "Then you'd better get to the salon and get those moles lemoned-off or whatever they do- because they're starting to show up again, and bigger than usual. Actually dear, you look like someone threw a bucket of mud at you!"

Dawn flinched at the insult about her freckles. Her eyes squinted into cat-eyed slits, her bottom teeth pushed forward. "Well darling Mother, maybe some new slimy gigolo will see you on TV and you can get yourself a fifth husband that doesn't mind a slatternly fat cow for a wif-"

"Listen you little slut, don't you talk to me that way, I'll-"

"*Shut up Camelia*," Maeve commanded in a whispered shout. "You too, Dawn. This behavior is deplorable and I will not have it!" She slammed her hand on the table. Her head jerked towards the kitchen door. "Where is that useless, poor excuse for a maid-"

The door swung open, Christine entered with a huge platter of scrambled eggs in her hands.

Soon the table was completely silent as everyone concentrated on eating. Dawn still smirked at her mother as she spooned eggs and bacon into her mouth

Giving up on trying to be discreet, Camelia took her purse off the back of her chair and pulled out the small flask of bourbon she had inside. Twisting the top off, she dumped the whole bottle into her coffee cup. Sipping her brew, she ignored the ferocious look Maeve shot at her.

Jaime gobbled his breakfast as fast as he could and left without a word.

As soon as Chloe was finished, she set her napkin next to her place and turned to Shanti. "How about a ride, Shanti?" she asked.

Shanti smiled at Chloe.

Chloe was wearing a long sleeved denim shirt that matched her jeans. Her face as always was scrubbed clean, devoid of makeup and her eyes sparkled at her friend. Shanti chewed quickly and swallowed, nodding vigorously.

"I'd love to, Chloe," she agreed happily. A ride would help chase away the demons that had her up all night with nightmares.

"Great! Finish up and get your jacket, I'll go get the horses ready." Chloe stood up then leaned over and whispered in Shanti's ear. "I can't wait to hear about you, the fire, the marshal, and…the kiss…"

Shanti's head turned swiftly, her eyes wide surprise at Chloe.

"What? But how did-" Shanti was puzzled. No one could have seen her and Jarrett out in the fields.

Chloe grinned and winked. "I could tell, girlfriend, by the way you two clung to each other, you couldn't take your eyes off one another. He was staring at your lips like he wanted to suck them off your face! I wasn't positive, but you've confirmed it now! Anyway, I want to hear all about it- everything!" She giggled and skipped lightly out of the room.

Shanti glanced around the table without moving her head to see if anyone had heard what Chloe had said. But no one was paying any attention.

She ate her breakfast as fast as she could, she couldn't wait to get on a horse and have the wind run through her hair. She also wanted the time to regroup and think about Jarrett. He was coming over later for the viewing of the painting.

Shivers of excitement ran up her arms. Closing her eyes, she pictured him, tall and lean with the broadest shoulders, thick dark hair with eyes the color of the sea. His lopsided grin, and the way he looked at her– goose bumps popped up on her skin.

Time to go.

Chapter Fifty-One

Chloe and Shanti rode for little more than an hour, chatting and rehashing the past few weeks, relieved that the frightening ordeals the Lawtons and Shanti had been through were now over.

Yet, mysteries still remained, lurking around them like a black shroud, thinly veiled, a lingering vaguely ominous feeling of unanswered questions.

They queried each other, who, and why were the diseased potatoes planted in the Vaughns' fields? The agriculture agents determined the fungus had been deliberately deposited in the soil. The girls pondered why were Langston, Serafina and Daisy killed? They concluded that they may never know the answers.

Shanti confided in Chloe her feelings for Jarrett, and their tender kiss.

The two young women giggling like schoolgirls teased and chased each other on horseback.

When they could feel the chill of the early winter day begin to creep into their bones, they decided it was time to head back to the house.

Maeve told them she planned a light lunch, later everyone would dress for the buffet and showing of Shanti's painting. Only a few close friends, neighbors, and some business acquaintances of the Lawtons' were invited to the small party.

Showering and quickly drying her hair, Shanti slipped into a white dress that clung to her body from her breasts down to her knees, then spread out in a mermaid fashion from there to her toes.

Spaghetti straps held the dress to her shapely shoulders, the bodice was covered in sequins that were widely spaced, then, became closer together and more numerous towards her slim waist, then began disappearing as they slid over her hips and down the length of her legs.

The bottom part that flowed out from her knees to her satin high heels had only a few sequins interspersed throughout the ruffly skirt. The sequins gave the white gown an antique lacy look.

Tiny white bows held back only a few wisps of butter yellow hair off her face.

Cheeks whipped naturally rosy from the wind, only one swipe of mascara to each set of eyelashes and a pale, shimmering pink lipstick was all the makeup she needed.

Already 60 or 70 people were gathered in the huge room, mingling and tasting the delicious treats the caterers had laid out on the tables that spanned the entire back wall of the room.

Men and women in starched white uniforms meandered through the throng of guests carrying trays laden with champagne glasses, stopping here and there as people picked a glass off the tray, enjoying the bubbles that tickled their noses at each sip.

Dress was fancy and formal, men in tuxes and women in floor-length gowns.

Leaving her room, Shanti walked the length of the hallway until she reached the stairs. Hesitating at the top, she gazed down at the numerous people that had spilled out into the foyer to greet newcomers.

Wow, she thought, all these people here to view her work. This was a small party? It was a bit daunting. She took a deep breath to calm herself.

"There she is, the guest of honor!" someone announced.

Heads turned and looked up at Shanti standing at the top of the stairs. She looked like an angel about to take flight.

Everyone was smiling, welcoming her to come down from the clouds and join them.

Shanti's eyes traveled around the group, recognizing many faces. Now that the criminals were found out and Shanti was no longer a suspect, and the painting was done, it was going to be hard to go back to her home in California and leave all her new friends and acquaintances behind. Especially-

Her gaze caught a familiar face.

Jarrett was smiling broadly up at her. It's the first time she hadn't seen him in his police uniform.

He was dashing in a black tux matching many of the men surrounding him. Interestingly, the bow tie at his throat was the exact shade of white, almost antique, as Shanti's dress. He had a white rose bud in his lapel.

He hadn't had time to get his hair cut, it still hung an inch or so over his collar, but it was all combed straight back in one long line. He looked pretty rakish for a policeman!

His blue-green eyes shone up at Shanti, those along with his broad smile intangibly pulled her to come and stand beside him.

Shanti never took her eyes from Jarrett's as she swept gracefully down the same staircase she had envisioned the women of the grand house attired in glamorous gowns descending the first day she arrived at the mansion.

She never felt a step under her foot, it seemed she floated down the wide thickly carpeted stairs.

All eyes were on her. Rumors of her near demise in the fire and the thrilling rescue by their beloved sheriff were rife throughout the town.

They were an extraordinarily striking couple, the kind romantic fables were made of. The handsome prince coming to the aid of the lovely damsel in distress, a collective audible sigh could be heard in the entire area.

As she reached the bottom step, Jarrett was there waiting for her. He held out a hand. Suddenly she was shy, her eyes dropped to the floor. She heard him chuckle.

"Where's that sassy little gal with the blue fire spitting from her eyes that's ready to pop me one? Where's she hiding?" he whispered teasing, his face close to hers.

Her smile soft, she pretended to lightly punch him in the arm.

"Listen, Jar-" she started to warn him, but a voice cut her off.

"Everyone, please, join us in the great room, we're ready for the unveiling!" Montgomery announced. His normally implacable face couldn't help but grin at Shanti.

It was great to see the young lady happy and safe. His eyes rolled skyward. Langston would sure be mad up in heaven if anything had happened to his little artist.

Jarrett took Shanti's hand and they strolled through the crowd over to Montgomery.

The butler led the couple with the rest of the guests trailing behind to the great room. The decorated room, shining all golden and sparkling with extravagant flower arrangements and candles, held the many guests.

Shanti shook her head. It was always interesting to see Maeve's idea of a 'little party.'

Her painting was at the front of the room on an easel and covered with a cloth.

Maeve, Chloe, Dawn and Jaime were standing next to the painting waiting for her. Camelia was sitting at the closest bar, batting her eyelashes at the bartender that was mixing her third martini.

As soon as Shanti and Jarrett joined the Lawtons, Maeve clapped her hands to get everyone's attention. When the room quieted, she spoke.

"Thank you everyone, for joining us here today. We have been through...a lot...lately," her voice shook slightly, it was very un-Maeve like. In a stronger voice she went on, "And, today we celebrate a joyous event, a happy harbinger of the good times that will hopefully return to Red Gem Farm!"

Smiling and nodding, she slightly bowed her rigid back to the people clapping with enthusiasm their agreement with her words. Her brave words were eagerly accepted by the townspeople, they felt the black cloud that had been hanging over the Lawtons' farm was finally drifting away.

Guests mumbled to each other, "We always knew that voodoo lady was up to no good, and we were right!"

"And now," Maeve continued, raising her hand, "I would like to reveal the painting that you all know our beloved Langston had commissioned Miss Shantilly Lane to do of our home that has been in the family for generations. I only wish that he...my dear husband...was here to see it completed..."

Maeve bowed her head at the sniffs that could be heard in the room. There wasn't a dry eye in the place. Clearing her throat, she turned primly to the easel and grasped the cloth covering the painting.

"Here's to the bright future of Red Gem Farm, may all our dark days be behind us!" she exclaimed, pulling the sheet from the painting in one swoop.

Loud oo's and ahs and applause scampered around the room, eyes were wide and excited, huge grins of delight bounced from person to person. Eyes went to the painting, then to Shanti's shining face and back to the painting.

Jarrett squeezed the hand he held so tightly and smiled down at her. She was all a-glow, like a blonde beam of bright light. He gave her a gentle push towards Maeve.

Shyly, Shanti joined Maeve standing next to the painting.

The sound of clapping was almost deafening. Shanti's grin was brilliant. *Wow*, she thought, *I guess they like it*!

Chloe leaned over and kissed her friend on the cheek. "It's fantastic, Shanti, really, it's breathtaking, you've totally captured the house. It breathes and, and...it seems to be...smiling," Chloe gushed, obviously in awe of the painting that held all the attention in the room.

Shanti had captured the realism and vast grandeur of the estate so precisely it looked almost like a photograph- only better- with feeling and dimension.

The pure blue sky in the background and the flowers she added softened the whole effect of the rough stones. Blooms of colorful roses, fuchsia rhododendrons and climbing ivy encircled the entire front of the immense stone building.

The winding driveway flowed through the wrought iron gate in a swirl, like a black snake curving in the green grass up to the front of the stately house.

She'd even put in such details as the cut glass design in the windows of the front double doors, and the words, 'Red Gem Farm' arched over the bronze gate.

"Well, Miss Lane, Granddaddy was right about you after all. And here I thought he was just a daft old man," Dawn drawled. Ignoring the swift indrawn breath of her Grandmother, she went on, "But," she held out a freckled hand and shook Shanti's hand.

"You are incredibly talented. The painting is absolutely outstanding. I am just, well, flabbergasted!"

Shanti blinked at the red-haired beauty pumping her hand so hard.

Dawn's navy blue dress skimmed her body as always, a slit up the front went to the top of her thighs, and the deeply dipping cleavage did its best to meet the slit.

Shanti checked her feline eyes for any dishonesty or trickery, but for once her face was clear of any deceit. Dawn was genuinely impressed with the painting and had searched for appropriate words to describe the feelings the awesome painting elicited in her.

"I must agree with my sister, Shanti." Jaime stood in front of her and shook her hand as well. "Your talent is incredible, just amazing, the painting is…dynamite!"

Shanti grinned in delight at the young man.

He was wearing the winter white suit he favored with a dark blue, silk tie. As usual, his red-brown hair was slicked back with mousse.

This was the first time Shanti had heard Jaime speak without sarcasm lacing his words. He was actually quite charming when he wasn't trying to act bored with the world or defensive.

Maeve clapped her hands again. "All right people, you are all welcome to come and peruse the painting up close. Then please help yourself to the food and enjoy the music."

The austere woman waved her hand, numerous gold bracelets bangeled together as she gestured towards the tables of food at the back of the room.

Immediately, a stringed band struck up a few chords moving right into a song. A wave of people quickly flowed towards the front of the room to get a close up look at the painting.

Within minutes, Shanti's arm was tired from well-wishers shaking it.

Jarrett waited for a little while, then he took Shanti's arm and pulled her away from the adoring crowd. He led her to a little alcove in the room that gave them a bit of quiet and privacy.

Her back against the wall, Shanti smiled up at the handsome marshal. Her eyes traveled from his strong jaw to his lips that looked so serious, then up to his remarkable eyes.

Jarrett put a forearm against the wall on either side of her head. Silently, he leaned in and gently kissed her. Shanti eagerly accepted his kiss.

They didn't notice the people nodding and winking in their direction.

"Hey Rett, quit monopolizing the artist!" Matthew Vaughn laughed at his friend and shook Shanti's hand. He and his sister Tori exclaimed their pleasure at the popular painting. The siblings were happy tonight, their father had been released from jail and was present with Dolly.

Tobias Vaughn harbored no hard feelings, he knew the evidence against him had looked bad. He was just grateful the true perpetrators were found out and he was no longer a suspect.

Unfortunately, there wasn't enough evidence yet to try the offenders for the murders of Langston, Serafina and Daisy. But the other charges were sufficient to ensure that they never experienced a free day again.

The younger set stood in a tight circle discussing the recent traumatic events culminating with the fabulous painting.

After a few minutes, Tori, sounding unsure, looked seriously up at Jarrett. "Rett, did they find Mrs. Li? Is it over?" The pretty brunet asked her longtime friend. She was draped in a pale pink floor length gown. A bow held a strap over one shoulder while the other shoulder was completely bare.

Tori looked longingly over at Jaime who was chattering away with a small group of men in a far corner. She finally came to the realization that he was unattainable, at least for her. It was time she showed some interest in other young men in her circle.

A handsome young man with sandy colored hair and dark brown eyes caught her attention when she'd first entered the room.

She planned as soon as she made her polite pleasantries to the Lawtons and Shanti, she'd make her way nonchalantly over to the young man.

The way he had looked at her when she stepped over the threshold gave her the courage to find a way to strike up a conversation with him. After all that happened lately there should be plenty to talk about!

Tori licked her lips and smoothed back her long hair. She forgot she'd asked Jarrett a question. She gave a quick shy smile across the room at the young man then turned her attention to the marshal when he started talking.

"Yeah," Jarrett said. "They picked Li up at the airport. She had a fake passport and was about to catch a plane to Thailand. We had men staked out at all the airports, train and bus stations. Plus, we had roadblocks all around the city. It was only a matter of time before we caught her."

"So, is she going to be tried for uh…the …murders…too?" Matthew asked, hesitantly.

Jarrett shook his head. "There's nothing to tie her or the others to any of the murders, even Serafina's. No," he shook his head again, "they claim it was just coincidence they were going to dump me in the same well she was hidden in. We can't prove they killed Serafina or anyone else. But we'll keep working on it, you can count on that!"

374

He unconsciously hugged Shanti tightly against his side. Damn, he thought, it sure felt good to hold her. He didn't like to think about what would have happened if he hadn't found her in time- he shivered and quickly pushed the vision of the burning barn away. He replaced the grisly image with thoughts of getting alone with her as soon as possible.

Shanti looked up at her courageous rescuer. She needed to think of a way to thank him for saving her life. Someone over by the doorway caught her eye. She stared at the petite woman speaking with Dolly Vaughn and Maeve.

It was Serafina's mother. The Vaughns had been so devastated from everything that had happened, they were trying to comfort the maid and thought it might help her get past the horrible death of her daughter by coming to the unveiling.

A quiet timid woman, Valena Vesela, kept fidgeting with the lace collar of her printed dress. Shanti's eye was drawn to the maid's freshly painted nails.

Suddenly, Shanti's mouth dropped open, she shook her head in disbelief. *Oh my gosh, now I know what's been bothering me!* She reached up and yanked at Jarrett's sleeve.

He tipped his head to look down at her, adoring the way her heart-shaped face and sparkling eyes smiled at him. He frowned.

She wasn't smiling. In fact, she looked quite distressed.

He took her arm and excusing them from Matthew and Tori, he guided her through the crowd and out of the room.

Wordlessly he led her down the hall to the library.

Chapter Fifty-Two

Jarrett flipped the light switch on and pulled Shanti into the room.

Even though no one was in the library, Maeve had had the help light the fire in the fireplace. A soft orange glow and warmth radiated from the stone fireplace. If Shanti didn't look so upset, it would have been a perfect place for romance, Jarrett thought.

But then again, the reminiscence of the flames might put a bit of a downer on romance.

Maybe later they could get to know each other better over a candlelight dinner and some slow dancing to a little bluesy music. However, right now, he needed to know what was causing the deeply disturbed look in her blue eyes.

The marshal drew her to the couch and motioned for her to sit.

Obviously distracted, Shanti sat on the edge of the couch, her back rigid.

Jarrett carefully sat down next to her and took her hand. He stared at the side of her head until she turned in his direction. Her eyes were wide and bewildered. He waited.

Shanti blinked, her smile wry. She shook her head. "You know Jarrett, there's been something bothering me, just a teeny thought poking at the back of my mind, always there, but I couldn't put my finger on it."

The marshal waited patiently. He was a cop. He knew people needed to organize their thoughts, feel the words and run them around inside their brains before voicing them.

"It was Serafina's nails." She took a deep breath and looked earnestly at Jarrett.

He was obviously confused. "Her nails?" he questioned, prodding her to continue. He still held her hand, their clasped hands rested on one of his thighs.

She nodded, her hair swished around her head. With her other hand she lifted the hair back up and off her neck, letting it tumble in big waves down past her shoulders. She leaned back against the couch. Her dress twinkled at her every breath.

Jarrett pulled his eyes from the dress that clung nicely to her curves and forced his gaze back up at her face.

"Yeah, weird, huh? Her nails, Jarrett, that's what has bothered me." She turned slightly and studied him, so strong and sure and solid, sitting patiently next to her, ready to support whatever fantastical idea she had.

Such pretty turquoise eyes, she thought, like a girl's, but the ruggedness of his face and fully masculine body weren't in the least bit girlish. She took a deep breath and sighed.

"Serafina's favorite color was pink. We visited a lot the first days I was here at the mansion, but then, for some reason, she grew cold. She wouldn't meet my eyes and refused to respond to my friendly questions.

"Then she suddenly became scarce. People kept asking and wondering where she was all the time. We should have known then, but she was so painfully shy we just didn't realize it..." Sighing, Shanti bit her lower lip.

"She obviously had a boyfriend, but for some reason they kept their relationship a secret, and somehow I don't think that was her idea." She shook her head, her hair fell back in front of her shoulders.

Jarrett reached over and picked up a thick lock of blonde hair that lay across her bosom, he caressed it absently then set it back behind her shoulders again.

"And…?" he murmured, keeping his voice patient and gentle.

"And, she always had her nails perfectly and freshly manicured. I think it was her only vanity. Tonight, when I saw her mother's nails, and before at the last party, Dawn waving her hand about almost made me realize…" She closed her eyes, thinking back.

Jarrett shook her hand lightly. "Realize what honey? What about her nails?"

She opened her eyes and looked at him, then she sat up. "Rett, when they pulled Serafina out of the well you said a few of her nails were broken. You could see the jagged tips of some. You figured she'd broken them when her hands scraped the rough brick wall of the well on the way down."

She gulped, pushing the picture of the dead girl that had been her friend out of her mind.

"I remembered that Serafina always did her nails in pink. Anyway, the night of Dawn's birthday party, you remember, when she almost drowned and Graham jumped in and saved her.

"He had told me to go to his room in the bunkhouse and get some blankets. I ran as fast as I could and found the blankets. However, when I pulled them down over my head from the shelf, they fell, hitting the desk and then landed on the floor.

"I looked down and saw a pinkish stain on the carpet and an empty glass lying next to it. I didn't realize until now, the glass had already been empty when it was knocked over."

Jarrett looked totally lost, his eyes were puzzled, he frowned. She held up a hand.

"Don't you see, I thought the pink stain was from the knocked over glass. But if that was so, there would still be some pink liquid somewhere in the glass, but there wasn't, it was dry. I tried to wipe up the stain but I didn't realize that was dry too.

"I figured the blankets had knocked over the glass and when it hit the floor the liquid had spilled causing the stain. I was in such a hurry I wasn't totally aware of everything I was seeing and doing." Her voice matter of fact, she held her palms open, shrugging.

Jarrett shook his head. "I don't get it, Shanti, what's the big deal about a stain?"

"I know, I'm sorry Rett, I'll get to the point." She didn't see Jarrett smile every time she said his nickname. She had attempted to keep him at a distance before by calling him Marshal, but now…well…it looked like her barriers were breaking down.

"I absently scrubbed at the stain with a towel that was probably still wet from Graham's shower. It made the stain lighten, and get a little damp. So I still figured it was freshly spilled. Now it's finally dawned on me that it wasn't a spilled liquid from a glass, but really was nail polish!" she declared with confidence, nodding her head.

Jarrett still looked bewildered. "Honey, I'm sorry, I must be the most thick-skulled man on the planet but, so what about nail polish? So maybe Graham was a little kinky-" he chuckled at the thought of the burly foreman painting his nails. "Or more probably, he had a girlfriend, so what? That's pretty normal."

"No, Jarrett, not just any girlfriend, but Serafina," she announced, waiting for his reaction.

His brows flew up. "Serafina? No, not her, she was a good girl, sweet, young. I mean he was a rough, older, no way-" his eyes narrowed when he saw Shanti's guilty expression.

She turned her head away. He cupped her chin and turned her face back towards him.

"What?" he asked.

She tried to remove her chin from his hand, shrugging like there was nothing to tell him, but she didn't meet his eyes.

He didn't let go. He repeated, sternly with an edge to his voice, "What?"

"Let go, Rett, you're hurting me." He wasn't, and they both knew it, but he let go.

He didn't remove his steady gaze from her face. She looked down at her hands that were now clasped in her lap.

"Um...I...uh...he...well, he kissed me." She tried to make it sound like it was no big deal.

"What!?" Jarrett took her shoulder, gripping it tightly. "What? That dirty old- old, ranch hand? He had the ball-"

"Jarrett!" Shanti blurted.

"He had the nerve to touch you? That filthy- I'll kill him- he had no fuc-" Jarrett, not recognizing the emotion of jealously that crept up his body to his throat, ready to strangle him. He couldn't swallow the picture of the rough foreman with his big callused hands all over Shanti's pure, delicate body-

"Damn him! Damn the bastard!" He jumped up, his face thunderous.

Shanti grabbed at him, pulling him back beside her on the couch. "Jarrett, come on, it was one kiss, it's not important. Listen to me."

Jarrett sat down, angrily setting his forearms on his knees, his back hunched. He glowered, trying to control the fierce emotions the picture of Shanti and Graham Duncan in an amorous embrace torched in him.

"Rett," she said quietly, calmly. "It explains her sudden coldness to me. I thought a couple of times when Graham and I were outside talking together that I saw a curtain in the house move, I felt someone was watching us, it must have been her.

"And the pink on the floor was the identical pink that Serafina always painted her nails. It was her favorite color, it matched most of her off-duty clothes, she loved pink.

"She commented on it several times to me. There's only one reason why her nail polish would be spilled in his room." She slid a glance at Jarrett.

He got a grip on his anger and nodded at her words. "I understand. She had to be very comfortable with him to be polishing her nails alone with him in his room in the bunkhouse. I get it; they were an item. But for some reason Duncan wanted it kept a secret. It must have been him that killed her, it had to be."

Shanti nodded her head, agreeing with him. "Yes, it was well known that Serafina had an incredible fear of the water. Nothing, no one would have been able to get her out in the woods near the river. She told me she lived here for over eighteen years and had never been within a hundred yards of the water. Only someone she loved and totally trusted could have lured her out there."

"Yes," Jarrett agreed. "The coroner said he felt she might not have been...uh... completely dead before she was thrown into the well."

Shanti's head swung towards him, her expression shocked. "What? Oh no, Rett, no! Her...her neck was broken they said-" she cried, her hand flew to her mouth.

Jarrett rolled an arm around her shoulder, comforting her. "I'm sorry honey, no one was to know. We didn't want her mother to know the truth and have to live with it. Someone broke her neck, there were bruises and, well, fingerprints around her throat.

"However, she was probably still barely alive when she was dropped into the well. She couldn't move...and well...drowned in the foot of water at the bottom of the well. There was well water in her lungs."

Shanti put her head in her hands and cried. *Poor, poor Serafina, what an ugly way to die...*

Jarrett pulled her head into his chest and stroked her hair, murmuring comforting words. He hated to see her in pain like this, he should have spared her the truth.

She pulled her head from the haven of his chest and looked up at him. Her eyes were dark blue pools. She pushed her hair back, a few strands caught in her eyelashes.

Jarrett tenderly plucked the strands out, pushing them back to join the rest of her hair. He bent his head to look into her eyes. His expression was serious.

"Listen baby, we don't want Mrs. Vesela to know about...about the way her daughter died...okay?"

Shanti nodded, smiling sadly through her tears. "I wouldn't add to that poor woman's pain, Rett, don't worry about me. But, the nail polish, I was thinking, did you guys do any, um, you know...like DNA tests on her broken nails? You know, to see if you could find out and identify if she scratched someone before she died?"

Jarrett nodded shortly. "CSI sent them in, but unfortunately for the moment, they've been misplaced. We have Miguel Perez in custody, but I have a feeling it might not be him. We'll need to lower someone back into the well to find more of the pieces of nails.

"I don't think the crime lab bothered to look too carefully in there because the water and bacteria in the well would probably have destroyed any evidence. However, it can't hurt to try. We need to send them back and do a better scouring of the area near the well too."

"Jarrett, I hate to say this, but I remember now, Graham Duncan had long deep gouges, like scratches that could have been made by nails on his forearms. I didn't think anything of it because he'd just rescued Dawn from the pool and I guess we all assumed she had scratched him while they were in the water and she was panicking."

Jarrett slapped himself in the forehead "You know, we've been idiots. We just figured whoever broke her neck, did it without much of a fight and then dumped the body in the well. I agree, like I said, I don't think it was Miguel, but, I'm starting to think you're onto something, it was-"

"And you'd be right, old man," Graham Duncan cut into Jarrett's thoughts. He was standing in the doorway calmly watching the couple on the couch. He had a revolver in his hand and it was aimed straight at Jarrett's heart.

"Aren't we cozy then, huh?" he commented sarcastically as he entered the room. He smiled wryly at Shanti.

Jarrett tried to push Shanti behind him the second he saw the gun.

"I guess that means I'm tossed to the curb, eh? And I had such dreams for us- don't-" Graham ordered as Jarrett started to jump to his feet.

"Don't be a hero, Marshal, I'm a good shot. And I owe you for that 'kinky' comment." He waved the gun at Jarrett to sit still.

The marshal sat on the edge of the couch staring at the barrel of the gun. He tried to judge the distance between the weapon and them wondering if he could get to Duncan before the foreman could get off a shot.

"What do you want, Duncan?" Jarrett asked, his face dark, he frowned threateningly at the foreman. Jarrett decided he wasn't close enough for him to be able to jump him.

He studied the foreman for a weakness that he could attack and get the gun away from him.

But, the ranch hand had grown up around weapons, he was quite comfortable with them and he was careful to keep his distance from Jarrett. He knew from his reputation that the marshal was quick, strong, and didn't hesitate to take chances.

Graham bumped his thick shoulders up and down. "I was afraid the girl-" he motioned to Shanti with the gun, "was starting to figure things out. I don't know how she could know anything, but I caught her looking at me kinda puzzled sometimes, I could see the wheels turning."

Shanti's terrified eyes went from the barrel of the gun to the foreman.

"I thought maybe she saw something, or stupid Serafina said something- sit still, Miss Lane." Duncan pointed the gun at Shanti who moved suddenly, angry that the foreman was maligning the poor dead maid.

"I saw you two leave the party, and I followed you. I've been standing outside the door listening. It's a good thing you weren't making out, Marshal," he laughed mirthlessly, "because I was starting to take a shine to that pretty girl," he nodded at Shanti who scowled at him from behind Jarrett's arm.

"I know girlie, that you didn't take to my kiss." He ignored the angry retort Jarrett muttered. "But you'll learn in time to like my rough ways, I'll teach you. You'll soon beg for them. Now," he waved the gun at the pair, "get up, slowly. Marshal, put your hands over your head. *Now*," he barked when they sat without moving and glared at him.

Graham took a threatening step closer and aimed the gun directly at Shanti's head.

"Get up now, Marshal, slowly, I mean it. It's only a matter of time before your people find those damned nails and test them, and me. I can't take the chance of the water deteriorating the evidence now can I?" He smiled evilly at Shanti.

"You're not just a pretty face are you, dear? You're right. The hot little maid scratched the crap out of me and must have broken her nails. I thought I had her totally in my power. We were kissing, when I brought my hands up and put them around her throat. She opened her eyes and looked straight into my soul, and immediately she knew. She fought like a wildcat for her life, so I had to break her neck."

He sighed, looking sad for a brief second, then shrugged the melancholy off.

"You're also right about it taking some doing to get her out to the river. There was no way I could kill her and get her body out there. There were just too many field hands milling about, I had to trick her. I pretended to let it slip that I was going to propose and wanted a romantic setting."

"But why Duncan? Why kill the poor girl?" Jarrett asked.

"She knew who killed the old man-" he laughed at their shocked expressions. "No, it wasn't me. I didn't know she was outside the room, tucked in the servant's staircase, when she heard me and the killer talking about Lawton's death. I heard a noise and saw a white skirt and bit of black hair, I knew it was her, I didn't let on at the time, but at that moment her fate was sealed."

He snapped his fingers, like he'd killed a mosquito. He looked straight at Jarrett, his face darkened menacingly. He still had the gun pointed at Shanti's head.

"Don't make me tell you again, Marshal, I'd just as soon quickly shoot you both and take my chances running."

His arm became more rigid, still pointing at Shanti, yet he was looking at Jarrett. "But I don't really want to kill you if I don't have to, not yet anyway, you're too heavy to drag. Plus, I have plans for Blondie there." He took a step towards the couple.

Jarrett could tell the foreman meant what he said, he obviously didn't care if he killed them or not, they would just be his safety pass out of the house and time for him to make his get-away.

No one else besides them knew he was a murderer. If he killed them and hid their bodies it would be some time before anyone figured out it was Graham, and that would give Graham the time to make his getaway and disappear.

Still, if he shot them now and ran, by time anyone gathered their wits enough to chase him, he could be long gone. Jarrett didn't like what the foreman said about Shanti, or the way he looked at her.

The marshal figured Duncan would use them as hostages to get out, but then will probably kill Jarrett as soon as they were clear of the house, but it sounded like he planned to keep Shanti around for a while.

He didn't like that plan, he needed to do something, but for now, he'd have to play along and wait for an opportunity to get to the foreman. Jarrett stood up.

Duncan waved the gun at Shanti who was still sitting, looking up at Jarrett. "You too, girlie." His voice was cold, he was done playing cat and mouse. Shanti stood up next to Jarrett.

"Marshal, take off your jacket," Duncan ordered.

Jarrett raised one eyebrow, but unbuttoned the tux and pulled it off. His white tie and shirt gleamed in the flashing firelight.

"Toss it on the couch," Graham told him.

Jarrett gave the foreman a cockeyed smile, but did as he said.

"Step away from the girl and put your hands over your head."

Slowly, the sheriff did as he was told. The white shirt strained over the muscles of his arms when he raised them to put his hands on his head.

Cautiously, Graham moved near Jarrett, carefully keeping the gun aimed at him.

"One move tough guy, and I blow yours and then her brains out all over the fancy walls." Graham pointed the gun at Jarrett's head.

Jarrett glared at the foreman, but he didn't flinch while Graham carefully patted him down.

Satisfied Jarrett didn't have a gun tucked into his belt, Graham stood back and waved the gun again at Shanti.

"Lift up his pant legs," he instructed her. She looked at him, confused. "Now!" he barked.

Shanti knelt next to Jarrett and lifted first one then the other pant leg. When she lifted the second one, a small revolver in a miniature holster strapped above his ankle was revealed.

Graham smiled at Jarrett. Jarrett shrugged and smiled back.

"Take it out and slowly lay it under his jacket," Graham told her, nodding towards the couch behind the couple.

With shaking fingers, Shanti unsnapped the holster and took out the little gun then gingerly pushed it under the tux Jarrett had dropped on the couch.

"Now Marshal, put your hands in your pockets and head out the door. You girlie, you walk behind him. Don't try anything heroic Marshal, as I said, I'd just as soon shoot you and take off running, but I do want time to get to the bank."

Jarrett lowered his arms and shoved his hands in his pockets. He shot a glance at Shanti.

She looked petrified. He wished he could remove the fear from her eyes. If it were just him and the foreman he'd take his chances and try to get the gun away from him. But with Shanti between them, which is exactly why Graham put her there, he didn't dare take any chances. He'd have to wait and bide his time.

Jarrett walked slowly out of the library, looking up and down the hall, hoping someone would see them. He could hear the noise from the party way on the other side of the house, but no one was wandering about in this wing.

That's why he'd brought Shanti here, for privacy. It'd probably be hours before they were really missed. He turned to the left, to head towards the front of the house.

"No," Graham barked again. His voice low, he didn't want to alert anyone to their presence, he said, "The other way, we're going out the back."

Jarrett turned and arched his brows at the foreman.

Graham's face was rock hard. His eyes had the strange vacant look of a reptile's. He had the gun aimed at Jarrett, but he had his hand on Shanti's waist.

Jarrett looked down at Graham's hand, his brows drew down in straight lines.

"Move Marshal, don't annoy me." Graham grinned meanly at Jarrett, he knew it bothered the sheriff to see him touching the girl. He squeezed Shanti's waist and whispered in her ear.

"You stay right between us girlie, or I'll blow his handsome head right off his shoulders. Understand?" he snarled, giving her a little push.

Shanti cringed, but nodded. She was trying to walk, but her legs were shaking so badly she thought she'd collapse.

They moved silently down the inside hall that ran parallel with the main hall to the kitchen.

When they reached the kitchen, Jarrett pushed the door open with his shoulder. He kept his hands in his pockets, he didn't want to give Duncan any reason to shoot him.

It was dark in the kitchen, Jarrett stopped in the middle of the room and waited. Shanti stopped next to him. Jarrett resisted the urge to look at her, to reassure her. He didn't want to do anything to anger the foreman.

"Go on, we're goin' out back." Graham pointed to the kitchen door with the gun.

"Outside? Listen Duncan, she only has on that little dress, she'll freeze to death." Jarrett motioned to Shanti with his head, keeping his hands tucked in his pockets.

Graham looked Shanti up and down, his eyes lingered on her breasts.

She resisted the temptation to cover herself with her hands, she stared steadily at the foreman. She wasn't going to show him how afraid she really was.

Never moving the gun away from the couple, Graham walked over to a closet and opened it. He pulled out a white chef's jacket and threw it to Shanti.

"Put it on. You," he nodded to Jarrett, "open the door, let's go."

Shanti pulled the jacket on, it went almost to her knees. The cotton material wouldn't really keep her warm, not in the frigid night air, but it would be better than leaving her shoulders completely bare.

Jarrett opened the door and stepped outside. He looked at Graham and slowly pulled one hand out of his pocket and undid his tie, it hung down on either side of his collar. Then he pulled his collar up around his neck. Shanti followed him out into the dark evening.

"Hands back in your pockets, Marshal," Graham growled. He followed Shanti out and closed the door behind them. He was wearing a suit jacket and tie. It was freezing outside. He pulled his collar up around his neck too.

Their breaths were visible white puffs.

Chapter Fifty-Three

"We're going to my room, do you know where that is, Marshal?" Graham asked, but Jarrett was looking at Shanti, trying to think of a way out of this situation.

She was gazing fearfully yet tenderly back at him.

"Knock off the lovers' looks you two- I don't need it. I asked you a question, do you know where my room is?" Graham ground out the words between clenched teeth.

Jarrett shifted his eyes to Graham. He shook his head.

The foreman nodded to Shanti, motioning with the gun. "You know where it is, you lead. But I'm warning you, Marshal, no fast moves, keep your hands in your pockets, you keep right next to her."

The three walked side-by-side, with Shanti between the two men just a step ahead.

Shivering, Shanti turned her head slightly towards Graham.

"I really would like to know, Graham, why did you kill Mr. Lawton? Or…did you…?" she put a questioning finger to her lips in contemplation.

The foreman chuckled. "The wheels are turning again, aren't they girlie?"

Jarrett kept his eyes forward, looking for cover, or a chance to take Duncan by surprise. But he was also intently listening, his forehead wrinkled in confusion at Duncan's words.

Almost tripping, Shanti dropped her head and looked down at the ground. It was hard to walk on the uneven ground covered with grass and stones in high heels and a tight skirt. She couldn't hold onto Jarrett to steady herself because Graham kept them a few feet apart. She stopped.

"Keep moving," Graham ordered, waving the gun at her.

Shanti closely scrutinized him through narrowed, thoughtful eyes. "Poison is not usually a man's way to murder, is it? And, how could you have gotten near enough to poison Mr. Lawton's food? You were in another room playing cards at the party."

Jarrett stopped as well and watched the two.

Graham laughed again and shook his head. "Nope, you got that right little girl. I told you it wasn't me. But you got it figured out though, don't you?"

Shanti sighed and looked down at the ground. She brought her hands up and smoothed back her hair that was tossing around in the light wind.

Thank goodness the biting wind had settled down to just a cold breeze. When she brought her arms up, the chef's jacket opened. Graham's eyes fell to her rounded cleavage. His tongue unconsciously ran around his lips.

"I can't wait until I get you alone-" he took a step towards her, the hand not holding the gun was reaching out to touch her.

Jarrett moved forward, stepping between the pair. Graham quickly raised the gun and aimed it between Jarrett's eyes.

"Don't move buddy boy, don't move a muscle." His voice was low with sincere threat.

Jarrett froze. Graham stepped back from the sheriff and the girl. Smirking, he said to Shanti, "Go on honey, tell us what you figured out."

Shanti tucked one hand in a jacket pocket to warm it and pulled the wide collar tight across her chest with the other to block the chilling wind. She clenched her teeth to still them from chattering.

"I was thinking, you know, about poison being a woman's method of murder. Then I was going through the women that had opportunity to kill Mr. Lawton in my head. I dismissed Mrs. Li."

They stood in a circle, Jarrett, his hands in his pockets and his shoulders hunched from the cold.

Graham had the gun aimed at Shanti's head again. He knew that would keep the marshal from trying anything. The wind blew through the trio, ruffling the men's pants and stirring Shanti's skirt.

She was thankful her gown was floor length, it helped keep her legs warm, yet there's no way she would be able to run in it if they had the opportunity to escape.

She could hear the trees rustling in the distance but otherwise the night was completely silent. They were too far away to even hear the party in the house.

Graham raised one eyebrow. "Why did you dismiss the Asian?" he asked her, curious.

Shanti shrugged one shoulder. "She had her own thing going on, the smuggling, there was no reason for her to call attention to her operation by killing him. Besides, poison would only draw attention to her anyway. People always thought she was mixing potions and stuff, you know, all that voodoo talk around town."

Graham nodded. "Yes that's true, but, what if he'd seen or heard her talking about the gas?"

They were standing halfway between the big house and the bunkhouse. Graham motioned to Jarrett with the gun to start moving.

The marshal silently obliged. His head down, the wind pushed his hair back, but the renegade lock still flopped over one eye, he didn't dare take a hand out and push it out of the way in case Graham decided it was an aggressive move and shoot him.

The sky was clear, no clouds blocking the stars or making them twinkle. The wind had pushed the puffy whites away from covering the tiny crescent sliver that was now left of the moon.

There was no sound except their hushed voices and feet trouncing across the fields along the dirt path made by farmhands and animals traveling back and forth.

Shanti shook her head. "No, she was too careful a person to be overheard. Besides, she always spoke so low half the time no one could hear her anyway. I think she gave her instructions only when she was way out in the fields, where no one could eavesdrop.

"Plus, Mr. Lawton barely left the house anymore, he couldn't have seen any more than I had, a few very bundled up people visiting out past the stables."

They were nearing the bunkhouse, they slowed then stopped just outside Graham's door. They were standing in the shadows of the building, there were no outside lights on.

"Well then, eliminating the housekeeper, who?" Graham was interested in how the artist abstractly thought about the occupants of the house and whether or not each of them could be a murderer.

Pulling his tie off, he unbuttoned the top button of his collar. He stuffed the tie into his jacket pocket, he didn't get it all in, part of it stuck out. He checked Jarrett.

The marshal was barely concealing his rage. His jaw was grit tight, eyes narrowed under eyebrows that were drawn hard over them. The white of the shirt accentuated the tan he had from being outside year round. His bow tie was untied and hanging around his neck, the top two buttons of his shirt were undone. His body was taut, he was obviously waiting for a chance to spring at Graham.

Graham considered how he was going to get rid of the large man's body. He planned on taking the girl with him. He needed a hostage, and the nights were cold…He could feel Jarrett reading his mind. He smiled a mock at the marshal, then, turned his attention back to Shanti.

"A process of elimination, Graham, and means and motive. I don't know the motive yet, but I do know the means." Both men's eyebrows shot up in surprise.

Shanti nodded, her expression serious. She held out a hand, palm up. "I realize it's another reason why Serafina had to be killed too."

Graham looked at the blonde with interest. "Oh really, do tell us, I'm on pins and needles." His smile and tone were sarcastic yet curious.

Shanti ignored the sarcasm, she was doing everything she could to stall for time. She drew her shoulders up and down, and clasped her hands together in front of her stomach.

"I remember when Mrs. Lawton took me to her friend, Catherine Scott's house. Mrs. Scott was so eager to show off her nursery and hothouse to me.

"She took us on a tour, well me anyway, Mrs. Lawton has been there a hundred times, she eventually wandered off and went back to wait in the parlor. Mrs. Scott stopped at every variegated orchid, every hybrid rose, to tell its story."

Graham nodded rapidly, he took a deep breath, he was getting antsy.

Jarrett stood impassively, waiting, like a lion patiently waiting to pounce on a fawn.

"Go on then, skip the flowers, what's your point?" Graham snapped impatiently.

"That is the point, Graham, the flowers, or rather the rare flowers and plants and herbs she had. Mrs. Lawton always brought Serafina with her to carry back special tea leaves, plants and herbs. She must have realized that sometime down the road, even though she wasn't the smartest girl in the world, Serafina would have heard something, then she would have remembered…"

Shanti trailed off, again the horrid picture of poor Serafina lying like a broken doll at the bottom of the filthy, mucky dark well sprung in front of her eyes.

Both men waited for her to continue.

She sighed. "The rosary pea bushes. Obviously, Mrs. Scott had them in her greenhouse."

Jarrett's head turned in surprise, his mouth dropped open.

"Serafina wouldn't have known what they were of course, and she would never hurt anyone, especially Mr. Lawton, she loved him as if he were her own grandfather." Shanti crossed her arms over her freezing chest.

"Mrs. Scott killed Langston? Whatever for?" Jarrett blurted with disbelief.

Graham chuckled.

"No, Rhett," Shanti said with a shake of her head, "not her."

"There was only one other person close enough to Langston to put the seeds on his food that night. That leaves-" Jarrett's brows shot to his hairline.

"Yeah," Shanti replied sadly.

Graham let out a snicker.

Chapter Fifty-Four

"So, you're saying Mrs. Lawton killed her own husband?"
Jarrett was incredulous, he watched Shanti in skepticism. "But, but she loved him, I know she did. I've seen them together for years...why...why...I don't believe it." Hearing Graham snort, he turned to the foreman.

"So, you knew you bastard, why?" Jarrett took a step towards Graham, his hands unconsciously came out of his pockets

Graham held the gun rigid at Jarrett and yelled, "Stop, don't move Marshal, or I swear, you're going right now!"

"Don't Jarrett, please! Do what he says!" Shanti stepped forward holding her hands up in front of the marshal. She pushed at him with her palms against his hard chest.

Jarrett was fuming. His hands clenched into tight fists, he looked down at Shanti. She was scared to death. He forced himself to calm down.

Graham was laughing at him, but the gun was steady at his head. He mocked Shanti, begging in a girl's voice, "No Jarrett honey, please, please don't hurt the big bad man!" Graham made a face at Jarrett, knowing the marshal was totally impotent to stop him from doing anything.

When he saw Jarrett wasn't going to attack him, he turned his attention back to Shanti.

She wanted to diffuse the situation, stall some more. "Yes, it had to be Mrs. Lawton that knew about the seeds, how poisonous they were, and she knew eventually Serafina would figure it out once everyone kept repeating the description of the bushes and the seeds."

Glowering furiously at Graham, she said, "We already know you killed Serafina. It was apparent from the start that you and Mrs. Lawton had some type of...uh...relationship. I thought it was loyalty, but now I wonder..." her thoughts tapered off with her words.

Then, "But why, Graham? I know she did it, but I don't know why she killed Mr. Lawton?"

His big arms folded over his beefy chest, Graham shrugged.

"It doesn't matter what you know now, you'll never be able to tell anyone anyway. I might as well tell you."

Shanti and Jarrett were both gaping wide-eyed at the foreman.

Graham tucked one hand in his trouser pocket and held the gun on the pair with the other as he confessed.

"The old man, not Lawton, it was the elder Vaughn, Magnus Vaughn, according to Maeve. Fifty years ago or so, Maeve's older sister, Genevieve and Magnus had an affair. It would hardly be called an affair- they were in their teens and in love. Maeve may be friends with Dolly but she's closer to Magnus' age.

"Well, as things happen, little Genevieve found herself pregnant. That was a total no-no in those days. Genevieve's parents would have sent her away to a home in another state, or even continent to have the baby, then they would have put it up for adoption, and the girl would have been shamed the rest of her life.

"Apparently, Genny confided in her little sister, Maeve. Maeve loved her sister and couldn't bear to see her in pain. She went and visited Magnus." Graham took a breath and looked at Jarrett and Shanti, he had their full and undivided attention.

"Maeve couldn't get her hands on any big money then, but she knew Magnus could. She talked Magnus into secreting Genny away, out of town, to have an abortion, which of course was illegal then. Maeve told her parents Genny was going to stay at a girlfriend's beach house on the coast off San Francisco for the summer.

"Maeve's parents always believed everything the steadfast Maeve told them, so they acquiesced, without checking with the make-believe girlfriend's parents."

Graham licked his lips, his mouth was getting dry. He could sure use a drink. As soon as he dumped the marshal's body he'd get that bottle of bourbon he had in his room. He pictured him and Shanti drinking. Alcohol should loosen the girl up, he thought, then-

"Duncan-" Jarrett's voice brought him back from his musings.

He must have been looking at Shanti like a cat ready to devour a parakeet. Graham chuckled then continued.

"Anyway, Magnus told his folks also that he was going to go visit some old school chums. However, apparently he was scared out of his mind. He'd never done anything wrong, ever, especially anything against the law.

"But Maeve was quite formidable even in those days, and he didn't dare cross her or not do exactly as she ordered. Maeve sent them off with firm instructions on how to get by boat to another country where abortion was legal. Then she sat back and waited, and waited and waited.

"Months and months went by, long after even when Genny should have had the baby, and there was no word from the couple. Maeve's parents were getting suspicious after not even a postcard or phone call from their daughter. They started to hound Maeve, asking where Genny was, who was she staying with? What were the people's names?

"Maeve tried to field their questions, but she was getting concerned herself when almost a year had gone by and still no word. Maeve finally lied to her parents and said she didn't know where Genny was, that Genny had sworn her to secrecy, that she must have gone away, eloped maybe.

"She couldn't contact Magnus herself because she didn't know where he was staying out of the country, and his family was vague on that issue and she didn't want to draw suspicion that she had a hand in her sister's disappearance." Graham sighed, running a hand over his brow, he switched the gun to the other hand.

"So, one day, two years had passed, a letter came to Maeve. It was from Magnus. He wrote that he was so sorry that he'd been silent for so long, but didn't know what to do, how to say what he had to say.

"He wrote that when they arrived in Switzerland, they got a small apartment and it took him quite a while to track down where to get the abortion. Genny was beside herself with fear, but she had the abortion and he brought her back to the apartment.

"She lay in bed for days without moving. She grew pale and sick with fever, and there was a lot of blood. Magnus panicked, unfortunately, he didn't get help. He just kept cleaning up the blood and washing out the cloths.

"And...Genny died. Magnus was so freaked, he was too scared to come home, so he just dropped the girl on the front door of a hospital in the middle of the night, leaving her as a Jane Doe then he ran off and joined the army.

"Years passed before he got up the nerve to write to Maeve. Maeve was devastated. She took to her room and didn't leave for months. Her parents feared for her health. She finally told them what happened, but left out the part of her own involvement.

"Her father suffered a heart attack, and within weeks was dead, and her mother just withered away, her heart broken. She died within the same year.

"Magnus returned home shortly after. Maeve acted like she was glad to see him, however, she hid her rage at what she believed he'd done. She blamed her sister's and then her parents' deaths on Magnus. He didn't know. He settled back on the farm next door and the families carried on as before.

"Maeve married Langston. He owned the house and farmland next to the Vaughns'." Graham chuckled, shaking his head.

"All those attempts on Magnus' life throughout the years?" Jarrett prompted, suspecting the truth now.

"Yeah, it was Maeve. She wanted him dead for what he'd done. But, somehow he managed to survive or miss each attempt. Her opportunities to get near enough to kill him without suspicion or other people around were few and far between over the years. Finally, she felt he had an angel protecting him, so she decided she'd hurt him another way. She was the one who planted the disease in the potato crop."

Shanti and Jarrett were stunned.

"But, I don't see how-" Jarrett started to say, but Graham cut him off.

"It wasn't her exactly of course, it was me. But she told me where to get the fungus and how to do it. I helped all the time with the harvests at the Vaughns, just like they sent help over to the Lawtons during harvests. It was easy to do the work undetected."

"But Graham, why would you do such a horrible thing?" Shanti asked. It was so shockingly unbelievable what he was saying, it was hard for her to take it all in.

"Yeah Duncan, what was in it for you?" Jarrett asked the foreman.

Graham's lips pushed out with his casual indolent shrug.

"The money of course. She paid me big. She paid me bigger for Serafina. I'm going to have an early retirement in Tahiti, or somewhere equally warm. I am so tired of this cold, hard ugly Godforsaken land. It's damned back-breaking work you know." He rolled his head to stretch his neck and switched hands again with the gun.

"But- but why would Mrs. Lawton want Mr. Lawton dead?" Shanti asked with astonished disbelief.

"Oh, he overheard us talking about the damned potatoes. We should have been more careful, like you say Mrs. Li would have been, but we weren't. Maeve was always so arrogant and had never gotten caught for her murder attempts, she got careless.

"We were discussing how well it had worked, you know, planting the mother tuber and it actually took- decimating half the crop, and ultimately- she had hoped- the Vaughns' entire livelihood. We were gloating I guess, she couldn't wait to see Magnus disgraced and losing his homestead. Her revenge would have been over the top spectacular." The corner of his lip crooked up before he shook his head and frowned.

"Anyway, the old man had been sleeping on the couch in the den. We didn't see him until it was too late, our voices woke him up. As soon as Maeve saw Langston and realized he'd heard us, she shooed me away, said she'd take care of things.

"And boy, did she take care of things. Honestly, I never thought she'd hurt the old guy, I swear." Graham held out a hand, palm up like he was swearing on a stack of Bibles to the pair staring so intensely at him, shock and horror written all over their faces.

"But you had no problem breaking the neck of a poor innocent girl," Jarrett said accusing the foreman of being dastardly in his own right.

Graham didn't look the least bit guilty. "Listen, the bitch was always following me around, she'd never leave me alone. They were starting to get on her for disappearing so much and not doing her job. Plus, she'd seen us together, she could tell I was interested in you-" Graham grinned at Shanti.

She turned away in distaste, Jarrett struggled to hold his tongue.

"Her jealousy was getting tiresome. Then, the little slut had the nerve to try to blackmail me into marrying her! She'd always eye Maeve and me with suspicion when she saw us talking. No reason really for us to ever share words.

"Maeve had nothing to do with the field work and looked down her haughty nose at us farmhands, we would hardly have been sharing buddy-buddy chit chat. She guessed what Maeve and I had done with the potatoes.

"Hey, once she tried the blackmail crap, I was done. She knew she'd gone too far. She started getting nervous and edgy. Besides, it was only a matter of time before it dawned on her about the pea seeds and she'd spill her guts to someone and then the

Maeve money tree would end. I tried to relax her, keep her off guard. I needed to get her away from the house to get rid of her.

"After we screwed one day, I told her I had a surprise for her out by the river. She balked at first, she hates the water, but I talked her into it. I made her think I was going to propose- propose to a maid- a foreign one at that! That's a laugh! Anyway, you know the rest." His brows rose at the pair to see if they were satisfied with all the facts laid out.

Shanti's eyes were round with horror.

"But what about Daisy?" Jarrett asked. He could tell the foreman was getting impatient and would end the conversation soon. He took a minuscule step towards Duncan.

Graham tugged at his lips and scratched his head. They needed to get moving, he was freezing and he could hear the girl's teeth chattering.

"I planned to lure you," he pointed at Shanti, "out to the barn. You didn't quite return my kiss the way I expected. I didn't know if that was because you were suspicious of me or what.

"Anyway, the dumb bitch saw me taping the note to your mirror. I knew she was pregnant, I told her I'd give her money if she kept her mouth shut. She was a greedy little bugger. I told her to meet me out at the farthest barn and I'd pay her. You know what happened after that." His eyes cut to Jarrett then shifted back to Shanti.

"I had planned on spending some quality time with you in the barn," he sighed heavily. "But Maeve followed us, she had other ideas. It was she who handed me the garden claw spade to stab Daisy with. I killed her and was about to hide her body when you came. You got there more quickly than I expected."

"Gee, sorry about that," Shanti snarled at him.

He chuckled. "Right. So, anyway, it was Maeve who threw in the match. I was actually stunned. I didn't want you dead yet. Get this," he chuckled.

"She tried to calm me by saying how much more your painting would be worth once you were dead!" He motioned with the gun. "Okay, enough chatter, let's boogie. Move- towards the river, Marshal. They'll never find your body after it's carried away with the current."

Shanti turned to do as he said, then abruptly stopped. "Just one more question, Graham, was it you that pushed me down the stairs?"

He smiled tenderly at her and shook his head. "No way honey. I'm telling you, I wanted you too badly to kill you before I could have you. I was actually very patient with you. I was being a gentleman. I knew I'd scare you off if I made my moves too fast. But I had come to the end of my patience."

"Someone took a shot at her in the woods, not you either?" Jarrett asked.

No," Graham scowled. "That was all Mrs. Lawton. You saw her with the plates at the festival, Shantilly. You were the only witness really to them eating together that night. She'd already poisoned Langston's green beans. The pea seeds blended in but were still possibly discernable.

"She had deliberately sat her and Langston at a table to eat where no one knew them very well- which wasn't easy! Then you sat with them, with that and the fact that you'd gone to Catherine Scott's house and might have seen the pea bushes and possibly put two-and-two together."

Shanti felt her face pale and stomach flip at the cold murderous malevolence that Maeve had managed to hide. And how near she had come to death. Make that twice, now.

Graham went on, "After she put Langston to bed, she came looking for you. She said she threw on an old khaki coat and pair of Jaime's pants and a pair of his soft soled boots- she couldn't sneak up behind you in heels you know..." his palms lifted with a small smile.

Shanti's eyes bounced in guilt at Jarrett. She had thought she had glimpsed his clothing that day. She should have known he wasn't the type of man that could ever hurt an innocent person.

"Anyway, she figured no one could suspect her because no one except you would have actually seen her give him his food. Plus, that was the only time she was alone with him. Even back at the house, Chloe was right by her side while she put Langston to bed.

"She had initially been slipping him little drops of herbicides here and there, she knew anyone and everyone could look guilty of that kind of poisoning. But she gave that up. Too easy to get caught by a maid or house member."

"That's our Mrs. Lawton," Jarrett said with sarcasm, "ever the one to think a project through."

"Anyway," Graham said continuing his saga. "Langston had been acting so peculiar because everything was dawning on him. It took time for it to truly sink in, all of it. All that Maeve had done.

"He realized after hearing the truth of the potato incident that it must have been Maeve that had made all the other attempts on Magnus Vaughn's life although Langston didn't know why.

"Langston didn't know what to do, but he knew with his high ethics that he absolutely must tell the authorities. And she knew that too. So, she acted, and...he's dead...as you will be soon, now move."

Graham motioned again with the gun. He didn't notice Jarrett had moved a few inches closer to him and his hands were no longer in his pockets. The foreman glanced towards the bunkhouse trying to make up his mind whether or not to go into his room.

He decided there was nothing right now that he needed in there, and besides, he didn't want to be in close quarters with the brawny marshal. When his eyes had turned away from the pair he held the gun on, he didn't catch the look that passed between Jarrett and Shanti.

He figured he'd better get this over with as soon as possible before people noticed the couple was missing and came looking for them.

Graham knew where Miguel had stashed one of the kayaks and he planned to use it to travel downriver to another spot he'd hidden an old truck and a go bag. Earlier that week he had assumed his days at Red Gem Farm were numbered and might have to leave in a hurry.

"Get going, to the river like I said, no more screwing around, no more questions," Graham barked. His face looked weathered and coarse in the darkness.

To Shanti, it appeared like the kind foreman she had befriended had been pushed aside by the very devil himself. Shanti wondered now how she could have thought him so attractive and safe.

Deep lines grooved alongside his mouth, already a five o'clock shadow darkened his face, and his eyes were cruel and menacing. He looked every bit an outlaw dragged straight out of the old west. Graham slipped an arm around Shanti's waist aiming the gun at Jarrett.

"Go on, you lead, we'll be behind you," he commanded the marshal.

Jarrett lowered his head and looked up at the foreman through the lock of hair that hung over his eyes. Then he glanced over at Shanti. She didn't object or struggle when the burly Graham put his hand on her waist.

Graham didn't take his eyes off of Jarrett.

Chapter Fifty-Five

Suddenly, Shanti screamed and pointed towards the river and yelled, "*Look out!*"

Graham jerked his head towards the river and instinctually ducked– at that moment Shanti jabbed him as hard as she could in his side with her elbow, taking the foreman by surprise!

Jarrett leaped, hurtling his body at Graham. He slammed into him, quickly grabbing the foreman's hands and tried to squeeze his wrist to get him to drop the gun.

From the momentum of Jarrett crashing against him, Graham stumbled backwards but still managed to hold onto the gun even though Jarrett shoved both the foreman's arms straight up into the air.

The two men struggled, their feet pushing against the earth, their bodies twisting and grinding, each trying to get the upper hand. Graham managed to hold tightly to the gun, Jarrett fought to force him drop it.

Shanti jumped out of the way of the huge men fighting like two bison on the range. Heads knocking together and clouds of dirt kicking up with loud grunts and groans and curses escaping as they fought for control of the pistol.

Shanti searched urgently around the area for a weapon to strike Graham with, a big rock or rake or something but she saw nothing except tall wheat grass and dirt.

"Shanti! Run! Get the hell out of here! Go!" Jarrett yelled without letting go of Graham's wrists or taking his eyes off the man.

Made of strong lean muscle, Jarrett was the taller of the two, but Graham was huskier and stockier. He was closer to the ground. Jarrett knew if the foreman was able to get his arms around the lower part of his body the older man would be able to knock him over or pull him to the ground then use his bulkier weight to try to hold him down.

He didn't dare let go of Graham. But he needed Shanti to get out of the area. He couldn't concentrate fully on the foreman when he was worried she might get hurt. And if he weren't able to overpower Graham, she'd be in danger again!

Shanti wasn't about to leave Jarrett alone in his struggle with possible death but she kept her distance from the men, she knew they were ten times stronger than her. She could see Jarrett's muscles bursting beneath his shirt as he worked to hold onto the equally strong foreman, and she didn't want to be close enough for Graham to be able to grab her and use her to stop Jarrett.

All at once the marshal used his full body weight and strength in a sudden lurch, hitting Graham as hard as he could in an attempt to knock him backwards - at the same time he shook Graham's wrist snapping it back and forth.

Struggling to keep his balance and the sudden push from Jarrett knocked the gun flying out of Graham's hand. Losing their footing, the two men crashed to the ground.

Before the foreman could get his bearings, Jarrett pulled his arm back then punched Graham almost square in the jaw, but he turned his head just in time deflecting the blow. The foreman scrambled out of Jarrett's reach and crouching low he jumped at the marshal knocking him off his feet.

Jarrett fell flat on his back, the wind knocked out of him. Taking the opportunity, Graham quickly climbed on top of Jarrett and started punching him in the face.

Frantically, Shanti ran to look for the gun. She tried to ignore the fact that Graham was on Jarrett and hurling hard blows to the lawman's head. She wanted to go and push the foreman off Jarrett but she knew it would be to no avail, her strength was so paltry compared to the powerfully built ranch hand. She'd seen him drop a two hundred plus calf on its back and tie its legs together in seconds.

Instead, she searched the high grass for the gun. It was dark and the gun had flown a good distance then skidded across the field when it got knocked out of Graham's hand.

Jarrett blocked a blow from Graham and ushered his own fist hard against the side of the foreman's head. Graham's head snapped back from the force of the blow. Jarrett rolled from beneath Graham and jumped to his feet.

The two powerful men scuffled in savage ferocity, each trying to get the upper hand. Graham brought his feet up and kicked viciously at Jarrett– knocking him backwards off his feet. Jarrett landed hard on the rocky ground.

The foreman bounced on his feet, his fists held out in front of his face like a boxer, waiting for Jarrett's assault.

"Go ahead Marshal, I'm going to kill you with great pleasure and then take my time with the girl…" Graham taunted Jarrett, he wanted the lawman to act without thinking, his unbridled fury would make him easier to combat.

Jarrett wiped his face across a sleeve then rolled both sleeves up revealing sinewy arms, equally as muscular as the foreman's.

Pushing the lock of hair back off his forehead, he smirked at Graham. "Give me all you got farm boy, I'll show you how the big guys fight," Jarrett mocked Graham. He wanted the foreman to make the first move so he could see him coming and prepare his siege.

Graham frowned darkly at the lawman, his face grisly, his eyes mere infuriated slits. He let the lawman get to him- he lost his temper and leaped at Jarrett, yelling furiously, his fists vehemently pummeling at the top of the marshal's head.

Springing back, Jarrett clasped his fists together and brought them down hard, brutally striking Graham's head. The foreman fell on the ground his face smacking the rough ground and Jarrett leaped onto his back continuing punching Graham in the head and neck.

Using all of his seeping strength, Graham bucked Jarrett off him then he ran at him like a bull at a waving cape.

Jarrett was just about to kick Graham in the head with a heavy boot, when the foreman reaching the side of the bunkhouse, sat down and leaned against the wall. Propping himself up on one arm, he held a hand up to Jarrett to ward him off.

"Okay, okay Marshal, I give up, I give up." He squinted up at Jarrett through the blood and sweat in his eyes. "You win."

Jarrett stood still. His hands still gripped in fists he stared suspiciously at the foreman.

Both men were panting, their clothes torn and dirty, each drenched in sweat. Warily, Jarrett eyed Graham. He certainly didn't trust him. But the foreman looked done in. The blood from gashes and nasty wounds on his face was blinding him, his shoulders slumped, his head dropped to his chest.

Taking a step back, his hands still in boxing mode, Jarrett told Graham to get up.

Graham peered at the lawman through streams of blood. He wiped his mouth and then his eyes with his sleeve. Shaking his head to clear it, rivulets of blood and perspiration flew out in all directions. He spat blood on the ground next to him.

Jarrett only slightly lowered his fists. "Get up Duncan, we're going back to the house." He tried to listen to where Shanti was, he didn't dare take his eyes off the foreman. He thought he could hear her still rustling a distance away in the weeds.

Graham looked over Jarrett's shoulder. "All right, give me a minute, you beat me near to death, boy." Graham spat again, slowly climbing to his knees. The foreman stood on shaking legs, hunching over he put his hands on his knees, breathing hard and moaning.

"Jarrett?" A timid voice spoke from behind the lawman. Jarrett didn't turn his head.

"Get away, Shanti, go to the house, now." His voice was hard and uncompromising. Jarrett was furious she had ignored him, exposing herself to the danger from the foreman.

With years of hard work out on the unforgiving land, Graham Duncan was as tough as they come. He only had 10 years or so on Jarrett and was hard as nails. It was really a toss-up who would come out the victor in their fight.

Jarrett had youth and agility on his side. He stood back another small step as Graham, wincing and groaning, still bent over, tried to stand up straight.

Suddenly – Graham threw a handful of dirt into Jarrett's face, instantly blinding him!

Shanti screamed, "Look out Jarrett, look out!"

The marshal jumped back, rubbing his eyes to clear out the dirt. He heard something creak, then screech– what the hell? He heard Shanti scream again, he ducked from pure intuition and he felt something whiz over his head.

Jumping back, Jarrett opened his eyes wide and could now see that Graham had pulled off a loose plank from the side of the old bunkhouse and was swinging it at him!

Shanti was still screaming, Jarrett gave her a hard push out of the way as he dove to the ground.

Graham swung the board as hard as he could at Jarrett's head. A huge nail, at least 6 inches long and an inch wide was sticking out of the end of the wood.

Jarrett rolled out of the way and the board crashed on the ground right where his head had been. Shanti jumped up and ran, tripping through the grass in her heels the long, tight dress hindering her speed.

The angry foreman chased after Jarrett swinging the plank back and forth slashing at him trying to slam the nail into the lawman's skull.

Jarrett groped in the grass for a rock, anything to hurl at Graham, but his hands only felt grass and dirt. He crouched again, his hands up in front of his face and open, he waited for the foreman to swing at him again.

Circling Jarrett like a vicious animal, Graham held the plank up over his head ready to strike, Jarrett moved too, preparing to duck.

Then, Jarrett slightly inclined his head, barely turning away, like he was listening for something, almost looking to the side-

Graham saw his chance and took it! He ran the few steps at Jarrett swinging the plank as hard as he could, screaming with exertion as swung the board with all the strength he could muster directly at the lawman's head.

But Jarrett planned the deliberate ruse. Pretending to look away to get Graham to move, just as the foreman swung the board and it came within inches of his head, Graham was virtually extended up in the air- running and swinging and screaming.

Jarrett bent at the waist, then turning deftly he jumped and shoved Graham as hard as he could.

Graham continued flying through the air, totally out of control. The momentum of pushing Graham caused Jarrett to fall to his knees, he watched as the foreman flew several feet then landed with a bang and a crash, skidding on his belly a few feet across the craggy ground.

Jarrett heard a cry, almost a wail. Graham's arms flung up then his entire body flopped, his arms flailed once or twice, his body trembled, then was still.

Jarrett didn't move, he could hear Shanti's running footsteps as she approached. Her footsteps slowed as she reached Jarrett's side. He still knelt, waiting. The foreman didn't move.

"Stay here," Jarrett instructed Shanti. He straightened and cautiously approached Graham, ready for another trick.

When he reached the foreman, Jarrett stood out of arm's reach and looked down at him.

Graham was belly down, his face against the hard dirt of the earth, he wasn't moving.

Gingerly, the marshal reached out with a foot and placed it against Graham's side. The foreman still didn't flinch.

Chapter Fifty-Six

Jarrett pushed against his side, rolling Graham over.

He rolled onto his back and laid still, his eyes wide open and staring. The plank was across his chest. It looked like the nail had impaled him, piercing his heart. The front of his shirt was a mass of blood.

Jarrett carefully and slowly knelt down next to the foreman. He looked into his eyes. Graham's pupils were flat there was no reflection of light in them. Jarrett put a hand to Graham's throat to feel for a pulse, there was none.

Shaking his head sadly, but with profound relief, the marshal slowly stood up, still looking down at the foreman's lifeless body.

Shanti walked hesitantly towards Jarrett. Reaching his side, she touched him lightly on the arm and looked down at Graham. Hearing her gasp, Jarrett quickly put an arm around her and pulled her head into his chest.

"He's dead, honey, you don't want to see him." He could hear her crying softly.

Jarrett, keeping her head against his chest so she couldn't see the body, turned moving them away from Graham. His arm tightly around her shoulders, he guided them across the rough land through the dark night.

Rubbing the blood and sweat from his eyes on his shirtsleeve, Jarrett's breathing was still rapid from the fight but he held tightly onto Shanti.

Halfway back to the mansion, Jarrett stopped. Shanti's crying slowed, sniffing, she looked up at him.

Standing tall and strong, his eyes matched the sorrow in hers. She reached up a shaking hand and pushed that recalcitrant lock back out of his eye. He smiled wearily.

"It's finally over, Rett, finally." Shanti sighed deeply, smiling tenderly up at her courageous hero.

He nodded and took both her hands in his. Dipping his head, he leaned over and gently kissed her soft lips. When she responded, he let go of her hands and wrapped his arms around her waist, pulling her close to him.

The kiss strengthened, deepened, Shanti brushed her hands up around his neck and pulled his head lower, pushing her lips harder against his. The sweet kiss quickly turned into a passionate, fiery heart-melting embrace.

Keeping one strong hand at her back pressing her even more tightly against his body, Jarrett raised his other hand and netting it behind her head, he wrapped her hair around his fist, pulling her lips harder against his.

Their searing lips caressed, eagerly exploring each other. He drew away, then ran his mouth down her neck, hesitating at the base, he licked and gently sucked, little feather kisses fluttered against her throat.

Shanti moaned, the sound urged him into further, increasing excitement. She could feel his breath against her neck, his body hot against hers, she could feel her eyes glazing, her pulse quickening, the blood flowing through her veins, her heart pulsating and beating so hard she could hear the roar in her ears.

Shanti cupped his face with her hands, pulling his lips back up to hers. They ground their mouths hard against each other. She could feel his heart thumping through the sheer dress, beating against her own heart.

Jarrett unbuttoned the chef's jacket and slid his hands inside, relishing the soft warmth of her body. He ran his hands up and down her back then caressed the slim sides of her waist. Her body melded with his, she felt she was drowning in pure white-hot sensation.

Reluctantly, Jarrett pulled his head back, releasing her lips, his hands still clenched the curve of her waist. He looked down at her.

Her lips were parted, inviting, waiting for his to return, her head tilted back slightly. When he didn't move, she opened her eyes slowly and looked up at him. Her eyes were blue pools of unshed tears, desire burned so brightly in them Jarrett swore he could feel the fire blazing out at him. Then her eyes closed again.

He leaned down and gently kissed first one of her eyelids and then the other. She opened her eyes and smiled lovingly at him.

Jarrett stood back from her and took her hands again, lightly clasping them in his. She looked up at him, puzzled. He smiled, the luster the burning feelings she so intensely instilled in him still radiant in his eyes, the color of them now like a dark stormy wind tossed sea.

"Listen honey, we have to stop right now, unless you want to feel that cold hard ground under your back- because any more of your enchantingly sexy body touching mine so crazily, I'm afraid I won't be able to restrain myself from totally, voraciously devouring you, greedily ravishing you-"

His eyes hooded now to hide his hunger for her moved slowly, painstakingly from the golden lashes framing those fantastic eyes that stared so enticingly at him, down the slender throat, her pulse throbbing so hard it was all he could do to stop himself from putting his lips to her trembling neck and suck her satiny skin.

He continued his heated perusal of her body as his gaze traveled over the lovely curve of her breasts, roving down further still. Resisting the temptation to touch her flat belly, he sighed heavily at the slim roundness of her hips then down to the shapely length of her legs to her petite feet.

His gaze swept back up to her lips so sable soft they begged to be kissed, parted again in desire as she watched him beholding her beauty.

His eyes, still hooded, the pupils black and enlarged with the craving he felt for her, Jarrett could feel the fire in his own belly waiting to engulf him, burning him up like the barn they had so desperately escaped.

He was entirely captivated by her, he needed to step back or he'd be all over her like a wild rapacious animal. He took a deep, beleaguered breath and ran a trembling hand through his thick hair.

She reached out to caress his face, but he captured her hand before it touched him. With the gentleness that he'd hold a butterfly, he kissed her hand, then let it go.

"You have totally snared my heart, beautiful Shantilly Lane. But we need to go, or I won't be responsible for my actions." One side of his mouth pulled back in a wry grin, but his eyes warned her of the heat he so barely kept in check.

Bereft of the warmth of his body, Shanti shivered suddenly, her teeth chattered uncontrollably.

"Okay, let's go before you turn as blue as your eyes!" he said to break the tension. "Besides, I have a matriarch to arrest."

Shanti moved back into the circle of his arms, they started walking back to the house.

"We really need to build a cabin out here, Rett, between the house and the river, we seem to be here a lot!"

They laughed together, Jarrett holding her tightly as she tripped alongside him.

Epilogue

Shanti stayed for only a few days, it was awkward being in the house.

At first, Maeve tried to staunchly deny her involvement in the deaths of her own beloved husband, Serafina and Daisy. But then they found bits of Serafina's broken nails in the weeds near the well. They easily matched the DNA that was still under the nails to Graham Duncan and it confirmed the ranch hand's story.

Once police knew it was Duncan that had obtained the potato fungus they traced his movements back to where he'd gotten it, and even found a paper trail, phone records and computer searches where Maeve had investigated and contacted ranches that had previously had the disease.

The claw hammer stuck in Daisy's chest had both Maeve's and Graham's prints on it indicating they had both been complicit in her death.

They had carelessly assumed the fire would destroy any evidence as everything in the barn was made out of mostly wood or straw. But they hadn't paid attention to the small wire band on the handle that was steel and their prints had clung to it like glue.

Alone, none of it would have been enough against them, but all the evidence put together including there was the same amount of thousands of dollars transferred from Maeve's account to Duncan's on several occasions.

With Shanti's information, the deputies found the rosary bushes in Catherine Scott's greenhouse.

Catherine was contacted by the police about her pea seed bushes. She had only known the plant by its technical name of Abrus, so the information about Langston dying from the pea seed poisoning hadn't registered with her.

When the police came to her house to discuss the plants with her, she examined her plant and advised that part of it was missing.

She recalled the plant had been intact prior to Maeve's last visit because she had moved it to another area that offered more sun.

At that point, Maeve finally confessed all, including the attempts on Magnus' life.

Even with her hands secured behind her back in handcuffs, Maeve still held her head regally high and her back ever rigid as the police led her out the door to the waiting patrol car.

She claimed no remorse, only stating that it was her duty to avenge her dear sister's death and Magnus Vaughn should burn in hell.

Langston had understood, she stated matter-of-factly, he knew what duty to one's family and honor was and he would never begrudge her that duty.

With both Langston and Maeve gone, someone had to take over the running of the farm and it fell on Chloe's trim shoulders. She attacked the job with gusto! It was just what she needed to recharge her battery and lift her from the lethargy of her grandmother's trial.

And, Langston's will had stated that if anything incapacitated Maeve, full ownership of the farm and estate would go to level-headed Chloe.

Chloe laid down the ground rules right away. Mother was to clean up her act and she could stay in the manor as long as she didn't drink, didn't bring home slimy men and contributed in some way to the running of the house or farm.

Reluctantly at first, Camelia took over the housekeeping duties. But as she worked daily, she found she enjoyed the constantly challenging events that were ever present in a large household like the Lawtons'.

Cleaning the mansion she found helped cleanse her own mind and soul, sweeping away the angst of her past. She reached out to her children for the first time in their lives, and they reached back. She finally felt part of the family.

Equally, the same rules more or less were touted to Chloe's brother and sister.

At first, Dawn squawked about having to put in a real day's work. However, as time went on, she fully immersed herself in the business side of the farm, mainly with getting the beets to distilleries and also the exporting of the beets after they leave the distillery.

Networking, making important connections and even the bookkeeping thrilled her. She got up every morning now and looked forward eagerly to each challenging new day.

Jaime got mad at first and ran off to live in a seedy apartment with other men of extremely loose morals. He soon tired of the lifestyle and the fear of dying from an overdose or a dreaded deadly disease.

A healthy relationship burgeoned between him and another young man and he moved back home to help out in the fields. He grew strong and tanned and healthy, and happier than he'd ever been in his life.

He thoroughly loved the feel of the mud in his hands and the grass beneath his feet. He was now always the first to mend a broken fence or sit atop a piler feeling deeply proud and for once content as he planned his future wedding to Edmund.

Montgomery of course was kept on and it became his sole decision on all help hired, inside and out and their supervision. He moved from his room far from the rest of the mansion to as close to heart of it that he could get.

His gut had told him something had been wrong for a long time but he had squelched it, not wanting to make waves, and it cost the life of his beloved master and best friend.

In the future, he would be where he could keep his finger on the pulse of the household, and where he would always be nearby to assist the new Lady of the Manor, Chloe.

His eyes searched through the open window for her until he found her.

Chloe was standing in the center of the fields with dirt pouring from both hands, her magnificent russet hair billowing in a cloud around her, and she was grinning across the open land all the way straight to him.

Everyone breathed a sigh of relief when Mrs. Li and the rest of her gang were rounded up and adjudicated guilty for their parts in the plot to release the deadly Amiton gas onto the world. Sentenced as terrorists, they would never again see freedom from prison.

Even poor old Logan Thayne got his comeuppance. He married his new con before fully divorcing Camelia and was arrested for bigamy. While in jail, other corrupting charges started piling on him, thefts of his past conquests, and another wife in his past he hadn't properly divorced. His prison sentence continues to grow as more women pop up to file charges against him.

Shanti made her good-byes with promises to write and keep in touch. She would be back sooner than she thought in the next year to be a maid of honor in Dawn and Matthew Vaughn's wedding.

It would be held in the spring when all is green and pure and fresh and the land abundant with colorful flowers and new life, and the hope of good and exciting things to come.

Jarrett drove her to the airport in a patrol car as his Bronco was in the repair shop.

Shanti giggled when he helped her into the passenger seat.

"Wow Rett, this is the first time I've ever been in a police car!"

Jarrett climbed into the driver's seat after he put her luggage in the trunk. He turned on the car and looked over at her.

418

She was all blonde brilliance as usual, smiling that dazzling smile of hers at him. He wished he were driving her to his mountain cabin for a long romantic weekend alone, to get to really know each other. To fish and drift in a canoe, take long walks through the mountains, make love all day and into the night, instead of to the damned airport.

"I hope it's the first time you've ever been in a police car, if not, you sure have some explaining to do!" He chuckled, returning her smile, his warm and loving. He pulled out of the driveway, drove through the wrought iron gate then out onto the street.

Shanti was waving forlornly out the side window at the Lawtons and Montgomery that were standing on the front lawn waving back.

Too soon they were at the airport. Her plane's boarding was already being announced. Jarrett took Shanti's hand and pulled her over next to a column that went from floor to ceiling. He set her against it and stared longingly down at her.

"I'm going to miss you badly, remember to call me the second you get home," he ordered her, his voice stern, but his eyes were warm.

Her smile turned sad. "I'm going to miss you too, Rett. I can't wait until you come and visit. I wish you were coming with me. Two months is a long time to wait!"

He nodded in agreement. "I know, but it's the soonest I can get away from work." His head bowed at the speaker system announcing the last of the boarding.

"I have to go, Rett." Her eyes filled with tears.

Jarrett leaned down and kissed her long and slow, he couldn't bear to take his lips from hers. They separated, he gave her a gentle push. "Go before I force you to stay!" he warned.

She peered up at him through her heavy fringe of lashes, a weak smile on her lips, then she turned and walked towards the entrance to board the plane.

They were now announcing last chance to board. She held out her ticket to the airport personnel who checked it and handed it back to her. Absently nodding to the man in uniform when he told her to have a nice trip, she stepped into the hallway then turned back and looked over at Jarrett.

The lawman was staring at her, his eyes like a puppy's, big and sad, his desolate smile longing for her to turn and run back into his arms. But, he knew for now that was impossible, they both had other lives and jobs to do, they'd have to wait. And the waiting would be painful and bittersweet.

He tucked one hand in his jacket pocket, the other he raised in a slow wave.

She waved somberly at him. Brushing a tear from her eye, she hesitated, gave one last look back, his hand was still in a mournful wave, but he smiled and watched her turn and disappear down the hall.

Jarrett stood by the window until her plane flew out of sight. He headed out to his car, his step suddenly light, he needed to get going, the sooner he got home, the sooner he could get things tied up neatly in Mooserock, get his affairs in order, cancel his rental lease, hand in his resignation.

Jiggling the small ring box in his pocket, he almost regretted not giving it to her before she left. However, he knew Shanti would want to share the event with her sister.

He couldn't wait though, to get on one knee and beg her to be his wife. As soon as he started his new job as sheriff in Shanti's home town, he would do the deed with Shanti's family and friends surrounding them.

"Yeah," he grinned. "I can't wait to get started with our new life!"

The End

Dear Reader, thank you for choosing <u>Murder at Red Gem Farm</u>!

I know you could have picked any number of books to read, but you chose this story and for that I am extremely grateful.

I hope you enjoyed this novel, and if you did, **please leave a review where you acquired it**, *and look for other exciting titles in my name!*

About the Author

Louise Furley loves writing romance with a huge helping of suspense. Sunny Florida is home where Louise is a graduate of St. Thomas University with a master's degree in Mental Health and lives with Bob, her own hero.

Louise is the author of numerous published novels. When not researching or writing, she is dreaming of unique plots, and discovering fresh ventures she hasn't yet experienced in the world. Ride along with her as she travels new and thrilling journeys!

LOUISE FURLEY